Sylvia Baker was born in Hertfordshire and married a man from a travelling family before she was twenty. They had two children but their family life was disrupted in 1971 when Sylvia's father was murdered by the notorious poisoner Graham Young. The trauma prompted Sylvia and her family to move to Devon with the intention of becoming self-sufficient. They didn't quite succeed but many happy years followed until Sylvia's son became involved with drugs and in 1989 died as a result.

Sylvia Baker has won many prizes for her short stories, including an Ian St James Award.

Her previous novels, *A Certain Seduction* and *The Loving Game* are also available from Review and have been highly praised:

'For emotional intensity it's on a par with Josephine Hart'
Independent

'Engrossing . . . for the reader it is a hugely enjoyable trip'
Time Out

'Hauntingly resonant . . . about the power of sex, the pain of love and the magic of both'
Western Morning News

Also by Sylvia Baker from Review

A Certain Seduction
The Loving Game

Falling in Deep

Sylvia Baker

First published in 1997
by HEADLINE BOOK PUBLISHING

First published in paperback in 1998
by HEADLINE BOOK PUBLISHING

A REVIEW paperback

10 9 8 7 6 5 4 3 2 1

ISBN 0 7472 5844 9

Typeset by
Letterpart Limited, Reigate, Surrey

Printed and bound in Great Britain by
Clays Ltd, St Ives plc

HEADLINE BOOK PUBLISHING
A division of Hodder Headline PLC
338 Euston Road
London NW1 3BH

For my Aquarian daughter, Donna Juliette, with love.

Acknowledgements

Thanks to Judith for her encouragement and to Kirsty for some very practical suggestions. To Geraldene Holt for help with food, Declan Evans for information about Ireland. To Vikki and Bernie Murphy who first introduced me to Lough Ine – the most magical place on earth!

Chapter 1

Last night I thought it would end in violence. After the door had slammed there was a thud and one of them shouted an anguished, *No!* Or was it, *Go!*? I had only just woken, or rather *been* woken and their raised voices filtered down to me in a jumble of disjointed words. I was angry at first. How dare they do this again? How dare they slam doors in my house? Then there was that cry, that one word that had me holding my breath in fear of what would happen next. But there was only silence. I waited, wondering what had caused such an abrupt and total silence. I stared up at the ceiling in the darkness. Perhaps they were standing there above me, facing each other. Perhaps one of them was no longer standing. Able to stand. I felt I knew which one. I closed my eyes and reminded myself that I have references from a bank manager and a doctor. I told myself that nothing awful had happened or would happen. To them or to me. Or to the furniture and fittings of my house. I'd just finished reassuring myself about all this when I heard one of them walk across the room. A door closed; quietly this time. I listened for ages but was quite sure that only one person had left the room. I sat up and switched on my lamp. My ceiling looked as white as ever. Newly painted when I'd had the upper floors decorated before they moved in. There was no red stain seeping through, no huge scarlet blot resembling an ace of hearts. I couldn't think where I'd got this description. But later, when I'd fallen asleep, I dreamed about it and I knew. I was Tess of the d'Urbervilles running off with Angel after she'd knifed Alec through the heart. But it wasn't blood seeping through the ceiling that I dreamed about, it was water that came dripping down from upstairs.

In the morning my head is sort of tilted upwards and my neck cricked as though I've been keeping watch all night. I blink up at my ceiling, remembering the shouting and my dream. Perhaps in the dark I was confused about where one ended and the other began. Working as I do on subjects concerning the human mind, my imagination has become overdeveloped. During the day I'm fine. But at night, especially in those dead hours before dawn, it goes into overdrive. Jolted awake at two in the morning I would be at my worst. So I can't be certain of what happened. And this makes me anxious, the uncertainty, and I have to start the day with three aspirin and four cups of strong tea. Taken in quick succession, tea, aspirin, tea, aspirin, the ritual alone soothes me. Even makes me smile at myself. But it's a temporary measure, I know that. I'm well aware that a hundred cups of tea and a whole bottle of aspirin won't alter what I've done. I've let my house, the main part, the three floors above my basement flat, to two men. Two brothers. And I wish I hadn't.

The aspirins and tea clog my brain a little and I counteract their effects with a cold shower. It's while I'm under the water shivering and planning my day, that I hear the postman arrive. 'Oh shit,' I mutter, knowing by his loud knock that I have a parcel, and knowing that he will not leave parcels on the step even in this quiet square. 'Shit,' I say louder, emerging too late to catch him. I dress quickly, glancing at my ceiling once or twice. Blaming my late rising on the men upstairs. I wonder whether to chase after the postman, and I'm halfway to my front door, zipping up my jeans, when I see Lewis Kaye, the elder of the two brothers, walk past my window. Neither of them has ever been down here. What does he want? I think. To apologise for last night? I doubt it; he never has before.

But when I open the door, he smiles and presents me with a parcel. 'The postman,' he says, 'he couldn't make you hear.'

'Oh no, I was in the shower.' For some reason I feel flustered. Which isn't like me at all. I might have weird dreams and imagine murders in the dark, but I don't get flustered with people. And I should be annoyed with this man. 'Come in,' I say, thinking I might broach the subject of late-night noise. 'Come and have a look at the bottom floor.'

He steps inside and I go to put the parcel on my kitchen

table. It's square and heavy. 'Books,' I say over my shoulder.

He smiles then looks up at the ceiling. Probably wondering if I can hear them. 'It's bigger than you'd think from the outside,' he says, glancing round.

'It used to be one of those huge Victorian kitchens.' I point to the wooden partition half hidden behind my fridge. 'The stairs are behind that. I expect you've noticed where they're sealed off up in your hallway.' I stop short of adding, and voices travel down clearer than you obviously realise. Perhaps he will realise after seeing down here.

'Ah, yes,' he says, nodding. On the two occasions that I've met this man before, he wasn't all that communicative; polite, pleasant but not communicative. Most of what I know about him and his brother has come from listening to their raised voices. And to my friend Evie's gossip. All too late. The tenancy agreement was already signed.

But this morning I'm determined to get more out of him. 'How are you settling in?' I say.

'Fine.' He nods and smiles.

'You find it big enough? When your daughters are staying, I mean.'

'Yes, plenty. They're here at the moment,' he adds as though he ought to tell me. 'I did mention that they come to me during the school holidays, didn't I?'

'Yes, you did,' I say, surprised that he thinks I might be concerned about his two little girls when his brother was bellowing like a madman two days ago. Fortunately it was a short-lived row and stopped when a woman left the house. A split with a girlfriend, I decided, as Lewis was at work. There are no women living with them, I know that. Normally there are just the two men, with Lewis's daughters joining them at weekends.

The four of them came when they viewed the house. They toured round behind me as I showed them each room. Well, Lewis and the girls did. His brother hung back, looking out of windows and lounging in corners. He didn't speak once. But they were all very quiet. Even the little girls spoke in hushed tones as though they'd been told to behave. It was their quietness that impressed me. My top priority was to find a quiet family who would not disturb me or the other residents of the Square. And Lewis himself seemed just the sort of person I wanted. A respectable family man – well, sort of – and too old at forty, or thereabouts, to be playing loud music half the night. It wasn't until afterwards, after I'd said they could move in, that I thought much about the brother. But when I did I knew that if he had come alone, I would not have let my house to him.

'They live with their mother in term time,' says Lewis. 'There's a school within walking distance. Though Lydia's not been very happy there lately. We'll have to see what happens next year when she's eleven.'

'And the other one?' I ask, pleased that he seems to be opening up. 'Is she at school?'

'Just. She started at Easter.' He gives another of his little smiles, but it's too brief to hide his concern. In fact I've noticed that despite the smiles, his face has a permanent look of sadness. People's expressions intrigue me. A smile, a frown, and your whole perception of someone can change in a flash. The trick is to discover what lies behind an expression. I've been reading about this, the masks we put on in public and how deceptive they can be. 'She cried every morning for the first week,' he says. 'Sobbed her heart out, according to her mother.'

'Oh so did I,' I say, anxious to seem understanding. 'And when I went to boarding school I howled so much that I ended up spending the first night in the matron's office.'

'Missing your parents, I expect,' he says. There's no smile this time and his added, 'Oh well,' implies that he's about to draw the conversation to a close.

It occurs to me that I haven't mentioned last night, and I add quickly, 'Actually, it was a dream I had. I dream a lot – especially if I'm disturbed.'

'Must have been a nightmare.' He glances towards the parcel. 'Hope you enjoy your books.'

'Daddy?' a child's voice calls from my front door, which we've left ajar. 'Daddy, are you there?'

'Yes he is,' I call back. 'Come in.' His eldest daughter, Lydia, appears, followed closely by her little sister, Mimi, which I think is short for Jemima.

Mimi races over to her father but Lydia stands just inside the door. 'Daddy, I need to tell you something,' she says, beckoning to him, one eye on me.

'I'm coming up now,' Lewis says. He bends down to lift Mimi into his arms.

She looks at me, smiles shyly, then whispers very loudly into her father's ear, 'Janus said he's going to phone Mummy again. He might break the phone.'

Lydia comes marching over and slaps at her sister's legs. 'He didn't say that. Shut up.' Mimi immediately bursts into tears.

'Sorry about this,' says Lewis, forcing a smile. 'I'd better go.'

My own smile is forced as well. I'm thinking of the broken phone and of all Gerald's beautiful furniture. And the fact that I haven't said what I meant to. And how can I in front of his children?

'Say goodbye to Mrs Harker,' Lewis instructs the two of them. 'Though you haven't even said hello properly.'

'Goodbye Mrs Harker ,' says Mimi with a pathetic little sob. A bit forced like our smiles, I think.

'My name's Verity,' I say, touching her lightly on the leg.

'Goodbye, Verity,' says Lydia. She has big clever eyes and a bold air of maturity.

I watch from the window as they go up the steps to the pavement. Since the interior stairs were sealed off the basement has only this one entrance. I hear Lydia say, 'He did really,' and Lewis tell her to be quiet, it doesn't matter. A door slams upstairs and then Mimi is crying again.

I go to sit at my kitchen table, wondering what I'm going to do. I'm none the wiser. I still don't know why Lewis and his brother shout at one another or why they have late-night phone calls or slam doors. All I've learned is that Janus seems to be the one responsible. Which doesn't surprise me. No wonder Lewis has such a troubled look about him. It makes me reluctant to complain. Perhaps I'll see how things go. Give it another week or two. Let them settle down. Yes, I think, that's what I'll do. I'll top up my wine supply, keep my aspirin bottle filled and ignore them. Maybe I'll even start to play loud music. Like Evie, who has hers blaring away all the time to keep out the noise of her neighbours.

But later, deep in a book called *The Planets and Human Behaviour*, a work which usually absorbs me totally, I find myself thinking about them. All of them. And I find myself slightly depressed. It's not just the noise, or the fears that they arouse in me, it's more a general feeling, as though my whole sense of tranquillity has been disturbed. I don't want to think about them. I don't want to know anything about them apart from what is necessary for my peace of mind. I'm happy with my solitary life. I have little interest in men these days. Or in children. In fact I have never been interested in children. Whether I shall ever have any of my own, I don't know. I'm thirty-three years old. I've been divorced and widowed but never wanted children. That night, my first at boarding school, the one I mentioned to Lewis, I told Matron that I wasn't ever going to have a baby. I was only eight but I knew all about babies and birth.

'Tell me,' Matron kept saying while I sat on a chair in her office. 'What is it that's making you cry?'

And finally I had to tell her. The truth. At eight I only knew about truth. 'I had a dream about being born,' I sobbed. 'My head got stuck and I died.'

Matron was quiet for a very long time, then she said, 'That was a horrible dream, Verity. But it's not the truth so you must stop crying and forget all about it.'

'But it is the truth,' I protested, collapsing into more tears. 'My mother told me it nearly happened.'

'Things like that don't happen these days,' she said firmly. 'Your mother has frightened you unnecessarily. She has made you nervous over too many things and it won't do.'

Thinking about it, the words she used which I still remember very clearly, makes me smile. And what I said next.

'Have you ever had a baby?' I asked her.

'No,' she said. 'I've never been in that situation.'

It was nearly light when she took me back to the dormitory. As she tucked me in I whispered, 'I'm never going to be in that situation either.'

Late Saturday night I'm not sure whether another row is brewing or if it's just that Janus finds it impossible to leave the house without slamming a couple of doors on the way. Shortly before slamming out he shouted, I'll fucking walk then, which makes me wonder where he's going. Especially as it's nearly midnight.

Where would anyone walk to round here at midnight? Or could it be that he's leaving for good? No, I think, wrapping the pillow round my head, that's too much to hope for.

And I was right. Early Sunday he's home again. He arrives on the back of a motorbike which roars twice round the Square before stopping outside the house. There's a noisy exchange of laughter between Janus and his leather-clad friend – one of those Hooray-Henry types by the sound of it. Janus himself is clad only in jeans and a ripped T-shirt – no crash helmet. I'm furious. Most of the people who live in the Square emerge around nine or ten, stroll round the corner for the Sunday papers then disappear back indoors for the rest of the day. We have minor politicians, company executives, owners of London stores. They are people who work late during the week and, if they are not out of town, prefer to relax on Sundays. They don't expect this sort of racket at the crack of dawn.

I drag a coat on over my nightie, buttoning it as I go. Halfway up the steps I see that Janus is off the motorbike and standing in the bushes of the central communal garden. Even from the back it's obvious what he's doing. He's probably under the impression that he can't be seen, and to be fair I doubt that anyone from the four houses this side of the Square is even up yet, though they'll certainly be awake now. But I'm still incensed. He's no delinquent teenager; he must be my age, or thirty at least. I stand there a moment, bracing myself. I'm only going to get one go at this. And if he tells me to mind my own business what am I going to do? I don't want it to turn into a shouting match and cause more disturbance. He's good at shouting.

The next thing I know Lewis is out on the pavement. He doesn't notice me, he's too intent on marching over to Janus. The motorbike speeds off, drowning out the sound of what Lewis is saying but I see Janus step back, palms raised in mock surrender. I think I also see him smile, but I don't wait to find out what happens next.

Back indoors my Siamese cat, Pisces, comes to rub round my legs. He's become suspiciously plump lately and I wouldn't be surprised if he hasn't been creeping in upstairs and getting fed. Lewis is a chef and runs his own restaurant near Piccadilly. I've seen him cross the pavement from his car laden with trays of food. Evie is convinced that I'll soon be dining on cordon bleu leftovers, but only my cat seems to have benefited so far.

For the next few hours they're so quiet that I simmer down. In fact when they all emerge around midday while I'm watering my pots of daffodils, I don't even hear them at first. One side of the tiny courtyard outside my door catches the sun and I can even grow tomatoes and peppers there. Well, I would be able to if Pisces didn't use the pots as a toilet. I thought the plants had some terrible disease when the leaves developed rusty patches and began to curl up. Then I caught Pisces one day and decided my poor plants were just reacting with disgust. The daffodils seem to be more tolerant, though they never look quite as good as other people's.

Pisces watches me. 'You men,' I say, thinking of this morning, 'will piss anywhere.'

'Excuse me.' The voice comes from above my head. I look up and find Janus leaning over the cast-iron railings that prevent people falling the ten feet or so from the pavement. 'I'm sorry if I disturbed you this morning,' he says. He's well-spoken like his brother but his tone isn't even faintly apologetic.

'Actually I was awake, but I don't suppose the neighbours were.'

'Well, I'm sorry. It won't happen again.'

'Just one thing.' Whether he heard what I said to Pisces or not, I don't know, but I might as well make the most of it. I leave my watering and go to stand below him. 'I'd rather you didn't make a habit of pissing in the middle of the Square.'

He looks taken aback, which is what I intended. I'm tempted to add that if he thinks because I'm a woman on her own he can walk all over me, then he'd better think again. But Lydia comes pushing in beside him. She smiles down at me. 'We're going out for lunch,' she says, 'to my father's restaurant.' There is a hint of boastfulness in her voice. Understandable, I suppose; what little girl wouldn't be proud of a father who had a restaurant in the centre of London?

Mimi runs up now. 'Do you want to come with us?' she says, peering down through the railings.

I see Janus smile to himself. Contemplating my embarrassment, no doubt.

'Oh, I've got a friend coming to lunch with me,' I say quickly.

To my surprise, Lydia says, 'Perhaps you'd like to come with us another time, when you're free.'

Before I have time to think of an answer to this Janus gives her a push and says, 'Come on, your father's waiting.' It's a harder push than a man should give a little girl but she rounds on him instantly.

'Don't shove me,' she says, punching him in the side.

For a moment I think he's going to retaliate. Then Lewis appears. I have the four of them now, all looking down at me; the two men towering above me, and the little girls with their inquisitive eyes taking everything in.

'Has he apologised?' says Lewis, resting a hand on Janus's shoulder.

Ah, I think, he was told to. Perhaps I should try to see the funny side of this: Janus, who's even taller than his brother, being treated like a naughty schoolboy. And me reprimanding him for something that I've just scolded my cat about.

'Yes, he has,' I say, smiling up at Lewis. But I don't feel in the least light-hearted. There are some people in this world whom you can never feel easy about however hard you try. Janus, I believe, is one of them.

They come home late, but they're quiet. There's no more than a light patter of footsteps across the floor before they're all in bed. Or so I imagine. I should think the girls must be, anyway. I wonder which room they sleep in. The smaller bedroom on the first floor, I expect. Janus sleeps in the attic room. I know that because Lewis mentioned something about it when they came to view the place. The attic room is very important to me. I know how it looks at every moment of the day. How the shadows move across its beamed ceiling at night, and how the sunlight pours in through its one window in the morning. I've stood naked in that sunlight, and I don't want anyone else to be up there. I should have had it sealed off like I have the stairs. I drift towards sleep, thinking of the partition and wondering how well it's fixed in place. Was it screwed or nailed to the wall? And why is the wood so thin? Could somebody break through it? Could it be smashed with a hammer? I wake suddenly, sure I hear someone coming down the stairs. I switch on my lamp and creep into the kitchen. What I heard was someone coming downstairs up in the house. Their phone is ringing in the hallway. It stops but a few minutes later it rings again. It's answered almost at once. I should have had the stairs bricked up. If I'd known my new tenants would get calls this late, I would have done. I can hear their voices when they answer the phone. Not always clearly. But this time I do. I hear Janus say that Lewis is not there. When I know very well that he is.

Evie calls round Wednesday afternoon after her art class. Her visits to me have increased now that I have two men in my house. But so far she hasn't caught them at home.

'They're out,' I say without looking up from my desk. She comes marching straight through to the back room, which is both my bedroom and study. Evie has a key to my flat as I do to hers. A safety precaution as we both live on our own and have no relatives nearby.

'Oh shit, they're always out,' she laughs, coming to hook an arm round my neck and kiss the top of my head. She leans over my shoulder to read the chart I'm working on. Her understanding of astrology is pretty basic although we actually met at the College of Astrological Studies. It was twelve years ago and although Evie didn't complete the course, we've been friends ever since. Evie's commitment to jobs, hobbies and men never lasts long. She's the proverbial butterfly, happily flitting from one thing to the next. She dips her little nose in here and there, staying for a bit when something pleases her. Given the lives we each lead, I should be a stabilising influence on her. Someone she can run to with problems. Ironically, it is Evie who sorts me out most of the time. For example, the day that I signed the rental agreement with Lewis Kaye, Evie was here until midnight reassuring me that I'd done the right thing. I'm not sure why I got cold feet at that point. Premonition? Intuition? Or simply that I didn't want my life to change?

'So?' She straightens up. 'How are things? Are they behaving themselves?'

'Bit noisy. Apart from that they're OK.' For once I'm keeping my worries to myself.

'You sure?'

'Yes.' I look up at her. She opens her mouth then closes it again. Evie is keeping quiet about something too. I draw another line on my chart. She'll tell me when she's ready.

'Are you going to stop work and talk to me then?' she says.

We go through to the kitchen and open a packet of shortbread biscuits and a cheap bottle of Lambrusco which Evie likes when she's thirsty. She knocks her first glass back in two gulps then asks for tea.

'Obviously a hard day,' I say as I go to put the kettle on.

'Sitting in a draughty classroom for two hours with no clothes on isn't much fun in this weather.'

'Don't you have any heating?'

'It has to be turned down low. The students get sweaty ogling me.'

'I thought they viewed you in a purely detached and impersonal way.'

'That's how it's supposed to be,' she says, refilling her glass while she waits for the tea. 'But I can't help it if I turn them on.'

'No, of course you can't, Evie,' I say.

You could pass Evie in the street and not look twice. She's a year older than me, and she's also shorter, almost stubby in fact. Most of the time she walks around in thick tights and Doc Martens, with her long red hair coiled up under a black beret. But once she shakes her hair down, smiles with her wide red mouth and strikes a pose, she's capable of turning any head she wants. She has life truly sussed. I've never known anyone so in control of themselves as Evie. I envy her this; not her life, I don't envy the way she lives. I'm happy here writing my horoscope column and working on my interpretations of dreams. But I should like the ability she has to make things happen and not to worry about the consequences. Her bravery.

'Oh by the way,' she says, 'I've heard something more about your Lewis Kaye.'

'Have you now?' So that's it, I think. 'I'd rather you didn't call him *my* Lewis Kaye.'

'He's *your* tenant.'

'Big difference.'

She smiles at me over her glass. 'You're so sensitive about men.'

'Evie, get to the point.'

'It might only be a rumour.' She pauses, sniffing at Pisces who has just sprung onto her lap from the top of the fridge, his favourite perch. He hangs his rump over the back to catch the warm air expelled by the motor. She tugs at his ears. 'You smell like a man,' she growls into his ruff. He dribbles with pleasure, rubbing his head under her chin and arching his back until his legs tremble. 'The restaurant may not be doing so well,' she says finally. 'I've heard that he's having problems. Financial ones.'

'Is that all?'

'Aren't you worried about your rent?'

'He paid three months in advance.' I shrug. 'I've had the rental agreement drawn up by my solicitor. It shouldn't be a problem to get him out if he doesn't pay.'

'We should go to the restaurant one evening,' she says mischievously. 'See what's going on.'

'Too embarrassing. He'll think I'm after a free meal.'

'So?' She looks at me sideways. 'What's wrong with that?'

'Here.' I put a cup of tea in front of her. 'Drink that and stop making my life more complicated than it is.'

'How can having a rich eligible bachelor living in your house make your life complicated?'

'He's not a bachelor, he's divorced. And you just said that he could be going broke.'

'Well, it might only be a rumour. He was doing very well at one stage apparently.'

'I know. You told me. Three times.'

'I thought you wanted information about him,' she says indignantly.

'I do. But not your hints. I don't need a man. I don't even want a man. Rich or poor, married or single.'

She laughs and kisses Pisces on the nose.

'He caught a rat this morning,' I tell her.

'Ugh.' She wipes her mouth with the back of her hand, smearing her lipstick, then wipes her hand on my tea towel.

'You wear far too much lipstick,' I say.

She jumps up and goes to find the hand mirror that I keep in the cutlery drawer. 'Lips are important,' she says, pouting at herself. 'They need emphasising. Like all of one's erogenous zones.' She holds the mirror up higher, catching my reflection. 'I think yours may be getting rusty.'

'And I think it's about time you were going home, Evie. I have a mountain of work to finish.' We do talk about sex but it's mostly in general terms: opinions, jokes, and it's usually Evie who has the most to say. Her crudeness can be comforting. She cuts everything down to size. I once told her how I hated smear tests, and she said yes so did she, and wasn't it amazing to think of all the inconsiderate bastards women welcome up there, and then we cringe at the sight of that dear little nurse?

But I don't feel much like talking today and I really do have a lot of work to get through. The deadline for my horoscope column is tomorrow lunch time.

She smiles sweetly and dabs her lips clean with my dishcloth. 'Well, walk me down to the station then.'

On the old railway bridge where the pavement is sealed off from traffic, kids are skateboarding. One of them zips by so close that we have to jump out of the way. He pulls up and scoots back to apologise, shading his eyes from the sun and saying he didn't see us.

'What manners!' says Evie, walking backwards to watch him. 'It's so nice round here. The kids over my way are like wild animals.' She plunges her hands in her pockets. Despite the sun it's still quite cold. 'The other day a young black kid shouted after me, did I want a good fucking? He couldn't have been much more than eleven or twelve. I do envy you living here.'

'Yes, it is nice and quiet. I've got a lot to thank Gerald for.'

She slips her arm through mine. 'Do you still miss him?'

Do I miss him? Nobody has ever asked me this, not even her. People presume I miss him, I suppose.

'In some ways I do.'

She pulls me closer to her. 'I know what you mean. His company, you miss his company.'

And I know what *she* means. Once she asked me if I'd been faithful to him all the time he was ill. Yes, I told her, I've never looked at another man. I wasn't offended. Plenty of people said worse. Nobody actually understood about Gerald. And I never tried to explain.

We've come to the main road and we stand and wait as a lorry rumbles past, then a line of cars. We should have walked up to the crossing. I look towards it, surprised to see Janus, Lydia and Mimi coming out of the station subway.

I turn quickly back to Evie. 'I'll leave you here. I want to get a paper.'

We kiss goodbye. 'See you Friday,' she says, and I'm in the newsagent before she has managed to cross the road.

I buy a paper and some sweets. I don't normally eat sweets but I have this sudden idea that I might catch up Lydia and Mimi and offer them some. I've seen them a couple of times since Sunday – only briefly, but they smiled and called out to me. Lydia was hanging around on the pavement when I watered my pots this morning. She asked me what my cat's name was. I could see that my answer intrigued her but then Janus came and called her back indoors. Her eyes narrowed as though she were about to defy him. He ought to have been put down at birth, she said. I watched her skip off and wondered just where she got that from.

They must have walked quite fast because I don't see them again until I turn the last corner before the Square. Janus is way in front of the girls, head down and smoking. He looks wrapped up in his thoughts, unaware that Lydia and Mimi are straggling so far behind. Mimi is walking with one foot on the pavement, the other in the gutter, hopping up and down with outstretched arms, a doll dangling from her hand. Suddenly Lydia snatches the doll and tosses it over a wall into someone's garden. Mimi runs at her, crying. Janus swings round and marches back to them. He points a threatening finger at Lydia and I hear her say, 'Temper, temper,' then she ducks quickly away from him. Janus vaults over the garden wall and retrieves the doll. As he hands it back to Mimi, he notices me.

'Hi,' I say with a bright smile. But he hardly bothers to answer, just nods in my direction then grabs Mimi by the hand. Perhaps he sensed that my smile was a bit too bright. Lydia comes running up to me but Mimi is forced to trot along beside Janus. When she tries to look back at us, he promptly picks her up and walks on even faster.

'Have you been to work?' Lydia asks, falling in step with me.

'No, I've been down to get a paper.' I decide to leave the sweets until I can get both girls together.

'Are you on holiday?'

'No, I do most of my work at home.'

'What do you do?'

'I write for a magazine. Do you know what a horoscope is?'

'Is it like a horror film?'

'No,' I laugh. 'It's to do with birthdays. I draw charts and write . . .' I pause over the word predictions. 'I write about what is going to happen to people.'

She looks up at me her big eyes glowing with interest. 'Can I come and see the charts?'

We've reached the house now. Janus puts Mimi down and flicks the end of his cigarette on to the steps.

'Can I?' Lydia repeats.

'Yes, I expect you could.' For the moment I'm more concerned about the burning cigarette on the front step of my house.

'Before we have to go home?' She looks up at me again, spots what is taking my attention and runs over to crush the cigarette stub with her foot.

Janus is fitting the key into the door. Mimi is treading on the cigarette now, grinding it with the toe of her shoe until there are tiny shreds of tobacco spread all over the step. I suppose he must smoke in the house. In bed in the attic room where Gerald's old books and astrology magazines are stored. I should have said no smokers. I should have had a clause put in the rental agreement saying no smoking in the house. Janus opens the front door and raises his arm to let Mimi in.

'When can I come?' Lydia asks me.

'You'd better ask your father first,' I tell her.

'Lydia,' Janus says, pointing a thumb through the open door. 'Get inside and stop pestering.'

'Stop pestering,' she mimics, and dashes past him after Mimi.

'She wasn't pestering me,' I say.

'Lewis doesn't want them to be a nuisance.' He gives a sudden unexpected smile. It makes him look more like his brother. More approachable.

'They're not,' I say quickly. Encouraged by the smile, I add, 'Are you babysitting?'

The smile vanishes. 'Yeah,' he nods, already halfway through the door and closing it while I'm still standing there.

Ignorant bastard, I think. Evie would have said it. To his face. I go down my steps into the comfort of my kitchen and an instant welcome from Pisces. He purrs and dances on top of the fridge before leaping into my arms. On second thoughts, Evie probably would not have said that. Or she'd have said it in a flirtatious way. Evie can make most things sound flirtatious if she wants to. And Janus is her type. He has a certain challenging quality which I know she likes. You don't find it in married men, she once told me. They've been smoothed down, no rough edges left to graze you. As far as looks are concerned, she's flexible as long as they're dark. Both Janus and Lewis are dark.

Pisces starts to wash my left ear, distracting me from my thoughts. Next he will nibble the lobe. It's his way of asking to be fed. As I'm opening a tin for him and wondering what to have myself, I hear Lewis's car pull up. It's funny how quickly you come to recognise new sounds. But just to make sure, I go to the window. It's difficult to see anything from down here. Sometimes, if I really need to know what's happening up on the pavement, I stand on a chair and lean out of the window. Evie's second-floor flat in Vauxhall is so much better for seeing things. Though the things that happen there are very different. Her windows look out across a stretch of concrete that was once a playground, and into a park. We've watched drug deals, fights, we even saw a mugging once but got so absorbed that we didn't think to phone the police until it was too late. All I can see from my basement at the moment is a pair of legs which I presume belong to Lewis.

I listen now, standing at the bottom of the blocked off stairs. It's all very quiet, so I go back to feeding Pisces. But as soon as I've put his bowl down for him, I find myself listening again. I nearly jump out of my skin when the phone rings. It's only Miss Campion next door, calling to tell me that my tenant has dropped some keys on the pavement. How considerate of her, I think, and how observant of her to notice. Then I realise that she must have been watching too. Or rather, I was watching like she was. I laugh to myself but I can't help thinking: goodness, am I becoming like her? Will I be an old maid who spends her time watching others? I bet she saw Janus throw his dog-end on the step.

I phone to tell them about the keys; easier than going up. Janus answers. He's politer than he was earlier. Coolly polite. Aloof. A minute later he dashes across the pavement in socks and underpants. At least I think it's him. I once read that young men have much hairier legs than older men. With age the hair migrates to the chest. I can't imagine what sort of book I read it in.

This will be something to make Evie laugh. Not Janus's legs but me watching one side and Miss Campion the other.

Chapter 2

Yes, I have a lot to thank Gerald for, a lot more than this house, a lot more than anyone knows. The house, after all, is only a temporary gift that I have to sell in four years' time. A quarter of the proceeds will be mine, the rest goes to Gerald's three children.

I used to feel as though they were waiting like vultures, wishing something would happen to me, that I'd fall under a train or get robbed and knifed in some deserted backstreet. Or even have a fatal accident in the house, get electrocuted changing a bulb, or choke on a fish bone. I began to avoid anything that was even remotely dangerous and plenty of things that were not, imagining that the combined willpower of the three of them alone would precipitate my early death. It took a year before I came to my senses and accepted that it was all tied up with my anxiety and guilt and the whole process of mourning. And only partly to do with the fact that they didn't understand about Gerald and me. I rarely think about them now, and I never see them. They came and took away some of his things after he died. One of his sons wanted some of the books from the vast collection that Gerald had built up over the years. I told him to help himself, and he was halfway up the attic stairs before I remembered the magazines. I panicked, for Gerald's sake. I didn't want his family jumping to the wrong conclusions; Gerald was fifty-nine when we got married, and I was twenty-four. I raced up the attic stairs just in time. You mustn't touch them, I told his son. I've just remembered, my solicitor said that none of Gerald's books must be removed yet because some of them are valuable and will have to be included in his estate. Evie reckons I'm a bad liar, but when I'm desperate for someone to believe me, they do, including her.

Gerald was my tutor on the astrology course. From the start he took an interest in me because I was his keenest pupil. Not the best, not by a long way, but I threw myself into the work with such fervour that he took it for commitment. He said he prized that most of all. And he said he thought I had an instinct for the subject. That was probably true at the time. I was becoming very detached from reality, the way you do when you want to avoid it. And I was light-headed with so much difficult reading. Kepler, Copernicus, Newton, anyone he mentioned who was eminent in the field, I read so that I could ask questions to impress him, so that he'd notice me.

Later, when I was having private lessons in his attic room and couldn't bear to think of the day that I would no longer have his praise and reassurance, I resorted to simpler methods to capture his attention. I started wearing low-cut blouses or just leaving an extra button undone. He had a chart of what's called proportional logarithms. They're used in calculating the position of planets, column after column of tiny close-packed figures. Like many of his charts the paper was curling at the edges with use and he had pinned it to his desk to keep it flat. I had to lean across him to read it.

He set me tests, giving me the dates and times of birth of different people. One day we did my chart. I said I didn't know the time of my birth. Lots of people don't. We'd covered this before on the course using a speculative time for those who didn't know, but he wanted my chart to be accurate.

'Phone your mother,' he said. 'Ask her.'

'She died,' I said, 'when I was born.'

'But I thought you went to visit her at Christmas?'

'Did I say that?' I started to sharpen my pencil. The lead kept snapping but I went on turning the sharpener, ramming the pencil into it until he took it away. 'I think I need to see a doctor,' I said.

'Because you forgot about Christmas?' he asked gently.

'No, it's not that.'

He put a hand on my arm and waited but all I did was tilt my chair back on two legs and brace my knees against the desk so that my skirt slid up my thighs.

'Are you sick?' he asked after a while. He twisted his head

round to look at me and the concern in his eyes gave me courage.

'My husband says I am.'

'Your husband? I didn't know you were married.'

'Yes. But I'll soon be divorced.' I spread out the fingers of my left hand. 'I gave my ring to a beggar outside Waterloo Station.'

His eyes widened a fraction. He's convinced now, I thought.

'Why did you do that?'

'Because I wanted to get rid of it. I tried to give it back to my husband but he . . .'

'He what?' Gerald sat very still. His breath had a slight wheeze in it though not as bad as when he climbed up the stairs.

I kept my eyes on the logarithms, staring so hard that the figures blurred and merged together.

'He told me to . . .' I had to stop again because I couldn't repeat what Mark had told me to do with my wedding ring, where he'd said I could shove it, not the word he'd used. Neither could I use the proper word for that particular part of my body. Any of the words for it. They were all seized up inside me, the way that my body had seized up. I dropped forward and covered my face with my hands. Then I slumped right over with my arms and my head on the desk.

Gerald said I should have a lie down. There was a sofa bed in the attic room. He pulled it out and dusted it off. When I curled up on it he fetched me a pillow and a silk-covered eiderdown that smelled of mothballs.

'Can I phone anyone for you?' he said.

'No. There's no one. I live on my own now.'

'And you travel all the way home on your own? In the dark?'

I nodded. 'Yes, on the tube. It doesn't bother me.'

'Well it bothers *me*. You can have your lessons earlier in future.'

I can't recall how he came to suggest that I stay the night. All I remember is that I asked him not to leave me alone.

'Is it the attic that frightens you?' he said. 'I have a spare bedroom downstairs.'

'No, it's not the attic. It's what I dream.'

He didn't mention about dream control then, though it

would have been the ideal moment. That came later. He just said, 'So you want me to stay up here with you?'

'Yes.' I held back the eiderdown. There was plenty of room for two on the sofa bed.

'Do you mean what I think you mean?'

'Yes.'

His hesitation, his lack of excitement, made it easy. I tried to think of the name of the hormone that makes men eager, aggressive. All I could remember was the second syllable. It made me think of Mark, angry and turning away from me to 'toss myself off', as he put it, purposely crude in his frustration with me. One day, I thought, I will stand in a crowded shop or somewhere, and shout out all these words that I cannot say.

Gerald's penis was small and soft as I imagined all old men's would be. But, of course, it didn't stay that way. He didn't get impatient. He sat up beside me and said, 'Have you been raped or abused or something?'

'No, nothing like that. I don't really have an excuse.'

He turned on the light and I could see he was frowning but he looked interested as well. And he'd lost his hard-on, which made it easier to talk. Mark could never listen properly because he was in a perpetual state of frustration. When this turned to not caring, we were finished.

'How many times have you actually had intercourse?' Gerald asked in the same tone he might use to ask if I were having trouble finding the aspect between two planets.

'A few times.'

'Just with your husband?'

'No. Twice before him.'

'But you've never enjoyed it.' This was a statement, not a question, and he was kind enough not to say, but you've always hated it. Gerald had got the picture. I never faked anything, I would have found that impossible. You have to know about enjoyment before you can fake it well enough to be convincing.

'No, and I didn't want to do it.'

'Is it a man's body that frightens you?'

I said yes but that wasn't the whole truth. My own body frightened me too, and all that can happen to it. The next day he bought me the magazines. I was amazed; I couldn't believe that he'd actually gone into a shop and put these on the counter to pay for them.

'Whatever must the shop assistant have thought?' I said.

'I told her they were one of the tricks that an old man has to resort to in order to stimulate a young woman.'

I didn't believe he'd said that but it made me laugh and I didn't feel so shy about looking at the magazines.

Gerald's wife had left him for another man years ago.

'She doesn't know what she's missing,' I sighed one afternoon as I lay stretched out naked on the sofa bed, Gerald's cheek resting on my stomach. His forefinger was still on my clitoris, light as a feather, hardly moving but enough to prolong the spasms of pleasure until I was ready to let them go.

'She found a younger man,' he said. 'More stamina, I suppose.'

I stroked his hair, cut very short and not much grey for his age. Stamina, I thought, yes maybe, but patience, I don't think so. And this was only stage one. Planet one, Gerald called it. I said it was Venus because I was loving it. I didn't say that I loved Gerald because I wasn't sure about that yet.

By the end of a week I was eager for stage two. It was funny but I didn't mind the way he talked, treating this like one of his astrology lessons. And when he asked me was I ready for the next stage, I answered by climbing on top of him.

'I thought this might be Mars,' he said.

'Mars?'

'War, a struggle. Was I wrong?'

I sat astride his stomach and took his hands to cover my breasts, then dragged them down over my hips. I felt so hot, inside and out. 'The sun,' I said. 'Stage two is the sun.'

He smiled up at me. From this angle he looked younger. Or maybe it was what we were doing. Maybe every vein and artery in his body was being rejuvenated with the same quick rush of blood that swelled in his penis. 'Kiss me,' he said. 'Kiss me like you kissed your first love.'

'You are my first love,' I told him. I caught sight of his expression before I closed my eyes and I knew what he was thinking. But neither the future nor the past seemed important.

I was concentrating on the present and the new freedom I had found.

'The sun,' he said, sliding his hands round the inside of my thighs until he could open me up with his thumbs.

'The penetrating heat of the sun,' I said easily.

I hadn't been home all week; I'd hardly left Gerald's house. I loved the space of it and all the stairs. Instead of a jog round the park I now ran up the stairs from the basement to the attic in one go, and down again. Miss Campion next door spread it round the Square that she could hear the noise of his chasing me. We had a laugh about that but secretly it made me sad because Gerald struggled to get up just one flight of stairs.

One day, we were watching a wildlife programme on the TV. It was about seals. There was a close-up of a baby seal being born. I was mesmerised; it was the first time I'd actually watched a birth, any birth. The mother seal hardly seemed distressed at all. With a couple of heaves and grunts it was over and the little pup slithered out, sleek and mottled and big-eyed with surprise.

'Do you think a human birth could be as easy as that?' I asked Gerald.

'Rarely, I should imagine.' He leaned back in his chair and closed his eyes. Sometimes he slept in the afternoons. I'd even found him asleep at his desk and persuaded him to move to the sofa bed.

'I suppose it's easier to have a Caesarean,' I said.

'Mmm?' He opened one eye. 'What are you fretting about now?'

'Birth,' I told him.

Both eyes opened. 'Do you want babies, Verity?' he said calmly, with just a little emphasis on the want.

'No, never.' Perhaps I said it too quickly, too vehemently because he stared at me a while, then shook his head as though he didn't believe me. I knew he'd had a vasectomy. That was fine, more than fine with me. I couldn't have wished for better. 'I don't much like kids,' I added to convince him. 'All the noise and the work doesn't appeal to me at all,' really laying it on with a trowel.

That night I had a bad dream about the seals. The one giving birth was my mother, only it was the same dream I'd had before. I was in her belly and she couldn't get me out. While she was straining and groaning, a man came up and clubbed her to death. It was like the adverts for Save the Seals, blood pooling around her while the man stood over her, gripping the wooden club. I was inside her and watching her at the same time.

The dream really upset me. I tried to explain it to Gerald without sounding too ridiculous. And of course it wasn't that I feared getting pregnant any longer. It was just that connection between making love and giving birth. I was still terrified at the thought of giving birth, and now that I enjoyed sex so much I didn't want them to be connected. I told Gerald this. I don't want them to be anything to do with each other, I said in desperation at trying to explain something I couldn't even understand myself. He didn't say I was being ridiculous. He said we mustn't always expect to understand our fears. And sometimes it's easier if we don't try. But he was so concerned that he asked a friend of his, a psychologist called Lenny, to come to talk to me. They had done a research project together some years ago about the influence that zodiacal signs have on dreams.

Lenny and I sat in the drawing room while Gerald went downstairs to make tea. I felt uncomfortable right away because Lenny was much younger than I'd expected, thirty-five at the most. There were things in my dream that I wouldn't be able to tell him. He was Swedish, typically Swedish, I thought, with blond hair and a curiously upfront manner, direct but disinterested. We chatted for a while and I answered his questions, background information like my age, my parents' ages, where I was born. He said if there was anything I didn't want to answer, I could just say 'no comment'. After a minute or two I wanted to say no comment to the whole thing and I think he sensed this because he left off questioning me and said, 'Let's get started then. Tell me your dream.'

I made it sound like a gruesome fairy tale, more childish than horrific – a big fat mother seal with a human face about to give birth when a wicked seal hunter comes along and kills her.

'Is that all?' he said, eyebrows raised, face blank so I couldn't tell what he was thinking. He had wire-rimmed spectacles and very smooth skin. 'Can you describe the seal perhaps?'

'It had bulging eyes and a very bulging stomach,' I said, putting my hands on my own stomach without thinking. I quickly took them away and screwed up my eyes to make out I was trying to remember more. I wished I had the courage to tell him that the seal's vagina was like a woman's, stretched and grotesque and tearing like my mother's.

'Your own eyes bulge a little,' he said. 'Did the seal look like you?'

'No. Its eyes were black and mine are blue.'

He peered closer at me as though he were checking. 'And you don't bulge anywhere,' he said with a puppet-like smile.

'Not so's you'd notice.' I got up and went downstairs. Gerald was reading a paper. 'Tea's a long time,' I said.

He closed the paper. 'Don't you like Lenny?'

'No.' I sat on his lap and kissed him. 'Tell him to go away.'

He went upstairs and did as I asked. They were together a while, obviously talking about me, before I heard the front door open and close.

'What's the verdict then?' I said when Gerald came back down. 'What did Professor Clever Dick have to say about me?'

'Verity,' he said, head to one side, scolding me a little, 'I thought he might help, that's all.'

'I don't need help. I just want to be here with you. What did he say?'

Gerald tried to smile. 'He said that you're obsessed with pregnancy and birth.'

'The stupid shit. I wouldn't be here with you if I was, would I?' I think that hurt him, which was just the opposite of what I'd intended. So I said, 'Gerald, why don't we get married?' I would be divorced from Mark in just a few weeks.

He shook his head. 'I'm not well. You're too young for me.'

But the next day I went home and packed up all my stuff and took my keys back to the landlord. I had virtually nothing in the bank and I wasn't sure if I still had a job. I worked in the marketing department of a magazine publishing company. I'd only been there three months but had already decided it wasn't what I wanted to be doing – much how I felt about the rest of my life at that time. Gerald had phoned in to say I was sick but

I hadn't sent in a doctor's certificate or anything. Maybe they'd phoned me at my flat. I didn't know and I didn't care. For as long as I could remember I'd been pinned down, hung up, inhibited, obsessed. No more.

I arrived back on Gerald's doorstep with a cab, full of my worldly possessions, ticking away at the kerb. He came to help me carry them in, bemused, I think.

By that evening my potato masher and egg slice were hanging beside his in the basement kitchen; my deodorant and razor were with his on the bathroom shelf and my books were piled on the floor in the attic. And I was there lying naked between the smooth Egyptian cotton sheets of his double bed.

'All right,' he said, when he came in from the bathroom. 'I'll marry you. You've got your own way.' He pulled back the sheet and, very slowly, ran a finger all the way down from my neck to my navel. Then he walked two fingers into my pubic hair and a little further. 'Is it just this?' he said.

'No, it's everything.' Then I laughed because he was tickling me and because for the first time that I could remember, I had not one single thing to worry about.

He slumped down on the bed. 'I just hope I can last out until you grow tired of me,' he said.

'I'll never grow tired of you,' I said. And I meant it because I was happy.

Three years later he became ill. It started with a bout of pleurisy. I nursed him, devotedly I would say. He had money in the bank but I carried on with the horoscopes he wrote for two magazines and a paper. The editors knew I did them but we all agreed to keep his name on them. For the next few years he was a semi-invalid. We did the horoscopes together and he taught me more when he was feeling well enough. I didn't go out much; I never complained; I was in a kind of vacuum, I suppose, but content. And I was never unfaithful to him.

It was during this time that my friendship with Evie really developed. She would come and spend an evening with me most weeks and she always went upstairs to sit with Gerald for half an hour. Her language and her jokes, which she never tones down for anyone, amused him, though I knew he had his reservations about her. She brought the outside world into our quiet house: gossip about the men who pursued her, risky encounters in pubs, that landscape of hers where excitement and danger were one and the same thing. Once or twice he asked me if I wanted to go out with her but I always said no. And later when he was more or less bedridden, he asked me again and said he wished I would.

'Better to do it and tell me,' he said, 'than to go behind my back.'

'Do what?' I said, trying to look at him without pity. So much of him was gone, his big body caving in while his lungs rotted away. And I could no longer see the man I'd seduced in the attic room six years before. I wanted to. It made me feel very vulnerable to know that soon he'd be leaving me. He had always been sure that one day I'd leave him. Nothing I could say would alter this conviction of his. 'You're only waiting,' he'd say, 'you're waiting until you're as confident as Evie, then you'll go chasing life the way she does.'

So now when I asked him what he thought I'd do behind his back, he raised his head from the pillow and said, 'Go chasing life.' By this time even such a short sentence was enough to exhaust him.

Some nights I'd lie beside him on the bed until he slept. His breathing was so bad now that the sound of it filled the room, a horrible wet rasping sound which I tried not to mind. I'd close my eyes and dream about how we had been during that first year together. I did this so that I could still feel good about him. And he knew. Knew what I was dreaming. I'd feel his hand reach for mine and hold on as tight as he was able. His nails had become yellowy and thick. They reminded me of a piano teacher I'd had at school. Her nails were so thick and long that they made a clicking sound on the keys as she played. I thought of this and I thought of school and Mark and my mother. But most of all I thought of how we had been, Gerald and I.

One night he lifted my hand and placed it between my legs. He was murmuring something. I leaned close to catch what he was saying. I smiled and kissed the side of his mouth to please him. But I couldn't do it. And later when he was asleep I went downstairs and cried for the first time in years. They were angry tears. And guilty tears. Mostly because what he said was true, I did want to go chasing life. I wanted to pick up men the way Evie did. I wanted to be fucked by men I hardly knew and worry about what would happen to me. Gerald had built a wonderful loving wall of protection around me and it was about to crumble. Soon I could do whatever I wanted but I had this awful confused feeling that if I didn't have Gerald to run back to, then I didn't want to go.

We had the basement converted to a flat for a nurse but Gerald went to his sister in Hove to die. She was a nurse herself, retired now but willing and able to care for him. He didn't want me to see him die. I understood why; it was to release me. But it had the opposite effect. It made me feel as though I had left him after all.

Two years later I think I've come to terms with all this. I know what I want from life and it's not to be like Evie, or anyone else come to that. I like my work, my privacy, my home. And as for men, well, I've come to wonder if I really need them after all.

Chapter 3

Lydia was knocking at my door before I was up this morning. I scrambled out of bed imagining the house must be on fire or something, then the knock came again, a little too polite for an emergency. I pulled on jeans and a cardigan over my nightie. Probably the postman with another parcel. I send off for a lot of things: books, clothes, gadgets; saves me going to the shops. It was ten past eight; about time I was up anyway.

They'd come to look at my charts, Lydia and Mimi. 'We have to go home on Saturday,' said Lydia when I didn't show any immediate sign of welcome. I'm not at my best first thing in the morning. I need three cups of tea and half an hour in the bathroom before I'm fit to see anyone. It's what happens when you live alone and work freelance, you tend to start the day when you feel like it. Freedom becomes laziness. You become too solitary. But I let them in.

'You'll have to wait while I get dressed and have my breakfast,' I said, conscious that I was putting up some sort of barrier in case they tried to make a habit of this. 'Have you had your breakfast?' It didn't occur to me to ask whether their father knew where they were.

'Ages ago,' said Lydia, her eyes swivelling round my kitchen, taking everything in. She has very dark eyes like her father. I presume they must get their blonde hair from their mother. Although it does happen, blonde-haired children from dark parents. I'm almost an example myself but not as extreme as these two. Their hair is almost silver. I've only ever seen them with plaits before but this morning their hair was loose except for one side of Mimi's, which had a partly unravelled plait. It made her look a bit waiflike, neglected almost.

Lydia bent down to scoop up Pisces, holding him cradled like a baby. Sometimes people are nervous of him because of the reputation Siamese cats have for being unpredictable, even spiteful. Pisces knows this; show any sign of fear and he can be very intimidating.

'Don't drop him,' I said as she began bouncing him up and down.

She clasped him tighter. 'I'll make your breakfast for you while you get dressed, if you like,' she said.

'That's very enterprising.'

'What does enterprising mean?'

'It means having initiative.'

'Oh,' she said as if she knew.

I left her making my tea and toast while I went for a shower. When I came back she had made a huge pile of toast, all buttered, and a pot of tea. Mimi was standing by the table, arms resting on it. She smiled at me but didn't speak.

'You must have used up all my loaf,' I said.

'It was getting stale,' said Lydia. 'It was out of date.'

Hmm, I thought, is this what children of divorced parents are like? I took a sip of the tea that she'd poured and looked from one to the other of them. It had just occurred to me that here was the perfect opportunity to find out more about my tenants.

'So you have to go back to your mother on Saturday, do you?' I said.

Lydia nodded. Mimi eyed the toast. I pushed the plate towards her.

'Take some then,' said Lydia, shoving her. 'You're allowed.'

'Do you always boss her about?' I asked.

'I'm looking after her.'

'Oh, I see.' I fetched marmalade. 'You look after her and Janus looks after you both. Is that it?'

'Just while Daddy's at work.'

'Has Janus always lived with your daddy?'

She pursed her lips, thinking. 'Mostly.'

'Did he when your mummy and daddy lived together?' I wasn't sure where my questions were leading. I just wanted to keep them going so that she didn't have time to evade anything. Because my instincts told me that is what would happen if I showed too much interest.

'Not all the time.'

'Why was that?'

She looked at me sideways, wary, and filled her mouth with toast. Oh, I thought, so I'm already on dangerous ground. Maybe I should have felt ashamed about interrogating her like this but I told myself that I had a good excuse. I have a right to know about them. They're not quite what they seemed that first day they came here, so I've a right to find out about them any way I can.

Lydia's eyes switched to the marmalade I was piling on my toast. 'You'll get fat,' she smiled.

'No, I've never been fat. Want some?' I offered her the jar but she shook her head. 'Didn't you have room for Janus when your mummy and daddy lived together?' I said.

'Yes, we had a big house.' She shrugged. 'Mummy didn't want him there.'

Mimi, who hadn't spoken a word until now, suddenly seemed to catch on to what we were talking about. 'Mummy shouted at Janus,' she said, putting a hand to her mouth as though she'd revealed something dreadful.

'Shut up, Mimi,' said Lydia.

Mimi eyed her defiantly.

'What did she shout at him for?' I said as casually as I could.

'I can't remember,' said Lydia.

'He burned things,' said Mimi, hopping up and down with excitement.

Lydia was beside her in an instant. She slapped her on the bottom. 'I'm telling Daddy,' she said, slapping her again.

'Stop it.' I pulled Lydia away. 'You shouldn't hit your sister.'

Mimi was crying out of all proportion to the light smack Lydia had given her but she looked so pathetic with her half-plaited hair and the tears rolling down her cheeks that I took her on my lap. She clung to me, making loud sobbing noises, and I stroked her back until she stopped.

Lydia stood there, a hand on her hip, her own eyes filling with tears. 'She's not supposed to talk about it,' she said.

'Is it a secret then?' I asked softly.

Lydia shook her head and turned away to rub a quick hand

over her face. I started to unravel the remains of Mimi's plait, surprised at the feel of her hair. So very thick and soft and heavy. All of a sudden she put her arms round my neck and kissed me on the cheek.

'Oh,' I said even more surprised. 'What was that for?'

Lydia smiled now and raised her eyes briefly to the ceiling. 'She does that to everyone,' she said. 'When are you going to show us your charts?'

At that moment the phone rang.

It was Lewis. 'Are my girls with you?' he said. I was astounded. Here we were barely four miles from the centre of London, a few minutes' walk from streets teeming with God knows what dregs of society and he didn't actually know where his two little daughters were.

'Yes,' I said, 'they are.'

I must have sounded disapproving because he said: 'I thought they must be. I knew they wouldn't go far. Lydia's very sensible.' There was a pause then he said, 'I'm sorry if they've bothered you. I overslept.'

'They're not bothering me. It's your father,' I said over my shoulder to Lydia.

She pulled a face. 'Tell him I left a note.'

'I heard that,' he said. 'Can you send them back, please? I have to leave soon.'

Lydia pulled another face but didn't argue. Mimi had crawled under the table after Pisces.

I was reluctant to let them go yet, and before I knew it, I was saying, 'Look, would you like me to have them for the morning? Lydia wants to see my astrology stuff. They can stay here until you get home.'

'Don't you have to work?'

'Not today. I could take them out for a walk later.'

'Are you sure?'

'Yes, or I wouldn't have offered. I'll send them up for their coats.'

There was another pause before he said: 'They won't keep pestering you. After today, I mean. They'll be back with their mother.'

I sent Lydia up for their coats and fetched a brush. Without her sister, Mimi became very quiet again and edged over towards the door. I crouched in front of her and gently brushed first one side of her hair and then the other. She stood there with a finger in her mouth, obviously worried about being left alone with me. But I couldn't resist questioning her some more. 'What did Janus burn?' I asked.

'Mummy's clothes,' she whispered, avoiding my eyes.

I felt like the wicked witch but I had to know. 'What happened then?' I said, lowering my voice to match hers.

'He cried,' she said, barely audible now.

'Was Daddy cross?'

She shook her head.

'Did Janus burn anything else?'

She shook her head again and then Lydia was pushing the door open. 'You have to come and say goodbye to Daddy,' she said, taking hold of Mimi's hand.

Now I don't panic easily. I worry, I tie myself into knots with wondering about the significance of things and whether it's safer to do something this way or that. Funnily enough I don't believe that my future is in any way predictable. I believe that we're all in charge of our destinies, which I feel is an awful responsibility. So I'm careful about what I do. But right now I feel that I've been very careless and that there is nothing I can do about it. And I'm panicking.

So I phone Evie. But she takes so long to answer that I change my mind about telling her what it is that has upset me. Instead I say, 'Can you come over? I'm babysitting two little girls and I need help.'

'Babysitting?' she laughs.

'Yes. I offered. I don't know what possessed me.'

'Oh,' she says as it dawns on her what I'm talking about. 'I know what you're up to.'

'Evie, can you just get over here?'

'OK. We'll pick their little brains to bits.'

We end up in St James's Park with a carrier bag full of shop-bought sandwiches, which the girls are now feeding to the ducks.

'Simple tastes, these two,' says Evie wryly, as we sit on a bench and watch Mimi throw garlic bread, prawns and lettuce coated with mayonnaise into the air. The bread reaches the water but the lettuce and prawns land on the path not far from her feet.

We have walked here from Selfridges where Lydia spent half an hour choosing a pair of earrings for her mother. Lewis has given them ten pounds each and Lydia was insistent that we went to Selfridges. Evie's suggestion that we go to the Toy Museum was dismissed with a 'We've been there.' These two seem to have visited every attraction in the whole of London. Shopping was all Lydia wanted to do. Mimi shopped too – ten pounds' worth of sandwiches to feed the ducks! Though we did persuade her to part with a couple to eat for our lunch.

Evie finds them amusing. She is not like me, wondering whether they are enjoying themselves and worried about crossing roads and not getting lost in the shops. She treats them as though they are two little dogs trotting along behind her, doing their best to keep up, stopping when she stops and starting when she starts.

Luckily the weather's good, it's even warm for April. The sun has brought people out, or I presume it has as I've never been in this park before so I don't know if it's always this crowded on a sunny spring day. It's funny, I feel as though I've been shut indoors for months, the sun is making my eyes water and everything looks very bright. Perhaps it's seeing the city through a child's eyes, taking in things that I'd normally miss, looking to left and right and even up and down rather than just straight ahead. Mimi and Lydia have competed with each other to give a running commentary on everything we've passed. 'Do you two ever shut up?' said Evie, which made them laugh for some reason. I wish I could talk to them as Evie does but it doesn't come naturally to me.

A short distance away from us on the grass, three men are lounging, three young men. Lads. I knew the minute I saw them that Evie would choose this bench. They look as though they are from a building site, muscular, dusty and already slightly tanned. That's all I notice; I don't have the inclination to eye up strangers the way Evie does. It isn't that I'm shy, I just don't flirt with strangers. Evie thinks it's a powerful feminist thing to do. I think she can't help it. Her birthday is

22 May, a fickle Gemini with the sensual quality of Taurus, a woman who is truly aware of the power of her body – with or without clothes as far as Evie is concerned. Today she is wearing a long skirt split to the thigh and, beneath her leather jacket, a tight cropped top like Indian women wear beneath their saris. I am wearing the same jeans that I dragged on when Lydia came knocking at my door earlier, and a black sweater, a uniform for blondes, Evie calls it.

The man in the middle of the group is showing an interest. He says something to his friends and they both look towards us.

'I think you can take your pick now, Evie,' I say.

'I only want the one nearest us. He keeps adjusting his balls in his jeans, haven't you noticed?'

'No I have not,' I say, smiling and turning away from her.

She calls Lydia over. Mimi comes too. 'Go and ask that man over there what his name is,' she says to Lydia.

Lydia glances towards them. 'No,' she says, 'ask him yourself.' But she looks again, interested in what Evie is up to.

'Do you think he looks sexy?' says Evie.

Lydia smiles, unsure how to answer, too old to giggle and too young to blush.

'Evie, stop it,' I say.

She ignores me. 'Have you got a boyfriend?' she asks Lydia.

'No.' Lydia wrinkles her nose with disgust.

'Bet you have,' says Evie. 'What sort of boys do you like?'

Lydia begins to smile again but doesn't answer.

'Has your daddy got a girlfriend?' says Evie.

'Evie!' I scold and try to gag her with a hand.

Mimi is hopping up and down with delight at our fooling around and I grab her and pull her on to my lap. 'You mustn't listen to Evie, she's very naughty.' Mimi cuddles against me. Her hands are greasy from the sandwiches. They leave smudges on the front of my sweater but I don't mind.

The men are gathering up flasks and lunch boxes but the one nearest is still watching us. Evie stands up and props her foot on the arm of the bench to tie the lace of her boot. She doesn't have particularly good legs; her calves are short and muscular. But it is the performance with Evie. The promise.

I lean back, Mimi still cuddled in my arms. The sun is no

longer making my eyes water. I feel relaxed, relaxed enough to think calmly and logically about what Mimi told me earlier. If it was a vindictive act, then it's not likely that Janus will repeat it against me who has done nothing more than tell him not to piss in the Square. And if it was an accident then he is probably more careful these days. People who smoke do have accidents, I know that. Gerald once fell asleep while he was smoking and set fire to the sheet. He gave up after that, though sadly it was too late for his health by then. If I believed in fate, which I don't, it would be easy to assume that his smoking would be the death of him, one way or another. It was Gerald who made sure there were fire extinguishers in the house. I know there's one in the kitchen and I think there's one in the attic room. I try to remember; try to picture exactly where it is.

Mimi wriggles from my lap and I look up at Evie, still playing to her audience. 'I thought you were dating the art teacher from your Tuesday sessions,' I say.

'No, I've stopped seeing him. It was embarrassing. Every time he looked at me in class, I'd think of the night before and my nipples got stiff.'

'Oh, Evie,' I laugh.

She straightens up and laughs too. 'You've got real colour in your cheeks,' she says, touching me with the back of her hand to test whether I'm hot or cold. I'm warm. I feel warm all through. We smile at each other. 'Come on,' she says. 'We'll walk along the embankment. Lydia can tell us what she knows about the Thames.'

'I don't know anything about the Thames,' says Lydia.

'Well, you can tell us about Daddy's restaurant then,' says Evie with a wink at me. 'We haven't heard much about that yet.'

In the event we don't learn too much about the restaurant but we do discover that Lewis's ex-wife is called Nicole and lives in Fulham with a man who is some sort of dealer in property, mainly abroad. And Lydia also tells us that her father is always phoning her mother in Fulham.

'And do they talk for long?' asks Evie.

'Sometimes,' says Lydia. She skips on ahead for a bit then announces that she wants to go home. 'Mimi's getting tired,' she says. 'So am I.'

'Tired of answering questions,' Evie says out of the side of her mouth.

We walk back to Westminster station and part beneath ground with a warm wind blowing our hair round our faces. Evie goes west and we go east. As we turn to wave, Evie calls out, 'Lydia, ask your dad if he needs any waitresses.'

'She's only joking,' I say, taking her hand as well as Mimi's. 'Evie jokes about a lot of things.'

On the train, Mimi falls asleep. Lydia is very quiet, chewing at her nails, inspecting each one then chewing some more. Completely absorbed. Or maybe lost in thought. I leave her in peace. In fact, I feel slightly ashamed at the way we've questioned them. It must be hard always to be separated from one parent.

When I return them home, Lewis is there and invites me in. I step inside the hall knowing that he is just being polite. He looks tired. His face is drained of colour except for the dark circles under his eyes and a bluish tinge of beard. From what I can tell, he works very long hours, often not coming home until after midnight. But he is usually home at this time, mid-afternoon, for a couple of hours.

'Have you had a good time?' he asks Lydia.

'Yeah, brilliant,' she says unconvincingly.

'And did you see Verity's er . . . astrology things?'

'Oh they had a quick look,' I break in. I think he's trying to coax Lydia into a more enthusiastic response. 'It's a bit complicated for a ten-year-old.'

'Ten going on twenty,' he smiles.

Lydia has gone to switch on the TV. We're standing in the hall and I can see right through to the kitchen, which was once part of Gerald's drawing room. In the corner I spot the fire extinguisher.

'Well, thank you very much for having them.'

'I've enjoyed it.'

Mimi is clamouring round his legs and he stoops to pick her up, pressing his lips against her cheek. She rubs both hands round his face, then pats it. 'You're scratchy,' she scolds him.

'Daddy,' calls out Lydia, 'Verity's friend Evie said do you need a waitress?'

He looks at me. 'Unfortunately I only employ men. But I'll ask—'

'No, no.' I wave a hand in front of me. 'She was only joking. She has a perfectly good job, she didn't mean it.' Which isn't strictly true. Evie is always on the lookout for a new job, a new situation, a new man.

Mimi is still fondling Lewis, her little fingers exploring his chin and neck. And I can't help thinking of something Evie once said to me about there being only one place to be kissed by a man who needs a shave. Something I don't know much about as Gerald had a beard which was soft as velvet.

'Daddy, I'm starving,' calls Lydia from the sitting room.

'I'd better go,' I say. 'Let you feed these two.'

I turn to the front door, still ajar. Lewis pulls it open for me. 'Say thank you to Verity,' he instructs Mimi. She stretches out from his arms to kiss me. I feel slightly flustered held in her grasp, inches from Lewis. Near enough to discover that he doesn't smell of food, as I'd imagined all chefs do; he smells of Ralph Lauren. 'Lydia,' he calls.

Lydia comes to the sitting room door and waves a hand. 'Thank you,' she says.

'It's been a nice change for me,' I smile. 'I might borrow them again sometime.'

Lydia eyes me a moment, then suddenly swivels round and runs back into the sitting room. 'Don't turn it over,' she shouts. 'I was watching that,' and I realise that Janus must be there. Keeping very quiet, I think.

I go to bed early with a chunk of halva, a bottle of wine, a file of work and some old books of Gerald's. This is not unusual for me, I like to work in bed. It's a way of getting to sleep. Often I wake in the middle of the night having fallen asleep in a clutter of papers and books, and even one time with half a tomato sandwich in the bed. If I worked at my desk until I was tired, it would not be the same. Ideas come easier when I'm in bed. I can rest my head on the pillow, close my eyes over a problem and think of answers that would not occur to me in any other situation. It is close to dreaming, not sleep dreaming but the other kind of dreaming where you let your mind wander until reality and imagination merge. Until they become one and the same. After all, there is only a thin dividing line between them. So Gerald led me to believe. And once you learn how to cross this border at will, you have the secret to controlling the dreams of sleep. That is how he explained it to me, all this in a soothing voice like that of a hypnotist. Telling me I could dream about whatever I wanted.

But I am too unsettled to think of dreams right now. And I'm wondering if today hasn't been a mistake from beginning to end. Too many thoughts are whizzing around in my head. Thoughts that I don't particularly want there. For example, I have never desired or sought the company or affection of small children but I can't stop thinking of Mimi's little arms round my neck. It may be that my maternal instincts are emerging from the hiding place where my mother has driven them. That's OK, I can accept that. And I can even accept that I might want to have a child of my own one day after all. The desire would need to be very strong, I know that, but I haven't discounted the possibility of this happening to me. The thing I can't accept – and it's a feeling that has only sprung up today – is the possibility that I am, or could be, jealous of Evie. And over something that hasn't even happened.

I am not a jealous person. I don't envy or want what others have. And I'm not competitive. It's probably the reason why I am so content with my solitary life, although some people might see it as a fault. At school I was good at sports because I was tall and agile, but if another girl was alongside me in a race and in danger of overtaking, I didn't try any harder, I'd let her win. So why do I feel upset at the thought that Evie really will try to get a job at Lewis's restaurant, and that she will march in and capture him?

When she first knew that he was coming to live here, she said that having two men in the house would affect my libido. 'The smell of them will get you going,' was what she actually said. It made me think of certain animals, apes, I believe it is, who only become receptive to mating when the act is about to take place. It was on one of the wildlife programmes that Gerald and I used to watch. Oestrus is stimulated by the male attempting to mate, was how the commentator explained it. Well, I don't think I'm about to throw myself at Lewis over a whiff of Ralph Lauren. But I have to acknowledge the fact that

I don't want Evie to have him. It would make me jealous.

I finish the halva and my first glass of wine and start to work on the file. Once a month the editor of the magazine I freelance for sends me a parcel of readers' letters detailing their dreams. Out of these I must choose three and interpret the dreams for publication. First I sift through and set aside any that I know will be considered too disturbing or too *risqué* in content. There are always a few that fall into this category and sometimes one or two that are simply pornographic.

Working on this should be easier and quicker than horoscopes; I have several books to consult and notes of Gerald's covering almost every possibility. But I always find myself lingering over these letters, wondering about the writers, especially the ones I mustn't choose. Do people really dream of being fucked by animals? Sometimes it's the family pet, but goats are the favourite; perhaps it's all those connections with the devil. The ones containing violence really alarm me and I usually tear them up after the first line. They seem more fabricated than the ones that are purely about sex, and I feel sure that they are written by men who assume, quite rightly, that a woman will be opening them.

My first choice is from a woman. A dream about swimming naked in a goldfish bowl. Being naked in a goldfish bowl is a bit of a cliché, I suppose, but I like the part about how she is tipped in the sink while the bowl is cleaned. This one will be humorous, acceptably *risqué* with scope for a mildly sexy picture, and plenty for me to enlarge on; water has such a multitude of meanings in the world of dreams. Freud wrote that those who often dream of swimming, especially swimming in waves with great enjoyment, are usually those who wetted their beds when children. I shouldn't think you get many waves in a goldfish bowl.

Sometimes I am so intrigued by the letters that I feel like talking to the people themselves. Especially the ones that I believe are made up. I should like to say, I don't believe you dreamed this but I'm interested to know where the idea came from. But of course I never do. And I don't know who they are anyway. All I'm given are their initials, their sex and the town where they live.

By the time I have written up notes for the first one, I'm tired and a little tipsy. I shove the books on to the floor and stretch out in my bed. It's the same one I used to share with Gerald and too big for this room where I work and sleep. Sometimes I feel that the whole basement is too small for me and I think with longing of how I used to run up and down the stairs when I first came to live here. And how Miss Campion would listen to me.

I lean over and pick up one of the books. Freud's *The Interpretation of Dreams*. In the front is a sheet of paper in Gerald's handwriting. It's headed 'Notes on the "id", the "ego" and the "superego".' The words fill the paper from top to bottom and side to side. No margins, and extra words squeezed in on every line. They are hard to understand, both in their form and their meaning. I feel suffocated by them. He taught me so much yet I know so little. I read a sentence which says, 'The sea is a fine example because of its many faces – it can be both male and female; as seductive as the female, as cruel as the male.' Or vice versa, I think.

I sit up so that I can see myself in the mirror opposite. I think I am more unusual than pretty. I have a small flat face not unlike those Peruvians who inhabit the Andes, wearing coloured blankets and tending llamas and alpacas. Gerald told me that. He said that if I had black hair I would look exactly like them. When I've had a couple of drinks I see myself differently. I imagine that I'm as seductive as Evie.

I throw back the duvet and take off my nightie. The sight of my naked body in the mirror arouses me. I stare at myself, wanting further stimulation, wanting to become intensely stimulated and then hold myself back. I wish I had the magazines that Gerald bought for me all those years ago. The pictures in them are still very clear to me. I can conjure them up easily. One had a woman holding her breasts in her hands, pushing them upwards, her fingers pulling the skin taut so that her nipples protruded. She was watched by a man chained to a wall opposite. The mere thought of being tied up terrifies me, but for some reason I found that picture the most arousing.

Keeping my eyes on the mirror I recreate the picture. As usual I feel a second or two of shame, of reluctance, and it's like that first time when Gerald said, 'Now do it by yourself.' In the end he had to manipulate my fingers, kick-start me.

Tonight I'm unusually hesitant to carry on. Though I desperately want to. I place my hand with spread fingers like a fig leaf but cannot move my finger because I have the feeling that I'm being watched. Or listened to. I imagine that they can hear me upstairs. I am still stopping and starting and teasing myself with all the images I can think of, when I hear Lewis's car pull up. I can only hear it because I have my bedroom door open and the sash on the front window pulled down a fraction. Not enough for anyone to get in. It's so that I can hear Pisces scratch at the glass if he should grow tired of his night-time prowling.

Lewis closes his car door very quietly but I hear him cross the pavement and put his key in the lock. He is extra quiet tonight. No visiting the kitchen or the sitting room but straight upstairs. Probably so tired that all he wants to do is fall into bed. I remember how tired he looked earlier. And Mimi holding his face. His scratchy chin. Then I do something I have never done before. I roll over and take my hairbrush from on top of the chest of drawers. It's real bristle. Short stubbly bristle that I was told by a hairdresser would not damage my fine hair. I run my palm over it and then circle it gently against the innermost corner of my thigh.

Chapter 4

On Saturday Lydia and Mimi's mother comes to collect them. I hear the car pull up and I hear them all out on the pavement but I close my bedroom door and get on with my work. The next thing I know, Lewis is phoning to say that Mimi has been knocking on my door but he can't make me hear. 'She has something for you,' he says.

When I go to the door I find Mimi standing there almost hidden behind a pot plant. She thrusts it at me.

'Thank you for taking me out,' she says, and runs back up the steps.

It's a wonderful plant with stripy maroon leaves and exotic-looking pink powers. A New Guinea Impatiens I read on the label, and on the back the price, three pounds fifty from a garage. I look up the steps. Lydia and Mimi are there with their mother.

'Thank you,' I say, going halfway up to them. 'But there was no need.'

'They phoned to tell me what a good day they'd had.'

My first thought is that the name Nicole suits her. I like to make some quick assumptions when I meet new people because on the whole I think first impressions are important. Later, when you know them better, it's interesting to see where you went wrong. If of course you did. And I also believe that looks are important when summing a person up. It's that whole intriguing business of the masks that we wear in public. Evie and I describe people to each other by likening them to well-known film stars or singers or anyone famous. Sometimes we say bits of this person and bits of that person. We got the idea from a board game that she bought in America. It has large cardboard faces cut up like a jigsaw and you have to try to guess who it is using as few pieces as possible. I would say Nicole was a younger version of Jane Seymour. But fairer, more Jerry Hall perhaps, especially with the height, though she is wearing stiletto heels. Classic oval face, good figure – slim but curvy. Confident.

'I don't get much time to go feeding ducks,' she says.

At that moment I spot Miss Campion peering round her door. When she sees me she waves and comes out. 'Good morning, Verity dear,' she calls, then smiles another more restrained good morning to Nicole. She holds up a bulging polythene bag. 'Just going to do my good deed,' she says.

Miss Campion puts mixed seed on the birdtable in the central garden every week, but always on Sundays. Her curiosity has obviously got the better of her. She beckons me across. I put the plant on the top step and go to see what she wants, hugging my arms round my chest to hint that I'm cold and don't feel like standing around out here.

'Did you hear about Mrs Dorrell?' she asks, looking over my shoulder as she speaks.

'Yes I did.' Mrs Dorrell, who lives opposite, was mugged on her way up from the station over a week ago. It's old news and not something I particularly want to hear all over again.

'Awful business. The poor thing has a black eye and a broken finger.'

'Yes, awful.'

'You ought to be careful when you go out, dear.' Her eyes are on me now. 'You should take a cab home if you're out late.'

'Yes, I will.'

'If you're on your own, I mean.'

I smile noncommittally but her attention is caught by the group behind me once more. I hear Lewis's voice but don't turn round.

'It's such a shame,' whispers Miss Campion. 'Such beautiful children as well.'

I nod, wondering why divorce should be worse if you have children who are beautiful.

Miss Campion waggles her fingers in the air. 'Good morning, Mr Kaye,' she trills, and I have no alternative but to turn round and greet him too. 'Oh well, duty calls.' She holds her birdseed aloft once more and I stroll across the road with her because I've spotted Pisces lurking in the bushes. He thinks that he's hidden from us but the end of his tail betrays him, flicking away on the grass like a little silver snake. He is probably deciding whether to hang around for the birds or make a dash for one of the open front doors.

I look back towards the group on the pavement, wondering whether I will be able to grab Pisces before he makes a move and embarrasses me. Lewis is holding Nicole by the shoulders. As I watch he bends and kisses her on the lips. It's a brief kiss but not the sort you'd give your sister or mother, or how I imagine you'd kiss someone from whom you were divorced. Even from across the road I can see that. Nicole steps back. The girls are already in her car – an expensive-looking model though I'm not good enough on cars to know what type. Nicole takes another step away, then removes each of Lewis's hands from her shoulders and gets into the car.

'I hope she doesn't wear those shoes on your wood floors,' says Miss Campion from behind me.

'Oh, I don't think she's been in the house.' I crouch down to see where Pisces has disappeared to.

'She did the other day she was here. But I'm not sure what shoes she was wearing then.'

I glance up at her. How different people look from ground level. This is how we must appear to small children and cats. All the sagging flesh below the chin. I make a mental note to start doing the facial exercises that my mother has been doing fastidiously for the last thirty-three years. Ever since she had me, in fact, after which she announced that she didn't want both ends of her falling apart.

Miss Campion invites me in for coffee but I refuse, making the excuse that I'm expecting a phone call, a lie which I'm slightly ashamed of. She is lonely, I'm not. I'm supposed to be having lunch with Gerald's elderly uncle, who lives in a huge house on Clapham Common, but I phone and cancel this with another lie. I tell him that I have a cold and don't want to pass on my germs. We used to go there once a month and it's something I've kept up out of respect for Gerald. The only attraction, I'm afraid, is the lunch prepared by his Greek housekeeper. But today, for some reason, I don't feel any more like eating than I do like making conversation.

I could, if I needed company, call Evie and join her for whatever she has planned for tonight. She's given up inviting me but I know that even if she has a date she would conjure up someone for me. She has this mental file like a dating agency, where she keeps details of men she considers would suit me. Her descriptions of them amaze and amuse me. Lusty, brawny types barely out of their teens. To stop her nagging, I tell her I'll try one of them soon. We have even discussed what I shall wear for this coming-out party. Evie has a dress of crushed velvet the colour of crème de menthe and no bigger than a tea towel. She is irresistible in it. According to her, so would I be. But I don't think tonight will be the night.

Even my little basement looks gloomy today, the corners festooned with cobwebs that I hadn't noticed before. Spiders love this house, probably because they know I won't kill them or put a tumbler over them and leave them to starve as Miss Campion does, though Pisces is free from both superstition and squeamishness, and ruthlessly hunts the ones that are foolish enough to venture within his reach, even eating them on occasion.

I fetch a feather duster and swat away a few of the biggest cobwebs, then clean up the dusty deposits that have fallen down with them. Cleaning is something I save for days such as this, days when I don't want to do anything in particular. Usually I listen to music while I work, or sometimes one of Gerald's old lecture tapes. It's while I'm sifting through the tapes, wondering if I should try one labelled *The Ascendant and the Midheaven* with *Jung and the Persona* in brackets beneath it, that I hear Lewis and Janus go out. I carry on with what I'm doing but I cannot help but hear them slam the front door and Janus arguing loudly that he wants to drive. The tape will be beyond my understanding but I put it on all the same, turning up the volume so that Gerald's voice fills the room. It is only then that I admit to myself that I feel a little depressed.

One of the many important things that Gerald taught me was to be honest with myself. It's the only way to be in control, he said. And it works, I know it works, it's how I live my life. So why has it suddenly stopped working? I will admit that yes

I do feel a frisson of something when I'm in Lewis's presence, so why do I seem to have lost control? It's not that I want him to notice me. And it has nothing to do with the fact that he is still, so obviously, in love with his ex-wife. It's that I have fantasised about him for the last three nights.

The next morning, finding myself still depressed, I make the decision to visit my parents in Hampshire. A long overdue visit. In fact I've not been to see them for six months. They don't come here because my mother can't, won't, travel, though she did manage to get to her sister in Scotland for Christmas. It's not that I expect they will cheer me up, quite the reverse. It's like the housework: something I do when nothing else inspires me. Nevertheless, the idea of getting away for a few days does make me feel a little better.

Later on, Evie phones. 'I'm back with Rick,' she says. 'We went out to celebrate last night.'

'Rick?' I say, wondering why she is calling to tell me this. 'Oh, the one who makes your nipples stiffen in class.'

Unusually for her she doesn't enlarge on this remark but says, 'We had a wonderful meal. Bet you can't guess where.'

Oh, but I can. 'Are you going to tell me the gory details now?' I ask lightly. 'Or will it wait until you come over?'

She laughs. 'You've guessed. Are you still there?' she asks.

'Yes, I'm just taking some aspirin.'

'What for?' she demands.

'Because I've got a feeling you're going to give me a headache.'

'You take too many pills.'

'You take too many men.'

'Stop being bitchy and listen.'

'I'm listening. Oh, before I forget, I'm going away for a few days to see my parents.'

'That was sudden.'

'I need a change of scene. Now tell me about last night.'

'Ah, well,' she drawls, and I can almost see her settling with the phone, probably half-naked, with the adoring Rick watching her while he poaches eggs and butters toast. 'You've been keeping secrets from me.'

'Have I?' This I can't guess.

'You didn't tell me the brother worked at the restaurant as well.'

'I didn't know. Doing what?'

'Waiting on tables.' She lowers her voice; so I'm right, Rick is there. 'And looking like Rufus Sewell.'

'Oh, Evie,' I laugh, 'you must have put your contact lenses in upside down.'

'Actually,' she says, her voice back to normal, 'I've lost one so people do look a bit odd at the moment. But I don't need to see the fine detail when it comes to men. The outline is enough.'

'And what about Lewis's outline? Did you manage to see that?'

'Yes I did. In fact once I'd sussed out who was who and introduced myself, he came over to thank me for keeping his daughters amused the other day.'

I'm about to tell her about my plant but decide not to go into that. 'So who would you say Lewis was like?' I ask instead.

'Mmm, hard to say. He had his chef's hat and jacket on. Maybe the guy in the Peugeot advert. Same soft eyes. Do you know it?'

'No, I can't say I do,' I lie.

'Well, I'll give you a tip. Next time you see him drive up, go out and say, "Nice car," then lean against it and close your eyes.'

I realise I've dropped myself in it here. If I don't ask why, she'll know I've lied. And if I do she'll go into a long description of what is a very sexy kiss. 'Hang on,' I say, 'Pisces is scratching at the window.' I walk to the window and back. 'I'll have to go and feed him,' I tell her.

'Don't you want to know what Lewis said about you?'

'Be quick then.'

She laughs. 'Don't give me that, Verity. You're dying to know.'

'I hate being told what I'm thinking.'

'Don't get arseholey with me.' She laughs again, to herself. 'It's nothing special anyway. He just said he was a bit embarrassed the way his daughters had barged in on you because he knows how busy you are with work. He said they all try not to make too much noise.'

'They don't try very hard,' I say irritably, knowing I'm giving exactly the impression I don't want to give. It's not like me. I'm just glad we're not face to face. 'Look, Evie, I have to go. Thanks for the very exciting account of your evening. I'll call you when I get back from my parents.'

'OK. By the way, you'll be pleased to know that Rick spent nearly eighty quid last night, so that's something towards next month's rent.'

'What were you wearing?' I say.

'What was I wearing?'

'Oh, never mind. Pisces sends his love,' I say quickly to distract her and to make up for being crabby. 'I'll speak to you when I get back.'

I spend the rest of the day cleaning my cooker and fridge while I listen to Gerald's tape on *The Ascendant and Midheaven.* The bits quoting Jung are quite interesting after all. They enlarge on his theory about man having two personalities, the introvert and the extrovert, two faces, one he shows the world, the Persona; the other hidden from view, our natural self. 'It's not necessarily deliberate, this mask we put on,' Gerald's voice tells me. 'But once we recognise it and seek to understand our true selves, then we can also look for that same truth in other people.' The sound of Gerald's voice is soothing, so real and familiar. I replay sections of the tape. Then I play the whole thing again and try to understand more of it. The theory about the two faces stirs something way back in my head but I can't quite remember what it is. I play the tape three times in all, stopping and starting it, repeating sentences aloud and squeezing my eyes shut to force this memory out. But still it eludes me. In the end I switch off the tape and go to make some supper.

Sunday night and I'm eating toast and a tub of hummus for my main meal. I finish off two pieces of toast and stick another slice of bread in the toaster, practising for bigger meals with my parents. That's the first thing my mother will ask: are you eating enough? Not, are you happy? Do you put the chain on the door at night? Do you still miss Gerald? Perhaps it's an instinctive thing for mothers to say, something to do with the first needs of a newborn baby. Funnily enough I don't know whether I was breast-fed, though I doubt it.

Lewis and Janus come home early, making more noise than when they left. I think they are having a row. I switch on the tape again to drown them out but can hear all three voices: the precise and almost tender way that Gerald would speak when trying to explain something, Janus protesting loudly that it wasn't his fault, and Lewis interrupting him to shout for fuck's sake shut up.

I wouldn't have thought Lewis was the sort of person who would shout and swear in a quiet place like this at half-past ten on a Sunday night. I think of Miss Campion and feel annoyed on her behalf. In fact I feel so annoyed that I forget my toast and go for a shower instead. Upstairs one of them is doing the same. In this house as in many old houses, I suspect, the plumbing talks. It tells me when they fill a kettle and when they are using the washing machine. And right now, I know that one of them is taking a shower, as I am. I wish I didn't track these actions of theirs. And I wish I could stop thinking about Lewis in his chef's jacket, the starchy white cotton and what it would feel like against my skin if he came up behind me now. The coarse feel of his jacket and the soft touch of his slender chef's fingers, perhaps a little slippery with olive oil the way mine are with soap.

I slide to my knees on the floor of the shower, my forehead resting against the tiles. Gerald is still talking away in the other room; his words are nearly lost in the swish of water around me but not quite. I hear him say something about dreams being the key to our internal lives. What does he mean by an internal life? A hidden life? A dream life? And what life does fantasising belong to? Is it a dream or is it reality? What I do know is that I am fantasising about someone who is very real. What he is doing to me with his soapy invasive fingers on the floor of my shower is a dream but one which I should like to turn into reality.

At the point of no return, when every nerve strains towards the attainment of that final overwhelming pleasure, I forget Lewis. Nothing exists outside the one small focus of that pleasure. Afterwards I kneel there for a moment, smiling to myself and thinking that perhaps I do understand what Gerald means after all. It even makes me laugh quietly to think of tomorrow at my parents when I shall sit with them, my

Persona in place and my father asking, 'Well, what have you been up to, Verity?'

I stand up and wrap myself in a towel, feeling lazy and almost content. But as I open the bathroom door I smell burning and my smoke alarm is bleeping like crazy.

A few panicky seconds go by before I realise that it is only the slice of bread that I stuck in the toaster earlier. I've cut it too thick and it has jammed and burned black at the bottom. I'm not superstitious. I walk under ladders and could spill a whole packet of salt without worrying about the devil standing behind me. But the billows of smoke in my kitchen make me uneasy. I turn the Expelair fan on full and open a window. The smoke starts to drift up towards the pavement, then seems to change its mind and hovers like a little cloud outside my door. It's trapped between the cold air outside and the warmth from my window, I tell myself. And I tell myself that I'm not overreacting when I hunt out my insurance broker's phone number so that I can call them first thing in the morning and ask them to check the position should my tenants set fire to the house.

Of course I don't put it to them like that, nor do I tell them that I have reason to suspect there could be increased risk. I just say could they please check what is covered by the massive new premium I have to pay. It seems I am well protected so I am determined not to worry about it while I'm away. But when I go to ask Miss Campion if she'll feed Pisces for me, I add casually that I'd be grateful if she could keep an eye on the house as well.

'Of course, dear,' she says. 'I'll pop round every day.'

'Well, you know what men are like,' I say without thinking. 'They could easily go off and leave the front door open or something.' Miss Campion probably *doesn't* know what men are like, and this is unnecessary anyway because she spends half her life at the window watching our comings and goings.

'Quite easily,' she smiles, as though she suspects my tenants are capable of far worse. 'But I must say, they were very quiet this morning. I didn't even hear them go.'

I didn't either, come to think of it. I haven't heard a sound but the car has gone. 'Probably trying to make up for last night,' I say.

'Why? What did they do last night?'

'Oh, just raised voices. You know.'

She nods as though she does, then smiles. 'I never used to hear a sound when dear Gerald was alive.'

'No,' I say.

'Still the past is the past. Unfortunately.' She pats my hand. I give her my spare keys and make my escape. Back indoors I call Evie but she's not there so I leave a message on her answerphone.

'Nothing important,' I say. 'I just felt like a quick chat because I didn't want to go straight from Miss Campion to my parents. And Evie, I might take you up on your offer of a blind date when I get back.'

Chapter 5

My father picks me up at the station. He seems a little preoccupied but I put it down to the fact that he has had just twenty-four hours' notice of my visit. He does all the shopping and perhaps he was worried about what to buy to feed this daughter whom he hardly sees and doesn't really know any longer. If he ever did.

As we drive away from the station he says, 'I'm sorry about Christmas, Verity.'

Oh, so this is what's bothering him. 'Don't worry, Dad. Really, it's OK.'

'Did you have a good time with Evie?'

'Yes, not bad.' This is a necessary lie to save his guilt. I could have gone to Brighton with Evie, but I didn't. My father thinks that he and my mother should invite me home every year. As I suppose most parents do. So when they told me that they had been asked to stay with my aunt in her tiny two-bedroomed flat in Edinburgh, I saved them by saying that actually I had thought of joining Evie and her family for a change. Evie also feels duty-bound to include me in her plans at Christmas now that I'm alone. No one seems to understand that I'm quite content with my own company.

'The other thing I wanted to talk to you about, while we're on our own, is to do with money.'

I look across at him, wary. 'Money?'

'Yes. I want to make sure you have something.'

'Can't we discuss this some other time, Dad?'

'I'm not talking about my will.'

I'm relieved; even the word makes me shrink away. The memory of Gerald's eldest son grabbing me by the arm and asking me if I was disappointed not to have it all is still upsetting to me. I rarely cry. Apart from when Gerald was ill and when he died, I can't remember crying since those first days at boarding school when I slept on a sodden pillow for the whole of the first week. But I cried over being misjudged by Gerald's family. Not openly. I think I managed to smile at his son and say something silly like, blood is obviously thicker than love.

'I want you to have enough so that you can buy somewhere when you have to sell the house,' my father says.

'Do you realise what a quarter-share will be?' I say. 'Do you know how much the value of property in the Square has risen?'

'I should think you'll end up with about a hundred thousand,' he says with a little smile. 'Am I right?'

I nod, surprised that he's so well-informed.

'But that's not enough to buy anywhere else in that area.'

'Let me worry about that, Dad.'

'The thing is, we've remortgaged. What with all the extras we need these days, my pension isn't enough.'

We're turning into the drive now. I notice that the bus shelter near to their front entrance has 'Saints Are Wankers' sprayed in giant letters across its roof, and that there are discarded beer cans at the top of the footpath that runs the length of their back garden. These things make me feel a sudden protectiveness towards my father. And a puzzling guilt, as though I am part of the brutal outside world that constantly threatens his quiet existence. He was an army chaplain before his retirement. Brutality is not alien to him, but I know that it has always offended him. I don't think I've ever heard him swear or even use a coarse word.

'I'm going to sell Kyle-dortha,' he's saying. 'I can give you the proceeds as a gift, so much each year. I have to check how much.'

'Kyle-dortha? I didn't know you still had it.'

He manoeuvres the car carefully into the garage from where a side door leads directly into the house. 'We shall never go there again,' he says, 'and I doubt that I'll get much for it. It's not in very good repair. But I can't afford to do anything to it. I haven't even kept up the insurance.'

'Oh, insurance,' I sigh.

He blinks at me, waiting for me to enlarge, but I just touch his arm, then get out of the car.

Later on we talk of Kyle-dortha again. I think my father wants to purge himself of any lingering nostalgia about the place. Or maybe he wants to remind me that we did have happy times together as a family. Ironically, my most vivid memory of our lough-side holiday cottage in Southern Ireland is the nightmares that the sound of water, constantly slapping against the stone parapet below my bedroom window, used to give me. At night and in bad weather it was always much louder.

'The water in the lough is so clean that it's used as a marine biology research site,' says my father. 'Did you know that, Verity?'

'No, I don't think so.' I'm distracted by the novelty of our thoughts running on such similar lines. And I have just remembered another thing about Lough Ine: the terrible stitch I used to get when we climbed the mountain that rises from its shore. Oh, and the little grotto in the woods where a plaster Virgin Mary stands beside a pool. I always wanted to remove one of the strings of plastic beads that hung around her neck and wear it myself. But I could never pluck up the courage. A girl at school had told me that Catholics have things called mortal sins that make the Virgin Mary weep. I was sure that stealing the beads would be one. Another one, my friend told me, was putting your hand inside your knickers. This, I decided, was far less risky than theft and, I discovered, far more thrilling. I'm not sure how old I was then, or whether it's shameful or ironic that I discovered these secret pleasures when I was still at school but had become almost frigid by the time I was married.

'Did you let it to anyone last summer?' I ask, pushing these thoughts away lest they show on my face.

'Only once, and the people complained about the sleeping arrangements. And the kitchen needs completely refitting. Things have disappeared over the years. Apparently there's no longer an iron or a toaster, and the shower fitment has been removed from the bath.'

'The trials and tribulations of letting property,' I say

absent-mindedly, my thoughts on my own toaster and the ominous smoke pouring from it.

My father nods to himself for a second or two, then slaps a hand on the arm of his chair. 'I'd forgotten. How are things going with your tenants?'

'All right. It pays my council tax and a few bills.'

'Is it a family you've got in there?' he asks.

'Yes,' I say to save explanations. My father won't enquire any more. He is not an inquisitive person, and as far as my welfare is concerned he requires to know only that I am not in need of anything.

My mother has been looking bored but now she clears her throat to join in the conversation. This throat clearing is a ploy, an announcement to make sure that we stop talking and listen to her.

'Can you get them out if you want to?' she says. 'That's what I want to know.'

'Yes, it's all been done through my solicitor.' I have asked my father not to tell her the details of Gerald's will. She would consider it an outrage, not a fair way of dealing with his estate as I did. According to my mother, a man must put his wife before any other mortal on earth.

'You'd need the whole house if you wanted to get married again,' she says.

'Well, I don't. Want to get married again.'

'How do you know what you might want in the future?'

'I'm glad you've come before the daffodils have finished,' says my father, strolling over to the window, hands clasped behind his back. 'We'll have a walk round the garden in a minute if you like.'

My mother ignores him. 'Your father and I don't have a lot to look forward to,' she says. 'It would be nice for us to see you married again.'

I stare her straight in the face. Her make-up is perfect. She applies it every day with the help of the nurse who comes each morning to assist her with bathing and dressing. The nurse is from a private agency so stays as long as my mother wishes. And, once a week, a hairdresser comes to the house to style her hair. She cannot do these things on her own because of her latest ailment, numbness in her fingers. When she told me about it, I thought to myself, well, at least she can't blame that on me. It's crippling, she maintains, though her doctor can find nothing wrong. Her medical problems seem to be moving outwards. Last year it was stiffness in her joints. Once upon a time all her complaints were closely connected to her womb and the damage wreaked upon her body by my birth. Perhaps as she has grown older, and sex and all its consequences have lost their importance, she has adjusted her suffering for a different use. I know that my father does all the cooking as well as the shopping. He will probably have to do the cleaning when they can no longer afford someone to do it for them.

'Nice?' I say. 'In what way?'

She looks towards my father but he is staring out at the garden. Her profile, eyebrows raised and lips pursed as though she is considering my question, surprises me. Never before have I thought I was like her. She looks too haughty, too stormy at times, and not amiable as I imagine myself to appear. But her profile is mine. Our strange flat profiles. And her once-dark hair is now tawny blonde, subtly tinted to disguise the fact that it is completely white. Even the once-brilliant blue of her eyes has faded to resemble mine. It takes a moment to sink in, this recognition that I resemble her so closely. Well, at least I know I won't look too bad when I'm seventy.

'Do you mean that you think another husband will be third time lucky?' My flippancy is a form of defence, I know, or rather a delaying tactic. I want her to say what is on her mind but not yet, not until I've decided whether to retaliate. I never have. And it's probably too late now anyway. The day before I married Gerald she took me aside and asked me was I pregnant? And when I told her no, Gerald had had a vasectomy, she shook me by the shoulders and said, 'Why are you doing this then?'

'No, that isn't what I meant. Though I hope that will be the case. Your father and I would like to see you happy. And we should like grandchildren. Or one at least. You are our only child, after all.'

'I'm happy as I am,' I say, but wonder if I've actually said it aloud because she goes on speaking.

'I know that babies can be a nuisance if you're working,' she says. 'But you could do your work in the evenings when it's in bed.'

I want to laugh at the absurdity of her. 'Hang on, Mother. I don't have a husband. I don't even have a boyfriend.' The only sex I have is by myself.

She stares at me, her face devoid of expression. There is so much I would like to say but I don't have enough bitterness left any more. And anyway, the equation is fading even for me now, the conviction that to have sex with a man can, and eventually will, lead to that most terrible of experiences, childbirth.

'No boyfriend,' she says. 'You're thirty-three years old.'

I do laugh now, a peal of laughter more suited to a three-year-old. I see my father glance round and wait until he turns away again. 'Well, I might remedy that soon,' I said quietly. 'Evie has someone lined up for me.' And I can't resist adding, 'Someone young.'

'Evie,' she says disparagingly.

My father opens the French doors. 'I saw a squirrel in the garden yesterday,' he says, looking out.

'I'll be with you in a minute, Dad,' I say. My mother is struggling to get out of her chair, her hands pressing feebly on the arms. I take hold of her elbow. 'What would be the best idea,' I whisper, 'is if I could find a nice divorcé with a couple of small children. That would solve everything, wouldn't it?' Her head twists round. I know that she thinks I'm being sarcastic but that's all. I don't know why I expected anything else or why I imagined I was being daring.

'I read your horoscopes,' she says, pointing to a pile of magazines on the bookshelves. 'Do you make them up?'

'No, of course I don't. I work them out properly with charts and tables.'

My father looks briefly over his shoulder again then goes out into the garden. He has never approved of astrology. It could be why I took it up in the first place. I can't really remember, but I hope not. I help my mother across the room to a sofa where she can watch us, and join my father out on the lawn.

'I've been thinking about giving it up,' I say. 'The astrology, I mean.'

He smiles but doesn't say anything and we walk together under the apple trees, skirting the clumps of daffodils which do look very pretty and even have a faint scent.

'There's only so much work you can do with books. The interpretation is the main thing. Gerald was brilliant at that, but I don't seem to have . . .' I shrug, 'whatever it takes.'

'I'm sure you do your best.'

'But it doesn't satisfy me. I feel as though I'm conning people.'

'Perhaps you take it too seriously.'

If I challenge him he will back down and I can't bear him to do this so I say, 'I might do some studying. Something different. Psychology maybe. Gerald's other subject.'

We have reached the bottom of the garden where a high laurel hedge, glossy with recent rain, divides it from playing fields. 'The money could help you with that,' he says. 'You could study full time if you had a decent sum.'

'Yes. Yes, thanks, Dad. I might do that.'

We turn and walk back up the lawn. My father picks a few daffodils on the way. 'Now then,' he says as we go back into the house. 'I can't remember what you like for a nightcap. Is it cocoa or Horlicks?'

'Coffee,' I say, wondering how I'm going to cope with five more days of this.

In the event, I don't have to. On the morning of the third day Miss Campion phones.

'I don't want to spoil your holiday.' She pauses long enough for my imagination to have my house burned down. 'And I don't suppose there's anything to worry about but I thought I should let you know. I think Pisces may be locked in the house. I haven't seen him since you left.'

'Have you checked my bedroom?' I say. 'He often sleeps for hours on my bed.'

'Yes, it was the first place I looked.'

'Well, perhaps you could knock at the house and ask.'

'I don't think there's anybody there. I haven't seen them for a couple of days.'

'Not even at night?'

'No. And the car's not there either.'

'Maybe they're away as well then. And Pisces could be off after some female.'

'Yes, there is that possibility, dear, but . . .'

'But what?'

'I thought I heard a cat mewing in the house last night. I knocked this morning but there was no answer.'

Unfortunately it's impossible for Miss Campion to look in the downstairs windows. You can't get close enough to the front windows because of the drop to my basement, and the only entrance to the back garden is through the house. I don't know what else to suggest and I don't want Miss Campion to have the worry of it.

'I think I'll come home,' I say.

'Oh, don't do that,' she says quickly. 'I'll knock again this evening.'

'No, don't bother, I'll come home. I'd only planned to stay for a couple more days anyway.'

'Well, if you're sure. Er . . . there is something else I ought to mention, Verity.' She sounds worried and my heart sinks. 'They had a battle of words soon after you left. Very loud. Very unpleasant.'

Poor Miss Campion, I think, and for a moment I experience the same sense of responsibility as I did about the graffiti on the bus shelter. 'I'll get the next train,' I tell her.

My father has the train times checked and the car out of the garage before I have time to do much worrying. Though, as my mother points out, cats can go for a long time without food. And I tell her that I once saw him perched on the side of the toilet bowl taking a drink, so that shouldn't be any problem. Her only reply to this is that all male animals do disgusting things. Good job I didn't tell her that the attraction for Pisces, so I believe, was that Evie had used my loo and not flushed it. Evie has told this story to half the men in London as indisputable evidence of her sexual magnetism. Disturbingly, most seem turned on by it.

I take a cab from Waterloo station and am home shortly before midday. Miss Campion is waiting for me.

'I've definitely heard Pisces mewing,' she tells me.

I hand her the bunch of daffodils that my father picked for her this morning and look up at the windows of my house. It all seems very quiet. The bottom sash of the attic room is pushed up a few inches and the net curtain that has been there since I first moved in with Gerald is hanging out. Even if they have gone away, there would be no reason to secure this window. It would take a very long ladder to reach it.

'I expect your parents were disappointed that you've had to come home.'

'Oh, yes.' I'd almost forgotten Miss Campion standing there beside me.

'I didn't know what to do for the best. I know it's none of my business, but they don't owe you any rent, do they?'

'No, no. It's all paid in advance.' I was lost in thoughts of my parents' farewell. Disappointment wasn't something I'd noticed. Miss Campion, I think, is in fact quite lucky to have all this excitement on her doorstep; it saves her from becoming totally enmeshed in routine like my parents.

'You go back indoors,' I say. 'I'll go and get my keys to the house.'

'Do be careful,' she says.

It doesn't occur to me to try phoning. I feel sure there's nobody in and that the explanation is simply that they have stayed with friends or something, oblivious to the fact that they have left Pisces locked in the house. I don't even hurry. I pick up the mail and make coffee, glad to be back with my own brand and not my mother's awful bottle of Camp.

There's a get well card, which alarms me for a moment especially as the writing on the envelope suggests the sender is pretty ill themselves. Then I see that it's from Gerald's uncle and remember the excuse I gave for not having lunch with him. Someone once told me that selfish lies turn into truths sooner or later. Nonsense, of course. But my throat *was* feeling a bit tickly on the train. I take a couple of aspirins with my coffee, just in case. For some reason people are always imparting this sort of doom-laden information to me. It might be because of what I do. People imagine it's a psychic thing when really it's a science.

I know by the personalised postmark that the white Jiffy envelope contains my bundle of dream letters for the next month. I would like to sit with my coffee and read through them. See if there are any of those dubious ones. Let myself become aroused a little as a homecoming treat. But first things first. My poor cat could be lying in a corner, weak and miserable with hunger. Or maybe dying of thirst because both Lewis and Janus are the kind of men who always put the toilet lid down. But somehow I cannot imagine Pisces pining away in a corner. What I can imagine is him ripping up the expensive Axminster stair carpet in a fury at being shut in. This thought spurs me into action and I go and hunt out my spare keys.

I ring the front doorbell and bang the old-fashioned brass knocker up and down a couple of times. There is no intercom system. Gerald considered a spyhole and a good strong door chain were enough. After his death I felt too miserable to worry about things like safety. Besides, I always liked the spyhole. I doubt whether Lewis or Janus ever bother with it. There is certainly no one peeping out at me now and not a sound from inside the house. I push the key into the lock. It's a bit stiff. I'd forgotten that. And I'd forgotten what it feels like to be in this house of my own. Though it's not quite the same. It smells different, and there are other people's coats in the hall. At least they haven't done a moonlight flit with Gerald's mother's Staffordshire flatbacks or his grandmother's Victorian mother-of-pearl firescreen. Knowing what I know now, I wish I hadn't left them in here but it's too late to start removing stuff.

I check the sitting room and kitchen. The kitchen looks almost unused but there are papers and accounts books piled on the coffee table in the sitting room, and every cushion on the sofa could do with plumping up. Over on the corner cupboard are photographs, quite a few and very tempting to me. But I don't go and look any closer; I'm nervous enough as it is, imagining that someone might come home. I shouldn't be; it's my house and I have a right to check what is going on.

Upstairs the main bedroom door is closed. 'Pisces,' I call, my fingers resting on the door handle. 'Pisces. Puss.' Then I wait and listen. Not a sound, so I don't open it. The other bedroom has obviously been used by Lydia and Mimi. The beds are unmade, the pillows still indented with the shape of their heads. The room smells of flowers, honeysuckle I think. Probably some Junior Miss scent like the one my mother used to buy me from the Avon lady for Christmas. That and other useful toiletries.

I stick my head round the bathroom door. Both the lid and the seat of the toilet are up. But no cat is balanced there. The bathroom is a mess, not dirty but scattered with discarded clothes, the glass shelves stained with white rings, tops off of tubes. Gerald had this bathroom redecorated as a present for me on our first anniversary. The porcelain tiles are from Italy, hand-painted with copies of Japanese erotica, and there is a large mirror set into the ceiling. I was a bit embarrassed when I showed Lewis round the house and he looked in here.

There is only the attic room left. I can't imagine that Pisces is shut in there; Miss Campion would never have heard him crying. But I had better check. And I have an odd desire to walk up to that room again, now that I no longer live here. I go slowly, quietly, trying to recapture how I felt when I used to climb these stairs for my extra lessons with Gerald. But it's difficult. I am not the same person. I am no longer neurotic nor unhappy; sex is no longer a monster to me. It's very encouraging to confirm all this about myself. It makes me feel powerful. Lately, I've been slipping back a little, worrying about things that might, could, happen. Not thinking things through logically.

The door to the attic room is pulled up but not properly closed. As I open it I feel a draught from the open window. It brings with it the smell of smoke, not that of flames but the stale smell of cigarettes. This is definitely where Janus sleeps, I think. Opposite me, under the window, is the single divan that replaced the old sofa bed from long ago. On the divan, beneath a duvet patterned with signs of the zodiac, lies Janus fast asleep with my cat curled in the crook of his arm.

If I make a quick exit I will look stupid. Pisces is already stirring, ears flicking, head emerging from its resting place under Janus's chin. When he sees me he stretches out on his back, his front legs stiffening until his paws are pressing into Janus's cheek. And of course, Janus wakes up too.

He gives a little grunt of surprise, then raises himself on his elbows to look at me. 'It must be time to get up,' he smiles.

'I'm sorry.' I find my voice at last. 'I thought you and Lewis had gone away and Pisces had got shut in by mistake.'

'Away? No.' He takes hold of Pisces, his hand under the cat's belly, and lifts him into the air. My stupid cat hangs there, all four legs dangling. 'He comes in here every day. I thought you knew.' Janus shakes him a bit but Pisces remains as floppy as a rag doll. 'He doesn't mind what you do to him, does he?'

'The rougher the better,' I say. 'Well, now I know that everything's all right . . . It was the car not being here, that's why I came in.'

'Oh, the car.' Janus sinks back down, Pisces still held aloft. 'It's in the garage. A small collision. Some old prat who should have been dead years ago.'

I think of my father and the graffiti on the bus shelter. And Miss Campion worried about being mugged, and upset by the way her new neighbours shout and swear at one another.

'And you were driving, I suppose,' I say calmly, though I feel suddenly angry.

'However did you guess?' he says with a little smile.

So that's what the latest row was about. The car. I recently saw Lewis meticulously remove every last petal of some cherry blossom that had blown from the centre garden on to his windscreen. Some of it had become trapped under the wipers. He poked it all out with his fingers, then fetched a J Cloth to finish the job.

Janus has dropped my cat on to the duvet. 'So you like rough stuff, do you?' he says, rolling him from side to side.

Pisces' tail begins to flick a warning, but I'm reluctant to go over and lift him from the bed, so I say, 'Be careful, he can be spiteful.'

'I know.' Janus holds up his right arm. On the underside is a long red scratch, vividly fresh against the paler skin between wrist and elbow. 'It was my own fault, I was teasing him with a piece of chicken. His claws are like bloody razors. And he stinks.'

'You'll have to kick him out if he's a nuisance. He forgets this isn't his home any longer.'

'No, I shan't do that,' says Janus. 'I like him. He's funny.'

'Well, that's up to you. Shall I take him now? Pisces,' I call.

But Pisces' attention is suddenly caught by something above their heads. There are low rafters in this room that slope up towards the pitch of the roof. Pisces wriggles into a crouching position, neck craned upwards, tail twitching with excitement. Then he springs on to one of the rafters. The next second he has batted down a giant spider. It lands on Janus's bare chest.

I start to laugh. But Janus reacts as though it is a black widow that has fallen on him. He goes rigid, his arms stiff by his sides, his chin tucked in, his eyes fixed on the spider. The duvet has become bunched over his thighs and I cannot help but see that he sleeps naked. Perhaps three seconds pass before he screams and jumps up from the bed, slapping frantically at his chest with both hands. If it wasn't for the terror in his eyes, I might think that he was doing this to shock me.

He laughs a little himself now. 'I'm sorry,' he says, backing away and snatching a pair of underpants from a pile of clothes on a chair. 'Sorry.'

And right in the middle of this awkward situation the thing that I was trying to remember the other day when I was listening to Gerald's tape, comes to me. But I don't think this is the moment to ask Janus if he knows about the Roman god with two faces, one in front and one behind, whose job it was to open the sky at daybreak.

'Forget you saw that,' he says, smiling and pulling on jeans as well.

I smile back, showing it doesn't bother me. 'Once you've seen one, you've seen . . .' I break off, wondering if I've got it wrong and he means me to forget his display of fear not of his genitals. 'As my friend Evie would say,' I finish lamely.

'Oh, yeah, your friend Evie,' he says with an appreciative raise of his eyebrows. 'She'd say that, would she?'

'She has hundreds of boyfriends.'

'I bet.' He goes over and yanks off the duvet, then brushes down every inch of the bottom sheet with the flat of his hand. Finally, he looks up at the rafters and pulls the divan out from the wall.

'I should think it's dead,' I say, crouching down to check the carpet.

Pisces comes to see what I'm doing, his tail erect with delight at the mischief he's caused. I could pick him up and go but I don't want Janus to think that he's shocked me in any way. 'Are you really that frightened?' I ask.

'A lot of people hate spiders,' he says defensively.

'Yes, they do.' I run my hand over the carpet. It feels gritty and I can see an accumulation of fluff and dust and tiny fragments of cotton trapped in the pile. But no spiders. 'Oh well,' I say, getting to my feet and picking up Pisces at the same time. 'I can't see the body but I'm sure you killed it.'

'It's my mother's fault.'

I'm half turned to go but I stop and wait. I know that people do not generally make statements like this unless they wish to tell you more. The reason I know this is because I've done it myself. But what really interests me and makes me stand there waiting for him to go on is the word 'mother'.

'I even dream about the bastard things.'

'That's quite common. To dream about a fear, I mean.'

'Some things you just can't get out of your head,' he says, facing me but careful not to meet my eyes.

'Yes I know,' I say very quietly. He looks at me now. But his expression has become so troubled that I lose courage. I look away. Then back. 'What did your mother do? Did she say, close your eyes and open your mouth, and then pop in a spider instead of a sweet?'

He frowns, then lets out a short angry breath. 'Fucking stupid,' he says, turning away. I feel sorry. This is a bad habit I have, making flippant remarks when things get serious. It's not that I misjudge the depth of other people's feelings or that I'm not interested. I am. It's that I shy away from them.

Janus flings the duvet back on the bed with such force that it goes flying off the other side. In the gap he's just made by moving the bed out. And where, almost certainly, there are more spiders.

'Evie told me you work at the restaurant,' I say after a second or two. It's a feeble attempt at making amends, but he does brighten up.

'Yes, I do sometimes.'

'Do you enjoy it?'

'Good tips,' he says with a little smile.

'I'd better go,' I say. Then add jokingly, 'Sorry to have disturbed you at this unearthly hour.'

I'm at the top of the stairs when he calls out, 'Hang on a minute.'

I turn round. He's standing in the doorway, a hand on each

side of the frame. For a split second my imagination has him as he was when he jumped out of bed. His very thin body, which doesn't appeal to me, and the abundance of black pubic hair, which does.

'Yes?' I say, looking him in the face.

'What was it you said you came round for?'

'To look for Pisces. I told you.'

'Oh, yes. You'd thought we'd gone away. Me and Lewis.'

'Yes.' I have the feeling that he's accusing me of something. 'I wouldn't have let myself in here otherwise. It was an emergency.'

'It's OK.' He smiles and raises a hand as though he's saying goodbye.

I carry on down the stairs with Pisces hanging on to my shoulder. He's beginning to wriggle and I pray he won't dig his claws in and make his escape back up to the attic room. At the bottom I stop to get a firmer grip on him, hooking my fingers under his collar. And I notice that Janus is still standing there, watching me.

Chapter 6

I gave Evie *carte blanche* to arrange this date any way she wanted, so of course we've ended up at Lewis's restaurant. She's pleased with herself, imagining that she has surrounded me with men I could get interested in.

But I can't complain about my date. I told Evie I didn't want anyone younger than me and Chris is forty next week. That came out because we've been discussing horoscopes. He seems quite knowledgeable about astrology but in a superficial way, as though he has been swotting up. I expect Evie has primed him. She knows that I prefer muscular or big men, and that conversation is important to me. Chris is a teacher at the same college as Rick. He teaches history and PE. An odd mixture but in theory he should be perfect for me. Should be.

'So you studied with Gerald Harker?' he says, airing his knowledge. But a lot of people have heard of Gerald. The sort of people who never buy a newspaper or magazine but ask their friends to 'read my stars' have heard of Gerald.

'She was married to him,' says Evie.

'Really? How long for?'

'Seven years.' Why do people say "Really?" like that, as though they need confirmation of what you've said? 'Until he died. I'm a widow.' There's a little silence in which the waiter arrives. It's not Janus. I don't think he's here tonight. I haven't seen Lewis either and I've made Evie promise not to summon him from the kitchens. I haven't told her about my encounter with Janus. What I did tell her when she came round on Wednesday is that I've decided to have a holiday, a couple of weeks in my parents' cottage in Ireland, the one my father is going to sell so that he can give me some money. Not on your own, she said, you can't stay there all on your own. Why not? I said. The next day she phoned and said she was coming with me, just for the first week to make sure I was all right. I'm worried about you, she said. You're not the only one, I thought, wondering if I wanted her company. I decided, on balance, that I probably did or I wouldn't have mentioned it. And the contrast between a whole week with Evie and a week of solitude might be the catalyst I needed to sort myself out. Think about my future. And the present, come to that.

I've chosen my starter but the others are still making up their minds. Goat's cheese on roasted red peppers. Chris takes his time. While he's reading the menu he looks sideways at me and smiles, and for the first time I wonder how this evening is going to end. What has he in mind, or rather what is on my mind? I have my suspicions that he's married. It was the way he said that his ex-wife swears by my horoscope column. He used the present tense, which doesn't sound like ex to me. Not that it bothers me either way. A married man wanting extra sex is probably my best bet for now.

Rick and Evie both ask for sweetcorn soup, and Chris finally opts for goujons of sole after keeping the waiter hanging around for a good five minutes. Is he this slow with everything? I wonder.

When it comes to the main course I ask for goat's cheese soufflé, which is really another starter.

'You're going a bit overboard on this Greek shit,' says Evie with a frown.

'I don't think goat's cheese is especially Greek.'

'Well, it's a fad,' she says. 'One of your food fads.'

'Do you like Greek food?' says Chris.

'Not especially,' I say wondering why I keep saying especially.

'What about all those Greek yoghurts you eat?' says Evie. 'And that other stuff, that mushy pea shit?'

'She means hummus,' I tell Chris.

'Yes, that shit,' says Evie a bit too loudly. Rick puts a finger to his lips which I could have told him was a silly thing to do to Evie. Especially as she's been seeing him for a few weeks now.

'What's up with you?' she says, leaning back, her arms

folded under her breasts. Evie has amazing breasts. They are so versatile. At the moment they are perfect half-circles bulging over the top of her Jane Austen-style dress. Not the green one tonight. But at the switch of a bra or minus one, they can become small and budding for her androgynous look.

'Have you ever been to Greece?' asks Chris. He seems determined to hang on to this subject. Probably easier for him than astrology.

I shake my head, an eye on Evie, who is still frowning at Rick. He seems very subdued. Unless he's just a naturally quiet person. Or maybe Evie's nipples no longer stiffen when their eyes meet. Whatever. I don't want him and Evie falling out this evening, not in here anyway.

'No, no I haven't,' I say, turning to smile at Chris.

'Are you going anywhere this year?'

'Yes, I'm going to Ireland.'

'*We're* going to Ireland,' says Evie, leaning over to put her arm through mine. 'Verity and I are going to a place where everything is totally unpolluted – the air, the water, the men's minds . . .'

'I shouldn't bank on that,' says Chris.

'No,' mutters Rick. 'She'd be disappointed.'

I feel Evie draw in her breath. Not to calm herself, more likely the prelude to an explosion. I slap her hand and fill up her glass from our second bottle of wine. It's a 1991 Hunter Valley Chardonnay chosen by Chris – his treat, he insisted. Nobody argued. We've agreed to split the bill between the four of us and this wine was nearly twenty quid a bottle.

'Not exactly packed in here, is it?' I say to Evie. 'Was it like this when you came before?'

'Similar. I don't know why.'

'Actually, the place had a bad review from one of the food writers,' says Rick. 'It was in your magazine.' He looks across at me, pleased with himself as though it's in some way my fault. The bad review and the fact that Evie is growing tired of him.

'I don't have a magazine,' I say.

Evie gives a little smirk. 'Probably written by a discarded lover. I expect Lewis has plenty of those, doesn't he, Verity?' She clasps my arm as though it's me and her against Rick. Now and again she goes in for these bitchy tangled exits out of boredom.

Rick tries to snap off a piece of the crackling from his pork but it peels off in one leathery strip instead. He dangles it from his fingers as though it's proof of bad cooking. But as I couldn't bear to eat the skin of an animal, crisp or not, this gesture is wasted on me. He looks at Evie forking up chunks of her monkfish with one hand. 'I thought you wanted to go to Venice,' he says.

'I do. But I'm not letting Verity stay all on her own in some godforsaken place where anything could happen to her.'

'Is this cottage out in the wilds then?' says Chris, sounding interested.

'Not completely,' I tell him, though I can't actually remember if there are other houses nearby. Except for a bungalow whose windows I once peered through. The image of it comes to me now. A table with an abandoned meal, yet no one ever seemed to be there. I remember thinking of the *Marie Celeste* though I couldn't have been more than twelve because that was the last year I went to Kyle-dortha. 'I wouldn't describe it as godforsaken. In fact I'd say it was heavenly.'

Evie, on her fourth glass of wine, laughs at my wit.

'But neither of you drive,' says Rick.

'No, we'll be cut off from the world,' says Evie. 'It'll be paradise.'

'We might be able to hire a couple of bikes,' I say, laughing myself as I imagine Evie and me wobbling along the Irish lanes.

'I'll give you three days,' says Rick. 'Top whack.'

'Shall I tell you something?' says Evie. 'Do you want to know the reason why Verity and I have been friends for so long, the reason why we never have rows?' She pauses for effect, not for Rick to make a decision whether he would like to know or not. 'The reason we get on so well is because we have not allowed our relationship to become sexual.'

He doesn't flinch, just says quietly, 'You might, holed up in that cottage for a week.' And I have to hand it to him, it's about the best answer he could have given her.

By the time we've finished our main course we're all a little drunk and Evie is being kinder to Rick. I've always thought it strange how some people become nasty after too much alcohol and others become embarrassingly benevolent. Evie goes on a curve, like a learning curve. She gets a bit bolshie then settles down into a kind of serene generosity. If I were to say to her, I really like your earrings, Evie, she would take them off and give them to me. At the moment she's touching up Rick under the table. She once told me that she likes to give a man an erection when he's had a lot to drink because he can't piss. That's another strange thing. When I had my first orgasm, with Gerald, I thought I was going to wet myself at the same time.

'Anybody having pudding?' says Chris, looking round for the waiter who is actually coming our way with a tray of drinks. When he gets to us I can see that they're liqueurs that we haven't ordered.

'Petite Liquorelle,' he says, and starts to distribute them amongst us. 'With compliments. Also your coffee.'

We all look at each other. This waiter doesn't speak very good English but he is certainly decorative which is, I believe, the most important thing for waiters these days.

'We haven't ordered liqueurs yet,' says Chris. 'I'm not sure if this is what we want.'

Evie is the first to catch on. 'Did you say these are free?' she asks the waiter.

'Yes, correct,' he says, nodding for emphasis.

Evie slides her eyes towards me. 'For the landlady, I think,' she smiles.

'Oh. I see. From Lewis.'

'From Lewis, correct,' says the waiter.

'Oh, well,' says Evie lifting her glass, 'here's to landladies.'

And, as we sit there sipping these delicious liqueurs, which taste like concentrated champagne, the thing I wanted to avoid happens. Lewis comes out from the kitchens. Our table is at the other end of the restaurant but I spot him the minute he comes through the swing door and makes towards us. He's not wearing his chef's whites, not a jacket anyway, but white trousers and T-shirt. I watch him over Rick's shoulder while I carry on the conversation I'm having with Chris. We've been talking about Freud, a bit drunkenly on my behalf. Chris has just quoted him. A quote that he has learned for this evening, no doubt. Especially for this evening. ' "I have not yet been able to answer the great question . . . what does a woman want?" '

'Perhaps he didn't ask,' I say.

'Is that how we men find out, by asking?' Chris leans a little closer to me and drops his head level with mine.

A dullness settles round my heart. I don't answer him but look up as Lewis reaches our table. Evie looks up too. 'Hi,' she beams at him, surprised. She hasn't watched him walk the whole length of the restaurant as I have. 'Thanks for the liqueurs.'

'My pleasure. Did you enjoy your meal?'

Evie kisses a finger and thumb at him. 'Delicious.' We all murmur our agreement.

'Would you like coffee? On the house as well. Did my waiter tell you?' He catches my eye and smiles.

'If you insist,' says Evie brightly. 'Make it four Gaelic.'

'We do eight different kinds.'

'No, we must have Irish. Verity and I are off on holiday there next month.'

'Oh, whereabouts?' He leans a hand flat on the wall beside him. The sleeves of his T-shirt are too tight. He is heavier built than Janus. I suppose he is always dipping his fingers into this and that, tasting and testing whether something needs more seasoning. Easy to put on the pounds in this job, I should think. His hands are scrubbed-looking, pinkish and smooth in contrast to his forearms, which are covered with dark hair.

Evie nudges me. 'Where is it we're going?' she says. 'What's it called?'

I look up. 'County Cork.'

'What part?' says Lewis.

'Near Skibbereen. Do you know it?'

'I've never been there but I've heard of it. My father has a restaurant in Kinsale.'

'Where's that?' says Evie.

'County Cork.'

'Small world. Perhaps we'll visit him,' she says.

I feel like a child who's been made to share her toys.

'Is he a chef as well?' says Chris.

'He was but he just runs the restaurant now.'

'Isn't Kinsale supposed to be some kind of Mecca for gourmets?' says Chris.

'Chris?' says Evie, smiling kindly. 'Is there anything you *don't* know?'

Lewis has turned away, called by one of the waiters. 'Excuse me,' he says, 'I have to go.'

'The *Lusitania* was sunk near Kinsale,' says Chris.

'Shut up, for fuck's sake,' says Evie.

Chris and I take the tube home together as he lives further up the line at East Finchley. But he insists on getting off at my stop and walking me to my door. 'I want to see where someone like you lives,' he says.

I have no idea what he means by this or whether I am going to invite him in. Deciding what to do makes me feel a little sick. Or maybe it's the mix of alcohol. Chardonnay, a champagne liqueur and very strong Gaelic coffee prepared in front of us by the decorative waiter who spread the cream with such panache that we all clapped. I burned my tongue drinking mine too soon. Chris pushed an ice cube between my lips. I had the feeling he wanted to push his fingers in as well. The ice melted almost at once and dribbled down my chin so that I looked drunker than I was. On the tube I talked about the physiological connections of our zodiac signs to show that I was still sober. And I was still sober enough not to mention that Chris might have a tendency to troubles with his genitals and bladder.

'There it is,' I say as we turn into the Square. 'That's where someone like me lives.'

The house looks taller and narrower at night, as though it were squashed in as an afterthought. There is a glimmer of light from the lamp I've left on in the basement but all the other floors are in darkness. Chris peers over my iron railings. 'It looks very cosy,' he says.

'Would you respect a woman who invited you in for coffee on a first date?' I say.

'As long as it's not Gaelic. All I could taste was the whiskey. There was more than a jigger in mine.'

'A jigger? What's a jigger?'

'The amount of whiskey you put in Gaelic coffee.'

'And an Irish dancer,' I laugh. Chris just smiles. I'm beginning to think he doesn't have much of a sense of humour.

He hasn't much restraint either. While I'm making the coffee he comes up and puts his arms round me from behind and kisses my ear. I wear my hair very short so my ear is the first thing he comes to. I put down the jug I'm holding and take a deep breath. I have already made the decision that I am not going to see Chris again but now I have to decide whether I am going to have a one-night stand. Which is what I wanted when I asked Evie to arrange this date. And thought about earlier today when I cleaned and tidied my bedroom, and sprayed it with lavender to get rid of the smell of a fish curry that I ate in bed last night.

'Verity. *La vérité*. The truth,' he says. 'The truth is that I haven't met a girl like you for ages.'

If I were Evie, I would say cut the shit. But I'm me and I'm going to need a bit of flattery. I let him pull me back against him. He's not much taller than me and his erection presses into the base of my spine, just above the crease of my buttocks. A very sensitive area. Which makes me feel like I won't need too much flattery, after all.

He licks my ear, then my neck. I am not a tease, I would not let things get this far then stop, but I can tell that he's not sure yet. He runs a hand carefully over my stomach. I don't move. He presses a little harder, gathering up my skirt with his fingers, slipping them inside my pants, playing with my pubic hair. My breathing quickens. It sounds very loud to me. I try to gain control of it but I can't.

'Is it all right?' Chris whispers.

I don't answer. I don't want him talking. I want to forget he's there behind me. In the days before Gerald liberated me, I used to think I want the man but not his cock. Now, I could almost say that the reverse is true. Almost.

'Say it's all right. Say you . . .' he pauses and pushes two fingers against my clitoris. 'Say you want me. Say you like it.'

Oh no, I think, he wants to talk. Probably something his wife won't do.

'Come on,' he coaxes, 'just tell me.'

I'm crushed between him and the sink unit. Not a good place, not for someone who hasn't done this for a while. 'We'd better go in the bedroom,' I say.

He starts stripping off his clothes before we're hardly through the door. I'm slower because my hands are shaking. I feel incredibly aroused. I'm wet, I'm trembling, I can hardly wait to have him inside me, but I'm not happy. I feel sick, mentally and spiritually sick. Soul sick.

Our shadows are on the wall. His makes me think of a unicorn with his erection pointing upwards. I look very thin. I turn sideways and push my breasts up to make myself look better, curvier. Chris like this. He sits on the bed and watches me, rubbing himself.

'Wank yourself,' he says hoarsely. 'Here. Stand in front of me and wank yourself.'

I go to him and push hard on his shoulders. He falls back on the bed. And looking down at him, his face shapeless with desire, no mask, I see behind my own mask too. Why do I long for things that I don't really want? Why is there no logic to sex?

'Come on,' Chris whispers, reaching up to encircle my waist. I kneel over him, my legs either side of his hips. But the moment I feel him at the entrance to my vagina, I recoil and pull back. I take him in my hand and rub him against me. And the feel of him is enough. Enough to last me another year, I think spread-eagled on my back, my eyes closed while I swim in darkness and hang on to every last ripple of pleasure.

Chapter 7

What does one need to go babysitting? I'm standing in my bedroom looking around me as though I expect to see something that I should take. A cardigan for a start. It's been a warm showery day but the big sitting room upstairs could be cold later. I don't think they have the heating on and I can't blame them as they are out so much of the time. At least Lewis is and I think he's the one who pays the bills.

It's ten to seven. Lewis is coming back to collect Janus at seven so I'd better go up. I wish that I hadn't agreed to do this. I've been wishing it all day.

The front door is open. As I go in Mimi comes running through from the kitchen. She is ready for bed, wearing a long white nightgown edged with broderie anglaise. Her hair is loose and kinked from her plaits.

'Daddy said we can stay up until eight o'clock,' she says, holding her wrist under my nose. 'I've got a watch. I can tell the time.'

She looks so pretty, like a little Victorian girl. This alone, this prettiness, this resemblance to those appealing children you see in old paintings, clutching puppies or making daisy chains in some idyllic meadow, makes me want to gather her up in my arms and hug her. But the moment passes. I take hold of her wrist and admire her watch.

Janus comes downstairs, followed closely by Lydia. The black trousers and white-frilled shirt of his waiter's outfit have transformed him. And it's the first time I've seen him clean-shaven and with his hair neatly combed. Fortunately, his appearance doesn't have the same effect on me as Mimi's; I haven't the slightest desire to hug Janus. I wouldn't even chance taking hold of his wrist the way he's scowling.

'Aren't you going to clean your shoes?' says Lydia as they get to the bottom of the stairs. 'Daddy always does before he goes out.'

'Good for him,' says Janus. 'There's a bottle of wine in the kitchen,' he says to me, walking straight past to pull open the front door. No instructions about the girls but I don't suppose he'll worry too much once he's out of here. I feel like telling him that I'm doing this as a favour and that I expect gratitude not bad manners. But of course I'm doing it for Lewis, not for him. And I did offer.

It was when I was on my way to do some shopping this morning. Saturdays I get my bread at a bakers round the corner, and if I'm feeling in the mood I buy Danish pastries as well and take them in to Miss Campion to have coffee with her. I'd planned to do that this morning. I've been avoiding her all week, avoiding everyone, in fact. Why one rash sexual encounter should make me act like a fox gone to ground, I don't know. I've even put off calling Evie, despite her having left two messages on my answerphone. The first, as I expected, was last Sunday. But after some early-morning sex which I soon regretted, the last thing I wanted was her questioning me about Chris.

Setting off to the bakers I saw Pisces sitting on the bonnet of Lewis's car. It had rained in the night and he'd left smudgy footprints all over it. The fact that the engine was running didn't seem to bother him. But the driver's door was open, which bothered me as I knew his next move would be to climb into the car and curl up on one of the seats. I had just picked him up and was about to dash back down and shut him indoors, when Lewis came out, bustling Lydia and Mimi in front of him. Mimi kept her head down but I could see she had been crying. Lydia looked sulky but she ran up to stroke Pisces.

Lewis smiled a brief greeting and said, 'Come on, Lydia, quickly now.'

She ignored him so I tapped her on the shoulder. 'Your father's calling you.'

He came over. 'Lydia, please, I haven't much time.' He looked more drawn and tired than ever.

'Can't I stay with Verity instead?' said Lydia.

'No, of course not.' He took hold of her hand.

'Problems?' I said.

'As usual,' he nodded, trying to smile. 'My commis chef has had a punch-up with my new waiter. They've both walked out.'

'And I've got to stay with bloody Cynthia,' said Lydia.

'That's enough of that, Lydia. Come on. Verity doesn't want to hear all this.'

'No, wait.' I guessed what was going on. Lydia and Mimi were here for the weekend and Janus would be looking after them while Lewis was at work. But if Janus was needed at the restaurant . . . it all fell into place. 'They can stay with me. If that's the problem.'

'Can we?' said Lydia, pulling at his sleeve.

I looked at him and shrugged, having doubts whether I should have interfered.

Lewis shook his head. 'Thank you, but I won't have time to take them to their aunt's later. I need Janus for this evening as well as lunch time, you see.'

'I don't want to sleep at Cynthia's,' said Lydia, defiant and frowning. But beneath her sulky expression I saw that she too was not far from tears.

'I'll come and babysit this evening as well.' I felt that I had to offer; I'd already made things worse, rather than better. 'I'm not doing anything. And you come home in the afternoon, don't you?'

Lydia started begging, 'Please, Daddy, please,' and he gave in, heaving a sigh of relief and thanking me so profusely that I felt like putting my hand over his mouth and saying, it's all right, it's all right. But of course, I couldn't touch him, certainly not put my hand on his face.

I took the girls with me to Miss Campion's. I thought she'd be intrigued with them, which she was. She kept smoothing their hair and patting the backs of Mimi's plump little legs. They behaved very well at first, smiling and tolerant, answering Miss Campion's questions about school and where they lived. But after the initial fascination had worn off they began to fidget and eye Miss Campion's collection of brass animals and the knick-knacks crammed in behind the glass doors of her china cabinet. I decided it was time to go.

So here I am, babysitting, getting myself involved when I don't want to be. Janus lights up a cigarette as he stands in the doorway, waiting for Lewis. He has his back to us but I can tell that he's annoyed about something from the negative hunch of his shoulders. Perhaps he doesn't want to work despite the good tips. Perhaps he'd rather be here. Whatever it is, I have the feeling that he resents me being here, and I make up my mind not to do this again.

Lydia comes over to me. 'Do you want to watch a video? Or shall we have *Blind Date* on?'

'*Blind Date*?' I say disapprovingly.

She laughs. 'Don't you like it?' We've become friends today. She has even told me a secret. Her mother's boyfriend is taking them on holiday to France. She revealed it to me in such a way, fiddling with and chewing on a little silver cross she wears, that I know she's not entirely happy about it. But I resisted questioning her.

'I don't think blind dates are a good idea,' I murmur, more to myself than her.

Once Janus has gone, I suggest reading to them rather than watching TV. Mimi spins round in delighted circles, then rushes off to get her Postman Pat book. But Lydia has other ideas and wants me to read from one of the books which are stored in the attic room.

'Daddy said we mustn't touch them,' Mimi tells me as we go upstairs. 'But Janus has. I know. I saw him.'

And I know that there is nothing even remotely suitable for five-and ten-year-olds amongst Gerald's collection. Nor anything suitable for Janus, I would think. But I jump at this chance to check the room.

'*Applied Astrology* or *The Meaning of Truth*?' I ask, taking both books from the top shelf of the bookcase.'

'What are they about?' says Lydia.

'Nothing you'd understand.'

Lydia comes to look and I stroke the covers, then put them aside to take back with me. But seeing the name of one of the authors, William James, reminds me that, somewhere up here, there is a copy of *The Turn of the Screw* by his brother, Henry. Selected bits of that might interest them. I find it but know I must be careful. The book has some very scary passages. I remember sitting up here one night with just a small lamp for company and reading it from cover to cover. It was when I first moved in with Gerald. He came searching for me, barging in and switching on all the lights. It was the only time I ever remember him angry with me, though I never understood why.

'Oh, Quint and Jessel,' I say, remembering even now how the names conjured up such an excitement of fear. I sit down on the bed and Lydia squashes up close beside me as though she senses something of my thoughts. Mimi is wandering round, opening draws and peering into cupboards.

'Leave Jan's things alone,' says Lydia, 'or I'll tell him.'

'Perhaps we'd better go downstairs,' I say. I've seen that nothing much has altered in this room since I was last here, though there is an overflowing ashtray which I should like to empty but don't feel I have the right. 'Who cleans in here?' I ask Lydia.

'I don't know.' She shrugs, turning away, her fingers at her neck, seeking out the little cross to push it between her teeth. 'Read some, then we'll go down,' she says.

What I've forgotten about the book is that it's told in the first person in contemporary nineteenth-century language. Totally unsuitable for Lydia let alone Mimi. But if they don't understand it, then it won't frighten them. I open it at random and start reading the part where Flora escapes from the governess to meet the ghost of Miss Jessel by the lake. Mimi listens for a minute or so, then wanders off again, this time to look out of the window. Lydia sits quietly until I've finished the chapter, a mere three and a half pages.

'Does the girl fall out of the boat and drown?' she asks, showing that she has understood at least part of it.

'No, but your sister's going to fall out of the window and break her neck in a minute,' I say, jumping up to pull Mimi away.

We end up downstairs, watching a video of them taken one Christmas when, it appears, Lewis and Nicole were still together. It's mostly the girls, opening presents, sitting under the tree, Lydia pushing a little doll's pram. They have obviously seen it many times before and give me one of their running commentaries on what is happening. In some shots either Lewis or Nicole is with them but there is no sign of Janus.

Mimi comes to sit on my lap. She cuddles up to me, quiet now after all her chattering.

'How old were you when that was taken?' I ask Lydia.

'I was eight and Mimi was . . .' She stops to think. 'Two or three.'

'It's lovely.'

She nods, seemingly unconcerned. 'If she didn't drown, what happened to her?'

'Who? Oh, Flora you mean. I forget.' I don't but I feel it's too complicated to explain. 'I'm going to stay by a lake soon,' I tell her. 'It's in Ireland and they call them loughs there.'

'My granddad lives in Ireland,' she says. 'We're going to see him soon as well.'

Mimi sits up. 'Is Mummy coming?'

'All depends,' says Lydia.

'On what?' I venture.

'I don't know.' She jumps up. 'Mimi, it's time you were in bed.'

'I want to phone Mummy to say goodnight,' whines Mimi.

'Can she do that?' I ask Lydia, thinking this might be something they do when they stay here.

'No, she can't.'

'I want to,' says Mimi with pouted lips.

'You can't, she's out,' says Lydia. 'At a club.'

Mimi forces herself to cry. No tears, just a tired little grizzle.

'Come on,' I say, cuddling her against me, 'it's way past your bedtime,' and to my surprise they both go upstairs without any fuss whatsoever.

A couple of hours later the phone rings. I answer it a little cautiously; it's twenty minutes to midnight.

'Is Lewis there?' a woman's voice enquires.

'I'm afraid not. Can I take a message?'

'Is that Nicole?'

'No. I'm babysitting.'

'Oh, does that mean Janus isn't there?'

'Not at the moment.' It's probably OK to tell a woman that you're virtually alone in the house.

'Could you tell Lewis that Angela called?'

'Yes, certainly. Do you want to leave a number?'

'Er . . . this is a bit awkward.'

I wait, curious.

'Can you give the message to Lewis yourself? Not via Janus, I mean?'

'Yes, of course.'

'I don't want Janus to know that I've called.' There's another pause. 'Do you know them or are you from an agency?'

'I know them. Quite well,' I add, hoping for some sort of explanation.

'Oh, good. Then can you make sure you give my number to Lewis discreetly? If you wouldn't mind.'

'No, I don't mind.'

She gives me the number, thanks me and hangs up. When I put down the receiver I find Lydia at the bottom of the stairs.

'Who was that?' she says.

It is probably *not* OK to tell a little girl whose parents are divorced that a woman who could be interested in her father has just called.

'A lady for Daddy?' she says.

'Well, yes it was,' I admit. 'Someone called Angela.'

Her brow creases a fraction. 'Oh. I don't know her.'

'Lydia,' I begin, 'she asked me not to let Janus know she called.'

Her face becomes a mask of indifference. It strikes a chord in me. Saying goodbye to my parents, withholding the tears until my tongue feels as though it's swollen into a big fat choking sausage.

'Perhaps it's a secret,' she says, and marches through to the kitchen. She comes back with a handful of biscuits and a glass of milk. 'You forgot our supper,' she says.

'Oh, I'm sorry.'

'It's all right. Janus always forget. He's bloody pathetic. Good night.'

I watch her go back upstairs and try to remember if I even knew the word 'bloody' when I was ten.

Carrying out Angela's request is perfectly easy as Lewis arrives home just before midnight, on his own.

I hand him the number and he pockets it without comment. 'What do I owe you for tonight?' he asks.

'Nothing at all. I don't want paying.'

'I feel embarrassed about this. I wouldn't have asked you.'

'You didn't; I volunteered. Anyway, I've enjoyed myself. Your daughters are very well behaved.'

'A meal then. Come in any time you want. Lunch time or evening.'

'Thanks. I will.'

'I'm sorry to have kept you so late.'

'It's all right. Have you left Janus doing the clearing up?'

'No, he's gone off somewhere,' Lewis smiles. 'He's making the most of his freedom.'

'Setting the town alight,' I say.

Lewis smiles again. But even when he smiles he looks tired and unhappy. Well, sad. Sad that he no longer has Nicole probably.

Evie has left a message on my answerphone threatening to call the police if I don't contact her.

Chris has left a message too: 'Hi, Chris here. Let's get together again soon. Call me if you're interested.'

I don't feel very interested in either of them at the moment. But I expect it will pass. Anyway, they both know where I live.

I'm feeling much brighter. Bright enough, in fact, to have taken up Lewis's offer of a free meal. Sunday lunch. Which is where I'm off to very shortly. Once Lewis arrives to give me a lift. At least I think that's what the arrangement is. He told me to wait here until Nicole comes to fetch the girls. They've been here for the second weekend running. Lewis picked them up from school on Friday and I looked after them again yesterday, just for a couple of hours. He has some temporary help in the restaurant now, so Janus is free to babysit most of the time.

I said I'd make my own way there but Lewis insisted on picking me up. Feeling he owes me, I suppose. All this juggling with home and work he has to do, rushing backwards and forwards so that he can see his daughters. No wonder he looks constantly exhausted.

And I've spoken to Evie. I told her I don't think that I'll see Chris again. She reckons I should have taken her advice and gone for a young and beautiful brainless boy, as she put it. According to her, the trick to enjoying men is to keep your sexual organs detached from your intellect just as they do. Verity, you get too involved, she said. At least she made me laugh. Not at what she said but because she's so wrong. And this morning my father rang to tell me that he has contacted Mrs Doyle who looks after the cottage for him. She said it is perfectly habitable and she'll make sure there is clean bedding ready for when we go.

So my spirits are considerably lifted. I've even decided to dress up a little, or a lot rather, because I'm wearing my very best, size ten and still room to spare, Edina Ronay white dress and jacket.

I'm putting the finishing touches to my hair when there's a couple of blasts from a car horn outside the house. Now it's unusual for me to go racing up my steps at any time. And why I take it for granted that this summons is for me, I'm not sure. But up I dash. And find myself face to face with Nicole. This could be an awkward situation and any number of silly remarks are already forming in my head. But she smiles pleasantly enough and asks if Lydia and Mimi have been behaving themselves.

'Yes. They're a credit to you,' I tell her, sure this is the thing that you're supposed to say to mothers about their children. And relieved that she knows about me babysitting and doesn't seem to mind.

'And you're off to lunch with Lewis?'

I'm also relieved that she knows about this, though there is something about her tone of voice, a seriousness, that makes me cautious.

'Not actually with him,' I say.

'Don't worry, I don't mind.' As she speaks the front door opens. Only Mimi appears. She runs over to us.

'Lydia's sewing a button on Jan's shirt for him,' she says.

'Where's Daddy?' says Nicole.

'He's gone to work.'

'But the car's here.' She points to Lewis's BMW parked further along than its usual place. I'm confused; I hadn't realised it was here. I heard someone drive off earlier and presumed it was Lewis. It must be that Janus has taken him to the restaurant and come back with the car. The lift I've been promised will be with Janus.

'Go and tell Lydia to hurry up. Let him sew his own buttons on.' Nicole gives Mimi a little push towards the house. As soon as she's out of earshot Nicole says, 'How do you find Janus?'

'In what way do you mean?'

'He's not causing any trouble?'

A lot of things come crowding into my head. Spiders and fires and late-night phone messages. I have the feeling that were I to mention any of these Nicole would know exactly what I mean. 'Trouble?' I say quietly, one eye on the door where any minute Janus will appear to drive me to lunch.

'You'll never get close to Lewis,' she says. 'Not while he's around.'

'I'm not trying to get close to Lewis.'

'I just thought I'd warn you. Whatever you do don't—' She stops, and I turn to see what has distracted her. 'Talk of the devil,' she says.

Janus is coming down the steps, buttoning his shirt. 'Are you ready?' he says to me, heading for the car and completely ignoring Nicole. Mimi and Lydia are close behind. Lydia is struggling with two bags, two school blazers and Mimi's doll. She bundles the lot under one arm and slams the front door shut with her free hand. Mimi comes skipping over with their school hats dangling from her wrist. Nicole goes to help them, ignoring Janus just as he has done to her.

'Looks like we're off,' I say. I stand there indecisive, reminding myself that I have decided not to become more involved with them. Not with her children, Janus, or her ex-husband. Especially her ex-husband, even if he does fuck me senseless in my dreams.

The girls are in the car now, waving and calling goodbye to me. Nicole takes my elbow. 'Be careful of him,' she says. Behind me I hear Janus revving the engine.

He drives just as I expected he would, too fast and badly. I know very little about the correct way to drive but I do know you are supposed to leave more than six inches between you and the car in front. And that you are obliged to stop when someone is already part-way across a perfectly legitimate pedestrian crossing.

I adjust my jacket. 'Perhaps I shouldn't have worn this,' I say.

He looks round. 'Why not? It's nice.'

'Because if I get it covered in blood it'll be ruined.'

He gives a disdainful snort and lights up a cigarette juggling matches, cigarettes and steering wheel in the process. I wonder why he doesn't use a lighter. So much easier than matches. And safer.

'What was Nicole yapping on about?' he says, opening his window to let the smoke out.

'Oh, this and that.'

'This and that and me, I bet.' He glances round again. I do wish he would keep his eyes on the road. 'What did she say? What did she call me? She's good at insults. She'd win prizes for dreaming things up about me.'

'She didn't insult you at all.' I don't think 'talk of the devil' could be classed as an insult. It's one of those things you say without thinking. But there was that sentence she didn't finish. What must I not do, I wonder. Judging by what I already know of Janus, it could be almost anything. 'Tell me,' I say, 'if Nicole and you have fallen out, how come she allows you to look after her daughters?'

'It suits her, that's why. She doesn't have to worry about them over the weekend when she wants to go out. Anyway, Lydia reports back on my every move.' He flicks the cigarette, half-smoked, into the path of an oncoming car. 'Don't be fooled by that angelic little face. She's got big ears and an even bigger mouth.'

I feel indignant on Lydia's behalf, given the loyal way she has avoided my attempts at prying. But I keep quiet. Trapped in a car that he's driving might not be the best place to get indignant. And I have to walk into the restaurant with him yet.

He slaps his hands against the steering wheel. 'I do it for Lewis,' he says. 'That's the only reason.'

He turns into a side street and manoeuvres the car into a parking space at the entrance to an alleyway, jolting to a stop a hair's-breadth from a brick wall.

'We can cut through there.' He points to where another alley leads off at right angles between the backs of buildings. It's littered with rubbish and stinks of rotting food. Not a place I'd choose to walk through in my Edina Ronay. Janus stands aside to let me go first.

'This is even more exciting than the drive,' I say, looking back at him.

'Watch where you're walking,' he says, which comes a bit late as I've stepped straight in a puddle.

'Is this meant to be some kind of endurance test?'

'No. We all come this way. Me, Lewis. And all his girlfriends.'

I look back again and catch my sleeve on an overflowing dustbin. 'Janus, let me tell you something. I'm not after your brother. And even if I were it's nothing to do with you.'

He comes up close behind me. 'And let me tell *you* something.' He pauses and I walk on a bit faster, glad I'm not wearing high heels. 'I've had enough of women trying to take advantage of Lewis.'

I stop and swing round to face him. 'Is that your interpretation of any woman who shows an interest in him?'

He stares at me. 'Are you interested in him?'

'I just told you. No. Not in the way you mean. I'm not interested in anyone. Now can we get out of here?'

'What about the guy who stayed with you the other night?' he says as we set off in single file again.

I take a deep breath, furious. 'Which one was that?' I say.

'Well, I've only seen one.'

'How observant of you.' We've come to the street. The noise and fumes of the traffic seem almost pleasurable after being stuck in that filthy alley with Janus. And safer. He comes alongside me. 'Amongst all her insults,' I say, 'did Nicole ever call you childish?'

'No, that's too tame for her.'

'Yes, I suppose so. Too tame a description of you, all things considered.'

'What do you mean?' His face changes.

'Oh,' I smile feeling confident with the restaurant just ahead. 'Just some words of warning she gave me. About you.'

'Do you want to know why she hates me?' he says loudly,

coming to a standstill in the middle of the street. A couple of passers-by glance at him. He glares back at them. They walk quickly on, and so do I. He comes running up behind me. We've reached the restaurant. He's breathing hard, but I don't think it's with exertion. It feels like a dragon is breathing flames down my neck.

'Can we stop this, Janus?' I say.

'Stop what?' He pushes open the door. Then pushes me too, his hand on my back, making out he's guiding me to my table. I pull out my own chair and sit down, wishing I hadn't come. Janus walks off without a word.

The table is by the window. The way the room is arranged many of the tables seem too close together and in gloomy corners. But mine is in one of the nicest positions in the restaurant. There's a card marked 'Reserved' propped against a crystal vase containing three roses. I've never seen any this colour, a pale mauvish blue, an almost perfect match with the table linen.

Janus returns with the menu. He hands it to me as though I'm a complete stranger. By now I haven't much of an appetite, and I choose quickly, picking out a dish because I recognise the French word for apricots, which I like.

'By the way, Janus,' I say, handing him back the menu. 'I won't be needing a lift home.'

'No? OK, I'll tell Lewis. He was going to take you.'

He allows himself a little smile of triumph standing over me to let it sink in. I notice that the middle button of his shirt is sewn on with black cotton. A thread hangs from it like a black hair peeping out from his chest. He frowns at me, then looks down at his shirt and brushes a hand over it as though he imagines that the thread is a piece of dust. When it still hangs there he brushes harder. The button pings on to the table. It's my turn to smile now. It's on the tip of my tongue to say, did you think it was another spider? But the frantic look on his face stops me.

Halfway through my meal, Lewis comes to join me. He brings a bottle of wine, apologising that Janus hasn't already done so.

'Is this OK?' he says. 'I remembered what you had the other night.'

'Perfect,' I smile. Wondering how he knows what we drank. Flattered that he took the interest to find out. Or did he just notice it on the table? 'Finished cooking?' I ask.

'For the time being.'

'This all looks very nice,' I say, fingering one of the roses. 'I don't think I've ever seen blue ones before. They're beautiful. Who chose them?'

He points a finger at his chest.

I start to eat again. Loin of venison with apricot filling. This is another thing I haven't seen, these little rings of venison stained with red wine, their centres stuffed with golden apricots. 'This tastes even better than it looks,' I say, slicing off a piece and dipping it in the surrounding pool of sauce. I feel a little awkward and wish I had someone else with me. Someone like Miss Campion. 'Don't feel you've got to sit with me,' I say. 'I'm used to eating alone and I'm sure you've got plenty to do.'

'I needed a break,' he says, closing his eyes for a moment as though he could fall asleep right there where he's sitting.

'Don't you have a day off?'

He shakes his head, smiling wearily. 'I haven't had a day off since I opened this place.'

'Then you're obviously working too hard.'

'It's the only way to survive. I can't afford any more staff. I'd like to spend more time with my daughters but it's impossible at the moment.'

'I'm sure Nicole appreciates that,' I say.

He nods and looks away. The three tables nearest to us are empty. I wish I could click my fingers and produce people to fill them. He leans his elbows on the table and touches one of the roses with the tip of his finger. Two petals fall on to the tablecloth. He looks surprised. 'They were two pounds each,' he says.

'At least they're real. You know something's real if it starts dying on you.'

He picks up the petals, weighing them in his palm. 'Nicole is planning to move to France,' he says quietly.

'Oh.' My fork is poised an inch from my mouth. I lower it a little. 'And take the girls presumably?'

'Yes. She's applying to the court.'

'Will you fight it?'

He shakes his head. 'Pointless.'

I eat a forkful of venison, chewing slowly, making it last. When I've finally swallowed it I say, 'Well, it could be worse. It could be Australia or somewhere.'

'Yes, I suppose so.' He looks even more downcast. 'Perhaps I should let you do my horoscope. You might discover something good in store for me.'

'I'd like to. Do your horoscope, I mean. And find something good for you.' I don't think he's really interested, but my mind's racing, already planning to invent an impending conjunction of planets, something which will signify good times ahead for him. 'You must come down and give me all your details sometime.'

He smiles. 'And you'll look into your crystal ball?'

'No, it's nothing like that. Astrology is a science.' I try to remember some of the impressive phrases that Gerald used to quote. But Lewis's sad smile makes it difficult for me to think clearly. 'Astrology doesn't solve problems but it helps you to find a pattern to them, learn by them. And even when we relate to this cosmic pattern, there are still many possibilities, we still have freedom of choice. You learn about yourself as much as anything.' I've been staring at the tablecloth while I try to explain what I mean. Searching for the right words has raked up a curious feeling of emotion, perhaps because so much of it reminds me of Gerald. I raise my eyes in a girlish desire to meet Lewis's. But there's no romantic exchange of glances; Lewis is looking across towards the kitchens. I look too. Janus is standing there, his arm in the air, a mobile phone in his hand.

'My biggest problem,' smiles Lewis, getting to his feet.

'Phone calls?'

'No, my brother.'

I watch him hurry off towards Janus.

Later, stretched out on my bed with one of Gerald's tapes to keep me company, I go back over all that has happened today. Mostly the things that have been said to me. And things that I've said myself. I seem to have lost control again. I'm getting tangled up with unsuitable people; people who all have problems of some kind. I've got my life exactly as I want it and I don't need this. And none of them means anything to me, nor I to them. I neither need nor want anyone else in my life. Especially not a man. I'm almost ashamed to think how I told Lewis, in that silly girlish way, to come down and give me his details. He may be divorced but he's not free. So, I think, no more one-night stands, no more fantasising about Lewis.

But I feel tense and wide awake and I cannot help thinking of Lewis, stroking a rose petal with his finger tip. And the way he kissed Nicole on the lips that day. The fingers idly stroking the inside of my thigh soon become his. And then everything male that I have encountered today, other days, becomes arousing. A faceless naked male lowers himself on to me. I moan under his weight and at the hardness of him. He's a stranger who will crush me and rape me. Then disappear at the point of orgasm and leave me to my pleasure and my recovery.

But this time I overdo it and fall asleep almost immediately. I dream of walking in the woods near Lough Ine and of taking a string of beads from the grotto. I put them round my neck and step into the pool. The water is cold and much deeper than it looks. The Virgin Mary smiles at me, but not kindly, and I begin to sink. A roaring sound fills my ears. It grows louder and louder. Gerald taught me how to wake from an unwanted dream but I can't make it work this time, although I know that I'm dreaming. Then the sound stops. And it feels as though it's the silence that wakes me.

And when I wake I have remembered something from a long time ago. I remember standing on a deserted quayside and listening to the sound of the tide rushing in through the narrow channel between Lough Ine and the sea. The roar of the water and then the strange silence that followed. It's when the tide turns, my father told me. The power of all that water forced through such a tiny gap.

I know that I won't be able to sleep again unless I have help. Somewhere I have a few temazepam. Evie hid them from me when she stayed overnight once. You'll only be able to find them in an emergency she told me. This is not an emergency, not yet, so perhaps I will have to wait until I'm frantic. I start searching the kitchen cupboards.

'Oh, fuck you, Evie,' I mutter, banging shut another door. 'You're supposed to be my best friend.' Then it comes to me. Of course. She didn't really hide them at all. I laugh, the tears rolling down my face, and find them on top of the bathroom cabinet.

It was Evie who gave them to me, after Gerald died. When I felt lonely, and when his family were demanding to sort through his things and trying to get me out of the house.

There are only three tablets left in the bottle. So I think do I really need one? Wouldn't a milky drink and a warm bath do the trick? I smile to myself. How circumspect I've become. I'll be turning into a second Miss Campion soon. I quickly pop a tablet into my mouth, wondering at what age you become tranquil enough to ignore your body.

Chapter 8

Something awful has happened. While I was blithely taking my one sleeping pill, Lewis was swallowing half a bottle of them.

A week later I still don't know all the details. But I do know that it was Nicole who called the ambulance. She drove up while I was in the kitchen searching for my pills. I remember thinking it must be Lewis and that he was later than ever. I looked out of the window to check and saw that it was Nicole, and that Lewis's car was already there. He must have arrived home while I was asleep and dreaming of Lough Ine. My memory of what happened next is vague, the sequence of events not clear. Maybe the temazepam was already beginning to work by the time the shouting started. I do remember that I was in bed and that I wrapped a pillow round my head to block out the noise. But it got worse; screaming and swearing: Janus and Nicole from what I could hear.

Buried under my pillow I must have fallen asleep. I woke to the sound of slamming doors, and got out of bed. I was very thirsty so I went to the kitchen and drank a can of Coke straight down. It fizzed in my stomach and I vomited most of it up again. That's when I heard Nicole and Janus out on the pavement. Janus sounded as though he had completely lost control. He was bellowing threats at her but he was in such a state it was impossible to make any sense of what he was saying. I thought he was going to kill her and I stood there in a stupid sleepy daze, wondering what I should do. In the end I picked up an old walking stick of Gerald's and went to the door. No sooner had I opened it than I heard Nicole's car start up. The only thought that registered in my sedated brain was, if she's driving then she must be alive.

Miss Campion, who was watching, told me that Janus had grabbed Nicole round the waist and thrown her into her car. 'And do you know what he did then?' she said.

I shook my head. I was trying to visualise how you can throw someone into the driver's seat of a car. We were discussing this at nine o'clock the following morning when Miss Campion had come knocking, disturbing me from a very profound sleep. I had taken another temazepam after being sick.

'He sat on the pavement smoking. Twelve o'clock on a Sunday night and he sits on the pavement smoking as though nothing has happened. My dear, I feel so sorry for you.'

I supposed she was referring to the fact that their tenancy agreement still has another four months to run. What interested me more for a moment was that Miss Campion was not reporting the facts correctly. After Nicole had driven off, I went to the top of my steps. And what I saw remains my clearest memory of the whole evening. Janus was not on the pavement but slumped against the front door shivering like an abandoned puppy. He may have been smoking, I didn't notice, but certainly not in the unconcerned way that Miss Campion has described. His head was thrown back, his eyes closed. I've never seen anyone look so horribly and utterly miserable. I crept back downstairs, bolted my door and went to bed. I didn't hear the ambulance arrive.

It has made the papers. Just a couple of paragraphs. Unavoidable because the restaurant is closed, until further notice, as they say. As far as our little community here in the Square is concerned, there has probably been nothing like it since the sixties when all sorts of Bohemian types lived here, creating a bit of havoc now and then, so Gerald once told me.

I sent Lewis some flowers even though he was home the next day. The girl in the florist shop gave me a funny look when I told her the delivery address. Whether it was because she knew what had happened and thought blue roses were a strange choice for someone who was obviously in a blue mood, I don't know. Or maybe it was because the shop is just round the corner and she knows where I live. When she'd filled in the address she told me to pick out a card and write my message. The cards had things like Best Wishes, Deepest Sympathy and Congratulations printed on them so I asked her to find me a blank one. After thinking about it for quite a long time, I couldn't come up with anything appropriate so I just signed my name. That was two days ago and I'm still worrying about it, wishing I'd thought of something sympathetic to write. I'm not sleeping well either. Though that's hardly surprising.

Evie brings me some more sleeping pills when she comes round. I prefer getting stuff from her rather than going through the rigmarole of a doctor's prescription. Evie never takes anything herself, not even for a headache, but she always seems to have whatever I need. Even if it is handed over with a lecture.

'I thought you'd be feeling awful,' she says, counting me out a few tablets and putting them in my empty bottle.

'I'm not feeling awful, just tired,' I tell her, aware that I sound snappy.

'Well, make sure you only take one at a time,' she says.

'Very funny.'

She gives a false clownish grin, then says, 'I suppose it was financial problems, was it?'

'I suppose so.' I've no intention of telling her about Nicole going to France. Lewis told me that in confidence. And it may or may not be a contributory factor for what he did.

'Apparently he's been in the shit before.'

'Has he?' I say without interest.

'Someone told me that his father bailed him out last time. Have you heard that?'

I shake my head. 'I don't know anything about his finances.'

'Let's hope the father pays his rent for him.'

I look at her and she leans towards me. 'Are you all right, babes?'

'No, Evie, I'm not all right. Someone I know has just felt so desperately unhappy that they don't want to live any more. So I'm not feeling one hundred per cent, no. And I'm not thinking of chasing after him for rent that isn't yet due, either.'

She pats my cheeks with both hands. 'You need a holiday.'

'Yes,' I say with a long sigh. 'Well, that's another problem.'

'Don't fret. We'll walk. Hitch.'

She thinks I mean the problem of how we're going to travel the sixty-odd miles from Cork Airport to Lough Ine. We shall probably have to hire a taxi and I can't seem to obtain a quote for this. My father says it will be all right, that the Irish are honest and won't overcharge us like some London cabbies do to foreigners. And I know that there are probably several ways of making the journey and that I'm making a mountain out of a molehill. But that isn't my main worry any longer. My main worry is here at home and what will be going on in my house while I'm away. I've even thought of cancelling the whole thing but Evie is so enthusiastic. She has read a tourist guide to Cork and is enchanted with names like Drimoleague and Timoleague, and the descriptions of the fretted Atlantic coast and the long peninsulas that trail into the sea.

'What about our luggage? Are we going to hire Sherpas?'

'We can travel light. With knapsacks. A few T-shirts, couple of pairs of shorts and a change of underwear. That's all we need.'

'Evie, this is Ireland not Majorca.'

'Pessimist,' she says. 'A few drops of rain won't kill us.' Then, in a hopeful tone of voice, she asks, 'Are we going anywhere near Connemara?'

'No, why?'

'Because I was talking to someone the other day who's been there. She said the men from there are all big and burly and wild. She said that there's nothing better than being fucked by a Connemara man.'

One thing about Evie, she can always make me laugh.

I've been trying to work up more enthusiasm for the holiday. I've even considered Evie's idea about hitching. It might do me good to rough it for a bit. If it rains then we'll shelter under a tree or in a pub. We'll be Girl Guides. Get ultra fit, or more likely collapse with blisters and fatigue. But our problems will be simple. The more I think about it, the more it appeals to me. Though I can't imagine that Evie will be able to pack all she needs for a week in one knapsack. She'll be cramming things in at the last minute: her make-up and hairspray and maybe that green dress in case any Connemara men happen to stray over to Cork.

I'm musing over this possibility, halfway through a bottle of wine and wondering what it is that Evie's friend finds unique about Connemara men, when I hear someone coming down my steps. It's a man's heavy tread. A slow heavy tread. And for a split second I experience that curious sensation, that fusion of dreaming and reality that has come to me more and more since I have been alone. By the time I go to the door, peeking first through the curtains to see who it is, I am myself again. Though having seen that it's Lewis, not all that composed.

Physically he doesn't look any different. Not like you'd expect someone who has had their stomach pumped would look. If that is what they did to him in the hospital. But he's nervous, I can tell. And if I'm not careful he'll make me nervous too. So I pull the door open wide and leave him to come in while I go and pour him a glass of wine. I do it quickly, confidently, so that he can't refuse.

His hand is shaking as he takes the glass from me and he puts it straight down on the worktop. 'I thought I owed you some sort of explanation,' he says, his hand to his mouth now to smother a little cough.

'No, no you don't,' I say, wanting to make him feel easier but immediately wishing I'd let him go on.

'Well, I certainly owe you a thank you. For the roses.'

'Oh, the roses. Two pounds each,' I smile.

He manages to smile too, though it's obviously an effort, then takes a large mouthful of wine. 'I expect you wish that you hadn't given me the tenancy,' he says.

'Too late now.'

'So you're willing to put up with us for another few months, are you?' He's standing with his back against the sink. There's a spotlight on the wall a little way along, its flexible stem angled towards him. It shows up the lines on his face, deepening them into shadows. I make a note never to stand in this same position if I have company because I think it would make me look less attractive, rather than more as it does Lewis. Faces etched with sadness appeal to me. Especially those of large handsome men. It makes them seem vulnerable. It touches me.

'If you want to stay that's fine with me.'

'I'm going to visit my father,' he says. 'I'm taking Lydia and

Mimi to see him. I thought I'd let you know. I didn't want you to think I'd disappeared. Not after all the—'

'That'll be nice for you,' I jump in again. 'A nice break.'

He takes another mouthful of wine. 'Before Nicole takes them to France.'

'She's definitely going then?'

'Not permanently, not yet. They're house-hunting.'

He is wearing a denim shirt, the cuffs undone and turned back. It gapes open over his stomach, not because he has a paunch but because there are two buttons missing.

'You'll have to get Lydia sewing,' I say.

'Sorry?'

'Your buttons.' I point at his middle and imagine slipping my hand inside his shirt.

'Oh.'

I cannot tell whether he's baffled or just not interested but I feel silly, which makes me blush. 'She was sewing buttons on for Janus the other day. Last Sunday. When I came to the restaurant. It reminded me.'

'Lydia can be very capable when she puts her mind to it. She's good with Janus. Very tolerant.' He pauses, finishes his wine. 'Which is more than I can say for her mother.'

I'm taken aback by this. Not the fact that Nicole isn't tolerant towards Janus, of course, but that Lewis has mentioned it, almost as if he's criticising her. I reach for the wine bottle, conveniently beside us on the drainer, and top up his glass. 'She's not so tolerant then?'

He takes a while to answer, letting his eyes wander round my kitchen, up over the walls as though he's searching for an answer there. 'I'm sorry,' he says at last. 'I shouldn't have said that. Janus is my problem, no one elses.' He puts down his glass beside the bottle and straightens up as though he's about to go. And I don't want him to.

'Did you know that he's named after a Roman god?' I say.

He smiles, surprised, visibly relaxing. 'Oh, you know that too, do you?'

'Yes. The one with two faces, isn't it?'

'That's right. Apparently it was his duty to guard the gates of heaven.' The smile widens. 'Janus used to tell girls that he did that.'

'Did it work?'

'I think most wanted to find out, yes.'

'Did your parents know about it? His name, I mean, not the girls.'

'My father did. He chose both our names. And my mother knew about the girls.' The smile blossoms into laughter. 'She used to tell him that he'd wear his er . . . his dick out before he was legally entitled to use it.'

There is a fondness in his voice. For Janus or their mother, I'm not sure. 'And what about you?' I ask, brave now that he seems happier. 'Did you wear out any part of your anatomy chasing girls?'

'No, I was more interested in becoming a chef.'

'You're the quiet one,' I say.

'Compared to Janus, yes,' he nods.

I nod too, frantically trying to think of something to stop the conversation fizzling out.

'I should go,' he says. 'I've kept you long enough. I just wanted to, well, show my face really.'

'I'm glad you have,' I say softly. 'I'm glad you're OK. Well, as OK as you can be.' I look at his glass. It's still full. 'Finish your wine before you go. I want to pick your brain.' It has just come to me; the perfect way to delay him.

'I don't think it's working all that well at the moment, but you can try.'

'You look in good working order to me,' I say lightly.

'Well, as long as you don't want advice on how to run a restaurant. Or a marriage come to that.'

I don't comment on this but pull out a chair at the kitchen table for him. 'Have a seat and I'll tell you.'

He turns to pick up his wine but stops and clutches at the sink with both hands. 'Do you mind if I have a glass of water?' he says.

'No, of course not.' I quickly pass him a tumbler. He's sweating. I can see beads of perspiration glistening across his brows and along his top lip. He wipes a hand over his face and gulps down a whole glass of water.

'Are you OK?' I put my hand very gently on his back, just my fingers really.

'Yes, yes, I'm fine, thank you.'

I watch as he lowers himself on to the chair. The sweat is pouring off him. He rubs a hand round his face again and I pass him a tissue from a box I keep on the worktop.

'Sure you're OK?' I ask.

He nods, clearly embarrassed and I wish I could help him in some way. Should I ask him if he wants to lie down? Take off that thick shirt that is making him sweat, and lie down? He rests his forehead in his hand a moment, pushing back the front of his hair. It sticks through his fingers, dark and damp, a little matted at the back. Lie down on my bed, I think, so I could smooth it. And smooth the lines on his forehead. And trail patterns through the dampness of his overheated body.

'I wanted to ask you about Ireland,' I say.

He looks up, licks his lips and wipes them with his knuckles. 'Fire away.'

'What's the best way to get from Cork Airport to Skibbereen if you don't have a car?'

'I'm not sure but I could find out. I don't think there are any trains. Is this for your holiday?'

'Yes. Evie wants to thumb it but I'm worried about the weather.'

'When are you going?'

'Next month, hopefully. Whenever we can book a flight.'

He picks up his glass, cupping the bowl in his palm, the stem between his middle fingers. 'Next month,' he repeats thoughtfully. Then, 'If you went by ferry instead you could come with me. I could take you to your cottage. Even pick you up.'

For one tiny sweet second I imagine that it's just the two of us. I draw in my breath. Let it out. 'But you won't have room. Don't forget Evie.'

'How could I forget Evie?' he smiles. 'There's plenty of room. Janus won't be coming.'

'Oh, well. Yes. Yes, please, that'll be great. You've solved a problem.'

'It's cheaper by ferry as well.'

'We'll help with the petrol.'

'You can help keep my daughters amused. It's a long drive.' He leans back in the chair and averts his eyes. 'Last time we went, it was all of us. Nicole as well.'

I have the feeling that he wants to talk about her some more.

But he looks back at me and carefully puts down his glass. 'I better not drink too much. But thanks. We'll discuss arrangements another time.'

A couple of days later Nicole phones me.

'Is it true that Lewis is giving you and your friend a lift to Ireland?' she asks.

'We've only talked about it.' Her tone isn't particularly friendly and I feel myself bristle. I'm also wondering how she knows my number. 'It's not definite.'

'I just wanted to make sure that Janus isn't going with him,' she says.

'Oh, I see. Well, I can tell you that. He's not.'

'Are you certain?' She sounds almost aggressive.

'You'll have to ask Lewis.'

'I have.' She gives a sigh of exasperation that could be meant for me. I don't know. 'But he might be lying. And I'm not having Lydia and Mimi anywhere near that maniac ever again.'

'You'll have to speak to Lewis.'

'He ought to be locked up,' she says – and I know she doesn't mean Lewis.

I put the receiver down before she has a chance to say any more; I don't want to hear all this – although the idea of Janus being locked up is not a bad one. It would save me worrying myself to death about what is going on in my house while I'm in Ireland.

Chapter 9

One worry solved, another takes its place. Janus is not alone in my house but here with me, in the middle of nowhere. And I want to die. I've just told Evie precisely that and she said why don't I go and jump overboard then.

'Come on, babes,' she says, lifting my head on to her lap. 'Sit up and fix your eyes on the horizon.'

'Can you see land?' I say miserably. 'Please say you can see land.' I was once travel-sick on a school coach outing. The driver stopped, reluctantly, in a layby where I was copiously and noisily sick in front of about thirty cars. Before I actually vomited, I wouldn't have cared if the whole world were gathered round to watch. Afterwards I felt devastating humiliation. I know it will be the same today as I lie stretched on a bench on the top deck of the Swansea to Cork ferry, soaked because it's raining. When I recover, as I keep telling myself I must, I will certainly feel ashamed of behaving in such a pathetic way. I've already staggered out of the restaurant with a hand over my mouth while the others were tucking into a meal. Evie says my face was bright green and I believe her.

The others are Evie, Lewis and Janus. Things have been happening again. Nicole wouldn't let Lewis bring the girls. She threatened to fight him in court and bring up his suicide attempt. When Lewis told me about all this he seemed only moderately depressed, rather than very upset about it. It made me think he must be dosed with sedatives. But it didn't stop him talking. He spent over an hour with me. He wanted to talk but not about himself so he told me about Janus and the spiders.

Everyone seems to be telling me animal stories. Or rather

creature stories. An Irish woman I met in the Ladies told me that she makes this crossing regularly and is always abysmally sick but it's the only way she can travel with her dog. The dog, a poodle, was with her and cocked its leg against the hot-water pipe while she was talking to me. 'Boys will be boys,' she said, ignoring the hot piss steaming off the pipe.

I had to get out in the fresh air after this so Evie collared a member of the crew who directed us up to this deck where the air is fresher than I've tasted in my whole life. He told us a story too – I think he wanted to delay Evie – about a dolphin somewhere off the Irish coast who comes out to meet the boats. There's a few of them dotted about apparently.

'A dolphin!' said Evie. 'I must get my camera.'

'I don't think we'll be seeing any of them fellows today,' said the man.

'It's too rough, isn't it?' I said, wanting him to confirm this because the others had maintained the movement of the ship was perfectly normal. It's all in the mind, Janus had said. I could have said the same about his spiders.

'Yes, it's a wee bit choppy,' smiled the man.

'I knew I'd end up in a watery grave.'

'I beg your pardon?' he said, a hand to his ear against the buffeting of the wind.

'Oh, take no notice of her,' said Evie. 'She has bad dreams about water. And she always wants her dreams to come true.'

I couldn't be bothered to dispute this. I was feeling too ill again.

We arrive at Kinsale late afternoon and Lewis drives us along by the harbour. Hundreds of yachts are moored there, the forest of masts turned to silver in the brilliant sunshine. There's not a cloud in sight. The sea's as tranquil and blue as the sky. Amazing, I think after the hard time it was giving me only a few hours ago. There are flowers everywhere, and music from a children's fairground. We turn into a back street packed with very old houses, most with shop fronts, or restaurant signs. It seems a long time since I've been in a place that has such an atmosphere of peace. I forget my seasickness and my worries about Janus and think to myself, yes, this is what holidays are supposed to feel like. Not those anxious weeks of my childhood, spoiled by my mother's semi-invalidity and her dislodged womb. Or the awful week of my honeymoon, protecting my own womb from ending up the same way. Gerald didn't care for holidays, and by then, neither did I.

Evie and I linger in the background while Lewis and Janus greet their father. They remind me of an Italian Mafia family the way they hug and kiss each other. I find it very poignant, given that this old man was supposed to be seeing his little granddaughters. Instead he has an elder son who has tried to kill himself, and a younger one who has brought tears to his eyes. I watch as he holds Janus at arm's-length and shakes his head, then pulls him close just as he done to Lewis. Evie takes my elbow and steers me outside.

'We'd better disappear for a bit,' she says. 'Did you see that Janus was crying?'

'Mmm.' I have a lump in my throat.

'Do you think he's the black sheep?'

'Probably.'

'Or maybe the prodigal son.'

'Same thing.'

We are staying at a bed and breakfast establishment for the night but have been invited to eat at the restaurant. For the next hour we wander round the town, hunting out the few estate agents so that I can gain some idea of how much the cottage is likely to fetch. But for some reason very few of the properties on display in their windows have prices on them.

The meal is a strange affair. Dacre, as their father is called, is charming but suspicious of Evie and me. Of Evie, more, I think. I would like to tell him, have no fear, this woman will not steal your sons, not permanently anyway. She would sleep with them, given the chance. The two of them together even. Then toss them back to you used and probably very happy. Me, now I'm a different matter because I don't know what I want.

We share a seafood platter, one great round plate bigger than you could circle with your arms, placed in the middle of the table. It's covered in squeaky clean seaweed over which is spread an amazing array of different shellfish. I've never seen anything quite like it; neither has Evie. Dacre seems amused by our delight and urges us to help ourselves, pointing out and naming different things.

'It looks so pretty,' says Evie, picking up a blue-striped mussel shell. 'And the smell.' She leans forward, her nose inches from the plate.

'It's all washed in sea water,' says Dacre.

Evie pulls a face. 'Isn't it polluted?'

'Not here. But it's salty. You'll need lots to drink.'

'Goody.' Evie rubs her hands together.

Dacre leans towards Lewis and whispers something. Lewis goes off and comes back with a shiny brown flagon stoppered with a wodge of muslin. They won't tell us what it is but I think it's what's known as elderflower champagne. Refreshing but not especially potent.

Janus scorns this and drinks Guinness. He's very quiet. Perhaps he received a lecture after the hugs and kisses. He could do with one. He could do with some table manners as well. He sucks the froth off his Guinness like a pig, and doesn't make any effort to join in the conversation. And now and again I catch him watching Evie. But Evie is being prudent for a change and pretends she is unaware of his interest.

We part at midnight. Lewis and Janus go up to their father's apartment above the restaurant, and Evie and I go across the road to our guesthouse. It's not exactly five-star accommodation. We have to share the family bathroom where socks are soaking in a bucket and books sit on top of the toilet cistern. I pick up the top one and find it's a bible. Beneath it is a biography of Anaïs Nin. Is this meant to tell me something? I wonder.

Our room is small and we keep bumping into one another as we unpack our overnight bags and get undressed. Besides two single beds, there is an old-fashioned dressing table covered with a lace runner, a worn armchair and a wardrobe whose door swings open every time we walk on a certain floorboard. But there are fluffy towels, which smell as though they've been blowing for hours in a sea breeze; brand-new soaps and, for our convenience, a glazed china chamber pot under one of the beds. We're both in fits of giggles by the time we discover this. I laugh so much that I feel as though the floor is sloping. Evie assures me that it really is.

'Is this what it was like at boarding school?' she says. 'Jolly jinks.'

'It wasn't jolly jinks. I hated it.'

'Couldn't you smuggle boys back to the dorm to liven things up?'

'No point,' I say, pulling a face of regret. 'I wouldn't have known what to do with them. Anyway, we were guarded.'

Evie sits on the bed and starts to remove her jewellery: an assortment of bracelets, gold chains and a large Gothic-style cross. She bundles them into her handbag and fumbles about to produce a packet of contraceptive pills.

'The one pill you don't mind taking,' I say.

'I like double protection.' She looks up. 'But now and again, Verity, just now and again, I come across a man I consider a safe bet for unsafe sex. And I treat myself.'

'Anyone in mind?' I say lightly.

She gives one of her big clownish smiles, inviting me to guess. When I ignore her she says, 'You ought to start taking it. You could do with a treat or two.'

I look away. 'I'm not prepared to live that dangerously.' She knows that I didn't need any contraception with Gerald, and that I've never bothered since simply because I haven't had much to do with men. And they all seem to use condoms these days anyway. All that, she knows. But what I'm not going to tell her is that since that night with Chris I've been considering going on the pill. For my peace of mind. Despite my intense longing for sex that night, I discovered that old fears could still surface. Taking the pill will make me feel safer. It's not that I plan to make a habit of casual affairs; loveless sex leaves me disappointed. But just lately masturbation leaves me disappointed too. Evie would say I need a man.

I watch her stuff the packet away in her bag. Carelessly, as though it's no more important than her chains and bangles.

'Your packet of excitement,' I say quietly.

'My packet of what?' she says.

I shake my head. 'Nothing.'

She lies back, stretching out full length, wriggling about until she's comfortable. The springs jangle in protest. 'This is unbelievable,' she sighs. 'Fucking unbelievable. Here we are with them two. And what are we doing? Sleeping in our little narrow beds with a potty underneath.'

'Which one of them were you actually thinking of treating yourself to?' I say.

She rolls on to her side to look at me. 'Darling, I don't mind.'

I get into bed as well and lie there with my hands behind my head. I don't feel at all sleepy. I'm relaxed but wide awake. And I've a feeling that it was something a little stronger than fermented elderflowers we've been drinking.

'Do you want a bedtime story?' I ask.

'Is it a sexy one?'

'No, it's about a little boy.'

'Go on then,' she yawns. 'But make him grow up by the end.'

'Once upon a time,' I begin. Janus's face is before me, sulky and withdrawn as he was tonight, and I have to try very hard to imagine him three years old with a child's sweet smile. Did he have Mimi's round peachy cheeks, I wonder, or has he always looked undernourished? But he would certainly have been appealing with those dark eyes and tumbling curls.

'Verity,' Evie calls, snapping her fingers in the air, 'I'm waiting.'

'Right. Once upon a time there was a little boy whose mother loved him very much. But she loved a lot of other people as well. She was very affectionate. Very affectionate.' I pause for breath, surprised at how I'm telling it. 'In other words, she fucked around. Her husband didn't go too much on this so he upped and left. But she still wasn't free. When you have children you can't do all the fucking around you want because they need looking after. One day, when the little boy was three, she had a phone call from one of her many lovers asking her to meet him. It was supposed to be just for lunch, and she thought that her little boy would be all right on his own for a couple of hours. After all, she had left him before on the odd occasion. And if she did happen to get delayed . . .'

'She's gonna get delayed,' sings Evie from her pillow.

'Shut up and listen. If she did get delayed then her older son would be home from school to look after his little brother. So with the utter lack of conscience common to all nymphos, off she goes.'

Evie chuckles to herself and I wonder why I feel the need to inject crude humour into this story.

'She has left the little boy with a pile of toys, a big picture book of nursery rhymes and a bag of sweets.' I'm embellishing now. I don't know for sure about the toys or the sweets but I think that's what a mother, even a bad one, would do. 'And she has impressed on him that he must not answer the door to anyone or poke anything in the electric sockets. But she does leave the gas fire on low because it's winter.'

'The cow,' murmurs Evie sleepily. 'I suppose he dies from carbon monoxide poisoning.'

'No he doesn't. Now shut up, you're spoiling my flow.' I'm into this now; I want to repeat it. Despite going over it in my head there seems to be something I'm not understanding properly. Evie might come out with the one remark which will make it simple and forgettable. 'The little boy plays with his toys for a while, then he starts to look at the picture book. It has "Bo-peep", "Jack Sprat", "Mary, Mary, Quite Contrary", all the nursery rhymes in big pictures. It's one of those books where the pictures pop up to give a 3-D effect. Now when he gets to "Miss Muffet" and the spider pops up, he doesn't like it. The spider has a big angry face. A *menacing* spider. More like a tarantula.'

'A three-year-old wouldn't know about tarantulas,' Evie pipes up.

'I know that. I'm just trying to emphasise how scared he was.'

'Did you know that women's fear of spiders is instinctive?' Evie props herself on her elbows. 'I read it somewhere. It's a primitive subconscious fear that a spider could dash up your vagina and harm your unborn child.'

'Where did you read that?' I'm always suspicious of remarks that Evie makes about fear because she doesn't really know what it is.

'Camille Paglia, I think.'

'You've read her?'

Evie smiles across at me. 'You're learning a lot of things about me tonight that you didn't know before, aren't you?'

'Do you want me to finish this or not?'

'Carry on,' she says, turning over as though she might fall asleep.

'Well, he gets so scared that he rips the spider out and throws it into the flames of the gas fire. The paper burns black, then drops into the grate. It wriggles about like burned paper can do. The little boy is terrified. He starts to cry. He cries and cries and calls for his mother. Because it's winter it gets dark early but he daren't turn on the light. He thinks it's the same as an electric socket. And as the room gets darker and darker, all the other pictures in the book come to life, like the spider. He runs and hides in the bathroom because it's the only door he can lock. The airing cupboard is in there and he crawls on to a shelf and hides between some sheets. When his brother comes home and knocks to be let in, the little boy doesn't hear him. The brother thinks they've gone out. So he goes off to his father's house, a bus ride away, and waits there until his father comes home from work. The father is furious. He phones his ex-wife but there's no answer. The following day he takes his son home early because he needs some things for school. They have to break in. And it's only then that they discover the little boy cowering in the airing cupboard. He's not crying any longer but he's traumatised and incoherent. All they can get out of him is the word "spider". The father thinks he means the big spider that's in the bath. He tries to show him that the spider in the bath can't hurt him because it cannot crawl up the sides. The boy just screams and screams. Then they find the torn book and the ashes.' I stop because I can hear that Evie is asleep. So it's not worth going on. Not aloud anyway.

In the morning she asks, 'What happened to the little boy? Did he burn the house down?'

'No.' I frown at her. What made her think that? 'No, no, he didn't,' I say realising that this might be a perfectly logical conclusion to come to. 'He developed a phobia about spiders.'

She is busy gathering up the numerous items she seems to need for a trip to the bathroom. 'How did you dream up such a crap story?'

'Too much elderflower champagne.'

She blinks and rubs at her eyes, which are panda-like because she is not as meticulous in removing her mascara as she is her jewellery. 'Yeah, I know what you mean. I dreamed I was being fucked by a dolphin. It wasn't bad either.'

'That's pornographic.'

'Yeah,' she said. 'You could use it for your dream page – liven up the magazine.'

'Mmm.' I'm hardly listening to her now. Not because she shocks me in any way; I know her too well for that. I'm thinking about fire again. About Janus burning the spider. And burning Nicole's clothes. But I mustn't worry. He's here, in Ireland. Not alone in my house smoking in bed, flicking his matches into an overfull ashtray, resentful at any woman who comes between him and Lewis.

'I don't think I've got any phobias,' says Evie, picking up one of the towels and holding it to her cheek.

'Well, I'm not scared of spiders.'

'No, but you're scared of most other things.' She laughs and ducks away as I throw one of the bars of soap at her.

It's been arranged that we shall have lunch at the restaurant and then Lewis will drive us to Lough Ine. He estimates that it will only take an hour or two, which gives him plenty of time to get back for the evening. In the meantime Evie and I are going to explore Kinsale and do some shopping, something we might find difficult once we are abandoned in the cottage.

There is a large shop in the centre of the town selling typical Irish goods. Sweaters from the woollen mills in Blarney, Waterford Crystal, Donegal Tweed, pottery and linen bedecked with shamrock and leprechauns. If you dropped in here from out of the sky you'd have no trouble sussing out in what country you'd landed.

We spend an hour buying postcards and gifts for home. Then, before we laden ourselves with the groceries, we sit in a small park on the edge of the town to write our postcards, me to my parents and Evie to numerous friends. We've bought cakes for a mid-morning snack but as soon as we take them out of the bag we are surrounded by a flock of large black birds. They strut at our feet, making a sinister grunting noise, bold and persistent like the pigeons in Trafalgar Square. When we try to shoo them away they hop sideways just out of reach, waiting for the chance to advance on us again.

We tell Lewis about them when we meet for lunch. He says they are ravens and that they are notorious not only for the unusual size of the flock but because they have been known to attack dogs being walked in the park.

'They're jackdaws,' interrupts Janus, who has been listening but not saying a word up until now.

'No, they're ravens,' says Lewis, 'you ask Dad.'

'I bet you a tenner.'

'Well, they looked like a bunch of old crows to me,' says Evie.

By the time we see Dacre we forget all about the birds because he comes on the run to tell Lewis that he's wanted on the phone. They go off together and come back a few minutes later smiling and talking quietly to each other. Janus watches them, his head slightly bent, looking up from beneath his brows, as though he is suspicious that something is going on behind his back. Dacre greets Evie and me and asks what we'd like to eat. I take the menu he hands me but keep an eye on Janus. He is staring intently at Lewis now, a challenging look. Twice Lewis glances at him. Then I hear him say, 'Nicole wanted the girls to say hello to Dad, that's all.' I read Janus's lips: 'Fucking woman.' He jumps up from the table and disappears through a side door of the restaurant. Lewis and his father exchange looks.

'Do you know what I fancy?' says Evie loudly, oblivious of the little drama going on under her nose.

Dacre smiles across at her. 'Not a seafood platter?' he says.

She smiles seductively back at him. 'How did you guess?'

'I'll have an individual one prepared especially for you,' he says.

She tilts her head to one side, holding back the hair from her face. It's a mannerism that she has perfected. 'How sweet of you. Now I know where your sons get their charm.'

Evie can say things like this without making people squirm. It's her theatrical tone. Dacre just raises an eyebrow. But I can almost read his thoughts. One of them, his eyes say.

I choose a salad. My stomach is not used to so much good food. But I'm cajoled into having a pudding by Dacre, who says we should make the most of this because we won't find food to match his once we have left Kinsale. The atmosphere has lightened; Janus has returned to the table and announced he is coming with us. 'I'll do you a favour,' he says, hooking an arm round Lewis's neck. 'I'll do half the driving for you.'

It's late afternoon when Janus pulls up in Skibbereen so that

Evie and I can buy bread and milk. His driving doesn't seem so bad on the wide empty roads of West Cork. We coasted along at a fast but surprisingly smooth pace, Evie and I enjoying the place names and Lewis dozing next to Janus. I'm pretty sure he is taking some kind of sedative and that Janus dishes them out. It's all done discreetly but I'm a discreet watcher when I put my mind to it.

We take a walk round Skibbereen to stretch our legs. In a pub window we see a large poster announcing that tonight is 'Kerry's Night'.

' "Live music with Kerry MacCarthy",' reads Evie. "Come early." ' She is lapping the place up just as she has done everything since she stepped on Irish soil. I've told her I suspect that she must have Irish blood in her veins as she is so entranced by all she sees. Even the squat bungalows that dot the countryside and the block walls that fill gaps in the hedges she finds intriguing rather than ugly.

'Let's come back here tonight,' she says. She's speaking to me but at the same time she links her arm through Janus's. 'We'll drive down to the cottage, drop off our things, then have a lift back here with these two.'

'But they want to get back to Kinsale, Evie,' I say.

'We'll be quick. Is that OK with you?' she says, looking up at Janus.

'It's fine by me,' he says. 'Lewis?'

'How will you get back to Lough Ine later on?' says Lewis.

'Easy.' She smiles and points across the road to where a hand-painted sign saying 'Taxi Hire' hangs outside yet another pub. She is still holding Janus by the arm. In her excitement and eagerness to organise everything I don't think she realises. But I know he does.

Once we reach Lough Ine, I am enchanted too. On this June evening the place is not far short of magical. And that's not a description I use very often. Despite my involvement with the stars, I find few things in life magical. I don't think I ever did. Bruno Bettelheim said that when children grow up they go on believing in magic if reality disappoints them. I have found other ways to escape reality.

All four of us stand on the shore, silent and still for a

moment. Apart from a couple in a boat on the far side of the lough there isn't a soul about.

Janus is the first to move. He goes to the car and starts to lift out our bags. I don't think his main objective is to help Evie and me but to save his brother the trouble. I've noticed how, in many little ways, he is mindful of Lewis's welfare. Perhaps to make up for the trouble he causes.

'Do you really want to go back to the pub tonight?' I ask Evie, once all our stuff is unloaded. 'We ought to get settled in here.'

She looks thoughtfully round the one downstairs room. It's a U-shape, or rather three sides of a square set round a chimney breast. One side forms a kitchen-diner; the bottom section is the sitting room with an open fire; and the other side has built-in cupboards and a sofa bed. It was once a fisherman's cottage and has never been extended, just modernised back in the sixties when my father bought it.

'It won't take a minute to get settled in,' says Evie, putting her radio on the mantelpiece and picking up one of our bags. She looks across at Janus. 'Or are you two in a rush to get back to Kinsale?'

Janus, in turn, looks at Lewis. 'There's no hurry is there? We've got time to have a beer with them before we go, haven't we?'

'I'm easy,' says Lewis.

He looks easy. His face is slightly puffy; his expression bemused as though his thoughts are far away. Probably the tablets, I think, and wonder if he should be drinking.

'Come on then,' says Evie, handing me a bag. 'Let's get a move on.'

It seems I'm outnumbered so I follow her up the cast-iron spiral staircase that leads to the first floor. I remember hating this staircase as a child because my mother found it difficult to negotiate. Laden with our bags we find it difficult too.

Upstairs there is a bathroom, tiny boxroom with a child-size bed, and a double bedroom. Evie and I decide to share the double bed and use the boxroom as a safety net if we fall out. Neither of us fancies sleeping alone downstairs.

Mrs Doyle has left clean linen on all the beds and we quickly make up the double, Evie disappearing off to the bathroom while I'm still struggling to get the very chunky pillows into their starched cotton cases. Another thing I remember: Mrs Doyle's laundry, all done by hand.

I'm not sure what one wears for a night out at an Irish pub so I change into a clean sweater and jeans. My hair is thickened with the salty air and rain from our sea crossing. I was too tired to wash it last night. I rub a blob of gel between my hands and rake it back from my face. The effect is not bad. In fact I look better than when I've spent two hours at the hairdresser's. Next door, Evie is very quiet. Probably putting on lipstick; that's the only time she's totally quiet. Downstairs it's very quiet too apart from the lapping of water. Lewis and Janus aren't putting on lipstick, that's for sure. But they could be whispering about us.

On the wall there is an old sepia photograph of the family who used to live here. My father hung it there after the room was decorated, carefully replacing it in the same spot that he'd found it. I take it down for a closer look, something I wasn't allowed to do when I was a child. On the back, in faded red ink, it says, 'Mary and John O'Brien with their eight surviving children, July 1910.' Eight surviving, I think, wondering if they, and the others who didn't survive, were born in this room. I imagine Mary O'Brien listening to the slap of water while she gave birth with only a whiff of chloroform to ease her pain. Or maybe she had to rely on whiskey. And maybe she gave birth alone while her husband was out fishing on the lough.

I go to look out of the window. No fishing is allowed now. At least I don't think it is. Nothing must be taken from the lough. I think that's what it says on the big notice board out on the road. It probably means that nothing *living* can be taken. It makes me wonder what Mary and John did with their dead babies. As I look the water is darkened by cloud. In the distance I can see where the lough narrows between the hills. It disappears into a long creek before widening out into what is really a land-locked arm of the sea. The gap, or 'cut' as it's known, that links it with the ocean, is so narrow and shallow that the tide rushes through it with enormous and terrifying power. Just as my father once explained. Anything floating in the lough would no doubt be sucked out through this gap when the tide changed. Destroyed on the rocks or washed out to sea.

Then Evie is there in the doorway, making me feel normal again. She looks like a Parisian with a pencil skirt split to the thigh and a little black beret pinned on her mass of hair.

'Ready?' she says.

Chapter 10

Gerald's theory about how to stay in control keeps coming back to me this evening. So I'm trying to be brutally honest with myself. Which isn't easy at the moment. I wish I believed in life after death so that I could contact him and ask him to explain a little better. But if Gerald is anywhere other than beneath the earth at Highgate Cemetery, it will be up amongst the stars. And he'll have far more interesting things to do than sort out a woman who even lies to herself about what she wants.

Evie gets to her feet and adjusts her little hat, giving me a secret wink from behind her hand. 'Which of you two is driving home?' she asks Lewis.

'I am,' says Janus, 'so I'll just have half of light ale this time.'

Evie has offered to buy our second round. Lewis bought the first. We are sitting on a leather bench seat in a bar that is only just beginning to fill with people despite it being half-past nine. The star attraction of the evening, Kerry MacCarthy, has not yet arrived. That is the reason why Lewis and Janus are still here. Janus wants to see Kerry. He likes the atmosphere in Irish pubs, especially when there's live music. He particularly likes this bar. He even likes the idea of driving back to Kinsale along dark country roads with a bellyful of beer. What he really likes, is Evie.

Kerry arrives while she is getting our drinks. Janus goes to help her. He stands close beside her. So close that as she turns her head to catch something he's saying, strands of her hair cling to the black T-shirt he's wearing. And even across the width of the bar, through the crowd of drinkers and the thick smoky air, I sense that the spark of attraction that has sprung up between them is flaring out of control.

There's intermittent clapping as Kerry makes his way across the floor and takes his place at an old upright piano. Someone has placed a brimming glass of Guinness on top of the piano – in fact when I look again there are three pints lined up for him. He takes his time, extracting a packet of Silk Cut from his waistcoat pocket, and lighting up before he finally lifts the lid of the piano. I'm torn between watching him and keeping an eye on Evie and Janus.

A cheer goes up as Kerry runs the fingers of one hand across the keys. Very lightly at first, then punching down with both hands while his feet work away at the pedals, making the music reverberate round the bar. I'm sitting at one end of the seat, Lewis at the other. It's just the way we sat down. Not wanting consciously to pair into couples. I look across at him and he smiles. I'm about to say something, make a comment as an excuse to move next to him, when Janus and Evie come back and squeeze into the space between us. Everyone is squeezed in now and it's standing room only for new arrivals.

Kerry bursts into song, his delivery so clear that we can hear every word, a heart-rending tale about a blacksmith who kills his wife's lover. Before long we are joining in the choruses of songs. Between each number Kerry pauses just long enough to swallow a few mouthfuls of Guinness and take a drag on his Silk Cut, propped waiting in the ashtray. He is very talented. His voice is rich and true but has a little rasp of hoarseness, a little catch like that of country-and-western singers. It suits the love and death themes of his songs, each one more poignant and tragic than the one before. And each glass of Guinness seems to enhance the sound.

At ten thirty he is joined by another two musicians, one with an accordion and one with a mandolin. The time is ticking away. Now and again I catch the hands of a clock on the far wall jerking forward a fraction. At least I think I do. The clock is wreathed in the smoke rising from more glowing cigarette ends than I've ever seen in one place before. It drifts in thick bands above our heads, blocking out most of the light from the bare electric bulbs. Janus buys another round of drinks. Hot toddies with cloves floating on the scalding liquid. It's almost impossible to make conversation, the music is too loud and everyone in the bar is trying to talk above it. Through the haze of smoke I watch the mandolin player. His bulk and his brush-like hair reminds me of Gerald. He is younger, maybe forty-five, fifty. His fingers pluck away at the strings, coaxing such a sweetness of sound that I can't stop watching him. The notes feel as though they're floating through the air, specially for me. They hit me somewhere a little lower than my heart. Now and again he catches my eye. I look away but instantly want to look back.

I notice that Evie has her hand on Janus's knee as she tries to tell him something above the din. The other side of them, Lewis looks sleepy, his eyelids drooping, his lips slightly parted. He has made no attempt to talk to us or even look in our direction for ages. All of this registers in a dreamlike way. I take longer and longer looks at the mandolin player, pretending it is a dream. He answers with tiny smiles and once runs his tongue along his top lip. How easy it is to build up excitement when you pretend. And how easy to maintain it. To pull it tight. We're exchanging looks more frequently now, becoming more daring, and I start to imagine what would happen next, what would be the conclusion, if this were real. Beside me Evie is doing something to the palm of Janus's hand. And I don't think she's telling his fortune. She doesn't need to. They know what the outcome of this will be. And so do I.

Eleven o'clock comes and goes. Then half-past. I buy more drinks and enquire what actually are the ingredients of a hot toddy? The barman smiles and points behind him to a kettle of steaming water. Next to the kettle I notice a catering tin of Nescafé and ask for a cup of that instead.

As I carry the tray back to our seat Evie stands up and says, 'It's not worth us getting a taxi now. They'll drive us home.' Her mouth is close to my ear. I can feel the heat coming off her. 'They'll drive us home,' she repeats, louder.

'I can hear you, don't shout.'

She smiles and lowers her voice. 'They might as well stay the night and drive back tomorrow.'

I put the tray down and she squeezes my neck. 'Want to take the mandolin player back with us?'

'All I'm worrying about is getting home safely,' I say irritably. The musicians are taking a break, talking amongst themselves at the bar. My fantasies have come to an abrupt end. Instead I'm having visions of the hill down to Lough Ine and the car spinning out of control and ending up in the water.

Out in the car park it's decided that I'll drive. I'm not sure how we come to this decision but I'm aware that it's to prevent Janus driving. He does however insist on sitting next to me as I've no idea how to handle the BMW and Lewis is apparently quite drunk as well.

After a mile or so I manage to get out of second gear, or rather Janus does, laughingly instructing me when to use the clutch and actually changing gear for me. And sometimes changing it wrongly on purpose. Evie leans between our seats giggling at his antics. It's a miracle that we do arrive safely.

And it'll be a miracle if both Evie and Janus don't end up with dislocated jaws. On the pretence of making coffee, they're devouring each other in the corner round by the cooker.

Lewis and I are seated either side of the fireplace where blocks of peat are stacked ready for a cold night. Janus comes and crouches down in front of Lewis. I don't hear everything he says – he's whispering, his hands resting on Lewis's knees. But I do hear him say that they can phone their father in the morning. Lewis nods. At the same time Evie comes up behind me.

'It's going to be easier if we have the bedroom, isn't it?' She's whispering as well. 'While you make up your mind.' She leans right over my shoulder and slips a small flat packet into my hand.

I feel exposed. Angry with her. I wish we were back in the bar.

'Do as you like,' I say. 'As you always do.' I slip the packet into the pocket of my jeans.

She kisses me goodnight on the cheek and hoists up her skirt to negotiate the spiral staircase. Janus walks up close behind her, grabbing her round the waist before they've reached the top.

I stand up and switch Evie's radio on. Lewis looks up and smiles.

'She was encouraging him,' he says. 'There's not much I could do.'

'Do? They're both free agents.' He's making me feel as though we're a middle-aged couple talking about our kids. I sink back into the armchair and close my eyes. To get to the toilets in the pub you had to go out through a back yard stacked with crates and aluminium kegs. I imagine going out there, signalling to the mandolin player to follow me. Exchanging hot frantic kisses in a dark corner of the yard.

I open my eyes but Lewis has closed his. 'Don't fall asleep in the chair,' I say. 'You'll get cramp. There's another bedroom upstairs. The bed's only five foot long but . . .' I stop and shrug. 'Or there's the sofa bed.'

He arches his back, then stretches out his legs as though testing them for size. I'm not sure how drunk he is. In fact he doesn't look very drunk at all to me, just sleepy. And I don't feel drunk now. I wish I did.

'I don't think either of us wants to go up there, do we?' he says.

I shake my head. I know what he means; it's not a proposition. 'But you look tired. You ought to get some sleep.'

'So do you.'

'We could lie head to toe on the sofa bed.'

He begins to laugh. I don't think I've ever heard him laugh. Perhaps he *is* drunk. 'Would you really sleep on there with me?' he says.

'Yes. Head to toe.' I fix my eyes on the blocks of peat. They remind me of big slabs of dark chocolate. Apparently people from Dublin drive out to the peat bogs of Wicklow at the weekend and fill carrier bags with the stuff, much as we might gather blackberries on the local common. 'We'll toss for who has which end.' I jump up before he can say anything else.

He follows me round the corner and helps me pull out the sofa bed. The mechanism gets stuck and he rolls up his sleeves and crouches down to fiddle with it. In the end he has to use brute force.

'It hasn't been used regularly,' I say. And inside my head I'm thinking, neither have I, neither have I. He helps me with the sheets and blankets. The only duvet is upstairs, probably on the floor by now. The pillows are not as bulky as those on the double bed and slide easily into their cases. I hold them against me and pummel them into shape, wasting time. And finally I put one at each end of the bed. For once, I don't seem able to think of any funny remarks to make this easier.

Lewis undoes the top button of his shirt and runs a hand round his neck.

'I'm going to get a drink of water,' I say. 'Do you want one?'

'No thanks.'

Round the corner I turn the cold tap on and watch the water cascade into the sink and gurgle away down the plughole. But I still hear the sounds of Lewis getting undressed and the creak of the sofa bed as he climbs in. When I go back his trousers and shirt are flung over the back of the armchair, and I can see the shape of him beneath the bedclothes. I quickly switch off the light. But it's darker than I thought it would be and I stumble against the fireplace, dislodging a pair of tongs that clatter down on to the stone hearth.

'Careful,' says Lewis.

'I'll pull back the curtains.'

I feel my way over to the window and pull the curtains wide open. The moon is half obscured by ribbons of cloud. It looks ghostly, romantic, ethereal but powerful – all the things a moon should be. Night birds call to one another across the water, two different voices with a little pause between while they wait for each other to answer. What I would really like is to go for a walk. A walk with Lewis. Round the lough in the moonlight. I'd like us to stop under the trees and kiss each other for a while. Kiss each other until we're desperate to get back here. Like Evie and Janus were.

The window is already open a fraction but I open it wider.

'What are you doing?' says Lewis, raising his head from the pillow.

'I'm delaying the moment that I have to get into bed with you,' I say.

He doesn't answer at once. Like the birds. Then he says so quietly that I only just hear him: 'Am I that repulsive?'

'You're not at all repulsive.'

He sits up and reaches for the pillow that I put at the foot of the bed. I stand there and watch while he places it beside his own. 'I'm not like Janus,' he says. 'I'll do whatever you want. If you want to lay here beside me and sleep, that's fine. If you want to kick me out, I'll sleep on the floor.'

'I don't want to kick you out. Too late for that.' I add in a nervous whisper. Then, under my breath, 'Especially the way I'm feeling.' My heart is racing now. I close the curtains but leave the window open. As I get undressed I can feel the cool air on my skin. I turn round in its draught my arms raised as though it's a cooling shower.

'You're cold,' says Lewis as I get into bed. He pulls me round so that we're face to face. It's all I need. I press up close to him. 'What do you want to do?' he whispers. 'I'm confused about you.'

'I'm confused about myself,' I say. There's only an inch between our mouths. I make the first move. I kiss him very lightly. He does the same to me. I touch his lips with my tongue. I want to push it between his lips, to push my fingers into his mouth as well. My breasts become painfully sensitive pressed against the roughness of hair on his chest. I want him to touch them but he doesn't. He takes my face between his hands and kisses me again. It lasts a little longer this time but he's too careful, too gentle. And I want this to be as I'd imagined, all the times I've dreamed about him and what I'd longed for out in the back yard of the pub crushed between beer kegs. But it's not. I suck at his lips. He's breathing hard, but I sense a certain reluctance to go on.

I turn my head sideways on the pillow and lay very still. The night is full of sounds. They merge together, none of them distinct any longer. Like my thoughts; nothing clear. Is it Nicole he wants? Am I only a substitute? Are we two dreamers making use of one another? I feel his hand on the side of my head, trying to turn me back to him. I resist the pressure for a moment. And then I don't care. Let him pretend I'm Nicole. And I'll imagine he's someone else too. A stranger. I'll make him lose control. If I'm not me I can do anything. So I run my hands down his body. There's spare flesh but it's solid and firm. He's still wearing underpants and I slip my hands beneath the waistband. He responds by kissing me more passionately. The way I like it. How I'd wanted the mandolin player to kiss me, his tongue up against the roof of my mouth. The sensation of choking, of spinning towards a new and longed for pleasure. He draws away, to get his breath, I think. But he sits up, throws off the bedclothes and pushes me down.

I lay spread-eagled stretching my arms and legs as far as they will go. My fists are clenched. I could pound him with them for no reason. And when he kneels between my legs, lifts my hips with spread hands and sucks my clitoris into his mouth, I do beat at him a little.

He knows when to slow down and when to stop. Sensitive, I think dreamily, as Gerald was. His grip on me slackens and I look up at him and smile. I feel powerful and weak at the same time. 'Lewis,' I whisper, 'I hate to bring this up but I have some condoms in my jeans pocket.'

He stares at me for a moment and I wonder if I've said the wrong thing. I try to take hold of his cock but he stops me. I try again but he grabs my hand, holding on to it while he rolls on to his side. He lies very still, his face against my shoulder. Very carefully I put my hand on his hip. He doesn't move. I'm bewildered and I lie there beside him, waiting for him to say or do something.

Finally, he says, 'I'm sorry. I've had too much to drink.' With this, he gets out of bed and goes to pee outside the back door. I listen to the sound of it going on and on. Above my head, the pad of heavy footsteps is followed by the toilet flushing. In a few hours it will be daylight. And time for these men to be gone. Good, I make myself think. Good.

I'm woken by the creak and thud of wood on wood. I think I'm back at home and that someone is climbing in through my kitchen window. A possibility that often occurs to me in the middle of the night. Heart pounding, I jerk upright and find it's neither the middle of the night, nor is any stranger standing in my bedroom doorway. It's Janus. He's just closed the window.

'It's freezing in here,' he says, arms clasped round his bare chest. 'You two'll end up with pneumonia.'

Lewis wakes as well. He squints at Janus, then looks round at me. I draw the bedclothes to my chin and manage a little smile.

'I've just put the kettle on,' says Janus.

The radio is blaring away and I wonder if it's been going like that all night. I don't remember leaving it on. Or leaving the window open, come to that.

'Jan, can you turn that down?' says Lewis. 'My head's thumping.'

Janus does as he's asked and disappears round the corner. I look at Lewis. His face is creased with sleep and shadowed with beard. I must look pretty rough myself. I rub my eyes and he ruffles my hair, then kisses me on the cheek. 'All right?' he says.

I nod, but I'm not, not really. I wish our awakening had been alone. My clothes discarded on the floor embarrass me. I'm not used to being with people first thing and I don't feel right. I also desperately need the loo. Lewis fetches his shirt for me to put on. He helps me into it and turns up the collar, holding it round my face to give me another little kiss, this time on the lips. I feel slightly better.

'Is Evie awake?' I call to Janus, trying to instil a naturalness into my voice.

'She was but she's gone back to sleep,' he says. 'Do you take sugar?'

'No thanks.' I wrap the shirt round me and go carefully up the spiral staircase.

The bathroom has been recently used. It's warm and steamy and dripping with condensation. The only towel is damp and the air is scented with the jasmine-like smell of Lux soap. It's a new bar put there by Mrs Doyle but the fragrance is so evocative that it could just as well be one of those that my mother used to bring here years ago. I turn on the bath taps and drop the soap under the gush of water.

When I go back down, the three of them are there drinking tea. Janus points to a mug on the mantelpiece but Evie jumps up to get it.

'It'll be cold. I'll make some fresh for you.' She takes my arm with her free hand and leads me round the corner. 'Nice bath?' she says. 'Was there enough hot water left?'

'Yeah. Plenty.' She seems a little edgy, a little excited. I'm not sure which.

'Lewis has put ten pounds in the meter for us. That should last a week or two.'

'A lot's been happening while I've been in the bath,' I say, spotting a pile of blackened toast in the sink.

'Well, there's no toaster. I had to do it under the grill.' She fills the kettle and plugs it in. 'There's nothing worse than lukewarm tea first thing, is there?' She's wearing a T-shirt and a pair of red knickers that wouldn't look out of place on a stripper. Her fringe has been combed but that's about all.

I hear one of the men unbolt the front door. 'Can you swim in the lake?' Janus calls to us.

'Lough,' I correct. 'I suppose so. But it's probably very cold.'

He comes round to us. 'Fancy a swim, Evie?' he says, taking hold of her arms from behind and nearly lifting her off the ground.

'No.' She elbows him off, smiling to herself. 'Not now.'

Not now? I think. I look at Evie but she's busy with the teapot, shaking old tea bags into the sink. 'What time are you going back to Kinsale?' I ask Janus.

He takes a step backwards, pretending to be affronted. 'Can't you wait to get rid of us?' he says.

Lewis comes to join us. 'Any chance of having my shirt back?' he says.

'She wants to know when we're going,' says Janus, putting his arm round Lewis.

'Why don't you pop upstairs and get dressed?' says Evie. 'While this brews.'

Brewing tea isn't something I'd normally expect from Evie. A tea bag dunked in a cup is more her style. Something has been going on in my absence. Lewis follows me up the stairs. The whole structure judders under his weight. I don't look round. He follows me into the bedroom where my bags lie on the floor with Evie's, still unpacked. I kneel down and start searching for clean underwear. Lewis shuts the door and goes to sit on the bed.

'We thought we might stay on here for a few days.'

'Oh did you?' I say, without looking up.

'Don't you want us to?'

'I don't think what I want comes into it. Janus and Evie aren't going to be separated until they've cooled off, that's for sure.'

He doesn't answer and I empty the bag out on the floor, playing for time, wanting him to say something, turn the conversation round from the way it's headed. In the end I bundle together some clothes and stand up.

'If you'll excuse me I'd like to get dressed. Then you can have your shirt back.'

'Why are you angry with me?' he says.

'I'm not angry.' I throw the clothes on the bed beside him. 'I'm not angry, I just feel that I've lost control, that's all. I came here to sort myself out. I wanted some peace and quiet to think about my future.'

'That was my intention too.' He tries to smile but it doesn't quite work, and it reminds me of how much more he has to worry about than I do. I sit down next to him. This would be far easier if last night had never happened. He looks at me and I can't help myself but take hold of his hand. 'I thought my life was falling apart,' he says. 'Even in Kinsale I felt depressed. But here. Here I feel different.'

'It's called atmosphere. It's very potent. But it doesn't solve problems.'

He sighs and squeezes my hand. 'You're probably right.'

We sit there holding hands, both lost in our own thoughts. Downstairs Evie shrieks at Janus to stop it, then it goes ominously quiet.

After a few minutes Lewis says, 'So? What's the verdict?'

'I can hardly send your brother away,' I smile.

'And what about me?' He puts an arm round my shoulders and plays his fingers along the hard ridge of my collarbone, puckering the soft material of his shirt. I can feel that his hand is shaking. 'Are you going to banish me to the five-foot bed?'

'Why would I do that?' I say very quietly.

I feel him take a deep breath; I even hear him swallow. All these little movements and sounds drawing me in. 'Because you're disappointed in me.'

'No,' I murmur. 'I'm not.'

'I had a lot to drink last night.'

'We all did.'

He pulls me closer. 'Tonight will be better.'

I feel a little flare of desire. But it's not quite the way I want it.

'We'll start again,' I say. 'Pretend we've just met.'

'Just met? Yeah, why not?'

I can tell that he likes the idea. 'Complete strangers,' I say.

He leans round to kiss me but I slip away to get dressed. I

turn my back on him and take off his shirt. This is something I've never done, never even dreamed of doing, putting on my clothes, slowly, while being watched. A striptease in reverse. Lewis doesn't move from the bed. And I don't want him to.

'One shirt, I say, holding it out for him to put on. He comes over to me, arms held out so that I can ease it on for him. I turn him round and begin to button it up but he steps back. 'Don't bother,' he says. 'I'm going to have a wash.'

When I go downstairs Evie and Janus are outside sitting on the low stone parapet that borders the lough at this end. Evie is still in her T-shirt and knickers, unconcerned that there are a couple of cars parked up by the road. The door is in two halves like a stable door. The top is open, letting in a chilly breeze that brings the smell of seaweed and brine into the cottage.

Evie comes to lean on the bottom part of the door, Janus close behind. As they stop he lifts her hair to kiss her neck.

'Your tea's cold again,' she smiles.

Janus looks at me over her shoulder. 'She doesn't need hot tea,' he says. 'She's got Lewis.'

To my annoyance I blush.

'They had to have the window open all night.' His eyes are fixed on me. They're very dark brown, harsh eyes with no hint of the softness that makes Lewis so attractive.

'Yes,' I say. 'We had to have the window open to let your smoke out.'

Janus encircles Evie's neck with his hands, sliding his thumbs up behind her ears. 'That's funny, I don't remember smoking in here last night.'

'Well, it must have been the accumulation of smoke on your clothes then.'

Evie smiles between us as though she's enjoying this. She leans back against him but immediately wrenches away. 'You fucking idiot!' she yells, her hand on her neck. 'You can kill someone by pressing them there.'

'What did I do?' he says, wide-eyed and trying to get hold of her again.

She slaps him away. 'It's a main nerve to the brain. Assassins use that trick to kill people.'

'I hardly touched you.'

'Yes you did. Don't fucking do it again.'

I think she's talking nonsense but I'm glad to see Janus feel the sharp edge of her tongue. 'You don't know your own strength, Janus,' I say, smiling sweetly at him.

His eyebrows lift a fraction. 'No? Don't you believe it.'

Lewis comes to see what's going on. 'Jan, what are you doing to these ladies?' he says.

'He's just being his usual innocent little self,' I say.

'Well, I've heard him called a lot of things but innocent isn't one of them,' says Lewis. Then he wraps an arm round me and pulls me against his side. He smells of Lux soap instead of his usual Ralph Lauren. I like it. It makes me want to sniff at him.

'Did you know that if I press very hard here,' I say, pushing my finger up behind his ear, 'it could kill you?'

That little forced smile comes and goes. Oh no, I think, how tactless of me to joke about death with him. He takes my hand away, holds it tight for a moment. 'Is that what you're planning to do to me?' he says. 'Press me to death?' And his tone is suggestive, not serious.

'Yes. Later. But not on your neck.'

He smiles properly now. 'I can't wait.'

We drive to Skibbereen so that I can book a visit from an estate agent to value the cottage. While I'm arranging this, the others are going off to buy the ingredients for a meal which Lewis has offered to cook for us. Being a chef, it seems, is unlike most jobs where you want a complete change while you're on holiday. Lewis stops to read nearly all the menus displayed in restaurant windows. And he spends ages staring at a pile of carrots and potatoes that look as though they have just been dug out of the ground.

'You don't see that in London,' he says, 'earth on the vegetables.'

'Can't we find some cleaner stuff?' says Evie, wrinkling her nose.

I leave them to it and go to the estate agents. When I join them again they have bought two ducks and a whole carrier bag full of the earthy vegetables weighed out into brown paper bags.

As I walk back to the car with them, the men carrying the

shopping and Evie with an apple which, after every bite of her own, she holds out for Janus, it strikes me how far removed this is from the life I normally lead. And how quickly everything has happened. I've never seen Evie act like this before either. Last night, caught up in the simmering atmosphere of the smoky bar, we were all acting a part, the way you can with dim lights and alcohol. But now, strolling along together in daylight amongst other shoppers and tourists, I feel that we're like actors still wearing our costumes and make-up after the play is finished. I can't work out where this is all leading, or what Evie and I are doing. She, especially, worries me. One night with Janus and she is behaving in a way she would despise in other women – apart from the fiasco over Janus squeezing her neck. And that little row was soon patched up. Within minutes they were all over one another again.

Lewis and I must appear like strangers compared to them. We walk along side by side but not touching. I'm not sure why; but for now I'm happy for it to be like this. I even feel an odd irritation with Evie. It's usually she who pulls the strings. Can't she see what's happening?

Beside me Lewis starts to whistle one of the songs from last night.

' "The Fields of Athenry",' I say.

He smiles. 'Is it?' The dark circles under his eyes have faded in the sunlight. Wearing the same clothes as yesterday and with a day's growth of beard, he seems to have changed from the person he is in London. Or maybe it's what we're doing, the ordinariness of shopping, the walking along a street in daytime with sunlight streaming down on us. Something I doubt he does much of back home. He looks and sounds relaxed. He rubs a hand round his chin as though I've commented on his appearance. 'I must look like a tramp,' he says. 'We'll have to nip back to Kinsale and get our things.'

'No, you look good,' I say lightly. 'The simple life obviously suits you.'

'Yeah, I could take to it. I like it here. No pressures.'

We've reached the car; Evie and Janus are a little way behind. 'So how long will you stay?' I ask.

He lowers his voice. 'How long will you have me?'

'I'm only here for two weeks.'

'And I should spend some time with my father.'

A hand suddenly clamps down on my shoulder, fingers digging in hard. I swing round, sure it's Janus, but it's Evie. 'What are you two whispering about?' she says, sticking her head between us.

I tap my nose and she gives me one of her tiny winks. Janus has stopped to light a cigarette. He has his head tilted to watch us while he cups the flaming match to protect it from the breeze. He winks too, as though to acknowledge I've caught him watching.

Lewis starts cooking as soon as we get back to the cottage. Janus helps him. I hang about for a while, seeing if there is anything I can do. But it soon becomes obvious that they don't need me. They work well together, not getting in each other's way as you might in such a small space. Janus follows Lewis's instructions with hardly a word, docile and obedient. At one point, when Lewis praises something he does, I see Janus's eyes sparkle with childish pleasure. It makes me think of them as children. And makes me wonder where it all went wrong for Janus. And for Lewis, come to that.

Evie is asleep on the settee. It's only a small two-seater but she's stretched out with one arm dangling on the floor and her hair trailing over the end like a drowned woman in a Pre-Raphaelite painting. I'm tired myself but there is too much going on in my head for sleep. Crammed in this cottage I feel as though I'm stuck in a crowd which is taking me along with it as it shifts this way and that. Even while Evie sleeps and the men are absorbed in their cooking, I still feel overpowered by them. Out numbered. Which I know is silly because I can't imagine that they'd unite against me over anything.

'I'm going out to get some fresh air,' I tell Lewis. 'I shan't be long.' I'd like to kiss him on the cheek, but Janus is beside him.

I walk up to the road and cross over into the woods. The track is muddy in places but it's easy to avoid the worst patches by cutting up through the higher ground on the left-hand side. There's a thick carpet of dead leaves and, here and there, perfect little circles of new pale grass.

I reach the grotto sooner than I think. It reminds me how many years it is since I've been here and how all the world seems smaller as you grow bigger and older. But the little plaster Virgin looks exactly the same as I remember her. How amazing, I think. She hasn't altered at all in over twenty years. Then I realise that it must be a replacement; the figure would be chipped and worn by now. She just *looks* the same, standing there in her tiny alcove of stone above the pool. At her feet are a number of smaller figures, plastic babies and animals, which I don't remember. There must be fifty of them, arranged haphazardly in a bed of pebbles as though people have stuck them there over the years. The rosaries are still there, at least I presume they're rosaries. Some are just plastic beads, the kind that we used to call poppers at school because you could push them into one another and pull them apart to swap around the colours. Others are made of glass or semi-precious stones, a hundred or more strung on silver chains and very thin twine. I finger one of them, wondering what the devout say as they count off the beads. Hail Mary, Holy Mother of God, I know is one of the things they have to say to ask forgiveness for sins.

Just beyond the grotto I notice something caught in the bushes. When I investigate I find numerous pieces of ribbon and strips of cloth tied both in the bushes and along the lower branches of trees. Beneath them, almost hidden by bracken, is another grotto-like structure but there is no Virgin Mary. It's built of darker stone and is half covered with moss. At the base is an inscription so worn that I can hardly read it. I crouch down, flattening the undergrowth with both hands. It looks like 'CI BAN SA'. I say it aloud a few times so that I can remember it and ask Mrs Doyle.

As I straighten up, one of the strips of cloth touches my cheek. It smells peculiar, unpleasant, like mushrooms or fungi. I wonder what they're for, what holy significance they have. Perhaps it could be similar to the prayer flags that are strung up in the holy places of Tibet. Gerald had been there and he told me about them. He said that each one is printed with a different prayer and as they flutter in the Himalayan winds, the Buddhist monks chant the prayers. It's sheltered here in the woods and the ribbons and scraps of cloth hang limply amongst the leaves. They look more pagan than holy, and I'm reminded of other things that Gerald told me about the monks and how the Na-Chung Monastery has grotesque and evil paintings all over its walls.

I go back to the Virgin's grotto, scoop up a handful of water from the pool and shower it over my head for protection. And laugh while I do it so that I know I'm only pretending to be frightened.

Our evening meal is ready when I get back. Janus is laying the table while Lewis halves the ducks. 'Only a small piece for me,' I say. I'm not a great meat eater, especially if it's fatty or greasy. Lewis trims me a special little portion and heaps it with a dark red sauce, not orange.

'Cranberry?' I say, but Lewis shakes his head and waits for me to make another guess. He leans back, elbows on the worktop. I go to stand in front of him.

'Give me a clue,' I say, yawning, though I don't really feel tired any longer. The walk has livened me up if anything.

He shakes his head again. He has his sleeves rolled up, his shirt unbuttoned and a tea towel tucked into the waist of his trousers. I want to lean against him. I can't be bothered with guessing games about food, I'd rather think about later when we'll sleep together on the sofa bed.

'Raspberry? Strawberry?' I say in a stupid flirtatious voice.

Janus turns round to frown at me as though I've gone mad. 'It's cherry,' he says.

'Oh good, I love cherries.'

'I told them you did,' says Evie from the settee. 'They've made you cherry tart for pudding.'

The urge to fall upon Lewis rises up in me like a wave. I'm flooded by it. 'This is the life,' I say.

'You'd better make the most of it,' says Janus bluntly. 'We're off on Friday.'

There's silence. Evie takes her place at the table and I do the same. Lewis starts to hand round the plates, each with its half of duck, the crispy bubbled skin coated with thick red sauce.

Janus brings the vegetables in an assortment of dishes, then sits down as well. 'We only planned to stay here a few days,' he says, smiling at me across the table. 'That's all.'

'That's fine.' I smile back at him. 'Evie and I *can* cook, you know. We're quite capable of looking after ourselves.'

'Good. You won't miss us then,' he says.

'No, Janus,' I say, 'I shan't miss you.'

★ ★ ★

We climb the mountain that evening. A couple of hours of daylight are left after we've eaten and we don't quite know what to do with them. The atmosphere has become a little tense, thanks to Janus. It shouldn't have; what he said was quite true, they did only plan to stay a few days. But that was hours and hours ago; a long time given the pace things are moving between us all.

I suggest the walk, hoping that only Lewis will agree. I want to show him the grotto. And I want to talk to him on his own. Be alone with him. But Janus and Evie decide to come with us.

I'm not sure whether the mountain isn't just a very high and steep hill. Evie called it a mountain when she first saw it and I think my father used to call it that too. It's thickly forested nearly to the summit, the trees in full leaf and still dripping from Saturday's rain. They probably never dry out completely, each layer shading the ones below, and so many thousands of leaves to catch the rain and hold it.

The path to the top doesn't spiral round the mountain like a helter-skelter, it zigzags its way up the flank overlooking the lough. This makes it steep and hard work in places. As we climb I think of the Himalayas again and the narrow passes where you have a sheer wall of snow-covered rock on one side, and on the other, a dizzying drop. Of course it's not like that here; we're sandwiched between a tree-studded wall of earth with only the occasional show of rock, and a slope that is steep but covered, reassuringly, in thick vegetation. Not dangerous, just a little precarious in the places where the path is narrow.

Halfway up Evie complains of a stitch in her side. I'm suffering too but keen to reach the top and see the view out over the sea.

'I can't go any further,' she says, coming to a halt, her hand on Janus's shoulder.

'Do you want me to carry you?' he says.

She takes a step back from him, laughing and wary, but he grabs hold of her and lifts her into his arms. She's still laughing when he goes to the edge of the path with her. It's obvious what he plans to do and I laugh as well. But Evie's face changes as he swings her out into the air. She clings to him and begins to scream. It's no longer a joke. She's tearing at his hair and screaming like a lunatic.

'Janus, cut it out,' Lewis orders him.

Janus dumps her on the path and walks off without us. Evie straightens her clothes and stares after him, her breath coming in dry angry sobs.

'He was only playing about, Evie,' I say. 'You encourage him half the time.'

'Well, I'm going back,' she spits. 'He can go on by himself.'

Janus turns round at this but carries on walking backwards up the path. The side of his face is bleeding. He rubs at it, then shouts, 'Why do women always have to scream their fucking heads off?'

'Fuck you too!' Evie shrieks at him. She turns and starts to run back down the way we've come.

I look at Lewis. 'What do you want to do?' he asks me.

'We'll go on. If they want to behave like a couple of kids, let them.' I try to shrug it off, but it seems this evening is irretrievably spoiled now. And I blame Evie as much as Janus.

No sooner have we started off again than Janus comes rushing past us after her. I hear him call out to her and look over my shoulder. Lewis looks too. She's stopped. Janus tries to put his arm round her. He has to make a couple of attempts before she lets him. It's like the games played by lovesick teenagers, the advances and retreats, the rows contrived for the fun of making up.

'Come on,' says Lewis, 'We'd better leave them to it.'

As we walk on once more, I can hear them talking in lowered voices, Evie making petulant and unconvincing protests to whatever it is that Janus is saying to her in a soft and coaxing tone. When I look round again he's kissing her, both hands up the back of her sweatshirt.

'Oh well, true love never runs smooth,' says Lewis.

'So they say,' I reply, disappointed that he could come out with something like this.

Chapter 11

Lewis and Janus go back to Kinsale the next morning to fetch some clothes and spend a day with their father. It's the first proper chance that Evie and I have had to talk on our own since we stayed at the guesthouse.

The weather is improving a little each day and this morning it's really warm. We put on swimsuits and shirts and go to sit on a stretch of rocky beach a short way from the cottage. The sun glints off the water. It's very still today. Last night a wind blew up, churning the whole surface of the lough into a mass of waves. Janus said the noise of them splashing against the stone parapet kept him awake. I never realised a lake could be so noisy, he said. Water is the most powerful of the elements, I told him. He looked interested so I told him how the sea pours in through that narrow channel, the cut. We must go and have a look, he said. So we're going to enquire about tides when we go to Baltimore, perhaps tomorrow. I hope the spectacle is as awe-inspiring as I've made it out to be, as I remember it.

A few people, probably tourists, are wandering along the road on the far side of the lough about a quarter of a mile away, but apart from that we're completely alone.

'I'm glad they'll be back tonight,' Evie says suddenly. 'It's more lonely here than I imagined. Are you really going to stay another week on your own?'

'That's what I'd planned to do, yes.'

'Verity?'

'What?'

'You haven't said one word about Lewis.'

'What particular word was it you wanted?'

'I just want to know that you're having a good time, that's all. I feel responsible for them being here.'

'Well, you are. But I'm not going to swap notes, if that's what you're thinking.'

She goes quiet for a moment, then says, 'Janus was the boy in your story, wasn't he?'

I'm surprised; I thought she'd forgotten. 'How did you know?'

'He stood on the bed with a paper, knocking all the cobwebs down.'

I laugh but she stares out across the lough, her face serious. 'He scares me a bit.'

'Evie, you know he was only playing about. You made a big fuss about nothing.'

'Oh, I don't mean yesterday. I don't mean I'm afraid of him. I mean scary as in . . .' She pauses and smiles. 'As in I might want to see more of him.'

'That *is* scary. Especially for you.'

'I have had some lasting relationships,' she says, indignant. 'I have been in love, you know.'

'Yes, I know you have. But I don't believe that you're in love with Janus.'

'No, I'm not,' she says quickly. 'Anyway, he's made it very clear that he doesn't want me to be.'

'Oh?' That's not what it looked like when they said goodbye this morning. A long drawn out parting that had sent their row on the mountain hurtling into oblivion. 'Did he actually tell you that? Rules of the game?'

'In a way.' She falls silent, raking her fingers through the pebbles and flaky shale that make up this beach. There are numerous shells scattered over its surface, some ugly and knobbly and more like pieces of warty rock. Others, like the one Evie has just picked up, exquisite in both form and colour. She holds it up to the light. It's shaped like the bowl of a soup spoon and almost transparent, the inside a swirl of pearly pinks and blues. She breathes on it and shines it with the corner of her shirt. 'A present for you,' she says, dropping it on to my legs.

I retrieve it and hold it in my palm. 'It would make a good ashtray. Better than a saucer, don't you think?'

She smiles grudgingly. 'I think there's a lack of understanding between you two.'

'I don't think I'm the only one who has a problem understanding Janus,' I say, wondering if I might tell her about Nicole. 'Not from what I've heard.'

But she doesn't seem to be listening. She's playing with a pebble, absently tossing it from hand to hand. 'He was asking about you,' she says.

'Janus was asking about me?'

'Yes.'

'Tell me then.'

'I'm not sure that I ought to.'

'Then you shouldn't have mentioned it.' I glance at her.

She throws the pebble across the beach and says, 'You mustn't tell him. He asked me about your marriages, your husbands. He said, is she the sort of woman who gets her claws into a man and won't let him go?'

I'm furious. The anger that pounds in my throat is difficult to control and out of all proportion to what she has just told me. I don't trust myself to answer for a moment.

'Don't take it too personally,' she says. 'I think it was aimed at me as well. A warning not to get too serious.'

'Well, I should take that warning, Evie,' I say, my voice tightly controlled, 'because I think he's the last person in the whole world that you, or any woman in her right mind, would want to get seriously involved with.'

She looks at me sideways. 'Don't lecture me, Verity. You're not exactly acting that sensibly yourself.'

'Lewis is different.'

'Oh, so you think you've got the best bet of the two, do you?'

'I think,' I say carefully, my anger subsiding now, 'I think that Lewis is, overall, a nicer person.'

'He's also the one who tried to kill himself. If I were you, I'd be just a teensy weensy bit uneasy about that. Or had that slipped your mind?'

'No,' I say, snapping the shell she gave me in half, 'I haven't forgotten.' Little silver flakes shower over my thighs.

'Whoops,' she says. 'There goes the ashtray. What a shame.'

'I don't want him smoking in the cottage anyway.'

'Do you know, Verity, you're getting to be a real old nag?'

I turn on her now. 'I'm amazed at you,' I say. 'I just can't believe you're so blind about him. He fills the place with smoke which we all hate. He touches you up the whole time, a thing you'd never stand from anyone else, and he . . . he discusses me as though I'm some desperate old spinster. And you stick up for him.'

'Finished?' she says.

'No, I haven't finished. I'm intrigued. I'd like to know what you see in him. What has he got that's so special? Do tell me because I can't for the life of me work it out.'

She stares at me. 'Can't you guess?' she says quite nastily.

I dash the pieces of shell from my legs. Some are quite sharp and leave red scratches on my skin. I take off my shirt, roll it into pillow and lie back on it.

'Verity?'

I have my eyes closed but she leans over and gently eases up one of my eyelids.

'We're not having a row are we, darling?' she says.

'No of course not.' I slap her away. 'Now leave me alone. I'm not Janus, I don't want to be mauled by you all the time.'

'He likes to be touched,' she says. 'Not just *touched* but sort of handled. Warmed. When he falls asleep he goes cold. He said that he always wakes up cold.'

I put my hands to my ears. 'Can we change the subject, Evie?'

She smiles. 'You never like talking about men, do you?'

'Of course I do. But not ones who slag me off like Janus has.'

'Oh, he talks a load of rubbish sometimes. Forget all about it.'

'You tell him then. Tell him I don't need, or want, to get my claws, as he calls it, in any man.'

'He's just so protective of Lewis. He doesn't want to see him hurt. Like he's been with Nicole. But I told him that you're not like that. I told him that Lewis would be perfectly safe with you.'

The men bring rain back with them. It comes lashing down as they step out of the car. Evie runs to open the door. I stay in the background, watching out of the window as the lough heaves and shifts under the onslaught.

Janus complains that the cottage is cold and sets about lighting the fire. I leave him to it. Or rather, leave them to it. Evie is already hanging over him. And I have to admit, he does look quite appealing this evening. He's full of quick little smiles and his eyes dance around in his face as though something has invigorated him. Maybe it's being back with Evie. I don't think it's the thought of Lewis being safe with me.

Lewis has brought in a large cardboard box packed with food from the restaurant. He starts laying it out on the table. His greeting has been perfunctory; he avoids looking at me. A day apart has made us strangers. And it doesn't work. Being strangers. It didn't when we played at it last night, anyway.

'What have you two been doing all day?' he asks, looking up for a moment.

'Oh, just relaxing. We sat out on that little beach for most of the time. It's been sunny here all day.'

'Good.'

We'll have to do better than this, I think. I start to help him with the food. Once I'm close enough to him, he whispers, 'Are you glad I'm back?'

'Yes.' I'd like to say more but Janus and Evie are behind us, and I'm not sure what I want to say either. What words I can say to make him feel better.

Lewis failed to make love to me again last night. Failed in the way he wants to make love to me. He didn't fail to give me pleasure. And I wish I could feel detached enough to be satisfied with this. But I'm neither detached nor satisfied. I'm worried that his problems will become mine. He has stirred up old fears in me. His failure makes me aware that however hard I try, however aroused I am, however wet and open and waiting, there is still a moment of instinctive resistance. I still flinch at that moment when a man's penis is about to enter me. The equation that my mother drummed into my head is still there. Buried under all the layers of Gerald's patient love and my own common sense. But not completely banished.

Lewis was prepared this time and I should have felt safe with a penis sheathed in rubber. But for just the briefest second I held him off. Whether it was that or not, I don't know, but he couldn't reach orgasm. When it became uncomfortable for both of us, he gave up. He said that it was probably the anti-depressant tablets he was taking. We didn't talk too much. I wanted to but he was too distressed about it. And later, listening to the wind kicking up loose slates on the roof, I wondered again if it's really Nicole he wants. And I told myself that the sooner this week comes to an end the better. But I was lying again. I don't want to be parted from Lewis. And if I could be sure that he's not still in love with Nicole, then who knows, perhaps we could fall in love. The idea appeals to me even more than it surprises me. And I make up my mind not to be disappointed about the sex. After all, if anybody should be able to understand, I should.

Janus crouches round the fire, warming his hands. The peat burns slowly and he prods at it and adds some driftwood. Evie has come to inspect the food.

'Mussels! Yum-yum,' she says. They are shelled and threaded on skewers together with rolled strips of bacon.

'They have to be grilled,' says Lewis. 'It won't take me long.' He turns round. 'Jan, you make the salad while I cook the fish.'

Janus stands up and salutes him. His face is flushed from the heat of the fire and when he comes to gather up the salad stuff Evie strokes his cheek.

'Warmed up?' she says.

The look he gives her makes me want to throw the pair of them out in the rain to cool down.

Lewis grills the mussels and fries fillets of lemon sole in butter. He's going to serve it with something called *crème de pamplemousse,* which is apparently grapefruit cream. Busy with his cooking he seems more relaxed. He turns on the oven to heat some crusty rolls. In less than ten minutes we're seated at the table, our mouths watering, the cottage cosy, a perfect scene of happy holidaymakers should anyone walk by and chance to look in the window. Not that it's likely anyone would walk by in this rain.

After our meal Janus mixes grapefruit juice with Jose Cuervo tequila and a splash of Rose's lime juice cordial. It's potent stuff in this small warm room with darkness and bedtime fast approaching.

Evie is sitting in one of the armchairs, Janus against her legs, his elbow on her knees while he smokes and flicks his ash into the grate. He's amusing himself by making bonfires with little pieces of snapped off driftwood. Now and again he looks up at me to see if I'm watching. But I won't be drawn. I'm determined to avoid a row with him. For Lewis's sake.

But I can't keep my eyes off those little heaps of flaming wood. In the end I go and scoop them up with the ash shovel in the pretence of making up the fire. Janus smiles to himself and picks up the bottle of tequila. He shakes it with both hands until the remaining liquid is frothing to the top of the bottle.

'Bubble bath,' says Evie.

'Actually you can use it to bathe in,' says Janus, perfectly serious. 'If you tip a bottle of it into a bath of water and soak in it for half an hour or so, it gives you sexual stamina.'

'You should try it then,' says Evie.

He shakes the bottle harder, then quickly unscrews the top and aims a shower of tequila into the fireplace. There's a mini explosion. The fire splutters and hisses while flames leap out, narrowly missing Evie's legs. She jumps up and kicks him and he throws what's left of the tequila straight into the fire. The flames go roaring up the chimney now, turning all shades of yellow and blue and green. Everything but red.

I'm not sure how, but the bottle ends up broken in the grate and Evie is crying. My first concern is for the cottage and I run outside to make sure the chimney is not on fire. The rain has eased a little and I stand there staring up at the roof. A few sparks emerge and float gently upwards but soon fizzle out in the damp air. Lewis comes out to me.

'The cottage isn't insured, you know.' I'm shaking.

'It's OK. I've thrown water on the fire.'

'We've got no phone, the whole lot could burn down before help arrived.'

'I'm sorry.'

'It's not you. You haven't done anything.' I wave an arm at the cottage. 'He's the one who should be apologising.' I can see Janus through the window. I see him shrug at something Evie says to him. He looks over his shoulder and catches sight of us.

'It was a joke,' he says, coming to the door. 'That's all.'

'Go and clear up the mess,' commands Lewis.

'And don't light the fire again,' I shout after him.

Later, in bed, Lewis asks me if I want them to go.

'You'll be gone at the weekend,' I say. 'I can put up with Janus until then. If it means keeping you here.'

He hasn't mentioned about staying on any longer again, and I don't want to get into a discussion about it now. I don't want to talk at all. We've been kissing. Every nerve in my body is straining to go on. He rubs the palm of his hand between my legs, sliding two fingers inside me. But I know this won't be enough. Not however good he does it. I pull his hand away and turn on my side to face him.

'I'll do anything,' I whisper. 'If there's anything you want to do.' I have ideas in my head that I can't tell him. Ideas of how I could make him lose control. 'Any position. Any way you want,' I say.

He starts to kiss me again, desperate open-mouthed kissing. I feel him grow hard against my stomach. I slide both hands down between us and caress him very gently as though I'm handling a delicate flower whose stem might snap if I don't take care. I stroke his balls and rub a finger backwards and forwards between them. They swell and contract in my hand. He smiles and sighs against my cheek and my desire for him is all mixed up with a tenderness that makes me want to cry. We carry on like this for ages. He's become a little softer and I'm torn between not rushing him and my need for him, so I wriggle down the bed and lick and bite at him. Finally I take him into my mouth. But he grows softer still and I feel a pang of frustration. This is not something I make a habit of and I feel a ridiculous sense of hurt that it isn't the answer. I lay my cheek on his thigh and wait.

After a few seconds he lifts me on top of him holding me under my arms, and I move up a little, pushing my breasts into his face. I feel his mouth open, his lips and teeth close round my nipple. He puts his fingers between my legs again but I pull him away, impatient, putting my own hand down to guide him into me.

'Not yet,' he says. I know why but I won't listen.

'Just for a while. It'll be OK.' And I'm making things worse, only I can't stop. I would rape him if it were possible. But there's no way you can make a man fuck you if he's not ready.

★ ★ ★

We take a trip to Killarney. Janus drives, and Lewis and I sit in the back holding hands. If I had known about the narrow mountain roads through the National Park I would have refused to be driven by Janus. It's hard to believe that he is terrified of a harmless spider the way he risks our lives with every bend. Surprisingly, Lewis says nothing. He sits beside me, silent and still, absorbed in the magnificent scenery. Maybe its danger appeals to him. Maybe he is wondering how it would feel to go careering off the road and bounce down the rocky mountain-side. An uglier death than a handful of temazepam, I would imagine. I squeeze his hand. He looks at me and smiles his sad smile. I want to be alone with him. Last night we fell asleep with exhaustion and without talking. And this morning Janus was down making tea at the crack of dawn. He pads down the spiral staircase like a panther but makes sure he wakes us once he's down. What Lewis and I need is a whole day and night alone together. Days and nights alone together.

We behave like tourists are supposed to behave. We ride in a jaunting cart up the long avenue to Muckross House and buy postcards and books in the souvenir shop. I buy the *The Love Story of Yeats and Maud Gonne* and an omnibus of Irish Folk Tales. Lewis buys three miniature books of traditional Irish recipes. Evie buys numerous postcards for friends, making a big deal about all the men on her mailing list. Boasting is unlike her and seems to me yet another way in which Janus is affecting her.

He is full of himself today; not a whisper of remorse for what he did yesterday with the tequila. Wandering around the gardens and then the house itself, I can't help wishing that it was just Lewis and I. Janus sets me on edge, makes me tense, when all I want is to relax and enjoy myself. He comes to peer over my shoulder as I look at a portrait of the Countess of Desmond.

'She looks like a man,' he says, then reads the inscription aloud. ' "As she appeared at ye court of our Sovereign Lord King James in 1614 and in ye 140th year of her age." '

'She died after a fall from a cherry tree,' Evie says, reading from the guide book.

Janus bursts out laughing. We are in the drawing room

surrounded by groups of other visitors. They are speaking in hushed reverential tones.

'Up a cherry tree at 140 years old,' Janus laughs. 'I bet she really was a man.'

'Shut up,' says Evie, laughing a little herself. She smiles round at me as though she expects me to join in but I can't see the joke.

'After a certain age people do begin to look sexless,' I say. 'You might look like a woman at eighty, Janus.'

To my surprise, he smiles. 'And what about you?' he says. 'How will you look? If you live that long.'

'Oh, Verity will live to at least a hundred,' says Evie. 'She hasn't any vices.'

'All women have vices,' says Janus.

'What are mine then?' Evie laughs.

I turn away to take another look at the Countess of Desmond. She has a vaguely apprehensive expression. Perhaps because she has lived half her life in a state of old age. Barren. So many years to long for lost youth.

Lewis takes the guidebook from Evie. 'She once danced with Richard the Third,' he says.

We flick through the pages together and come across the story of Lady Ellen MacCarthy who crossed a lake in moonlight for her romantic marriage ceremony at Muckross Abbey in 1588. She had previously been engaged to another man and marriage to him would have brought her lands under Elizabethan control. Her midnight wedding angered the Crown and the poor bridegroom was imprisoned in the Tower of London for the rest of his life.

'Do you think they came for him at the ceremony?' I say, struck with a picture of Lady Ellen and her new husband torn apart for ever.

Lewis reads on. 'Well, it says that the land eventually passed to his descendants, so I shouldn't think so. They must have had some time together.'

'Maybe they just had one night,' I say, preferring to think of my own tragic version of their story.

'How heartbreaking,' says Evie with a sigh. 'Perhaps he was fucking her in this very room when the soldiers came for him.'

Oddly, her choice of words makes them seem very real to

me, so I don't bother to tell her that this room didn't exist then; the house wasn't built until the nineteenth century. I close my eyes for a second and try to imagine their anguish. Janus spoils it by laughing again because he has just read that the bridegroom's Christian name was Florence.

'You just can't see the beauty in anything, can you?' I say.

He frowns slightly. 'They're all dead,' he says. 'I can't see any beauty in that.'

In the evening we go to Baltimore to eat out. We have a couple of drinks first in a bar that is dark, smoky and loud with conversation in accents so strong we can hardly understand a word. We have chosen it because of the dining room above and the menu which has fresh salmon at half the price you'd pay in London.

Lewis drinks lemonade. I don't enquire why but I think it's to do with his tablets. I saw Janus give him some earlier when we got back from Killarney. The two of them were round by the sink and didn't know that I could see them. I couldn't help watching as Janus put his arm round Lewis's shoulder and whispered something against his ear. I heard Lewis say, Yeah, don't worry, I'm fine. Janus rubbed him gently on the back. It was such a tender gesture, quite unlike the way he treats Evie.

Seated in the dining room, we hear music start up in the bar below. It's a mixture of fiddle and mandolin, the notes floating clear above the hubbub of talk. Our table is by the window and we have a wonderful view across Roaringwater Bay where the sun has just disappeared behind the offshore islands. We are all nibbling at freshly baked doughy rolls as we wait for our first course to arrive.

'Isn't this heaven?' I say suddenly.

'Sure is, babes,' says Evie.

'I almost wish,' I say, 'I almost wish that I could keep the cottage.'

'And I wish that I could keep you company for another week.'

I look at her but she shakes her head. 'I've got three good sessions next week, darling. I can't let them down.'

'No, of course not,' I say.

'And my flight's booked.'

'Don't worry.' I arrange my knife and fork. Next to me Lewis clears his throat.

'I don't like to think of you on your own here without transport,' he says.

We've still not discussed when he'll go back to Kinsale, though Janus is convinced that they're both staying with their father for next week. I can only assume that Lewis either plans to go with him or hasn't made up his mind what to do.

'If I need to get anywhere, Mrs Doyle's husband will give me a lift. They only live up the hill. And there're taxis in Skibbereen.'

'But you don't have a phone.'

'The Doyles do. I shall manage just as Evie and I would have done on our own.'

Evie looks from me to Lewis and back. 'He's worried about you,' she smiles.

'I'm thirty-three years old. I don't need to be worried about.'

Lewis remains silent; perhaps he doesn't want to discuss this in front of Janus. Oh well, I think, if he's going to put Janus first all the time it might be better if he does go back to Kinsale on Saturday.

Our salmon arrives. It looks delicious baked with a herb crust and accompanied by mangetout peas and potatoes boiled in their skins. But somehow I'm not very hungry anymore.

After we've eaten we go back down to the bar for a last drink. We also want to find someone who knows about the times of the tides so that we can catch the ocean in full flow when we finally get to visit the lower end of the lough. So far we have only received vague answers to our enquiries. But this time we're in luck. We get some firm information and a tale to go with it.

The barman introduces us to an old man who not only knows about tides but about the whole of the ocean around County Cork. Around all of Ireland, come to that. He squints at us from eyes whose lids are nearly closed, stuck down by an awful yellow crust. Understanding him takes great concentration but it's worth it for the intriguing tale he tells about the Seal Woman who has been seen on the rocks where the lough meets the sea. She comes here for a month either before or after the longest day.

'Oh, now, you mean,' says Evie.

He stops talking. Evie apologises for interrupting but still he doesn't go on. We look at each other then someone close by winks at us and taps his glass. Lewis sorts out a few Irish punts and spreads them on the bar. The old man nods his thanks and carries on. I think he could be blind, or nearly blind. His head turns slowly from side to side as he talks as though he's scanning us, feeling our presence rather than seeing us.

The Seal Woman's name is Ean, he tells us. He pronounces it to rhyme with rain but spells it out on the top of the bar with his finger as though it's important that we should know this. She has a black silk cloak which allows her to take human form just once a year. It's then that she comes ashore to mate with a man so that her offspring can also assume human form. This is how he tells it, using words that would be precise and clear if it wasn't for his accent. A story he has often told, no doubt. To gullible tourists, I think, as he beckons Janus nearer. Janus bends his head close to the old man's. One of the crusted eyes opens a little wider.

'You'd be the one,' he says. 'She knows that young men like yerself will chase after anything that looks as though it might have a cunt.' He pauses for breath. 'But you'd be wise to turn your back on this particular lady.'

Evie giggles. 'He won't,' she says. 'A fat seal would appeal to him.'

Janus looks daggers at her. 'Fucking rubbish,' he mutters.

The old man grabs Janus round the thigh. 'It's a strong leg,' he says. 'A good strong leg for swimming. She likes that.'

Evie looks at me and smiles cautiously while Janus fumes.

'I saw a seal give birth once,' I say, more to break the tension than anything else. 'On the TV I mean.' But no one takes any notice.

Janus drains the last of his Guinness in one swallow. 'Come on, let's clear off,' he says. 'I'm getting pissed off listening to all this crap.'

Lewis stretches and yawns. He has been near to sleep, elbows propped on the bar. A couple of times while the old man has been talking I've had to nudge him awake to stop him falling off the bar stool.

'Janus wants to go,' I tell him.

'OK.' He's about to stand up but I hold on to his arm.

'But I don't.'

They all look at me.

'Lewis is tired,' says Evie. 'We ought to go.'

'I'm all right.' Lewis settles back on his stool.

'Well, I'm shattered, anyway,' says Evie, forcing a yawn. She looks at me, swivels her eyes towards Lewis with a little frown, telling me that I'm being selfish.

Janus plays with the car keys, tossing them in the air.

'Let's go,' I say abruptly. Janus is smiling as I push past him. I stop in the middle of the crowded bar and make my way back to the old man. 'You didn't tell us,' I say loudly. 'What happens once the man has mated with the Seal Woman? What happens to him?'

He looks up at me. Through the slits in the yellow crust I can see his eyes, black and bright as a bird's. It takes him so long to answer that I think this is part of the story that he doesn't usually tell; he's inventing it while I wait.

He makes a motion with his hand like waves, then dives it down towards the floor. 'He's a nice little supper for the eels,' he says. 'They like a bit of young meat. Specially the bollocks on them.'

There's a ripple of laughter; eyes turn to Janus. He in turn looks at me. If looks could kill, I think, pleased with myself.

'You're talking to a young lady, Tommy,' says the barman.

The old man grins at me. I leave him the money for another drink and catch the others up at the door.

Chapter 12

Janus is very cool towards me the following morning. He ignores me when he comes down to make the tea. For once I'm up first. I woke early, troubled by bad dreams. I dreamed that I was being strangled with a loop of thick oily rope, the sort they use to tie up boats. I'd been swimming and got caught in it. When I woke I found Lewis's arm across my neck, his watch strap digging into my throat. He must have had bad dreams too because he was tossing and turning half the night and muttering in his sleep. Nothing intelligible. A good thing, I suppose because he probably dreams of Nicole sometimes. Just as I do of Gerald.

It's brilliantly sunny this morning. The lough is sparkling as though it's been sprinkled with diamonds. And the air is so clear that it's possible to see right across to the far side where it narrows into the long channel of the creek. The first tide change is due soon. We'll see it here from the way the water swells up against the parapet, the level rising a good few feet. But there won't be time to walk down to the lower end; it's a good mile or two from here.

Lewis sleeps on. I told him that I knew he had taken some tablets and that we should not attempt to make love. Not even touch one another. And no passionate kisses.

'But you like being kissed,' he whispered to me in the dark.

'I know,' I said, 'but if we hold back from doing anything, anything at all, it might help.'

He went very quiet. I should have shut up myself but I started telling him how I'd read it somewhere. The thing to do is to resist any contact for a day or so. Then build up with caresses avoiding the erogenous zones at first, taking it step by step but holding back from intercourse until it became irresistible. It was true, I had read about it. But the last thing Lewis needed was a detailed lecture. I heard his breathing grow uneven as though he were upset but still I couldn't shut up. 'What is it you want from me?' I asked him.

He buried his head against me. I cuddled him, kissed him all over his face and neck and wherever I could reach without moving away from him. After a while he said, 'Can I stay here with you another week?'

'Yes,' I murmured. 'Yes, yes, yes.'

Soon afterwards he was asleep. I lay awake for a long time, thinking to myself that now we would have all those days and nights alone together.

By breakfast time Janus seems to have got over his annoyance with me. Though if he knew that Lewis is planning to spend next week here instead of with him at Kinsale, I'm quite sure that it would come rushing back faster and more furious than the tide that is filling up the lough while we eat. He would not be smiling across the table at me, or asking me, 'Is it true that you can interpret dreams?'

'Well, it's part of my job.' Despite his pleasant tone, this change of mood makes me wary. 'But I'm not an expert. It's something that my late husband taught me, mostly from books. Freud especially.'

'Oh, Freud,' he says disparagingly. 'I don't need anyone delving into my psyche. I just wondered what it means to dream about fire.' He looks at me across the table, his expression carefully innocent but not so pleasant somehow.

'Fire?'

'Yes, fire.' He reaches for his matches and strikes one. 'As in flame.'

'What actually did you dream?' I say. 'That you set fire to my cottage?'

'No.' He laughs as Evie bats him away because he has held the match near to her hair. He shakes it out, sending a spiral of smoke above the breakfast table. 'I dreamed that I burned some clothes. I didn't mean to do it. It was an accident.'

'Whose clothes were they?' I say. Beside me Lewis goes on spooning up muesli. We bought it in a health food shop in

Killarney. There are so many Brazil nuts in it that it takes ages to eat a bowlful.

'I don't know. Does that matter?'

'I hope they weren't mine,' says Evie.

'Of course they weren't yours,' he snaps. 'Why would I burn your clothes?'

Evie shrugs and falls silent. Unusual for her. Well, not so unusual lately.

'Off hand,' I begin, lowering my eyes to make out I'm thinking about it, 'and from what I can remember,' I run a finger up and down the handle of my spoon, careful not to rush this, 'I would say that you were jealous of the person who owned the clothes. But that you don't wish them any real harm. It's more a display of emotion. Deep feelings that need bringing to the surface. That you want brought out. That's the significance of flames. You can't ignore them. This also ties in with your zodiac sign. And links up, in a complex way, with your basic water element. Fire is for feeling, you see, and water is for intuition.' I pause, surprised at my own inventiveness. Janus is staring at me. I feel myself start to blush and go on quickly to hide it. 'I think that you may have a fascination with fire. A love-hate relationship, fear and fascination. I have the same with water.' I'm running out of words now. 'If you could remember whose clothes they were . . .'

'Dreams don't have memories,' he says. 'You're talking rubbish. You're making it up as you go along.'

'Of course she's not,' says Lewis. 'She's studied it. You shouldn't have asked if you weren't prepared to accept the answer.'

This is the first time that I can recall that Lewis has stuck up for me against Janus. I would cheer aloud – if I weren't so sure that Janus will certainly hold this against me.

We decide to go our separate ways for the day. Evie and Janus drive off somewhere. Lewis and I take a walk down by the lough.

'When will you tell him about your staying on?' I ask.

'When we take Evie to Cork on Saturday. I'll stay the weekend in Kinsale and come back here on Monday morning. Or Sunday night if you want.'

'Whenever. I'm more concerned about your brother.'

'Don't be. It'll do him good to spend some time with our father on his own.'

'I don't mean that.' We have left the road and turned down a wide track. On one side there's a steep wooded drop to the creek, on the other a high bank, also wooded, divided from the track by a ditch running with water. A profusion of grasses and ferns grows here, sprouting up from the boggy ground, the dark wet green of it broken here and there by clumps of purple flowers. The sudden heat has made everything steam like a sauna. 'I mean that I'm concerned about his jealousy.'

Lewis doesn't answer for a moment, which makes me sure I'm right. I've found that making a bald statement is a good way of determining the truth. Most people will become understandably indignant over a false accusation. Once, when I was saying a tearful goodbye to my mother at the beginning of a school term, I blurted out, You're glad when I'm back at school aren't you? The delay until she reassured me that this was nonsense made me know I was right. Ten years later I tried it with Mark when I accused him of sleeping with someone else. Funnily enough, I really didn't know that he was cheating on me.

'Who told you about Nicole's clothes?' Lewis says at last.

'She did,' I lie. 'She warned me about him.'

There's another long pause before he speaks again. This time he gives a little sigh first. 'Nicole is an only child who had a very happy upbringing with two loving parents. She can't understand about Janus and me. She wouldn't even try.'

'But whatever happened, whatever the problems, he can't cling to you for the rest of his life.'

'I know that, Verity. Don't you think I know that?'

There are a few other walkers about this morning but we seem to lose them the further we go down the track. It's like a tunnel in places, with the branches meeting over our heads and the vegetation on either side encroaching on the path. Tree trunks are covered in lichen and there is a pervading scent of mildew and peaty earth. Everywhere is damp. A bit like my spirits after so much talk of Janus. But I want to know. I need to know exactly what it is I'm up against.

'Did your mother often leave you alone?' I ask.

'Yes. Regularly. But that time she left Janus all night was the worst. My father wanted us to go and live with him after that, but Janus didn't want to leave his mother. She had damaged him irreparably but he still adored her. It's hard to believe, thinking back, but she was a very loving mother in some ways.' He sighs again and shakes his head, lost in thought. I think of my own mother who never left me on my own but dumped me in a boarding school instead. And I didn't need any frightening picture books with all the images she painted for me.

'So did he stay with her?' I ask gently.

'Yes. And I had to make a choice. Whether to go with my father or stay with Janus and my mother.'

'How old were you?'

'Twelve, nearly twelve.'

'And you chose your brother?'

He nods. 'Janus didn't talk properly again until he went to school. He was like a baby, crying when he was put to bed and if he was left alone. When I was at home he followed me everywhere. Even when he grew up he wanted to be with me all the time.'

'Like a puppy dog.'

He smiles briefly.

'And now he's grown into a big bad dog who snaps at anyone who tries to get close to you.'

'No.' A quick denial. 'Only Nicole.'

'What about Angela?'

'Angela?'

'The phone call while I was babysitting.'

'Oh. Well. He may have been rude to her.'

'I suspect there's been others.'

He doesn't answer.

'And now there's me,' I say carefully, not wanting to presume but needing to know. 'And I don't want my clothes burned.' Or my cottage, I think.

'He's engrossed with Evie.'

'They have a little infatuation going, that's all. He has an eye on us, Lewis, you know he does.'

'He senses that I'm . . .' He is holding my hand but takes it between both of his now. 'That I'm serious about you.'

'Oh,' I say lightly as if I'm surprised. 'You didn't say.'

'I wasn't sure how long you'd put up with me.'

We have reached a turning in the track. A derelict house stands at the corner. The chimney is still perfect and it looks as though recent fires have been lit in the hearth below. Squatters? Tramps? Janus? Everyone needs a fire, I think. Behind the house a field slopes up the side of the hill, its nearest boundary marked by a thick hedge of fuchsia. As we investigate two donkeys appear the other side of the hedge. We scramble over fallen masonry and through tall spires of foxgloves to reach them. They poke hard furry noses at us, vying with each other for our attention. When we stroke them one starts braying loudly and bites the other on the rump until it runs off.

'Two brothers,' I say as we make our way back to the track. 'Perhaps that's what you should do to Janus.'

He doesn't even smile. 'I hope you wouldn't ask me to do that.'

'Nicole did, didn't she?'

'Yes.'

'But you wouldn't.'

'No.'

'Why?'

'Because I love him. I love him, Verity. Full stop.'

He walks on, head bowed. Dealing with all this stuff I've dragged up, I suppose. And I'm thinking too. I'm imagining someone saying they love me; love me, full stop.

The track comes to an end as we meet up with the last widening of the lough. There's a quay here. for boats. Obviously little used now, judging by the coarse grasses that grow between the slabs of stone along its edge. Though there are one or two ropes coiled by the heavy iron mooring rings, and a scatter of dilapidated lobster pots. The place is exactly as I remember it. Deep, dark blue water surrounded by rocky hills, like a fjord. The same feeling of depth and cold and silence which used to make me feel almost sick with awe.

'What a wonderful place,' says Lewis.

'Yes, it is.'

'And is that the famous gap you've been telling us about?' He points to the space between the hills about a quarter of a mile away where the sea is just visible.

'The cut,' I correct. 'Yes, that's it.' We watch in silence as wave after wave breaks against the rocks at the foot of the hills, sending a spray of foam high into the air. Even from this distance we can hear the thunder of the sea rushing into the lough and then the eerie silence as the tide gathers up speed to suck it back out. I feel excited to be here, and excited that Lewis is impressed. I want to explain to him how I feel. 'Whenever I hear someone say they get good vibes about a place, I always think of here. Even though it frightens me a bit.'

'I know what you mean. It's the feeling that you're witnessing immense power.'

'Yes, that's it. Power.'

'Perhaps I should jump in,' he says, taking a step towards the quayside.

The idea of it terrifies me. 'Lewis, please don't play about,' I say, grabbing his arm.

'You'd rather have me powerless, would you?'

'You won't be.' We have never discussed this out of bed, in the light. 'Not after next week.'

He looks fleetingly troubled, then suddenly points towards the far rocks. 'Good God, whatever's that?'

'Where?' I say, alarmed.

'The Seal Woman.'

I laugh and put my arm round his waist. His body is warm and damp with sweat through his shirt. I would like to touch him, put my hands on him and arouse him. Find a dry grassy hollow and lay down with him. The longing to do this is so strong that I look down at his zip and imagine undoing it, taking out his penis, rubbing it, kissing it, sucking it. I look out across the water and feel swamped with that same thrilling nausea that I used to experience as a child. It reminds me of something that Gerald once told me. Fear and sexual excitement are born in the stomach; don't confuse them with feelings that belong to the heart. Or he may have said loins. That was more like Gerald. And this feeling is definitely in my loins.

'So you *were* listening in the pub last night?'

'I heard some of it. Between catnaps,' he smiles.

'Did you take any tablets this morning?'

'Just one. I shan't take any more today.'

'Do they help?' I ask softly.

'Well, I don't feel depressed any longer. But that's probably because of you.'

'Me and my cottage,' I say, missing an opportunity.

'If I could just shake off this tiredness I'd be fine.'

'Do you want to go back?'

'Yeah, I think we'd better.'

After lunch I leave him sleeping and go off for another walk. This time up through the woods. I want to see the grotto in sunshine and take a photo of it. Evie and Janus came back earlier but they've gone out again, walking too, making the most of this hot day. Evie invited me to go with them but I pretended I wanted to stay here with Lewis. I need to take some time alone to think very carefully about all that is happening. Or what might happen.

Coming back this morning, Lewis and I talked about how it would be to live in Ireland. I joked that we could move into the cottage. That I could sell the house in London and live off my share of the proceeds. Lewis then said, quite seriously, that he had thought about going into business with his father. But first he has to sort out his finances back home. I wasn't sure which way the conversation was headed. Or had I said too much? I had the feeling that I was being swept along, losing my foothold on reality. I was worrying about it but not wanting it to stop. When the conversation flagged for a moment I said the first thing that came into my head. I said, well neither of us has any ties to keep us anywhere. As soon as the words were out, I realised how tactless I'd been. Lewis was looking straight ahead, but I saw the tears well up in his eyes. 'I have two daughters,' he said. Then he smiled. 'And a restaurant that isn't paying.'

I think I must be getting desperate because I found the way his smile forced its way through the shine of tears very sexy. But this time the feeling seemed to spiral up from my loins and into my heart.

So I have a good deal to think about. And whatever we do there will still be the fly in the ointment. A spider in the ointment. Perhaps I should tell Janus that the cottage becomes infested with spiders as the weather warms up. I could say that it's to do with the number of flies about, attracted to the lough by rotting fish. The law of nature: wherever there are good hunting grounds, predators move in. It could be true, but it doesn't sound very convincing.

Mrs Doyle popped in earlier. Lewis was boiling up some winkles we'd gathered on the way back from our walk and we had to put the lid on the pan very quickly. She had come to enquire if there was anything we wanted. You two girls on your own, she said. Then she spotted Lewis. I think she also smelled the winkles. So now she probably has me down for a hussy who plunders the lough. I made her coffee and told her about the estate agent who was coming next week. Lewis won her over by complimenting her on the black silk two-piece she was wearing. She was on her way home from church, she told us. Church on a Wednesday? But she'd stopped off to pick up one or two shells from the shore. It's acceptable to take empty ones, she stressed. Especially when they are being used, as these are, by Mrs Doyle's granddaughter to make a gift for the Virgin. I asked her if she meant for the grotto in the woods and she said, no not that tatty heathen thing, this was for the one on the Skibbereen road.

'Confession,' said Lewis when she'd gone.

'Confess that we took the winkles?'

'No, you idiot,' he laughs. 'Mrs Doyle has been to confession.'

'Oh, I see.' I laugh too. 'I shouldn't think she has much to confess.'

Perhaps I'll make my own little confession, I think as I walk to the grotto. If I confess to something awful I've done perhaps the Virgin will grant me a favour. Or a wish – that's what I need. And perhaps a tatty heathen grotto is the place to make a wish. But I haven't done anything awful. Unless not loving your mother or fantasising about sex with a mandolin player could be regarded as a sin. Probably.

My wish, of course, is to be rid of Janus because I believe that Nicole is right and that I will never get close to Lewis, properly close, while Janus is around. This is probably a big sin, wanting to be rid of someone. How big depends on how I want to get rid of him. And that is something I don't know myself.

Under the trees the ground is much drier than it was the other day. It's easier walking not having to avoid the puddles. Sunshine makes such a difference; you notice more, hear more. For instance, it sounds like a hundred birds are all singing at once. All beautifully in tune as birds always are. I love birds, they are so fragile and shy yet they have so many gifts. Their wonderful voices, of course. And then there's flight, and the way they can balance on a tiny twig. And the way they build nests with their beaks I find amazing. Are they singing for sheer happiness? I wonder. Or is it their nature, something they can't help, like cats can't help washing all the time?

As I'm thinking about all this, trying to work out what spontaneous thing human beings do to show they're happy, I hear a low moan. Not of pain. This person is very definitely happy. The grotto is a few yards in front of me. The undergrowth behind it is not thick enough to hide the two bodies on the ground. I quickly switch my eyes to the Virgin's passive face, my heart speeding, not sure whether to turn round and creep away – they haven't seen me. Nor are they likely to within the next few minutes. In common with most people, I suspect, I have never watched a couple that I know making love. And in these first few seconds it is neither embarrassing nor shocking, but surprising. I also learn what being rooted to the spot feels like.

All I can think of clearly, as I watch Janus's buttocks rise and fall with increasing speed, is that now I have seen both sides of him. Like turning a cardboard cut-out round. A cut-out doll like those I had as a child, all complete with sets of clothes for every occasion. Janus and Evie are minus most of their clothes. Her small hands are gripping the top of his thighs. A good strong leg for swimming. They could be swimming. Buffeted on the waves, the two of them clinging together. Janus is holding her head, giving her the kiss of life. Such desperation. As though this is their last fuck before drowning.

A whistle sounds above my head. I jump and step back behind a tree. But it is only the birdsong, startling me because I have not been hearing it for a moment or two. Evie is becoming noisier. I put my hands over my ears, trying to cover my eyes as well, although I am turned away from them. I want to get right away but I'm frightened to move. And then it's too late because I can hear Janus has got to his feet. I twist my head round, my cheek against the rough bark of the tree. He walks, still half naked, to the grotto and washes himself in the pool. Oh well, I think, it is only a tatty heathen grotto.

Evie is beside him now. She too washes, splashing the water up over her thighs. I hear her say, 'I wish semen came in powder form.' Then, 'What am I going to dry myself on?'

'You should wear knickers,' says Janus. His tone is irritable and when she splashes water at him he swears at her. So. He's one of those men who cannot wait to be off afterwards. Evie says that they're the sort who sweet-talk you silly before. Is that what she likes about him? I don't think so. I can't see her face but her silence is significant in itself. She goes to sit on a flat rock that juts from the lower part of the grotto, waiting while Janus gets dressed. Once he has zipped up his jeans he reaches out and touches her hair. She turns to look up at him and now I can see her face. This is not my Evie, not this submissive woman who leans her head against his hip, her arm round his leg. He pulls away and wades off through the undergrowth, coming back with some old pieces of cloth. It takes me a few seconds to work out where he has got them, and as it dawns on me I hear Evie say, 'No, I don't want those.'

'Why?' he says.

'You know why.' She jumps to her feet. She has her skirt on now and it catches on branches as she runs off down the track. Janus follows. 'Don't try and frighten me,' she shouts back at him, her voice ending on a sob.

Janus runs faster, his arms outstretched, laughing and whistling, for all the world like a great black bird.

Chapter 13

I am becoming convinced that Janus is set on preventing Evie and me from being alone together. For instance, Evie wanted to make a phone call yesterday so she and Janus decided to drive into Baltimore and pick up bread and milk at the same time. Lewis and I said we might go and sit on the beach. We might even take a swim if there was nobody about. When Evie heard this she changed her mind, tempted by the idea of swimming.

'Can you go and get the bread on your own?' she said to Janus.

'No,' he said. 'If you're staying here than so am I.'

'Are you joined at the hip?' I said without thinking.

'We're joined at both hips a lot of the time,' he said.

Evie didn't even smile. She seems to be less enchanted with him as the week draws to a close. Less enchanted with everything in fact. She has lost her brightness. This is not like her and I'll be glad when she is back home, away from him. And I'll be glad when Janus is back in Kinsale. He still doesn't know that Lewis plans to stay here with me next week. And I hope Lewis sticks to what he said about waiting until Saturday to break the news because I don't want to be around when he does. Janus deprived of both Evie and Lewis will not be a happy man. That's the one thing I am sure about at the moment.

But on Evie's last day I'm determined to snatch some time alone with her.

'Fancy a walk?' I say quietly as she comes downstairs after taking a bath. I'm not sure but I think Janus was in with her.

The two of them were upstairs together for a long time and all the hot water has gone. I didn't actually hear them but Janus has grown quieter over the last couple of days. Just as Evie has. It's more peaceful, but it makes me uneasy for some reason.

Lewis is reading a paper, flat on his back on the sofa bed. Every now and then it drops on to his face and he jolts awake and rustles it back into position. He is still tired much of the time. I think of him as battle-weary. Having to fight emotions that he cannot control; emotions that have turned on him like enemies. We don't talk about his suicide attempt. I'm sure it would depress him despite his having won that particular battle. In the sense that he's still alive. I would like us to talk about it. Not, I have to be honest, because I imagine that talking would help. I am curious to know if he really meant to kill himself. And I would like to know all about that big bust-up between Janus and Nicole. But that's another taboo subject. Perhaps next week. My plans for next week include another walk to watch the tide crashing through the cut; heart to heart conversations when we can reveal all sorts of secrets to one another; and long sessions of all-night sex. I'm sure things will be better once we're on our own. Maybe they'll get so good it'll be daytime sex as well. In the woods; down by the quay. What's good for Evie . . .

'Yes, let's,' she says in answer to my question. She comes to see what I'm doing. I have offered to cook this evening, being as I haven't so much as boiled an egg all week. The one thing I'm good at is boiling eggs. But I'm having a go at omelettes, whipping up the yolks and whites separately to show that I know what I'm doing. It's certainly a plus having a chef around; even Janus shines in that department.

'Just you and me, eh?' I say, glancing towards the stairs then across at Lewis who has fallen asleep yet again. Evie nods and I'm careful not to make a noise as I put the whisk down on the worktop. We manage to leave unobserved.

At the road there are four routes to choose from. Up the hill towards Skibbereen, which is really too narrow and steep for walking and talking at the same time. Left to Baltimore; again unsuitable because of the many bends, hazardous if you're not concentrating; this is the main route between the two places.

Or you can leave the road and walk down by the lough or up through the woods. Evie points left towards the lough. I point over the road to the mountain and the woods.

'Oh, all right,' she says, giving in as though she doesn't really care where we go. 'But not too far. These woods give me the creeps.'

'That's what woods are supposed to do. That's the point of them.'

She looks sideways at me. 'Verity,' she says patiently, 'I came here to get away from all the scary things in life.'

'Oh, you disappoint me. I've always thought you were one of the bravest people I know. I thought you thrived on risk. Travelling on the underground late at night; smiling over your shoulder at all those black boys who call out to you. Falling in love,' I add as I see her begin to smile.

She puts her arm through mine. 'Well, I wouldn't want to disappoint you, so I shall carry on doing one or two dangerous things. But I shan't be falling in love.'

'You've made up your mind then? You don't plan to see him once we're all back in London?'

'No, I told you. He doesn't want anything long term.'

'But do you?' We're no longer joking.

'No.'

The grotto is ahead. She doesn't comment on it. 'Have you seen the holy grotto?' I say.

'Yes. I've been up here with Jan.'

'What about the pool?'

'What about it?' she says.

'I just wondered if you'd noticed it.'

'I'm not blind, Verity.'

'What I really meant is, what do you think of it?' I know that it's too late now to reveal what I saw. Not that I could, anyway. But I feel mean, as though I'm spoiling our friendship, damaging the trust we have in each other.

'Nothing. It's just water.'

'Mrs Doyle said it was tatty and heathen.'

'She probably meant the other one. The one behind it.' Evie points in the direction of the second grotto.

'Oh?' I clear my throat. 'Why do you say that?'

'Something Jan told me.' She sounds uncomfortable; which

makes two of us. 'Can we stop talking about this. It's getting dark.'

It's not dark, just gloomy with no sunlight. The sun doesn't penetrate here at this time of the evening; the bulk of the mountain is in the way. 'What did he tell you?' I ask.

The pieces of cloth and ribbon are visible now. I hadn't noticed before but every one of them is white.

'Those,' Evie says pointing again. 'He said they come from the torn up clothes of dead people. They represent the shroud of Christ.'

'How does he know? Is he an expert on religion as well as sex?'

She frowns at me. 'I didn't say he was an expert on either.' She pulls her arm from mine. 'He and Lewis are Catholics, or were. Their father is.'

'I didn't know that.' I take her hand and slip it back through my arm. 'We always seem to end up arguing when we talk about him.'

'We're not arguing,' she says firmly.

'No, of course not.' I hug her arm against me but she feels tense.

'He said that women hang them there to ensure that they have healthy babies. They use them to wipe themselves after sex, then they bring them here. It's quite common apparently. What you mustn't do, ever, is touch them.'

'I wouldn't want to. It sounds disgusting.' I force a laugh because she looks so serious. 'But I don't believe it.'

'Well, I don't believe it either.' She sounds as though she has just made the decision not to believe it. As though my not believing has helped. As though she needed my support. 'Let's go back,' she says, suddenly pulling me round. 'Don't tell him I've told you all this, will you?'

'Why? I'd like to hear some more of his tales.'

'No. Don't you dare mention I've told you. He hates it when you don't believe him.'

'Too bad.'

'You don't know how intimidating he can be.'

'How do you mean?' I say quietly.

She walks on and I hurry after her. 'I can't really cope with him,' she says, head bent. 'That's all.'

'What's going on with you two? Has he threatened you or something?'

'No, he hasn't threatened me.' I'm beside her now and I hear her take a deep breath. 'He's threatened you.'

'Me? Why? What have I done?' I'm indignant, I'm laughing. Laughing crossly, I've heard, is a sign of nervousness. Now I know that it's true. 'What did he say?'

'Oh, don't worry about it. It was just one of those things men say. You know.' She squares her shoulders and imitates a man's voice, 'Don't fuck with my brother or you'll have me to answer to.'

'Is that what he actually said?'

'Something like that. Forget it. We'll all be splitting up soon, anyway.'

'No, Evie, we won't. You seem to have forgotten that they live in my house.' I step round in front of her, blocking her way. 'I want to know exactly what he said.'

'I wish I hadn't told you. You're going to make a big thing of it when it's nothing more than . . .' She suddenly breaks off and smiles over my shoulder. I look round and see Janus coming towards us.

'Been making your confessions?' he says, jerking his head in the direction of the grotto.

'Oh, that's what it's for,' I say. 'You tell the statue all your secrets, give her a few beads and you're forgiven. Is that it?'

The look he gives me would wither a tree. I feel slightly ashamed; perhaps he really is religious. Though I find that very hard to imagine.

'She's a heathen,' says Evie, smiling. 'She doesn't believe there's anything up there except the stars.'

Janus ignores her. 'It depends what you've done.'

'Or what you plan to do,' I say.

He smiles as well now. He has very white teeth for someone who smokes so much. Very even as well. Dental care was obviously something his mother didn't neglect. 'Come on,' he says. 'Lewis is cooking the omelettes. He sent me to find you.' He moves in between us, taking us both by our upper arms and propelling us forward. 'You're muscly for a woman,' he says, squeezing my biceps.

I try to pull away but he holds on. And after a few more

steps the track becomes too narrow for us to walk three abreast and he has to let go of me.

My first day alone feels curiously silent despite an influx of tourists, come to wander round the lough. This morning one of them knocked on my door wanting to know if it was possible to hire a boat anywhere. He was a man on his own with a back pack and an accent which I guessed, rightly, was German. I suggested he go to Baltimore and enquire there but he lingered at the door, asking me questions about the lough and where I was from. We must have talked for about ten minutes before I noticed that his eyes kept dropping to my legs. I was wearing my swimsuit with a shirt, thinking that I might take a sandwich to the beach later. I brought the conversation to a close and went back inside, shutting the top half of the door as well as the bottom. Lewis and Evie had bombarded me with warnings before they left. It made me see they were right and that I must be careful here on my own without a phone or a car.

But later, at dusk, I decide to take a walk. Not to the woods – I'm not feeling brave enough for that. Just up to the road where I hang about watching the ripples made by fish and the swarms of tiny insects hovering above the water. On the way back, I do feel a twinge of nerves about the night ahead, and I remind myself that I must make sure all the downstairs windows are closed. Fear, I tell myself, is all in the mind. But born in the stomach, I think, remembering again what Gerald told me. Like sexual excitement.

In the end, Lewis doesn't come back until midday on Monday. But he comes bursting through the door in a way that makes me think, hey, this man has been worth waiting for. He immediately apologises for not returning sooner but I tell him, 'Shush, you're not under any obligation to me. I was prepared to be alone.' I'm more interested in the change that seems to have taken place in him. For a start his expression seems mysteriously free of tiredness. The rest I can't quite put my finger on. He's just more alive than I've ever seen him.

'Would you rather be alone now?' he asks.

I pretend to think about it, then smile and shake my head. 'No. I was thinking about you all night.'

'Both nights?'

'Yes, both nights.'

'Tell me what you were thinking,' he says, putting his arms round me.

I'm tempted to say, let's go to bed and I'll tell you, but I'm suddenly cautious. I don't want to put him to the test. I don't even want to take the lead. Not yet. Not until I'm sure this is going to last longer than the first flush of pleasure at being together again. I hold him at arm's-length, my head to one side, eyes narrowed as though I'm trying to work something out. His only response is to blow a kiss at me.

We take blankets and go to sit on the beach. Or rather, lie on the beach. Few tourists come this far because it means passing through a pair of gates outside the cottage. They are never closed but give the impression of everything beyond being private. We start to kiss. Something has definitely happened while he's been away.

'What is it they say about absence?' I laugh, pulling away from him to get my breath. 'Or have you swapped those tranquillisers for pep pills?'

'Why?' he says, with a little crooked smile.

'You're so eager.'

'Don't you like it?'

'I love it.' I can't resist adding, 'Maybe it's because there's just the two of us.'

'Actually,' he says, after a little pause, 'I've stopped taking the tablets.' His voice has grown serious.

'Was that wise?' I ask. 'To stop just like that?'

'I don't care,' he says abruptly. 'I've never taken anything like that before. I wouldn't have taken them in the first place if I'd known what they'd do to me.'

'But they helped at the time, didn't they?' I lie very still, wondering if he'll go on. I would like to know more about his suicide attempt. I'd like to know a lot more about him than I do. Especially about Nicole and him.

'They got me over a bad patch. Yes.'

'But you can deal with er . . . with things now.'

'Yeah.'

'The worst problems are people, aren't they?' I say in an attempt to keep the conversation going. 'I mean, with money you know how you stand.'

'Not always.'

'But you don't get emotionally involved with money.'

'I suppose not.' He sighs. I feel his grip on me loosen. 'I had a long talk with my father. He reckons that Janus needs help of some kind. But I can't imagine him agreeing to that.'

'When I said people,' I venture, 'I really meant Nicole.'

'She's no problem. Not any longer.'

'Tell me,' I say very quietly, 'tell me truthfully. Did you ever fantasise that I was her?'

'Do what?' he says, propping himself on an elbow to look down into my face. 'You are joking?'

'Yes,' I say shamed into a lie. 'Sorry.'

'I can't believe you said that.'

'But you did want her back. At one time. I saw you kiss her once. I could tell.'

'One little thing and your imagination goes into overdrive.'

'I didn't imagine all those rows you had with Janus. They were about her, weren't they?'

'Some were.'

'And other women?'

'I did have other women, yes.'

'And Janus saw them all off.'

'It wasn't quite like that, Verity.'

'Nicole warned me about him.'

'We're back to her again, are we?'

I hear the irritation in his voice. I'm going to spoil this homecoming if I don't shut up. 'I just don't know what to believe,' I say.

'He's not here now, so what does it matter?'

'No, you're right.'

Once, at a party where I had become paired off with someone that I wasn't sure about, Evie scolded me; why didn't I just have fun without worrying about later, tonight, tomorrow? I don't know why I've remembered this. Lewis has everything I want. And if I'm worried about later, it's not the same worry I had then.

'Actually, I called Nicole from my father's. I was going to tell you. I spoke to my girls and I had a long conversation with Nicole about you.'

'About me?'

'She said that if I was with you, she'd be happy for the girls to come and stay.' He looks at me. Waiting for me to be pleased for him, and I can't disappoint him.

'Well, that's good. When did she mean?'

'Any time. Back home maybe. Or here. She's glad about you. She said she's glad I'm happy.'

'So you're happy, are you?' I say, pressing up against him, trying to get back to how we were ten minutes ago.

We move upstairs to the big bed. As I change the sheets I can hear Lewis singing in the bathroom next door. I get undressed and lie on top of the bed, reading. It's one of Gerald's books that I brought with me, wanting to make good use of all the hours I thought I'd be spending alone. From the wall opposite Mary and John O'Brien and their horde of children watch me. What would Mary O'Brien think if she could really see me lying here, waiting for my man with Nietzsche's *Beyond Good and Evil* propped on my naked stomach? Probably, that I was mad. Both to be lying here naked and to be struggling with a book which makes about as much sense to me as it would have done to her. Unless she was highly intelligent and had time for reading, with eight children to look after. And if she was able to read, of course. What little I know of her. Well, I do know that she slept in this room. And I know that on at least eight separate occasions a man, her husband, had an orgasm during sex with her. And there were the children who died. I'd forgotten those. Mary O'Brien, I think that it's safe to assume, had sex on a regular basis. Whether she liked it or not I'll never know. But I think I can also be pretty certain that she was never in the situation of trying to understand about the variety and problems of morality whilst also wondering if her man was going to be able to sustain an erection.

Or, because he has been lingering in the bathroom for nearly half an hour, if he was going to get one in the first place. I put Gerald's book down and reach for a paperback that Evie has left on the bedside table. More nakedness. *The Naked Lunch* this time. It falls open in my hands, at a certain page, the way that books with explicit sex always do. Reading quickly, I can't work out whether this is gay sex or what's termed AC/DC. Either way it seems the most disgusting stuff I've ever read. Worse than the dream letters, crude rather than erotic. But it turns me on all the same.

I get up and go over to the window. It has started to rain. The lough is all but obliterated in cloud and darkness. I lean out and the wind blows a shower of rain into my face and over my shoulders and breasts. The sound of water running away comes from the bathroom. I will stay here leaning out of the window, I think. Let him come into the room and be confronted with my backside.

The headlights of a car coming down the hill from the direction of Skibbereen catch my attention. The car stops a moment at the bottom of the hill, then carries on towards Baltimore. It's followed by another and another. Traffic, I think, here in this far corner of Cork there is still traffic. It's not so lonely. I would feel perfectly safe here on my own. Lock the doors, light the peat fire and I'd be snug and safe to work and dream. And what am I going to do with my week now?

The rain drives in harder and I'm about to close the window when I see a man walking down from the road. He is wearing a long dark coat with the collar turned up, his head bent and his chin tucked into his chest. Well, he's not walking for pleasure. And I can't see any sign of a rod so I don't think he's come here to do some illegal fishing. The German come back to ravish me? Rape me. Kill me. Or the Seal Woman in disguise. Or a man who has just been ravished by the Seal Woman and is now so traumatised that he is coming to the cottage for help. What endless possibilities there are for a lone man to be walking in the rain after dark along a dead-end lane. I'm just about to call Lewis when I realise that it's Janus.

Chapter 14

I'm halfway up the mountain. The path is slippery after the rain but I keep going on up to wear myself out, subdue myself. It seems the only place that doesn't disturb me in some way. Perhaps, when I reach the top, I shall stand there and scream. The thought makes me smile for the first time in hours. Nineteen to be precise, because that's how many hours that have passed since Janus arrived at the door last night.

I could hardly believe that he'd come back. He walked in and said to Lewis, 'You forgot your tablets.'

I stood there, open-mouthed. 'So you've come fifty miles to bring them, have you?'

'He needs them,' he said, dripping puddles on to the floor, not having taken off the long coat as though he wasn't sure if he could stay. Then Lewis started pulling it from his shoulders. No word of reproach. Nothing.

'I think I must be dreaming,' I said.

They both looked at me. Their dark eyes a matching pair. Or that's how it seemed. I was wrapped in a beach towel which I'd snatched up when I realised it was Janus coming down the road. Drips from his coat hit my bare legs. The door blew open where it hadn't been latched properly.

'Yes,' I said. 'I'm dreaming. And it's a nightmare.' With this I went off upstairs. At the top, I stopped and looked down through the spiral. 'Don't forget to take your tablets, Lewis,' I shouted. 'We don't want it to be a wasted journey, do we?'

I locked the bedroom door and lay there, listening to the hum of their voices. They went on and on, talking way into the night. I dozed for short spells, waking to darkness again and again. This is how it had been for the two nights I'd spent on my own. Now thanks to Janus, another night had passed without my sleeping properly. It was nearly dawn when I finally slept; a deep thick sleep of utter exhaustion. I didn't wake until nearly midday, and when I did, my head was spinning and my eyes felt sore. Lewis came knocking with tea but I told him to piss off.

'He's had a row with our father,' Lewis said through the door. 'He's been kicked out.'

'So he comes running straight back to you,' I said.

'He had no choice. He doesn't have any money.'

'Perhaps you'd both better go,' I muttered. But he heard me.

'Is that what you want?'

'I don't know what I want,' I yelled at him. 'I don't know.'

I stayed in bed for another hour or so, wondering what I was going to do. In the end I got dressed and went downstairs, planning to have this out with Lewis. Janus was crashed out on the sofa bed, face down, fully dressed. Lewis was crouched in the hearth, trying to light the fire. The cottage felt cold and damp.

'I'm sorry, Verity,' Lewis said, looking up, a ball of rolled-up newspaper in his hand. 'But what could I do? He thumbed it all that way. He had to walk some of it. In the pouring rain.'

'He's not a baby, Lewis.' I tried to stay calm. He looked so stressed and tired.

He bundled the paper into the fireplace and struck a match. The fire hadn't been lit since the fiasco with the tequila. When he lit the corner of the paper it fizzled out.

He stood up. 'Just tell me. Tell me what you want me to do?'

I felt my own tiredness seeping out. I glanced at Janus, his long legs spread out on the sofa bed, his feet hooked over the end. His dark curls had dried to an unruly mess. He coughed and started to heave himself up on all fours as though he had no idea where he was. And suddenly I couldn't bear the thought of being around when he came properly awake.

'Do what you like,' I said, slamming off out.

I don't make it to the top of the mountain because I begin to hit patches of mist so thick that I feel unsafe to go any higher. It occurs to me that I'm actually walking in cloud, a strange and slightly disappointing experience. It's just thin damp fog, nothing like the fleecy billows you see from ground level. As I make my way down, a fine drizzle begins to fall but I don't want to go back to the cottage yet. The damp air is clearing my head. The exercise has revitalised me. I have too much energy if anything; nervous energy, I suppose. I start to wander up the hill and I've only got a little way when Mr Doyle passes me in his battered Toyota. I don't recognise him at first; it seems that everyone here drives a Toyota. Then he reverses noisily and comes to a halt beside me. On the spur of the moment I ask him if he'll give me a lift to the nearest phone box. Instead, he takes me home to his bungalow, hidden in a fold of the hills above the lough.

Mrs Doyle greets me civilly but a little cooler than I've come to expect from the inhabitants of West Cork. Probably to do with the winkles. She shows me into their sitting room where the phone sits on a lace doily in the centre of a glass-topped coffee table. Then she switches off the television and she and Mr Doyle disappear into the kitchen, to put the kettle on, she says.

I get the number from the directory and dial it quickly before I have time to change my mind.

'Is that Mr Kaye?' I ask, though I know it is.

'Speaking.'

'This is Verity Harker. I thought I'd let you know that your son is back at Lough Ine with Lewis and me.'

'And spoiling your holiday, no doubt.'

I hadn't expected to get to the point this quickly. I stare at the scene of a Japanese garden on the Doyle's coffee table. Why is there so much from Japan here in Ireland?

'You should have sent him back to England with your friend,' he says.

'I don't think it's my responsibility to send him anywhere,' I say, finding my voice.

'No, of course not. But I don't think you've called to let me know that Janus is safe with you, have you?'

'No. What I've called you for is to ask . . .' I pause to collect myself, assemble my thoughts. 'Do you know what happened with Nicole? Did Janus really set fire to her clothes? And is he likely to do the same to me? To mine, I mean?' I breathe more easily now that it's all out.

'To answer the first of your questions, Verity, I don't know what happened with Nicole. Lewis said she dramatised the whole thing. And I'd like to believe that. He certainly set fire to something. It's just that their stories differ. And as for knowing if he'll do it again, I sincerely hope not.'

'I wouldn't have bothered you. Only I thought you might know. What he's likely to do.'

'Seeing as I'm his father.'

'Yes.'

'If anybody can guess what Janus is likely to do, it's Lewis. As you've probably realised, they're very close. I knew where he'd gone.' He doesn't sound at all angry; not as if they've just had a blazing row. I don't know too much about father and son relationships but it seems to me that it would take a pretty big row to throw your son out with no money in a foreign country.

'Perhaps I should talk to Nicole.'

He doesn't answer.

'You don't happen to have her number, do you?'

'Yes, I do. Have you got a pen?'

Next to the phone there's a pad printed with the name of a pub and a picture of a glass of Guinness. The attached pen is shaped like a bottle. I write down the number and read it back to him to check. 'Well, I won't keep you any longer.'

'Verity, just one thing.'

'Yes?'

'I wouldn't attempt to split them up.' For a second I think he means Lewis and Nicole. Then he says, 'If you attempt to do that, you'll make an enemy of Janus just as Nicole did.'

'I'm not trying to do that. I don't even want to.'

I put down the receiver and tear the top sheet from the Doyles' phone pad. Nicole's number is surrounded by nervous doodles. Mrs Doyle's head appears round the door just as I stuff it in my pocket.

'All finished?' she says. When I nod she opens the door with her hip and comes in with a loaded tray of tea and biscuits and little round cupcakes topped with chocolate half an inch thick.

'I'm sorry but I don't have any money on me,' I say, perched on the edge of her green moquette sofa while she pours the tea.

'We shan't fall out over that,' she smiles, and hands me a plate with two biscuits and a cupcake, which I really do fancy.

'And how are you enjoying yourself at the cottage?'

'Very much.'

'It'll be a shame when the place is sold. Your daddy's had it for so long. I remember you all coming here when you were a tiny wee girl. Before you can remember, I expect.'

'Oh, I do. I remember the first time we came. The lough especially. The sound of the water used to frighten me. I've never forgotten.'

'Ah, well, you can never have too much respect for the water. My father fished for his living so he drummed that into us. And the lough is part of the sea, after all.'

I drink the tea she has poured for me and she sits opposite, drinking her own, looking at me when she thinks I don't notice. Mr Doyle comes in with his cap on. 'Will I be giving you a lift back down now?' he says.

'Oh no, that's all right.' I get to my feet. 'I'd rather walk. I need the exercise. I do far too much sitting around.'

'Well, you'd never think so by the size of you,' says Mrs Doyle. 'But you young girls don't eat properly, that's the trouble. You all want to fade away to nothing.'

I smile to be called a young girl. 'I'll drop the money for the call in sometime.'

She waves a hand as though to say forget it. 'Your daddy sends me enough for looking after the cottage.'

'Can you see it from here?' I ask as we go to the front door.

'Only the chimney top,' she says. 'But we know when you light a fire. Looks like you've left one burning now.' She points down the valley to where a column of smoke rises straight up like a coil of grey rope.

'I could send you a smoke signal in an emergency,' I say, staring at the chimney, imagining the cosy scene round the fire.

'You could an' all,' laughs Mr Doyle. 'Fan it with a rug and they'd see it in Skibbereen.'

'Don't talk so daft,' says Mrs Doyle.

They stand and watch me until I lose sight of them on the long trek down the hill. It's stopped raining but the clouds have brought the evening closing in early. Everywhere looks dismal. I feel dismal. Mostly because I don't know what to do. Shall I order Janus out? Throw him out? The idea appeals to me but my natural caution makes me shrink from embarking on this. How would I enforce it? And would Lewis back me up? One minute he's talking as though we have a future together, the next he's calmly allowing the biggest threat to that future back into my cottage. I feel suddenly vulnerable. The way I used to feel as a child standing by the lough while my father went on about the power of water. And my mother about the weakness of her body. I don't want to feel weak or vulnerable. And I don't know why I keep getting myself into these situations. Falling in love with Lewis being a prime example.

The first thing I notice when I get back to the cottage is the black coat that Janus was wearing last night. It's now on a coat hanger hooked on the corner of the mantelpiece. Lewis is sitting by himself reading a paper.

'I was about to come looking for you,' he says.

'Where did he get that coat?' I ask.

'He's had it for years.' He frowns. At my sharp tone, my silly question, my expression. I don't know but I don't want him frowning at me.

'Where is he?' I demand.

'Upstairs, in bed.'

'Which bed?'

'Calm down. The little bed. I didn't think you'd want him down here.'

'No I don't.'

'Verity, he has no money. There's nowhere else he can go until we get the ferry home on Saturday.'

'It's not my problem.'

'No, but it's mine.'

I march over to the cooker. I'm starving and it's obvious they've already eaten. I lift the lid on the frying pan to find curry and rice. A little cloud of spicy steam hits me in the face. 'Is this for me?'

'Yes. Janus cooked it.'

I tip it on to a plate and take it round to sit by the fire. 'Is this what you had?'

'Yes. We would have waited for you, but I didn't know where you'd gone. Let alone what time you'd be back.'

I stir the curry with a fork. The rice looks very yellow. 'What's in it?'

He shrugs. 'I'm not sure. Janus did it all.'

'But you had some.'

'Yes.'

'Then you must fucking know what's in it.'

He stares at me, his sad expression, and I can't stand it. Neither can I eat the curry.

'I'm going up for a bath,' I say, dumping the tray on the settee. I curse the spiral staircase because you have to be either barefoot or clad in rubber-soled shoes to run up it. And I'm only wearing socks.

The door to the little room is not shut right up. I can see Janus asleep on the floor where he has dragged the mattress adding to its length with pillows. Beside him there's a saucer with a couple of dog-ends squashed into it. I feel like marching in and kicking him awake, shouting at him not to smoke in my cottage. But I know that it would escalate into a full-scale row. And I don't want that. I daren't risk it – I could end up losing what little control I have left.

Janus rolls over, mumbling and whimpering in his sleep. The room smells of smoke and curry. I pull the door to very carefully and go for my bath.

Afterwards I put on a long-sleeved nightdress which buttons right up to the neck. I packed it in case I was cold at night, remembering how I used to shiver here as a child. When I see the mug of cocoa and the boiled egg that Lewis has waiting for me, I feel like a maiden aunt.

He draws one of the armchairs nearer the fire and I sit down without a word.

'Are you all right?' he asks anxiously.

'Yes, I'm perfectly all right.'

'You don't sound it.'

'You've never heard me swear before, that's all.'

'You've every reason to get annoyed, I understand that.'

'Pass my egg,' I say, determined not to give in too easily.

He bends down to pick up the tray that he's put in the hearth and ends up crouching in front of me instead. He rests his arms in my lap and kisses me gently on the lips. 'This is pretty,' he says, running his hands over my shoulders and down to my elbows, all encased in thick cotton. 'But it's like armour.'

I can't help smiling. 'No, armour doesn't have buttons.'

'I'm no good at buttons.' He lifts my hem and slips his hands underneath. They feel cool against my skin still warm from the bath. He gently massages my thighs, working his way upwards. And I forget about not giving in and about not going to bed with him.

'Your brother might come down,' I whisper.

'No he won't. He's had a couple of my tablets. He felt a bit uptight.' He presses his knuckles between my legs and finds my clitoris with his thumb. 'But I haven't taken any. Remember?'

My surplus energy becomes focused in the exact spot that he's touching me. I pull his head against my breasts and he sucks my nipples through the cotton. It's almost as good as when his lips are against my skin. But not quite. So I undo the buttons, all of them, very quickly.

'I'm scorching,' he says, leaning away from the fire. He stands up, pulling me with him. As soon as I'm upright the nightdress falls around my ankles. 'Your egg will get cold,' he says, holding me tight against him, his hands splayed round my buttocks.

'Fuck the egg,' I say, and he laughs into my hair.

I undo his trousers while he holds me, remembering how I'd wanted to do this when we were down by the quay. He feels hard and smooth. But this is not unusual; he has no trouble getting an erection. The first flush of pleasure is always very intense for him. But I think even then the possibility of failure is on his mind. And he cannot relax – or reach orgasm.

I take a step towards the little settee and we tumble on to it in a tangle of Lewis's half-discarded clothes. It's uncomfortable. My legs are bent up and Lewis is half on the floor. But we mustn't lose this moment, we both know that. I ignore the spring that digs into my shoulder and grip hold of Lewis so that he won't fall off me. My head jams against the arm. Lewis's weight and the awkward position makes the settee rock and creak. The sound seems to fill the room. The whole cottage. I imagine that I hear the familiar vibration of the staircase. 'What was that?' I whisper.

'Nothing,' he says. But I can't help twisting round to see. And I hurt him. He has to separate from me.

'I'm sorry. I thought I heard Janus coming down,' I say. Making things worse.

He doesn't answer, and I know it's too late. I would try changing positions, even suggest we go up to bed. But I've learned how sensitive these moments are for him. Practical suggestions sound like criticism; starting again is not an option. We lay crammed there in sweaty silence until Lewis heaves himself off me. 'I'm sorry,' I say again. 'I really thought I heard him. I'm sorry.'

'It's not your fault,' he says, wrenching up his zip with enough force to castrate himself. He looks towards the staircase. 'It's mine.' He takes a gulp of my cold cocoa and marches off outside.

I stay where I am, telling myself he needs time alone. Vaguely hurt because lying quietly with me is not the answer. Perhaps he's out there cursing to himself. To the stars. Getting stuff out of his system. Out of his head. Well, I know how hard that can be.

I give him a few more minutes, then slip on my nightie and go to the door. He's left the top open and I can see him leaning on the car, hands in his pockets staring out across the lough.

'Lewis,' I call. 'Please come back in.'

He continues staring across the water. There's always a hum of noise from the lough at this time of the evening. Muffled and unidentifiable. Anonymous creatures and birds bedding down for the night. But even muted, the sounds have an underlying exuberance as though an orgy of squawking and screeching is about to break out. And the splashes. Every now and again they come. Some creature leaping out of the water to devour another. A whole night-time of violence going on out there in the darkness.

'Lewis,' I call again. 'I love standing here admiring your handsome profile. But I'm getting fucking cold.'

He smiles now and comes over to the door.

'It doesn't make any difference,' I say.

'Any difference?'

'To the way I feel about you.'

He leans his arms along the door, presses his forehead against mine.

'It'll probably take a while for those tablets to get cleared from your system,' I say.

'Maybe.'

Shut up, I tell myself, don't start spouting your theories.

He takes my face gently between his hands. 'Are you willing to wait?'

'Yes, of course,' I murmur.

'How long?'

'As long as you want.'

'I wish I could believe you.' His voice is a whisper, his lips against mine as he speaks. 'I really am serious about you. Tell me you feel the same.'

I nod. Shit, I think, this tenderness, this gentleness of his, gets to me. I loop my arms round his neck. We kiss with the bottom half of the door between us. It's a conciliatory, sweet and romantic kiss. But not passionate. Not on Lewis's part anyway. Me, I feel as though my body will burn a hole through the wood.

The man from the estate agents is on the doorstep at nine the following morning. Lewis and Janus have gone to fetch bread and milk and to find out where we can buy more peat. It's sunny again today but I want to keep the cottage warm while we're here; parts of it are showing definite signs of damp. There's a blackish mould under the bath and powdery speckles of mildew in the corners downstairs.

I'm clearing out the grate, dressed in my nightie and a cardigan, when he arrives. I'd completely forgotten about him and he has to wait outside while I dash off to put on a skirt.

He's pleasant and chatty, and tells me that I should get a good price despite the many repairs that need carrying out.

'It's the position,' he says. 'Wonderful. I've got buyers queuing up for places like this. People from abroad mostly. We should be able to shift it pretty quickly. How long are you staying?'

'For the rest of this week. Definitely. Could be longer. It all depends.'

He smiles. 'Your husband might take another week off work, will he?'

'No, it's not that. I'm not married. I'm just going through a funny patch in my life. You know, not sure what to do next.'

He nods and smiles again and I feel silly so I offer him a coffee to cover my embarrassment.

He follows me round to the sink. 'Well, if you're still here when we have the draft details typed up, I'll pop back to see you with them. It's nice to get out of the office.

'Good. That'll be good.'

'You're here on your own then, are you?'

There is a hint of something in his voice. I fill the kettle, wanting neither to encourage nor discourage him. Ashamed that I'm hesitating over telling him that I'm not here on my own. Excited at his interest. Amused even. Not at him but at myself. I plug in the kettle and realise that there is no milk. Then, like a miracle, Janus comes barging in with a bulging carrier bag. Saving me from myself.

While we finalise details Janus slouches on the settee with his coffee, flicking ash all over my clean grate. There were no peat blocks to be had at Baltimore so Lewis has gone on to Skibbereen. He dropped Janus off so that I could have my morning toast and coffee. If this is meant to gain Janus house points then Lewis has miscalculated. All the time that I'm talking, Janus is listening, stuck there in the middle of the room, rudely blowing smoke into the air. The final straw is when he switches on the radio turning the volume up and tuning into a different station.

'Right,' says the estate agent taking his leave. 'I'll be in touch. I might even come back with a buyer straight away.'

'No,' I say suddenly. 'No. What I want first . . . I did explain when I came to see you . . . I want a valuation.'

'Ah, yes. Yes, of course.'

'Before you do anything else,' I emphasise.

'I'll see to it.' His manner has changed slightly. Whether because he senses that I am having second thoughts about selling, or rather that I'm no longer worth his smiles, I don't know.

Janus sniggers as I close the door. 'What a prat,' he says.

I hesitate for only a second, then I snatch up his cigarettes and matches and throw them out of the window. He leaps from the settee but I'm already pointing a finger in his face. 'Keep your filthy smoke out of my cottage. Do you understand?'

Janus doesn't hesitate at all. 'And you keep your filthy hands off my brother.'

It's the nearest I have ever come to slapping a man round the face. I even raise my hand. But it drops to my side again. And not because he is over six feet tall. It's that old instinct of mine, caution, reasserting itself. You don't need to retaliate in this way, it tells me, you can win in other ways.

Janus has taken a step back but his head is thrust forward. 'He phoned Nicole and told her about you. Do you know why? Shall I tell you? To make her jealous, that's why. To make her want him back. That's the only reason he's here.' He pauses. 'The only reason,' he says, emphasising each word. 'You don't know half of it. You're fooling yourself.' He hasn't heard the car pull up. I let him go on without interrupting. 'You think you're clever with all that shit about dreams, but you're just a means to an end.' He pauses again. Any minute the car door will slam and alert him.

I'm shaking now but I say calmly, 'Not if I marry him.'

The door slams. Janus swings round. He quickly looks back at me and shakes his head. 'No way. Don't even think about it.' And off he goes, galloping up the awful staircase, negotiating it better than any of us have managed to do.

Lewis staggers in, his fingers hooked in the twine of two bundles of peat blocks, and a bottle of champagne tucked under his arm. I go to help him. I take the bottle and smile appreciatively even though I'm still shaking like a leaf. 'Bollinger 1988,' I say. 'What's this for?'

'For us. Tonight.'

'Are we celebrating?'

'Yes.' He dumps the peat in the hearth and I have to put the bottle down before I drop it. 'Where's Jan, upstairs?'

I nod.

He comes to take hold of me by the shoulders. 'Are you cold? You're shivering.'

I don't seem to be able to stop so I rub my hands together making out I really am cold. 'A bit,' I say, 'just a bit.'

'We'll light the fire.' He wraps his arms tight round me. 'You don't feel cold. You feel hot. Are you OK?'

'Yeah, course I am.' I nod enthusiastically to reassure him. 'Tell me then, why are we celebrating?'

'Last night. You said you were serious about me. But you've never actually said you loved me.' He pauses, bends his head to mine in that way he has of touching foreheads, looking closely at me. 'So I thought we could say it to each other tonight. Then we'll open the champagne.'

I don't know what to say. This should be a beautiful moment. It should be more important than all the sex. More important than all the failed sex. It's certainly original; making plans to tell someone you love them. I close my eyes to let the words sink in. Waiting for those little pinpricks of emotion behind my eyelids.

'I want us to stay together,' he says.

Standing the other side of the stable door last night I remember thinking to myself, it's love he wants, love. And the idea is very attractive to me. Surprisingly attractive. Even his problems with sex attract me. The wanting something that is just out of reach. You want it more. I open my eyes to look at him. I do love him, I'm sure I do.

'Don't frown at me like that,' he says. 'I thought you felt the same way.'

'You've taken me by surprise. That's all.'

He lets go of me and runs a hand through his hair. 'It's taken me by surprise too. I liked you from the beginning, but . . .' He shrugs. His eyes glisten with softness. Lewis was made for scenes like this. 'But if you're not sure . . .'

'I am sure.'

'Is it Janus?'

I look towards the stairs. You can't see to the top from here. I should tell him what's happened.

Lewis looks too. 'I'll deal with him. Don't worry about it.'

'Well, I don't think you ought to mention anything to him just yet. I'd like a peaceful couple of days before we go home.'

'OK.'

'What about this?' I pick up the bottle. 'He's not stupid.'

Lewis takes it from me and hides it under the settee. 'No sweat. He chatted up the girl in the paper shop. He's meeting her in Baltimore tonight.'

'Evie's soon forgotten.'

'Well, you said yourself it was just an infatuation.'

I get an even bigger surprise when Janus comes up behind me, or rather creeps up behind me because I don't know he's there until I feel a hand on my back, and apologises. It's a plain and simple sorry muttered from behind while he touches me very gently between my shoulder blades. I'm outside hanging towels on the rotary dryer and he has obviously followed me. I don't turn round immediately. I'm still angry from this morning. Still angry that he's here.

'I shouldn't have said what I did. I'm sorry.'

'Until the next time.'

'What do you mean?'

I turn to face him now. He's standing very close to me, which I find disconcerting but I brazen it out. 'Until the next time you decide to insult me.'

'There won't be a next time.'

'No there won't. Because if there is, you're out of here.' I go to push past him but he blocks my path.

'Why are you so aggressive towards me? Why do you always want me out of the way?'

I shove the plastic clothes basket against him. 'That's ludicrous. You know very well it is. It's you. You're the one who wants *me* out of the way.'

He grabs the other side of the basket, holding it away to protect himself. I jab it into him again, hard as I can. I'm aware that I'm provoking him unnecessarily. I should just demand he lets me past, and go back indoors. 'I think you have a problem, Janus,' I say. 'And I'm not the only one who thinks so.'

'Nicole,' he says. 'I knew she'd talked about me.'

'Yes. She did. She warned me about you.'

'Did she tell you that she wanted to sleep with me?' His eyebrows shoot up. 'No, I didn't think so. Or that I turned her down.'

'In your dreams,' I say. I snatch the clothes basket away and duck under the dryer to avoid him.

He comes after me. 'Verity, wait. I want to tell you something.'

'Piss off, I don't want to listen to anymore of your lies.'

'It's not lies,' he protests.

'I don't give a shit. I don't care what she did – I don't care what either of you did.'

'I only told you so that you know what she's like. To warn you not to listen to her.'

At the cottage door he quietens down and follows me in, meek as a lamb.

There is a small argument about the car. Janus wants it this evening, of course, and Lewis wants to know exactly where he'll be going with it. I leave them to it and go off to hunt for shells. I'm going to make something for the Virgin. The Woodland Virgin, as I've come to think of her. I wonder idly if the girl in the paper shop is a virgin. She looked very young from what I saw. She's probably a good Catholic girl with a band of strapping brothers ready to avenge her honour. Well, I hope so.

Coming back from the beach I happen to glance up and see Janus at the bedroom window. The big one, not his. He steps back, making me think he didn't want to be seen. Lewis is sitting on the wall, reading a paper. He is wearing shorts and has his feet dangling in the water.

'You look very sexy,' I say, hugging him from behind and pinning his arms to his sides. I kiss him on the ear and sniff at his neck. 'And you smell very sexy.'

A page of the newspaper flutters down into the water. It floats there for a second or two like a great square jellyfish. Lewis tries to retrieve it with a stick but it sinks beneath the surface, way out of reach.

'That was the horoscope page,' he says.

'Oh, no.'

'But I've read yours.'

'And?'

'It says that you have come to a decision regarding matters of the heart.'

'Liar,' I smile, hugging him tighter.

'Well, have you? You didn't sound too sure earlier.'

'I've got to give it a bit more thought,' I tease. 'Love's a very serious matter.'

He twists round to kiss me. 'Nothing seems very serious here.'

I wait a moment then ask him: 'What's Janus doing in our bedroom?'

'I said he could borrow one of my shirts. He's getting ready to go out.'

'Oh.' I look up at the window again but he's not there. 'So he's got your shirt and your car.'

'Anything to get rid of him for a few hours,' he says.

There are some cars parked up near the road and a few people strolling around. Two little girls are coming towards us. From a distance they remind me of Lydia and Mimi – they are similar ages and have the same long blonde hair. As they get nearer I see that the resemblance is remarkable. The dark eyes and straight thick brows. The older girl is taking careful but domineering charge of the little one.

Lewis has seen them too. He looks at me and gives a tiny smile.

'Not quite as pretty as your two,' I say.

They come to the gates then turn back and go skipping off towards the cars.

'Why did you and Nicole split up?'

He sighs and folds the paper. 'A number of things. It started off with my work. I had a lot of publicity a few years ago. TV, parties, you know. I hated it but I had to go along with it for the money. It kept us apart. We started leading separate lives.'

'Other women?'

'Oh, no. Never. I could have done. I had plenty of opportunity. But I didn't want to. I hated the whole scene. In the end I turned my back on that side of it.'

'But it was too late.'

'Not really. We bought a nice house and spent more time together.'

I instinctively look towards the cottage again. 'It was Janus, wasn't it?'

'Nicole suddenly decided she didn't want him around. If she'd only let me handle it my way. But she wouldn't listen.'

'Had they fallen out?'

'They'd never ever got on.'

'So you had to choose between them?'

'That's what she wanted. Or pretended to want. Because she knew I couldn't. But I've told you all this. Why do you keep questioning me about it?'

'It helps me understand,' I say, unable to ask the question I really want to. The thing I don't believe. That I don't want to believe. 'So they never got on at all?' I say.

He shakes his head, looks away. Subject closed, I think. Then he says, 'Nicole goaded Janus. She tormented him in all sorts of ways. You might not believe this, you don't know him well enough, but he didn't retaliate for ages.'

'So he did retaliate? In the end.'

'Yes.'

'How?'

'You know how. He burned some of her clothes.'

'Favourite things?'

'I expect they were.'

'Where were they?'

'In the house.'

'In the wardrobe or where?'

'I can't remember. Why?'

'She wasn't wearing them, that's what I mean. I mean he didn't harm her? Actual bodily harm, or anything.'

He stares steadily at me. 'What are you talking about, Verity?'

'About my safety,' I say with a smile. 'Forget it, forget it,' I add quickly before he can answer. I put two fingers against his lips. 'Shall we sneak out the champagne? Have it out here in the sunshine while he's busy getting ready?'

'Good idea. We'll bring out some of that French loaf and the Brie that I bought this morning. We'll have a picnic. A party.' Lewis starts to climb off the wall.

'No, you wait here. I'll fetch everything.'

While I'm deciding whether we shall drink from wine glasses or half-pint tumblers I hear Janus turn on a tap upstairs. This morning I put five pounds in the meter. It seems to gobble up money. And I know for a fact that Janus fills the bath tub to the top; he leaves the telltale ring for the next person. Well, not any more, I think, not now he's here on sufferance. As I go upstairs I'm making a list of rules in my head. He won't like it, not rules.

The bathroom door is open, letting steam escape through to the bedrooms. Adding to the problem of damp that we already have. And I don't expect he has opened the window. As I've asked him to on more than one occasion. There's not a sound. He's filled the bath and left it. Probably trying on Lewis's shirts in front of the long mirror in our room. Preening himself for the evening ahead. The seduction of the little shop assistant. I creep to the bathroom door. This is a lesson, I shall tell him when he finds that I've pulled out the plug. Never leave your bath water unattended. Or I may pretend ignorance and blame it on the Little People. Tormenting Janus is obviously something women are prone to. Or driven to, rather.

I'm almost through the door when I see that Janus is sitting in the bath with his eyes closed. One hand is resting on the side, a cigarette held between two fingers, the smoke curling up to mingle with the steam. In the other hand he has hold of his cock. I think to myself, this is the third time I've seen Janus naked and he's not even my lover. His brother is. I'm caught between a bizarre sense of amusement and sudden numbing arousal.

He doesn't open his eyes, makes no sign at all that he knows I'm there, just goes on rubbing his cock, silently and expertly. If he were a snake charmer and I a hooded cobra I couldn't be more hypnotised. Within seconds his expression softens, his lips part, his jaw tightens, the bath water ripples. I watch every detail. I cannot take my eyes from his cock. I see each spasm, watch even as the trails of semen dissolve in milky threads beneath the water. The sound of his breathing fills the room, harsh and loud as though he has his lips pressed to a microphone, making love to it the way pop singers do. I back out of the door, but not before he has opened his eyes and seen me.

Chapter 15

A postcard arrives from Evie this morning, posted from London the day she got back. I'm surprised enough to see the postman – the few items of mail to do with the cottage are normally sent directly to my father – and doubly surprised to receive something from Evie. The card has a picture of the Houses of Parliament, not the sort of thing Evie normally sends. I've known her spend half an hour choosing one Christmas card, and ever since we've been friends she has usually managed to find me a birthday card with something relating to astrology. Failing this she falls back on cats, but they're always Siamese. This one, I'm quite sure, was sent in a hurry.

As I turn it over to read the message, Lewis comes to peer over my shoulder, hooking an arm round me at the same time. There is an ease in the way he holds me. An extra warmth, as though we have been together, been involved with each other, for a long time. A new closeness which allows him to read my mail.

'Evie,' I say, then start to read aloud ' "Sat next to a nun on the plane so I felt extra safe – especially when she told me that she had a terminal illness and was flying back to see her family maybe for the last time. And smiling and cheerful as she told me! A quick way of getting to know someone, anyway, so I asked her about the grotto – you know which one . . ." ' At this point my voice trails off. Postcards, which anyone can read from the postman to whoever picks it up off the doormat, don't usually reveal secrets; I was worried this one might. I read the rest through quickly to myself, struggling with Evie's scrawl and the faintness of the ink, and decided it was OK. ' "We must talk," ' I read aloud again. ' "Phone me as *soon* as you can. Miss you, love and kisses, E." ' The 'soon' is underlined but only just, as her ballpoint was obviously down to its last drop of ink.

'She probably wants to know what Janus is up to,' says Lewis, raising his voice a little.

'Did I hear my name mentioned?' Janus calls from round the corner.

'Why would we want to talk about you?' says Lewis.

'Then my ears must be deceiving me.' Janus comes to see what's going on.

'Verity has a card. From a beautiful girl who you let slip through your fingers.'

'Let me see,' says Janus.

'No, it's private,' I say, hiding it behind my back, smiling and play-acting, worried that Janus will ask about the grotto. Worried that I might catch his eye, which so far this morning I've managed to avoid.

'You've shown it to Lewis.'

'So?'

'Please yourself.' He loses interest. 'I'll go and fetch the papers. Anything we need?'

'Verity'll come with you,' says Lewis. 'She wants to make a phone call.' He winks at me.

'She won't be up yet,' I say quickly.

'You want to phone Evie,' says Janus, catching on immediately. 'Is that it?'

'I'll do it later.'

'No, go on,' says Lewis. 'You said you wanted some shopping. I'll cook breakfast for when you get back.'

Janus takes hold of me round the wrist. 'Come along, Verity. We'll phone her together. I've got something I want to say to her.'

'It's me she wants to talk to.' I jerk my arm away. 'I don't expect she's got much to say to you.'

'You'd be surprised.'

'Why don't you tell her about last night?' says Lewis.

'I wouldn't even tell *you* about that,' says Janus, implying that there is plenty to tell.

Lewis smiles and winks at me again as though the three of us are bound together in an affectionate little conspiracy about what we've all been up to. He is happy. He thinks we're all happy. And I mustn't spoil the illusion by refusing to go with Janus. And I have to go with him. I need to prove to myself that what I did yesterday doesn't matter. Not watching Janus in the bath, not that. That wasn't intentional. It just happened to me. The list of unintentional sightings of Janus is growing but I don't consider any of them to be my fault: not the spider falling on him, not him fucking Evie in the woods, and definitely not him masturbating in the bath with the door left open. But fantasising about him last night while I was in bed with Lewis was entirely my fault. Even if I didn't mean to do it.

Gerald once told me that if the sight of his body put me off, then I should close my eyes and dream about a younger man. I protested that I'd never do that, to please him. But I did. And we both knew, and so it was all right. But Lewis didn't know why I was so keen to masturbate him. Or how I closed my eyes and thought of Janus, so quick, so sure of himself, so intent on reaching that private moment of orgasm. And as I rubbed Lewis, my head was full of Janus and those final moments. I was trembling with the desire to have it happen all over again. Nothing else mattered. And when Lewis was nearly there I talked to him. I'd never been able to do that before, not with anyone, not the things I said. But the words came easily. And I kept on talking, right the way through until Lewis lay there still and panting. Content. Grateful even. I was quiet then, my head spinning with excitement. I flexed my aching wrist and pulled his hand between my legs.

'Pretend it's my cock,' he said as he pushed two fingers inside me. 'Pretend it's my cock because it soon will be.' He kept saying it while he eased his fingers in and out. And I kept pretending.

Janus comes into the phone box with me. I can't stop him. I have felt powerless for the whole of the five-minute drive, dreading that he would say something about yesterday, and trying to work myself into a state of indignation in case he did. I had my defence ready, even the cross tone I would use. Reverse the situation, I would have said, and I'm quite sure that no man would have walked away. But he spoke only about the girl he took out last night. He told me that once he discovered that she was barely sixteen he had taken her home.

I stiffened with even greater indignation. On her behalf this time. And when he told me that he'd spent the rest of the evening in the pub playing cards so that Lewis and I could be alone, I looked out of the window as though I hadn't heard.

I dial Evie's number. Janus waits beside me in the tiny booth.

As soon as Evie answers I blurt out, 'I didn't know whether you'd be up but Janus wanted to get the papers, so I came with him.'

'Where is he?'

'Here with me.'

'In the phone box?'

'Yes, Evie,' I say very deliberately. 'He's right here next to me.'

'Can you get rid of him?' she says very quietly.

I laugh as though she's said something funny, then turn to Janus. 'I want to talk to Evie privately. Can you wait outside?'

He slips his arm quickly round behind me and tries to take the receiver trapping my hand under his. 'Evie!' he says. 'I'm pining for you.'

I don't hear her reply because he has dragged the receiver away.

'It's torture for me without you,' he goes on. 'Verity and Lewis have this very big thing going now. They're even talking about marriage, would you believe? Verity is, anyway.'

'Give me the phone, Janus,' I demand.

He laughs and hands it over, creating the impression that we're having fun and games.

'You two seem to be getting on OK,' says Evie, sounding surprised.

The pips go and I put more money in. 'Yes and no,' I say.

'We're fine,' Janus shouts. 'We're having a good time together. The three of us.'

'Janus, will you get out of here?' I elbow him away but he's simply too big for me to budge him.

'I've been worried about you,' Evie says, lowering her voice again. It drops to just above a whisper. 'Don't trust him, Verity.'

'Don't worry, I can handle it.'

Janus leans back against the glass, eyes on me, half smiling.

'What's this about marriage?' says Evie.

'Oh, I won't do anything without telling you,' I say.

'I knew I shouldn't have left you on your own.'

'I'm not on my own.'

'With them two, I mean.'

Something is wrong here and it suddenly dawns on me what it is. 'You knew Janus would be back with us then?' I glance at him as I speak. His expression gives nothing away.

'Yes. He told me at the airport. I was going to phone him in Kinsale when I got home but he said not to bother, he was going back to the cottage.'

The pips sound again. I realise I haven't asked her about the grotto. 'Evie, I'd better go. I'll call you again soon. Tomorrow. We'll talk on our own.'

'Yes do that. Are you all right?'

'Yes, of course.'

'Take care, babes, take care,' she gets in before the line goes dead.

Janus seems suddenly bored and walks out of the phone box ahead of me. I follow him into the shop. He buys papers and cigarettes while I look along the grocery shelves, trying to remember what it is we need. I hear him ask the man behind the counter, 'Where's Ann Marie this morning?'

'At school,' comes the less than friendly reply. I also get a cool reception.

Janus doesn't say a word on the drive back. I keep quiet too, reading the papers, which have reports of an IRA bombing in London. Funny that we should come here and escape danger, I think. Janus takes a bend too fast and we nearly hit a brewer's delivery truck coming the other way. The driver raises a hand in apology but Janus swears and makes a V sign at him although it was entirely his fault. An incident which makes me realise that you never escape danger anywhere.

The piece of paper on which I wrote Nicole's number has disappeared. I put it on the dressing table in our bedroom. Under *The Naked Lunch*, I think. I can't imagine that Lewis would have removed it without saying anything. He might have removed it *after* saying something. Like, why did I want to speak to Nicole? Because it would, to him, seem a strange thing for me to have her number. Especially written on a piece of paper headed 'Guinness On Tap at Sean Ogs', and decorated with enough flowers to fill Kew Gardens. No, I don't think it was Lewis. But I don't *want* to think it was Janus, and as the only other explanation is that I have mislaid it myself, I start to look under other books and on the floor. 'Stop watching me, Mary O'Brien,' I say, looking up at her. 'Or I'll turn you round to face the wall.' I'll take the photograph home as a surprise for my father. He can hang it in his bedroom. Let my mother look at the O'Brien family and see what some women are capable of.

I give up my search and am about to go downstairs when I hear that Lewis and Janus are having an argument.

'For fuck's sake, Lewis, what am I supposed to do without money?'

'I don't have any to spare.'

'I know Dad gave you some.'

'It has to last until we get back home.'

'You can afford to buy champagne. For her.'

'That's none of your business.'

'What am I supposed to do stuck in this fucking hole?'

'Keep your voice down.' Lewis sounds angry. 'I didn't ask you to come back here.'

'OK. I get the picture.'

I hear the door open and Lewis say, 'Jan, wait.' I go back into the bedroom and look out of the window. Janus is walking up towards the road, wearing the long black coat, his hands stuck in the pockets, his head bent. I hear the door close. Janus looks back a couple of time then goes slouching off again. Once I'm certain that Lewis is not following, I lean right out of the window and call after him. He looks back again, stops. I beckon him and he walks reluctantly towards me, his head raised to the window.

'Where are you going?'

He shrugs and squints up at me.

'Hang on. I'll lend you some money.'

His expression barely alters; he certainly doesn't seem all that delighted with my offer. A strong breeze is blowing from the direction of the mountain. It whips his hair up and away from his face. Despite a few days' growth of beard, he looks very young and thin and vulnerable.

'How much do you need to go for a drink?' I say, wondering

why I'm doing this; there must be better ways of getting rid of him. 'A tenner?'

He shakes his head. 'No thanks. I do have some pride, you know.' He's about to walk off again but I call him back.

'This isn't fair, Janus. It isn't fair on Lewis. You're putting stress on him all the time. You lied to get yourself back here. Now you're causing more trouble. He'll end up having another breakdown.'

He stares out across the lough.

'Don't you care?' I say when he fails to answer me.

'The trouble with you is,' he says, turning back to me, his eyes watering as the wind catches him once more, 'you watch people and you try to work them out with your books and your little theories, but you don't get it right. You can't because you've never been there. You're stuck in your own little world. Your safe little world.' He wipes a hand across his face, then shoves both hands back in his pockets. 'Tell Lewis I'll be back later.' With this he's gone, leaving me speechless. Not with anger. I have every reason to be angry, but I'm not. I sit on the edge of the bed and wonder if he's right.

I need to get away from them both for a while. Be on my own again. But I don't want to go wandering up the mountain, in the woods or even walk by the lough. None of these places will allow me to think clearly. In all of them I feel an overdeveloped sense of atmosphere that influences me to think this way or that. Even the mountain has turned against me. When I look at it now, it reminds me of the day I went to the Doyles and wrote on their phone pad. Nicole's number, which has disappeared. And I dreamed about the grotto again last night. Lewis was sleeping very soundly, his cheek pressed into the pillow, sent off in minutes with his tablets. I encouraged him to take them because he'd been worrying all day about a letter that his father had sent on to him from the bank. He didn't show me and told me only that it had the date and time of an appointment the manager had made to see him.

His worrying affects me. I'm trying not to become involved, not to worry about his problems. But it's impossible because I really do care about him. Sometimes it feels like a burden; others, I want to put my arms round him and smooth away the creases from his face. The confusion is making me edgy. My dream didn't help. It reminded me of when Gerald sent for his friend Lenny because he was so concerned about me. It was a similar dream, full of the kind of symbolism that I've come to understand. But I couldn't work it out this time. I dreamed that I was in the woods naked and the Virgin took off her blue robe and wrapped it round my shoulders. Like a cloak. 'Don't be ashamed,' she said to me. But as soon as I came out of the woods the robe changed colour and became the black cloak of the Seal Woman. A hugely pregnant Seal Women. Perhaps I don't want to work it out. But I know one thing, or three things rather: I'm not pregnant, don't want to be, and am not likely to be. If I'm avoiding anything, it's not that.

Lewis drops me off in Skibbereen. As far as he knows I'm going to see the estate agent, do some shopping and take Mrs Doyle to lunch as a thank you for looking after the cottage. She will then give me a lift back. Part true, part lies. I'm not taking Mrs Doyle to lunch but it was the best I could think of to get rid of him. And I shall get a taxi home and call in at the Doyles'.

The estate agent has come up with a valuation that sounds pretty good. Invested properly, the money would provide a large enough income to allow me to give up my columns and take up study of some kind. The psychology I want to do. I sit there on the other side of the estate agent's desk thinking about it, imagining the change in my lifestyle. And realising that it won't be that much of a change.

'It's a good price,' he says tentatively, as if he takes my silence for disappointment. 'For a quick sale. It wouldn't be wise to leave the place uninhabited for another winter.'

'No,' I say without conviction.

'Shall we go ahead then?'

'No,' I say again, this time more emphatically. I stand up. 'No. I'm sorry. I've wasted your time. I don't want to sell just yet. I'm sorry.' I stumble out of the office and walk very quickly to the square in the centre of town where I collapse on a wooden bench. A woman sits down beside me, heaving two bulging shopping bags between us.

'Fine day,' she says.

'Yes, it's lovely.'

'Too warm for shopping, though.'

'Yes, it is.' I smile at her but I feel strangely detached. 'Do you live in Skibbereen?' I ask her.

'No, I've come in from Castletownshend,' she says. 'We come in every week to look in at the cattle market and do a bit of shopping.'

'Oh, Castletownshend. I've heard of that.'

'Yes, well you would due to Somerville and Ross.'

I nod. The names sound familiar but I can't seem to remember why. I know that normally I would want to sit here and chat to her and find out more. But I don't feel like talking to a stranger for some reason. I want to talk to someone that I know well and who knows me well. I go over the road to the bank to change some more money into Irish punts and get some coins for the phone.

I try Evie first but she's not there. Then I start to dial my father's number but know that he'll ask about the cottage, so I put the receiver down. Maybe my blood sugar level is low, maybe that's what is making me feel so light-headed. There's a teashop not far from the phone box. It's crowded, today being market day, and full of smoke but I sit in a corner and eat a huge slice of carrot cake and drink a whole pot of tea. Afterwards I sit there for a while, watching a Japanese couple, obviously tourists, trying to make conversation with a family who are obviously locals. There's laughter and much signing with hands. Even the children of the Irish family join in, all trying to make sense of the Japanese couple's broken English. When a correct guess is made there's nodding of heads and clapping. A map is pulled from a rucksack. Bancheebay? says the Japanese man. The Irish family look at one another, baffled, then one of the younger ones shouts, Bantry Bay! and gets pats on the back from everyone.

I go to call Evie again, almost tearful that she's still not there. This time I leave a message on her answerphone to say I'll ring back later. Along from the phone box I notice the name 'Sean Ogs' above a pub, another reminder of the Doyles' phone pad. The dim light and the hum of voices attracts me. I'm not sure why. And I'm not sure why I order a Guinness; I'm not normally a beer drinker. But I drink it quickly, then order another. Walking back through the town I feel bloated and a bit happier. It's too early to go home yet and I end up in the library, writing a postcard to Miss Campion.

A group of schoolchildren are sitting near me. Older ones, sixth formers trusted to study out of school, I expect. I don't take much notice of them at first, or rather I try not to take much notice because everywhere I look in this town there are people with other people. Happy families and groups and couples. All making me feel acutely alone. Me, a woman who loves her own company. Who even, not so long ago, preferred sex on her own. Then one of the girls looks up and smiles at me. 'Hello,' she says as though she's not sure whether I'll recognise her.

I smile back, surprised. 'Oh, hi there. Anne Marie, isn't it?'

She gets up and comes over to me, a file held against her chest. 'How's Janus?' she says.

'He's fine.' She's enormously pretty in a plumpish dark hairy way. One day she'll be too plump and she'll have to use a depilatory on her top lip. But for now she's lovely.

'He said he might call in at the shop, but he hasn't.'

'Ah, well, actually we popped in this morning. But I don't think your father approves of the age gap.'

'Oh, it's not that. I've been out with a twenty-year-old before. But he thinks I should only go out with boys from round here. Not people on holiday.'

A twenty-year-old, I think to myself. Well, well. I smile again. 'I'll er . . . I'll tell him I saw you, anyway.'

She lingers there, hugging the file. 'I read your horoscopes.'

Another surprise. 'You get the magazine here?'

'Yes. Mrs Doyle told us it was you. That you were sort of famous.'

'I'm hardly famous.'

'You have your picture in a magazine every month.'

'That's fame?' I say raising an eyebrow.

'My family would think I was famous if it happened to me. So would my school friends.'

'Well, perhaps it will one day. What do you want to do'

'I'd like to train in psychiatric medicine.'

'Probably not the best way to get your picture in the paper.'

One of her friends comes to tap her on the arm and point to the clock.

'I have to go,' she says. 'I hope we meet again.' Still she

doesn't move, though her friends are gathering up their books. 'Tell Janus hello from me, won't you?'

'I know,' I say in a sudden rush of warmth. 'What are you doing this evening? Would you like to come out for a meal with us? Janus and his brother and me?'

Her face breaks into a beautiful smile. 'That would be lovely.' The smile fades for a second. 'He won't mind that you've asked me, will he?'

'No, he'll be delighted. Anyway, it's going to be my treat and I'd like you to come. Save me being outnumbered. We can talk about mental illness.'

She laughs. 'It's very nice of you.'

'We'll pick you up at six.'

'Thank you. I'll wait outside the shop.'

After she's gone, I wonder what I've done. But I feel a lot better for it and eager to get back to Lewis.

We drive out to Bantry first, my idea, and have a drink at The Kilgoban whose end wall is painted with an amazing mural of the bay and an invitation to 'Stop – and call in'. No wonder the Japanese are prepared to come halfway round the world to visit this place, I think. I'm beguiled by the beauty of the scenery once more, happy, and sure we won't be discussing mental illness. Anne Marie takes every remark of mine as though it's a personal compliment. Proud of her country though she plans to leave it and go to university in England. Janus is extraordinarily well behaved. No sarcastic comments, no overtly sexual pawing, and he even restricts his smoking until we're out of the car because Ann Marie mentions that she sometimes suffers from travel sickness.

The minute I got back from Skibbereen this afternoon I told him that I had invited her. I waited for his reaction, still high enough on the Guinness not to care what he said. He stared at me, making out he was shocked. 'Hey, Lewis,' he said. 'Verity's procured a woman for me.'

'Anne Marie will be delivered safely back to her door,' I said. 'I thought you'd like the company, that's all.'

'I'm touched by your concern.'

And I'm touched by his treatment of her. Touched because I hadn't thought him capable of acting respectfully or gently towards anyone. Apart from Lewis, that is. And touched because I'm feeling particularly sensitive this evening.

We go on to Ballydehob, a village between Bantry and Skibbereen, which at first sight looks full of pubs and not much else. But Ann Marie suggests it because her cousin has a restaurant here.

'He'll find us a nice table,' she smiles 'and we won't have to tip him.'

'And never mind about the food,' teases Janus.

'Oh,' she says, laughing, as she does at all his remarks. 'The food's pretty marvellous, don't worry about that.'

And it is. A wonderful starter of crab with cream cheese and salad nearly fills me. It sits on top of the carrot cake and Guinness I had earlier, comfort feeding in Skibbereen because everyone seemed part of a family or a group, matched up, needed, in love.

Anne Marie is reeling off the names and ages of her brothers and sisters to Janus. 'And the baby of the family is Michael,' she says, steadying her glass as Lewis tops us all up with a fruity dry wine from South Africa chosen for us by Anne Marie's cousin. He's young with a hint of shyness but eager to please, much as Lewis must have been when he started out. 'Do you have any brothers or sisters, Verity?' she asks me. She has become very talkative after just a glass and a half of the wine. But I'm on my third and don't care.

'Sadly, no. My mother didn't want any more after me.'

'I'm not surprised,' smiles Janus. His first sarcastic remark of the evening.

Anne Marie pulls a stern face at him.

'Oh, it wasn't anything about me. It was the birth. She found it such an awful experience. Violent and gory', I add, aware that I've read this somewhere. 'Camille Paglia,' I mutter, smiling to myself as I remember Evie and I discussing spiders that night in Kinsale. 'She said that the most common violence in the whole world is childbirth. My mother believed that too, or so she kept telling me.'

They all look at me.

'Sorry,' I say, a hand to my mouth. 'I think I've had too much to drink.'

'Well, I don't think that's necessarily true,' says Anne Marie, looking very concerned. Concerned for me perhaps. Her older sisters, the ones near my age, all have children. 'The commonest violence as far as women are concerned is rape, surely.' She blushes, an intelligent girl who would like to have a conversation about the things that concern her but hasn't the confidence. Not yet anyway. And by the time she does I suspect that she'll be settled down with a husband and children and have other things on her mind.

More of Camille Paglia comes to me, the bit about pregnancy resulting from rape being nature's heart of darkness. But Anne Maric is a good Catholic girl and this might be too difficult for her. 'No wonder women have more nightmares than men,' I say finally.

'Is that a fact?' she says, placing her elbows on the table, her eyes lighting with interest.

Janus groans. 'Don't start her off,' he says loudly. Talking about me of course.

'Oh, you men, you never want to discuss serious issues with women,' says Anne Marie, smiling at him, pulling his hands from his ears where he's holding them. Janus says something very quietly to her. She looks into his eyes, the subject of violence against women forgotten. I wish she knew about the gentle violence of persuasion. But that's something she wouldn't believe in right now.

'What did the estate agent say?' Lewis asks me.

'I made a fool of myself, actually. As soon as he'd told me how easy it would be to sell and what a good price we'd get, I told him I'd changed my mind and that I didn't want to sell. Then I walked out.'

He smiles at me in disbelief. 'Why?'

'I couldn't bear the thought of parting with the place.' I lean towards him. 'It's become very special to me.'

'I'm glad,' he says softly.

'I'll have to tell my father. Ask him if I can keep it, if that's possible. I expect there'll be all sorts of stupid regulations attached. But I'll sell the London house. Not before your tenancy runs out, of course.'

'We'll work something out.' He takes my hand.

'Are you really glad?'

He nods, mouths, I love you.

I hear Anne Marie laugh and I glance across the table. I'm startled for a moment. Janus, it seems to me, has one eye fixed on her, the other on us. An illusion that I put down to Guinness, South African wine, rich food and the notion that he is mythically able to look two ways at once.

Chapter 16

Last night ended in disaster. An idyllic evening turned into chaos. I'm trying to work out why, pinpoint the moment, the words that lit the fuse, not of Janus's temper but of Lewis's. I can't help thinking that it was my fault and that it all began on that spur-of-the-moment decision when I invited Anne Marie to come out with us. They say that things done spontaneously are often those which give the most pleasure. But I'm beginning to think that it doesn't work like that for me.

So I'm sitting here on the stone wall outside the cottage, letting the events of last night filter through my head like a film. Slowing it down and speeding it up to see if I could have done anything to stop what happened. It's not that I want to be in control of other people's lives, just my own.

There was a public phone box outside the restaurant and while we were debating whether to have coffee, Lewis decided to give his father a call. I thought that I might phone Evie as well when he'd finished. When he came back he seemed anxious, not smiling as he had been.

'Not bad news?' I said quietly as he sat down.

'Good and bad.'

Janus looked across at us and although I knew he couldn't hear what we were saying, I knew that he had picked up Lewis's mood, as he always does.

We finished our coffee, strong with cream but no whiskey this time, and I asked for the bill, taking charge of it as I'd said I would. Anne Marie tried to give me something towards it but I told her firmly that it was my treat. Her cousin had already been very generous.

'Well, let me get the coffees then,' she said, pushing a handful of coins towards me.

I pushed them back and Janus gathered them up and slipped them in the pocket of her jacket.

'She can afford it,' he said.

Now I know it wasn't meant as rudely as it sounded – I hardly took any notice – but Lewis reached across the table and caught Janus by the sleeve.

'She? She?'

'Sorry, I mean Verity,' Janus said immediately, but Lewis held on to him.

'Verity,' he said, stressing my name. 'Verity can't afford to throw money around any more than you or I.'

Janus gave a little shrug. Anne Marie blushed with embarrassment.

'Well, if this is what you call throwing it around,' I tried to make a joke of it to diffuse the situation, 'I'm all for it.'

Lewis didn't seem to hear; he was still staring at Janus. I looked across at Anne Marie and raised my eyes to the ceiling as though to say, men! She smiled nervously.

After a few moments Janus asked pleasantly, 'What did Dad have to say?'

'He's found a job for you.'

This was it, I think, the news that Lewis could, should have saved until later.

'Oh yeah?' said Janus.

'A friend of his needs an extra hand for the summer.'

'In a restaurant?' said Janus without enthusiasm.

'No, in a garage. Serving petrol.'

'Serving petrol,' repeated Janus, as though it was the most menial and degrading work anyone could possibly think of.

'It's a job,' said Lewis. 'With wages.'

Janus didn't answer and I stood up, gathering my bag and jacket, hoping that they wouldn't prolong this in front of Anne Marie. But as the others got up from the table Janus said 'And I suppose you're going back home?'

'I have to,' said Lewis curtly. 'I don't have any choice.'

Anne Marie stopped for a last word with her cousin. I lingered with her, complimenting him on the meal and thanking him for the reduction in the bill. Saving Anne Marie from the storm that I knew was brewing.

We followed the men out to the car. 'You and Verity,' I heard Janus say.

Lewis seemed to be ignoring him. I saw him feel his pockets for the keys. 'I've got them,' I said, producing them from my bag. Janus held out his hand and without thinking I gave them to him.

He dangled them in front of Lewis. 'Shall I drive?' he said. 'I've had less to drink than you.'

Lewis snatched the keys from him. 'I'm safer drunk than you are showing off,' he said.

'Oh, I wouldn't think so,' I intervened. For once I disagreed with Lewis. And I couldn't believe how he seemed intent on humiliating Janus. 'You don't want to risk losing your licence, do you?'

Lewis took a deep breath, threw the keys at Janus and got in the back. We left Ballydehob in silence, Janus driving more carefully than usual but, not surprisingly in the circumstances, going off in the wrong direction. Anne Marie suddenly asked where he was going. He pulled up. By now we were on a narrow road bordered by low-lying bog. He drove on again until the road widened and there was dry ground on either side. Lewis said he'd get out to see him round but Janus said there was no need. I swear I heard the scrape and crunch of metal colliding with stone seconds before it happened. The way you do when everything seems to be leading up to the one thing you dread will happen.

We all got out. The damage wasn't that bad. Not the damage to the car, anyway.

'It's a standing stone,' said Anne Marie as we all peered at the solid grey slab protruding from the turf. 'It'll be the marker for a dolmen, a tomb. My brother once rode into one on his bicycle and knocked his front teeth out. He said it had just sprung up out of the darkness.'

'I'll put that on the insurance claim,' said Lewis.

'Don't start on Anne Marie,' said Janus.

I closed my eyes for a moment. 'Shall we just go home and calm down,' I said.

We all got back in the car. Lewis drove the rest of the way, heaping more humiliation on Janus.

As we approached the lough Janus said, 'Stop here. I'll

drive Anne Marie home myself.'

Lewis refused to let him have the car. Anne Marie, holding back tears, said, 'I'll walk the rest of the way.'

'Good idea,' said Janus, also holding something back. Fury probably. He took her hand and helped her out. They disappeared into the darkness together. Janus had his arm round her.

Lewis turned the car down towards the cottage. The headlights lit our way, casting long beams on the deserted path, picking out the shapes of two lanky pines on the hill and the blue of an upturned rowing boat on the little beach.

'There was no need to do that,' I said.

'Do what?'

'Make him feel small in front of Anne Marie.'

'If he acts like a kid, I'll treat him like one.'

We went into the cottage in silence. I turned on the radio to fill it. An old Meat Loaf number echoed round the room. 'Paradise by the Dashboard Light'. Poor Janus, I thought, having to walk his girlfriend home like a teenager. With no dashboard or any other light. It's such a sexy number, so full of youthful passions. I hummed away to the music in a sort of grim defiance at Lewis's bad temper. And I couldn't help thinking of Janus and Anne Marie kissing goodnight outside the shop. Or maybe before that, out of the way of her father. They had four or five miles of dark road to kiss one another. I didn't think he'd try anything else. Not judging by the way he'd treated her. I didn't want to listen to the Meat Loaf song any more, so I turned the radio off and asked Lewis if he was coming to bed.

'I'll wait for Janus,' he said.

'Do you think that's a good idea?'

'He doesn't have a key. Anyway, I won't be able to sleep until he's back.'

I went upstairs on my own. Through the door of the little bedroom I could see the tumble of blankets and pillows left, by the looks of it, exactly as Janus had stepped out from them this morning. I went in and stood there, resisting the desire to straighten them. On the chair, the only other furniture besides the bed, was a bundle of clothes. On top, a pack of cards, a tin of throat pastilles, a hairbrush and a notepad. A young man's belongings. I wondered if the piece of paper with Nicole's phone number was hidden there. I could have looked but I didn't.

I went to bed and thought about last week when Janus and Evie were sleeping together in this room, under this same duvet. I wondered what they talked about in the dark, and if there had been times when Janus was as sweet with Evie as he'd been with Anne Marie. And I remembered that I hadn't phoned Evie and so I began to wonder as well what she wanted to tell me. And what I would tell her. And what anyone was telling anyone.

It was another couple of hours before Janus got back. I heard him come in. Just. He was very quiet, obviously trying not to make a noise, and he managed to get right up the stairs without a sound. The next thing I knew he was tapping at my bedroom door.

'Yes?' I whispered, sitting up.

He stuck his head round. 'Lewis is fast asleep. On the sofa bed. What do you want me to do, leave him or wake him?'

'Oh,' I hesitated, thinking. 'Best leave him. Is he warm enough?'

'I don't know. Should I go and put another blanket over him?'

'Do you mind?'

'No, of course I don't mind.' He smiled. 'I enjoyed tonight. Most of it, anyway.'

'Yes, same here. Anne Marie's a lovely girl.'

'He nodded. 'Verity?'

'What?'

'Could you have a word with Lewis?' His tone had changed slightly. I had the impression that he was having to make an effort to say this. 'Could you tell him that you don't mind me coming back to London with you?'

My first reaction was to throw in his face all the nasty things he'd said to me. But I couldn't do it. 'It's nothing to do with me, Janus. And I don't want to interfere. Anyway, wouldn't it be better if you were working?'

'So you won't do it?'

'I'm not going to interfere, that's all.'

He tilted his head to one side. His curls were springy and glossy with damp like a child's. And his expression was childish too, that same air of vulnerability as I'd noticed when he stood under my window and I'd offered him money. 'I thought we understood each other better,' he said. 'But I must have got that wrong.'

Before I could answer, he pulled my door to. I didn't hear him go back downstairs but I heard him through the night those few steps away across the landing. I could hear him cough every now and then, and several times I heard the rough sharp rasp of a match being struck.

So I'm sitting here on the wall with plenty to think about once more. My head aches a little and I have a dull pain low in my stomach. Not enough to bother me, just a niggle. I remember my mother saying she used to give thanks to God every time her period arrived. You might thank the moon, but not God, I should think. I don't thank anyone; I shall be irritable and bloated for the next couple of days before mine starts. Evie once told me that sex is the answer for PMT but I've never tried it. I prefer a painkiller and a lie-in. Which have worked to some extent. And staring across the water is soothing. It's so clear that I can see every pebble and strand of weed. At the moment it's too low to dip my feet in, and it's probably cold anyway.

Behind me Lewis is dismantling the rear light of his car while Janus hovers close by trying to help, but getting in the way from what I can hear. You could cut the atmosphere with a knife. I want to say, leave the damn car, let the garage fix it, that's what you pay your huge insurance premiums for. But I keep quiet. Unoccupied they would probably be worse.

'I'll have to make sure that we drive back in daylight,' says Lewis.

I look over my shoulder wondering who the 'we' includes. Janus is standing there with his arms hugged round his chest as though he's cold. He's barely spoken two words to me this morning and I've been careful what I've said to both of them. But I'm suddenly fed up with it, all this thinking before I speak.

'Are you seeing Anne Marie again before we go?' I ask, swinging my legs back over the wall so that I'm facing them.

'No.' Janus shakes his head squinting up at the sky. 'It's going to rain.'

I look up too. It's a mackerel sky but I can't be bothered to repeat the rhyme to him. 'Why not?'

'No time.'

'Will you keep in touch?'

He shrugs. I've been answered with worse than shrugs and silences before. And somehow I can't be angry with Janus this morning. He imagines that he has good reason to be upset both with Lewis and with me. And in some ways he does.

I jump off the wall. 'Who wants coffee?'

Lewis looks up, a piece of Perspex in his hand. 'Yes, please,' he says.

'Janus?' I say.

He shakes his head, his eyes on the sky once more. Lewis throws the piece of Perspex at him. 'Answer her,' he shouts. Then he picks up a spanner and throws that too. Janus doesn't flinch as the spanner hurtles towards him and drops at his feet.

I'm astounded. I look down at the heavy spanner, thinking of the damage it could have done. Janus picks it up and meekly holds it out to Lewis. Something is going on here that I don't like. It puts me in mind of the way animals in a pack behave. The dominant creature snarling at a weaker member, knowing that they never retaliate. That they're conditioned not to. A powerful ritual.

Lewis ignores Janus's outstretched hand and marches off indoors.

'There's no reasoning with him when he's like this,' says Janus. 'He's best left alone.' He smiles at me and goes to put the spanner and the rest of the tools away in the car.

I don't know what to say. I'm suspicious of him and irritated with the pair of them. 'I thought you two were supposed to be devoted to one another,' I say finally, 'but I'm beginning to wonder.'

'Is that what he told you? That we're devoted to each other?' He has his head bent over the boot and I can't see his face but I know that he's no longer smiling. He slams the boot shut, having to use extra force as the bottom of it is buckled. 'Well, he blames me for too much now.'

'Blames you for what?' I say quietly.

He looks up at the sky once more, staring hard as though the answer is hidden somewhere between all those little dapples of cloud. I look too and see that smoke is coming from the chimney. It erupts in little grey puffs like the smoke signals that I joked about with Mr Doyle.

'He's lit a fire,' says Janus, as though I can't see for myself. 'He always feels the cold when he's depressed.'

'I thought it was you who felt the cold,' I say. He's still gazing upwards so I leave him and go to make the coffee.

Lewis is sitting by the fire, writing figures in a notebook. 'I thought we might as well use up the peat,' he says.

'Good idea.'

'I'm preparing some figures for the bank.'

'Do you want any help?'

'No, thanks. I'll get my father to read through them.' He looks up at me, his face serious. 'You are coming back with us on Saturday, aren't you?'

Janus has come to look over the bottom half of the door. He swings it backwards and forwards, making it creak annoyingly.

'Yes, I think I will. I need to do some sorting out as well. And I expect my cat's missing me.' I crouch down beside him, a hand on his knee but he goes on with his writing. His figures are very untidy, dropping below the lines, some big, some small. 'Sure you don't need any help?' I say.

'I'm OK.'

You're not, I think, neither am I. My body is sending me messages. I feel delicate, overblown. Overflowing. I move my hand, willing him to take hold of it. Take hold of me. But he doesn't.

Out of the corner of my eye I see Janus unhook his black coat from the row of pegs by the door. He puts it on.

'I'm going for a walk,' he says.

'You won't need that,' I smile. 'The sun will be out in a minute.'

'Oh, you can't trust the weather here. And I'm going for a long walk.' He's out of the door, sliding the bolt to stop the bottom half blowing open. 'Do you want to come with me, Verity?' he says.

Lewis takes hold of my hand at last. 'Go and keep him company,' he says. 'Keep him out of my way.'

Chapter 17

'I dreamed about fire again last night,' Janus tells me as we walk together up to the road. He seems very subdued just as he was when Lewis threw the spanner at him. ' I wanted to tell you on your own because Lewis thinks I'm making it up to annoy you. And I'm not.'

'He thinks,' I say patiently, 'that it's about Nicole. And so do I.' Then I clap my hands over my ears. 'But I don't want to hear any more about it. I want to end this holiday peacefully. I want to go home with beautiful thoughts of this place.' I take my hands away and look up at him. 'Do you know?' I've spent half my life feeling anxious.'

'Anxious?' he says.

'Yes. Anxious about what's going on around me. Anxious about what might happen to me.'

'What do you think is going to happen to you then?'

'Oh, I don't know, Janus.' I shake my head in a fluster of impatience. 'Come on. I want to say goodbye to the Woodland Virgin and the mountain.'

He laughs and runs across the road ahead of me, disappearing amongst the trees, camouflaged in his black coat.

I've brought the shells that I collected the other day. I haven't got round to making them into something, maybe a cross, as I'd planned, but I've washed and polished them. I place them on the grotto, arranging them in a semicircle round the Virgin's feet. They look prettier and more natural than the plastic beads I used to covet as a child.

'A peace offering for calling you a statue,' I say, licking my finger and rubbing a smudge of dirt from her alabaster face. If she forgives me she doesn't show it. Not a flicker from those downcast eyes. Contemplating the sufferings of the world perhaps, oblivious of her pretty surroundings, the ferns and feverfew and wild strawberries. Strange companions. But maybe they have some kind of significance in their relation to women. Headaches and pregnant women's fancies.

Janus is leaning against a tree, hands in his pockets. I pick a few of the tiny strawberries and throw them at him. He ducks, then comes to pick some himself and eats them. 'Now the mountain,' he says. 'Let's go right to the top.'

'Oh, I don't think I can climb up there today. I have a slight cramp. I'll say goodbye from the road.'

'You don't want to go back yet, do you?'

'No, we'll walk a bit further.'

'The lough then. That place you took Lewis. Where the sea comes in.' He smiles, eager, like a child. 'Yeah?'

'It's quite a way.'

The smile fades. 'I'll go on my own if you don't want to come.'

'It would have been nice if Anne Marie could have spent the day with you.'

He doesn't answer.

'Or Evie.' I cock my head at him. 'Do you wish she were here?'

'No good wishing for people, is it?' he says, walking off without me.

I catch him up and fall into step. 'It doesn't hurt to wish.'

'I can't see the point of it.'

'You can be very stubborn, Janus.'

'Why? Because I don't agree with all you say?'

'No,' I laugh. 'Because you're determined to keep that coat on however hot it gets.'

He lets himself smile but says, 'I'm not hot. Not in the slightest.'

The path down to the quay is damper and steamier than ever, and when we reach the tunnel of trees it's like walking under a warm shower. It's impossible to avoid the drips; the trees are laden with moisture, their branches weighed down with it. And the path seems narrower somehow, as though the undergrowth is trying to spread right across it, meet in the middle and obliterate it. Not surprising in this continuous cycle of sunshine and rain. The ferns, I'm sure, have doubled in size. A quick spurt of growth as their fronds have uncurled like sleepers awakening. So many different types, and all so fresh and clean. Unlike my own potted ferns, which are always covered with a thin film of London grime. Ferns grow from spores not seeds; I remember that from biology at school when we had to draw the life cycle of a fern. An easy way of introducing nine-year-olds to how male sperm fertilises a female egg. An easy reproduction system too. No lady fern need struggle to expel her baby. And they've been around for 300 million years so they know a thing or two.

'Did you know that ferns date back 300 million years?' I ask Janus.

'The world's not that old,' he says.

I can't argue because I'm not absolutely sure about it. Maybe I've just remembered it wrong. But I'm inclined to think not. My memory is good in that it stores details away in little packages. A word, a reminder and it all comes back to me. Hart's-tongue, male fern, maidenhair, spleenwort and hard fern. And there actually is one species called lady fern. I'd never realised before what suggestive names they have. Even polypody and rustyback sound faintly indecent now I come to think of it.

'Look.' Janus points ahead. 'Donkeys.'

We've reached the derelict house. Both donkeys have their heads stuck through the fuchsia hedge, their ears flicking backwards and forwards amongst the sprays of crimson and violet flowers. Janus rips up a handful of ferns for them but they prefer his sleeve, nibbling and tugging at the material.

'Hey,' he laughs. 'My best coat. My only coat.' He pulls away and tosses the ferns into the fireplace. One of the lighter fronds hangs in mid-air, suspended there as if by magic. Janus steps back and I see that it's caught on a huge spider's web.

'Watch,' I say, and I blow very gently on the fern. Just enough to make it quiver. From behind one of the blackened stones of the chimney, a little yellow spider appears. It hesitates for a moment, checking the coast is clear. Then quick as lightning, it scurries across to investigate.

'Fuck that,' says Janus.

'Don't be silly, it's tiny.'
'But it's yellow.'
'What's that to do with it?' I laugh.
'It's unnatural. It could be poisonous.'
'Don't worry, there aren't even any snakes in Ireland, so I'm sure they don't allow poisonous spiders in.'
He frowns at my teasing and takes another couple of steps back. I know that his fear is genuine but it seems so pointless to be afraid of something that can't possibly harm you. Being as careful as I can, I pick the spider from its web, holding it by a leg between my two fingers.
'If you throw that at me . . .'
'I'm not going to throw it at you. I promise. Give me your hand.'
'No way.'
'I promise it'll be all right.' I take hold of his wrist. He holds it stiffly by his side. 'Come on,' I coax, and he lets me lift it. I can feel he's trembling. Only slightly, but I can feel it. 'Open your hand.'
'No.'
'Yes.'
He does.
'Ready?'
'No, don't,' he says. 'It'll run up my sleeve.'
'No, it won't. Watch.' Very gently I lower the spider on to his outstretched palm. It has become a shrivelled lifeless speck, smaller than a currant. Its legs have collapsed around its body. 'They pretend to be dead when they're frightened.' I keep a grip on his wrist. 'Close your hand.'
'I can't.'
'You can.'
Very slowly, his fingers meeting stiffly like those mechanical grabbers that lift toys in amusement arcades, he closes his hand. But he keeps his arm rigid and his head turned away as though he's about to have an injection. I hold his hand closed but after a few seconds he pulls free and shakes the spider to the ground.
'You've made me sweat,' he says, shrugging off his coat.
'No, it's your fear that made you sweat,' I smile, 'not me. And that coat.'

We walk on down the track. My cramp has gone. My body does this to me sometimes, making me assume it's up to something that I know about, then playing tricks on me. Inherited probably. My mother never knew where she was with hers.

It's very quiet beneath the trees. We haven't seen another soul since we left the cottage. Weekdays are usually quiet. It's not until the weekends and the school holidays that people come here in any number. And it must be nearing the time for preparing evening meals, or fetching the children from school. Not for wandering around the lough, anyway.

I take hold of Janus's arm. He looks startled. 'The time,' I say. 'What's the time?' Both he and Lewis wear expensive-looking gold watches. Presents to each other, apparently.

He holds up his wrist, waggles it and taps his watch. 'It's stopped.'

'Oh.' I come to a halt.

'It doesn't matter. What does it matter?'

'No, I suppose not.'

'You're being anxious again.'

'No, no I'm not. I said I *used* to be anxious. I'm not now. Not anymore.' Convincing myself. 'I'm more philosophical now.'

'What will be, will be, is that it?' He smiles round at me. 'Whatever the stars say.'

'Not exactly.' I feel a little uncomfortable for some reason. 'I think that your future depends, to a certain extent, on what choices you make.'

'Well, tell me, Verity.' He is looking straight ahead now. He swings his coat up into the air, aiming at a branch, catching it and bringing down leaves and a great shower of raindrops. 'Are you going to choose to marry my brother?'

I stop. Look at him and then concentrate on brushing the leaves from my hair and shoulders. 'Have you brought me all this way to ask me that?'

'I wanted to ask you sometime. I wasn't sure when it would be.'

For one tiny split second I'm afraid. Not exactly of Janus. But not of anything else either. 'What makes you think he's asked me?'

'He told me he's serious about you.' He's still not looking at me.

'Well, he may have. But he certainly hasn't mentioned marriage. Neither have I.'

'Would you say yes if he asked you?'

'It's really nothing to do with you,' I walk on, pulling out a tissue to wipe my face, 'whether I'd say yes or not.'

'I just wanted to tell you that I won't mind.' He catches my arm. 'Because I know you think I will. I know that Nicole has tried to turn you against me. With her lies.'

The cramp has returned a little. It's making me sweat. Janus takes the tissue from my hand and wipes it across my forehead. 'Are you OK? You look very white.'

'Yes, yes. Just hot.' I drag my sweatshirt over my head. Underneath I'm wearing a flimsy sleeveless blouse. It comes adrift from my skirt, letting cool air flow round my ribs. But I tuck it back in and loop the sweatshirt round my shoulders.

'I think you'd be very good for Lewis. You're patient. You won't mind when he has black moods.'

'Black moods?'

'You saw him earlier. You saw him throw that spanner at me.'

'Sometimes, Janus, sometimes, I've felt like throwing a spanner at you.'

'I know.' He smiles. 'But if you knew us better. If you really knew us, you'd know that I'm more docile than Lewis. Inside,' he taps his chest, 'I'm a very gentle quiet person.'

I laugh. 'You could have fooled me.'

'You ask Anne Marie. You ask Evie.'

'Not Evie. She . . . she . . .' My usual inventiveness deserts me.

'She what? Come on, tell me. What has Evie been saying about me?'

'Oh, nothing much.' I play for time, trying to think of something convincing. As convincing as any lie can be. 'She said you could be overpowering at times, that's all.'

He frowns, slowly smiling at the same time. 'Do you think I'm overpowering?'

'I think what she meant was, overpowering in a physical way.'

'The trouble with Evie,' he says, 'she doesn't know what she wants. Sex, love, sex. She swaps them about all the time. And when you think you've got it right, she changes her mind.'

'Well, Janus, I got the impression that there was only one thing on offer as far as you were concerned.'

His face contorts into that frowning smile again. 'You're so wrong about me.'

'I said it was an impression. That's all I seem to get of you. Impressions. You can be very hard to fathom.'

'How am I doing today?'

'So far, so good.'

He smiles with what I imagine is pleasure.

When we get to the last great bulge of the lough, the sky is no longer dappled with cloud but spread with a fine colourless haze. The water looks colourless too, and totally smooth, not a ripple, not the slightest movement anywhere. And no boats. It seems that nothing is moving except for those constantly breaking waves just visible in the distance. I slip off my sandals, which are wet from the walk, and prop them on a rock to dry. The rock feels warm to my touch and the slabs of stone on the quayside are warm under my feet.

Janus lays his coat on the rocks and stares out across the water, shading his eyes with his hand.

'Weird place,' he says. I watch him scan the whole scene, taking everything in. He drops to his haunches, looking down over the edge of the quay. 'The water's so clear. But I can't see the bottom. Must be very deep.'

'Tell me something, Janus,' I say, partly to distract him because I can't bear him hanging over the edge like that. 'Why aren't you smoking today?'

'I've had a sore throat. I promised Anne Marie I'd cut down.'

'Yes, I saw the throat pastilles on your chair.'

He turns to look at me, just his head swivelled round, chin against his shoulder. 'Oh, did you? Spying on me. Again.'

'The door was open.'

He continues to look over his shoulder at me.

'Well, it is my cottage.'

He smiles to himself, then goes back to staring down at the water. 'Do you fancy a swim?'

'No!' I say indignant, thinking only of what I would wear.

'You're scared.'

'No I'm not.'

'This place scares you. Lewis told me.'

'Well, there's more reason to be frightened of deep water than there is of a tiny harmless spider.'

'I'm not scared of spiders any more. You've cured me.'

'Fear doesn't come into it. It might be all right for you to jump in there in your knickers, but not for me.'

He laughs and stands up, stripping off his T-shirt at the same time. He tosses it on top of his coat and starts to unbuckle the belt on his jeans.

'I think you're a bit of an exhibitionist,' I say, looking round for somewhere to sit. The rocks are a bit too near the water's edge.

'Oh, come on, Verity, don't play the shocked spinster. You've seen me in less than my Y-fronts.'

To my surprise he is actually wearing Y-fronts. Navy blue with threads of elastic dangling from the waistband. I try to think of a male equivalent that sounds as insulting as spinster. I try to think of anything. Anything that I can blab on about.

He stands right on the edge of the quay, running his thumbs round under his waistband, adjusting it, preparing to dive in.

'I think it might be dangerous to swim here,' I say. 'I've never seen anyone swimming. There could be strong currents. From the sea. When the tide comes in.'

He drops down on the warm stones, sitting there with his legs stretched in front of him. I sit down too on a patch of grass that slopes up beyond the rocks. He has his back to me. There is so little spare flesh on him that you could pencil in the outline of his shoulder blades and vertebrae, every bone. The back of his hair is tangled, as usual. Hair like his needs brushing every day. You could curl it round your fingers into fat sausages.

'So you've given up smoking,' I say.

'Not for good.'

'Oh. Just until your throat's better.'

He stretches his neck and rubs his hand up and down it, fingering his Adam's apple as though the soreness is located right there. 'It's not too bad now.'

'Do you suffer from sore throats a lot?'

'No.' He looks round. 'I think I caught it off Evie.'

'Oh, Evie's always got the sniffles. It's all that sitting around in draughts.'

'So she said. Still, it's a way of making a living. If you've got the body for it, of course.'

'Do you miss her?' I say quickly.

'In a way.'

'What way?'

'What way? Do you really want me to tell you?'

'Not particularly. I expect I can guess.'

He lays back on the ground, hands behind his head, neck twisted so that he can see me. 'Yes I do miss the sex. But it's not an insurmountable problem. As you know.'

I could stop him right here. Change the subject. Leave him to his swim and go back on my own. Behave like a shocked spinster.

'Yes, well, we all know that it doesn't necessarily take two,' I say lightly.

'But it's not as good, is it?'

'Depends on your imagination.'

'Do you think so? Still, I expect you've got a really vivid imagination. All that studying about dreams. Does it help?'

'Oh, shut up, and go for your swim.'

'You didn't want me to a minute ago. Don't you like talking about sex?'

'Not with you, no.'

'You just like watching me.'

I've let this go too far. I know that's what I've done. Perhaps a boat will come sailing through that gap in the rocks and save me. Not from Janus. From myself. My limbs feel weightless. My body, heavy. Hot and heavy like I'm stuck to this spot. Like I'll melt here and spread all over the grass.

'Go for your swim,' I hear myself say again. It doesn't sound like me speaking. I wonder if he notices. 'If it's not too cold I might come in. Just on the edge.'

Janus sits up, scratches both hands around in his hair. 'I could do with a fag.'

'Have you got your cigarettes with you?'

'No,' he says, shaking his head as though he's lost in thoughts of other things. He stretches. 'Well, it's now or never.'

'Shouldn't you take your watch off?'

'It's waterproof.'

'But it might slip off in the water.' How desperate I sound about the safety of his watch.

He turns round, shifts nearer to me and places his arm on my knees. 'You take it off if you're that worried about it.'

Without looking at him, I undo the strap. It's a heavy, beautiful watch inscribed on the back of the case. I hold it in my hand without reading the inscription. Janus takes hold of my leg, his fingers pressing into my calf. I close my eyes and sit very still. Then I feel him take hold of my other leg.

I make no move to touch him, give him no encouragement, barely lift my hips from the ground as he takes off my pants. My eyes are still closed but I can feel him poised above me like someone about to do press-ups. We don't kiss. There is no beginning to this. No build-up. One minute we were two separate people, now we're joined. But my body has been secretly waiting and there is no moment of hesitation. Janus is fast. But he takes me with him. I feel impaled by him, over and over until I can't see or hear anything but the noise of us, like animals. And when he comes it's like an explosion filling me with heat and I'm frightened but I don't want him to stop. He begins to pull out of me but I hang on to him. I wrap my arms and legs tight round him. And he pushes hard into me once, twice more. Then it happens for me, and it goes on and on until I can't help crying out. 'Shh,' he says, 'shh,' and he puts a hand over my mouth.

His body is damp with sweat but feels very cold. He breaks free from me and curls on the grass at my side. I feel strange and light. As though I've been pumped full of air and that I'll go floating off into the sky like a big fat blow-up doll. I put my hand between my legs. It's so wet there. Wet with virility, I think, smearing it round the inside of my thighs. My elbow nudges something on the grass. It's his watch. I leave it there, move my arm away from it. Janus reaches over and picks it up. Soon we must speak. What will we say? Maybe he will apologise. But I don't think so and I don't want him to. And I don't want him to say, don't tell Lewis. Or will I say that?

'Will you tell him?' I say in a small voice.

'Of course not. He'd hate me.'

'This isn't what happened with Nicole then?'

'What?' His tone is abrupt. 'Did I fuck her and tell Lewis, you mean?'

'Yes,' I say, feeling as though I'm speaking from inside an empty shell. A big empty shell but with only a small opening, so that I'm trapped. 'To get rid of her.'

'And get rid of myself.'

'Lewis might forgive you.' I'm almost whispering.

Janus turns sideways and runs a hand across my breasts. I'm still dressed but my body is so sensitive that it feels as though his fingers are against my skin. They're cold.

'We won't tell him,' he says. 'We'll be together, the three of us. Do you understand what I'm saying? Does that appeal to you?'

'Yes, I understand.' I turn to look at him. He turns to me at the same time. He has an innocent expression, wide blank eyes and slightly parted lips. Childishly innocent. But he's not a child, not a boy or even a very young man. It's just a mask he wears. One of many. I feel a sudden desire to claw at him, tear the mask away, scream accusations. But all I say is, 'What are we going to do?'

'What are we going to do?' he mimics, rolling over to whisper in my ear. 'What have we done? Not everything has consequences. There's not a meaning and an answer for everything.'

'There is for most things.'

'Not this. It's not one of your dreams.'

But that's just what it is. A waking dream. Something in my head that I've allowed to come true. I sit up and reach for my sandals. They're nearly dry, but stiff with caked mud. Janus takes them from me and bangs them on a rock. Then taking each of my ankles in turn, he slips them on for me. This little gesture makes me feel slightly better. Though it shouldn't. I don't want to be won over by his concern, his tenderness, those flashes of gentleness that spring up to surprise me.

I get to my feet. Out towards the sea the sun is breaking through. The spray looks brighter, caught in its brilliance, leaping higher into the air.

Janus puts a hand on the back of my neck. 'What are you dreaming about now?'

'Nothing. Dreams are too risky. They're not worth it.' I take a step forward to escape from his hand. I don't want him to touch me. Or rather, I want him to touch me too much.

'Like stories?' he says. He snatches up his coat from the ground and swings it round my shoulders. 'There. You can be the Seal Woman. You've got her cloak. You've taken human form.' He stands back and spreads out his arms. His voice becomes teasingly dramatic. 'And I'm a stranger wandering along this lonely shore.'

'No, Janus.'

'Yes.' He comes over and grabs me from behind. 'Put your arms in the sleeves.'

'No, stop it.' He's holding me too tight, trying to force my right arm into the sleeve.

'Janus, don't!' I shout at him but he won't let go.

'You have to come from the sea. Dripping wet.'

I struggle with him as he grabs my left arm. Telling myself, reassuring myself, that he derives some kind of sexual pleasure from this.

'I don't want to get wet, I've got my clothes on. Let me go.' I'm struggling like crazy now.

'We'll jump in together. Don't be scared. I'll teach you not to be scared.' His words are punctuated with panting as he drags me to the edge of the quay. 'Like you taught me.'

'I'm not scared.' I am, very. 'I'll jump in by myself. Just let go of me.'

He loosens his grip but I can't move because I'm almost hanging over the edge. Below, more than an arm's-length below, the water pushes against the stone, swelling a little as though something is shifting under its surface.

'The tide,' I say in an odd high-pitched voice. 'The tide's coming in. Let's watch. It's what I've been waiting for.' I put my arms round his neck, press my face against his chest, kiss his cold skin. And then we're falling. For a moment I'm stunned. By the fall, his weight, the cold water. I feel myself sinking. A soundless roar starts up in my ears. Then the instinct for survival activates my legs. I kick madly, propelling myself upwards, gasping for air as I break the surface. The coat is dragging at me. I try to get it off but I can't. I'm aware that Janus is there but I can't see him, only sense his presence like a predator waiting to close in. Something hits me in the chest, hard. I go under. I feel hands on my shoulders pressing down, and the whole lough is rushing past me in a great wall of water as I sink. Then I'm free, swept along by the water, but free. I propel myself to the surface again. Take great gulps of air. I'm swimming now. Going with the water. If I could just get the black coat off I might stand a chance. But I have to keep swimming. I don't know where Janus is. I sense many things in the water, below me, around me. Touching me. But I must not panic. If I panic I'm lost. I will drown. I must concentrate on swimming. Nothing else. Not the creatures that are in this lough. Or Janus. Especially not Janus. That he is here somewhere, trying to drown me.

My arms are getting tired. And I could cry with the cold. I can barely feel my legs. I think that they're moving. I hope they are. I mustn't give up; no one will know what happened to me. Only Janus. So I can't give up. And for a moment it's easier. I surge ahead, lifted and dropped on a wave that breaks in my face and blinds me. At the same time I'm dragged back. I sob with fear as I feel the coat pulling at my shoulders. It slips away from my neck, and suddenly I know what to do. I know it, if only I have the courage to do it. I thrust my arms backwards keeping them as straight as possible. It's terrifying to be plunging face down into that great depth of water. But it works. The coat slides from me like a shedded skin. I force every aching muscle to one last effort. There's the sound of splashing behind me. The water rises and falls, breaking over my head as though I'm swimming in the wake of a large solid object. Wouldn't it be wonderful if it were a dolphin? I think. A dolphin trying to save me. I float there, dreamy with exhaustion. Then my head bangs into something that is not the flank of a dolphin. I put my hands up in defence and find that I've hit a boat. A small wooden boat. I sob with relief. Call out as I clutch its side. But there's no answer. It's simply moored there. It sways drunkenly under my grasp. On the third attempt I manage to hook a leg over the side. It tilts alarmingly but with one final desperate heave I'm over and in. The planks are wet and stinking but I press my cheek against them and give thanks, sobbing quietly into the wood.

I lie there absolutely still, listening. Nothing but the slap of water. Growing louder, stronger. The boat rocking. The lough filling as the tide pours in. Above me the sky, dappled again. If I keep staring at it, empty my head of all that has happened, detach myself from my wet and freezing limbs, then perhaps I will find myself back outside the cottage, watching Lewis fiddle with his car and Janus staring up at the sky.

Chapter 18

I'm saved. But I don't feel saved. Being with these strangers is not comforting. These people, this family on holiday from Dublin, don't know what has happened to me. They can't hug me and reassure me that I'm safe, that everything will be all right. I told them that I was climbing on the rocks and fell into the water. I'm not hurt, I assured them, not wanting to be whisked off to hospital somewhere, which would mean answering questions. The one thing I need is time to think, sort out what is true and what I've imagined. Or, more upsettingly, what I can repeat and what must stay secret. The grazes on my arms and legs are from climbing into the boat. I think. Their little fishing boat which hasn't been used since they came here last summer.

Or I may have banged myself climbing out of the boat and up the wooden jetty. Balancing on loose planks and fighting my way along the overgrown path to their holiday chalet. It's not easy, pushing aside brambles with your bare hands. For a moment I picture myself in a perfectly detached way – all that I've just been through. And I think of how all my life I've tried to avoid danger. I once said to Evie that she was risking her life, the way she travels round late at night on tubes and buses. You can't keep worrying about those thousand-to-one chances, she said, you just have to be aware, that's all, be aware of that one person amongst all the other thousands, the one who might wish to harm you.

At this point I start to cry. I sit on the fluffy bathroom mat in this strange house, amongst strangers, and sob my heart out into their big bath towel. Next door, in their kitchen, I can hear the sounds of the woman moving about. She's getting out cups, switching on appliances, the kettle to make me more hot sweet tea, the tumble dryer to dry my clothes. I passed them to her round the bathroom door. Of course, being a stranger, she couldn't ask me what had become of my pants. They must still be lying on the grass somewhere down by the quay. It occurs to me that if I had drowned they might have been used as important evidence. But Janus has probably found them and tossed them into the water. Not for a single second do I consider the possibility that he has drowned. I see him clambering up the rocks on to the quay, dripping wet, black hair plastered to his head. Drying himself as best he can; maybe even using my pants before he gets rid of them. Getting dressed, fastening on his watch, and all the while keeping an eye on the water. The picture is so real that it slots into the rest of what's stored in my memory. And I'm frightened because I can't distinguish the dividing line. Perhaps this is what happens when you've been very near to death. A sort of anaesthetising process. I pat my face dry. And when I've stopped crying I carefully pat my battered body dry.

'Are you sure you're up to going home now?' the woman asks me while I'm drinking my fourth cup of tea. 'Declan's gone to bring the car down. We have to park it up the end of the track.'

They've been very kind. My clothes have been dried and ironed. They've offered to take me to a doctor, even given me a pair of flip-flops to wear. And now the husband is going to drive me back to the cottage. I'm seized with fear. I want to be with Evie or my parents. I'd even settle for staying here a while longer. They have a patio with plastic chairs and sun loungers. It would be nice to sit there all evening, to lie back and close my eyes and pretend that I'm someone else. Someone who may have a *few* problems in her life. But not someone who has, quite willingly, no, very willingly, had sex with a man who wants her dead.

'Are you all right, dear?' The woman takes my elbow as I get to my feet. 'You look awful shocked. Sit yourself back down for a minute.' She gently pushes the hair from my temple. 'You've banged your head. You've a wee blue swelling under here. You might have concussion.'

I feel for myself but it's hard to tell what hurts and what

doesn't. I'm vaguely hurting all over. 'My veins stand out there,' I tell her. Her concern is beginning to overwhelm me. 'A drawback of being fair-skinned.'

She looks at me doubtfully. 'Well, you should have a checkup. You're white as death itself.'

'I swallowed a lot of water,' I say, placing my hand on my chest, then my stomach.

'Sea water and all,' she tuts, shaking her head. 'Oh well, it'll clean your insides out. It's good for that.'

My insides feel as though they're being cleaned out right this minute. A familiar ache has settled in my groin. I recognise it amongst all my other aches and pains. Soon I will need to lie down for an hour with a painkiller. Sooner rather than later.

Lewis meets me at the door. Declan, a shy man who hardly spoke two words to me, drove off once he saw the door opening. I feel as though I'm being handed from man to man.

'Verity, what happened to you? Whatever's been going on?' Lewis guides me in. Shuts the door. I mustn't cry, I think, I mustn't cry or I'll lose control.

'Is Janus back?' I say in a high tight voice.

'Yes. He's upstairs. He's distraught. He said you had a row.'

'Oh, yes. What did he say it was about?'

Lewis takes hold of me by the arms, draws me closer but not against him. 'I won't let him come between us. I promise you, Verity.'

'What did he tell you?' I say. My voice sounds hard and cold now. I don't want him gripping hold of me like this, or making promises to me.

'That he asked you if we were serious. If we planned to get married. And that he knew you'd want him out of the way, the same as Nicole did.'

'And?' I know that Janus will be listening. He could even be crouched on the top stair. Waiting. So that he can rush down and tell Lewis what we did. Shout me down. With something that sounds more believable.

'That's about it. He said you ran off down by the lough. And that he waited but you didn't come back. And he knew . . .' He stops, shrugs, struggles on, 'That he'd ruined my life once more.'

I step back from him, look down at my freshly ironed skirt, touch my clean dry hair, convinced for a moment that the grazes hidden under my sweatshirt will have disappeared. 'Ruined your life?' I say, as though the words don't make any sense.

'I won't let him.' He takes hold of me again but I pull away, wrench away.

'Go and ask him, I want you to go and ask him.' I'm finding it difficult to speak. The cramp in my stomach is spreading out, down into my thighs, up into my chest. Swelling in to a great ball of nausea. 'Can you go and ask him what he's done with his black coat. You remember. He was wearing it.'

'It's over there.' Lewis points. 'In the sink. He dropped it in the lough. Climbing over the rocks.'

I rush over to the sink. And then I'm vomiting up streams of brown liquid. It might look like four cups of strong tea. It even smells faintly sweet. But I know it's lough water, gushing out from the pit of my stomach, spraying and dribbling on to the Seal Woman's cloak. My head spins. Not a wise move to go searching for a man, I think, not a wise move at all.

'Oh God,' I moan, clutching hold of the sink while Lewis wipes my face with a towel. 'I'm going to lie down for a while. In bed. I want you to get rid of him before I go up there. Get him out of my cottage.'

'I've told him he has to go in the morning.'

'No, now.'

'Verity, it's past nine o'clock.'

I clutch my stomach; my insides are heaving again. 'Get rid of him. Now.'

'But where's he supposed to go?'

'Anywhere.' I'm hunched over and trembling from head to toe. 'I don't fucking care as long as it's away from me. Get him out of here. Get him away from me.' I'm on the verge of screaming. Lewis puts a hand on my shoulder but I push him away. I snatch the towel from him and hold it pressed over my mouth, to hold my hysteria in, the way you press a wound to stop the blood spurting out. I bite on it. Lewis stares at me. All this for a row? Is that what he's thinking. He lowers his eyes and nods, more to himself than me. 'All right,' he says. 'All right.'

He leaves me and goes upstairs. I can't bear to listen. I can't bear what they'll say to each other. When finally they come downstairs, Lewis is first, leading the way. They go straight to the door but at the last minute Janus looks back over his shoulder at me with mad accusing eyes. Lewis pushes him outside, then comes back to me. 'I'm taking him to Kinsale. I'll come straight back.' He touches my cheek. He looks worried. No wonder, I think, no wonder, caught between us two. 'Wait for me,' he says. A funny thing to say and I don't answer.

And later, as I get undressed, inspecting my arms and legs, the grazes, the scratches, the bruises and the thin trickle of blood on the insides of my thighs, I think to myself that he won't come back. They're off together, inseparable. Janus pouring lies into his brother's head. Truth as well. Either way, Lewis won't come back. And do I want him to? I have to sleep on it. I can't make any decisions. I can't even think about tomorrow and going home.

And I can't sleep on it either. Every time I close my eyes I hear the sound of water roaring in my ears. It doesn't surprise me that I have a new nightmare waiting for me. After all, it's my subject – I know all about it. So I lie there in the dark listening to the slap of water beneath the window. Waiting for morning and daylight, no, *longing* for morning and daylight. As I used to.

Lewis arrives back with the dawn, slipping in beside me with cold hands and feet. His arms go straight round me and I wriggle up close. His big body is comforting. I press my face into his chest with relief. The way I pressed against the planks of that boat.

'I didn't think you were coming back,' I murmur.

'Why?' He raises his head. 'Because you and Janus had a row?'

'Something like that.'

'You're too important to me now. More important than anyone.'

So Janus has made his decision. He is keeping our secret and letting me have Lewis back in return for *my* silence. So it's up to me now. But if I want to keep Lewis I must keep quiet. It's not a fair bargain but I can't risk testing its strength.

I get up early while Lewis is still sleeping. I creep downstairs and drag the black coat out of the sink. It leaves a trail of water across the floor as I carry it outside. Before I drop it over the parapet I feel in both pockets. Nothing in the first one. But in the second there's a very soggy box of matches. And deeper in the pocket, saved from floating away by the matches, there's a piece of paper. The writing on it is nothing more than smudged blue ink, but the printing on the top is still readable. 'Guinness on Tap at Sean Ogs'. Why do bad things always turn out as you expect they will? And good things . . .? Well, who knows. I fling the coat into the water. It lands with a slap, the arms sticking out as though it's about to start swimming. To glide forward, heading for the long creek and the deep, deep water nearer the sea.

As I go back indoors I wonder if I've done the wrong thing. The coat could get washed up on the shore somewhere. It could start a hunt for the owner. Or maybe it will drift out on the ebb tide. Get sucked through the cut or ripped to pieces on the rocks. Forget it, I tell myself. Forget, forget, forget. But the trail of water across the floor seems to tell me that I won't.

Chapter 19

In the first flush of shock over what I reveal to her, Evie commands me to go straight to the police.

We're sitting together in our nighties on the end of her bed. I came to her as soon as I arrived back in London last night. It was a mistake, I know that now, but I had to tell someone what happened to me, the part I could tell anyway. If I didn't talk about it, say aloud the things that were screaming around in my head, I feared I might have nightmares about water for ever. Especially that moment when Janus put his hands on my shoulders and I thought I was going to die. The need to talk was greater than my anxiety about keeping the other part of that afternoon secret. But from the start, when I began telling her how he'd put that coat on me, inventing a little to hide what had gone before, I sensed that Evie was hiding something too.

'The thing is,' I say, 'I don't have any proof. It would be his word against mine.' I pause and look at her, expecting her to overrule my dissembling with an indignant outburst. But she just stares back at me, sympathetic, doubtful, as though she's half convinced already. 'And I'm not sure,' I go on. 'How can I be sure what he meant to do? He might just have been trying to frighten me. You know what he's like. Over the top about everything.'

'But can you risk not going to the police?'

'What would I gain? Not protection, that's for sure. Anyway, I'm safe while he stays with his father in Ireland. And that's the main thing, I suppose.'

'Well, if you don't tell the police, you must tell Lewis.'

'Oh, how can I, Evie? Think of what it would do to him.' My

words seem to echo mockingly back at me. I have to look away. I don't want to hurt her any more than I do Lewis. It is one thing to tell your best friend that the man she was recently fucking day and night has tried to drown you; quite another to tell her that you fucked him too. 'And there's the chance that he might not believe me. He might think I'm making it up to get rid of Janus.'

'Don't be silly. You wouldn't make something like that up.'

'But he tries to protect Janus. He's done it before. With Nicole.' I stop, unsure what Evie knows about this. Unsure about so much.

'He can't go on protecting him,' she says. 'You were lucky. But I think we all know that Janus'll end up doing something really terrible.'

Her seriousness worries me; it's not like her. I wait, sensing again that she's keeping something from me. Something that she's on the verge of telling me.

'If I'm truthful, none of this surprises me,' she says at last. She clicks her tongue as though she's unhappy, as though she'd rather not go on. 'He frightened *me* a few times. Well, you know that. I would have said more on the phone that day, but you sounded as though you were getting on OK with him.'

'What would you have said?'

'It was just his stupid talk. It didn't mean anything. I just wanted to warn you not to trust him, that's all.'

'Tell me, tell me what he said.'

'It was at the grotto,' she says as though I'm forcing it out of her. 'He made a confession to that plaster figure. You know, I'm a sinner, forgive me, and all that. But he was whispering so I couldn't hear. I thought he was fooling around and I said had she sentenced him to burn in the fires of hell. I thought he was going to laugh, but he didn't. He picked the figure up and said she was a witch, like all women, and that she was the one who was going to burn in hell. Then he threw her in the pool. Well, you know I'm not religious, but I was a bit shocked.' She shrugs. 'And angry. I was angry. But even when he scooped her out and put her back on the pebbles, I was too scared to say anything.' She looks at me. 'I was too shit scared of him to make a fuss.'

I don't know what to say. Evie scared of a man makes me

feel very sad for some reason. But she's smiling again now. Albeit a little sheepishly.

'We made love there a couple of times. The first time, I thought it would be exciting because the place was so spooky. But I had this feeling that we were being watched, so I didn't want to do it again. But it's hard to say no to Janus.' She eyes me cautiously. 'There, now I've told you everything. A bit late, I know.'

And I've told her so little. 'I don't think it would have made any difference,' I say. 'Janus might be a little crazy, unbalanced, I mean, but he's clever too. And he can look so innocent, can't he?'

'Yeah,' she sighs, 'a dangerous combination. So what are you going to do? Are you going to tell Lewis?'

'I suppose I ought to,' I say to satisfy her. After what she's told me, she'll think I'm mad if I don't. 'I'll go home tomorrow. He's got an appointment at the bank in the morning. He might need cheering up.'

'I don't think what you're going to say will cheer him up.'

'No. Well.' I'm stuck for words again. Simply because I don't know how I'm going to get out of this. I've fallen even further into the trap that Janus set for me, now that I've told Evie so much.

Perhaps she senses I have a problem because she says, 'You will tell Lewis the truth, won't you? You're no good at telling lies and it'll show if you do. Get it all out in the open. I hate to see you in a state like this. Especially as it's partly my fault.'

'I'm not in a state. And it's not your fault.'

She tucks her nightie under her feet, holding it there and staring at me in such a concerned way that I feel my whole body flush with guilt. 'Do you remember that day on the beach,' she says, 'when we nearly had a row over Janus, and you said that you thought Lewis was the best of the two of them?'

I smile. 'Yes, I do.'

'I thought I had the best one at the time.' She sighs and rests her cheek on her knees. Lost in thought. Of Janus. Again.

'You must still feel something for him,' I say quietly. 'I mean, the way you were with him.'

'Sex,' she says. 'That's all it was. I know that now. You know the way it is,' she smiles. 'If they're really good at it, you believe you're in love.'

'Really good?' I hear myself say. 'Tell me then. Was he?'

'On a scale of ten . . .' She glances at me, smiles almost self-consciously. 'About twelve. And that's only for kissing,' she adds with another little smile.

'Kissing?' I say lightly, having trouble now keeping it going.

'Yes, you know, the kind of kissing that makes your toes curl.' She demonstrates, curling her toes round with her fingers. I nod, wondering if I do know, wondering what it was like. She presses her shoulder against mine. 'Have you ever come just by kissing?' she says. The next second she has her arms round me. 'Oh, babes, I'm sorry. How tactless of me. Here I am going on about sex, and he tried to kill you.' She cuddles me tight. 'He did, didn't he?' she whispers as though I might say it was all my imagination. And redeem him.

But my breath sticks in my throat; I can't say a word. We cling together silently until I start to cry. Sob out the whole mess of it on her shoulder.

I go home the following afternoon while Evie is at one of her classes. The Square is bathed in sunshine. It looks sleepy, safe, but different. For a moment I feel like a stranger arriving at somewhere I've never been before but which seems vaguely familiar. Then the scene falls into place: the central garden, the majestic columns of the bay windows, some stained grey with age, others painted in bright colours; and in the far corner my tall narrow house waiting for me. These things form a pattern that I know, a safe and reassuring landscape, the one I ran to that day I arrived on Gerald's doorstep with my belongings piled in a cab. A few steps further on, Pisces appears on the pavement as if by magic. The way he does when he's been waiting for me but doesn't want me to know. I phoned Miss Campion from Evie's to check that he was OK. He approaches me with his tail in the air but stops a few feet away, sitting down to wash a back foot, pretending he hasn't seen me. I call his bluff and walk by, then whip round and scoop him up.

'Pisces, my precious baby,' I say, kissing his head. He smells stronger than I remember. Fishy cat food and damp earth. I've just forgotten. He endures my cuddling for a minute or two, then nips me on the shoulder and leaps out of my arms. At this point I realise that the BMW is not here. Lewis can't still be with the bank manager. But he has a lot to sort out; he could be anywhere.

The flat smells musty when I first step inside but Miss Campion has put a vase of sweet peas on my kitchen table and their scent helps to freshen the air. Beside them is my mail, neatly stacked, and a loaf of bread. I must go and thank her soon and take her the linen tablecloth and matching napkins that I bought for her in Kinsale. I can't remember what they're like now, whether I chose a set with the shamrocks or not. So much has happened since that day Evie and I went gift shopping.

I flick through the mail but don't open any. There are bills, and letters from the magazine, all things which will drag me back into the routine of my life. And I have this odd feeling that once I'm back in this routine the past two weeks will melt away like footprints in wet sand. The good and the bad. So closely united that I won't be able to lose one without the other.

'Come on, Verity,' I say aloud, directing my voice towards Pisces who has followed me in. 'Pull yourself together.'

I shake some Munchies on to the table for Pisces, then put the kettle to boil while I sort out Miss Campion's present. To my surprise I find that not only is the tablecloth decorated with dozens of shamrocks, it is also bright green. I hope Miss Campion is not like my mother and considers green an unlucky colour. My father once bought a green Volvo and had to change it because she refused to travel further than the local shops in it. I've never much liked green either, probably her influence. I leave the tea and go to knock on Miss Campion's door.

Standing in her sitting room while she exclaims over the prettiness of the embroidery and the wonderful quality of the linen, things that are becoming harder and harder to find according to her, my return to normality feels complete. She has a large hexagonal-shaped mirror over her fireplace. It's hung in the same way as one my parents have, from a chain, tilted forward. The whole room is reflected there. I see the two of us, our pale heads. Hers, neat grey curls; mine, blonde and a little spiky. But not so different caught quickly. And at a brief glance it's easy to mistake the frailty of old age with the slimness of a young woman who does not eat as she should. The thing that startles me most is that I can see very clearly how I could become.

'I might sell the house,' I tell her. She's been asking me about the cottage. 'I'm not sure yet. I'm not sure what I'm going to do.' About anything, I add silently.

'I'm thinking of selling too,' Miss Campion says. 'I rather fancy Eastbourne. A nice little bungalow.' She sighs. 'I don't feel safe here any longer. It's not peaceful any more.'

'No,' I murmur, staring down at the tablecloth and the neat embroidery and the quality linen. And at Miss Campion's wrinkled ringless hand stroking away at it.

'By the way, dear,' the hand grasps my wrist, 'I was sorry to see Mr Kaye has had another accident. With his car,' she adds as I stare blankly at her. I was thinking about feeling safe and unsafe.

'Oh, yes,' I say. 'But only the back.'

'No one hurt, I hope?'

'No.' I turn to my reflection again. Check that I don't look too much of a wreck because it has just dawned on me that the BMW might have gone to be repaired, and Lewis could have been in the house all this time. Maybe sleeping, exhausted after the ordeal of sorting out his finances, and not heard me come home. I have the keys to the house in my hand. Miss Campion has just returned them to me. All my duplicate keys on my Piscean key ring, a present from Gerald, the two fishes trying to swim off in different directions. The front door key stands out from the rest, newly cut and still shiny. I'm in a strange situation now. What if there's no answer when I ring the front door bell? Do I let myself in? And if Lewis is not back . . . all sorts of possibilities present themselves. Hiding in his bed the most appealing of them.

It turns out that I do have to let myself in. Although there is a light on in the kitchen and I can hear the loud hum of the spin programme on the washing machine, I can't make him hear me. But once I'm in the hall I feel hesitant and stand there craning my head to see into the kitchen and the sitting room.

'Lewis,' I call, 'Lewis are you there? I've been ringing the bell.'

I can see the washing machine. The cycle is finished now and the red light flashing on and off. There is a heap of dirty laundry lying in front of it, one of Lewis's shirts on top. I go through, lift it up and sniff at the collar. His familiar smell fills my nostrils, warms me, arouses me. I suddenly want to see him very much. How amazing, I think, that a dirty shirt can do this to me.

At the bottom of the stairs I call out again. Still no answer. I become slightly anxious. Perhaps his meeting with the bank manager was worse than he expected. Perhaps there have been more demands for money amongst his letters. Nicole may have been in touch; or Lewis may have phoned her; he will certainly be wanting to speak to his daughters.

Halfway up the stairs a faint smell of smoke reminds me that Lewis has another problem bigger than all the others. I must remember to bring round some fresh air spray. I might even have to take all the curtains to the cleaners to get rid of the smell completely. I stand there a moment. There's another scent in the air. Lewis's Ralph Lauren. It comes drifting down from the landing where the air looks faintly steamy. So that's it; he's in the bath. Nothing like a good hot soak for easing troubles.

'Lewis,' I call. At the same moment the phone rings. I call him again but he doesn't hear. Probably got the tap running, so I dash back downstairs to answer the phone myself.

To my surprise it's Lewis.

'I thought you were in the bath,' I say.

'In the bath?' he laughs. 'I'm at Evie's.'

'I thought I could smell you.'

'Smell me?' he laughs again.

'I'm in the house,' I explain, laughing too. 'I came up here looking for you.'

'And I came looking for you. Evie said you'd gone home. I phoned there first. I guessed where you were. At least I hoped that's were you'd gone.'

'Are you coming home now?'

'Yeah, I've just got to take the car in to the garage. I should be back within an hour.'

'I'll be waiting.'

'I've missed you,' he murmurs.

'It's only been two days.'

'I know but I couldn't wait any longer. I came round here to get you.'

'To carry me off?' I say.

'Yes,' he whispers.

'Don't you two start running up my phone bill,' I hear Evie shout in the background.

'I'll see you later,' says Lewis.

'I'll be back in my flat. I've got a stack of mail to open. I'll leave the door on the catch for you. By the way. Did you have a bath earlier?'

'Why?' he says. 'What are you planning to do to me?'

'I'll see you later,' I laugh, resisting the desire to mention the steam, ask if he opened the window, nag like I did at Janus.

I feel a bit happier. His meeting at the bank obviously wasn't too bad. And Evie obviously hasn't mentioned anything to him. So I've got the choice now. To keep quiet. To keep Lewis. To keep safe.

I go back upstairs before I leave. The steam seems to have dispersed. But I can still smell the smoke. Steam and smoke. They look almost the same. Can even be confused with one another. But they represent water and fire. Opposites. Fire and water. Both dangerous to me.

I rake both hands through my hair. Shake my head to clear out all these negative thoughts. Then I run back downstairs, turn off the washing machine and go home to wait for Lewis.

I begin to open my letters, but I find my mind wandering. And in the end I'm just ripping open the envelopes and spreading their contents over the table in an untidy mess. Not reading or taking any of it in. Pisces stalks about, intent on having all my attention. He jumps on to my lap, butts me under the chin, and when this doesn't work he skids about on the table, sending paper flying everywhere. In a sudden flash of irritation I put him outside and shut the window. But a few minutes later, when I'm back at the table trying to concentrate, he comes pushing at the door. I smile to myself, relenting, not sure why I lost my temper with him in the first place. How clever of him to notice that I left the door on the catch. Or could it be Lewis? I swing round, knowing it can't be, not yet. And find Janus there.

He walks in without a word, closing the door behind him, pressing it firmly shut and clicking down the catch.

'Get out of here,' I say. I lick my lips, preparing to repeat it. Trying to stay calm. Knowing, suddenly, that he was in the house all the time. The smoke; the steam; even the washing machine maybe; they were all down to him. 'Does Lewis know you're here?' I ask when it's obvious that commanding him to leave is not going to work.

'No. No one knows.' He walks calmly over to me. But stops a few feet away, between me and the door.

'What do you want, Janus? Tell me what you want, and then get out.'

He looks down at my letters. 'You've been telling lies about me, haven't you? You've been trying to turn Lewis against me. That's why you didn't want me to come back with you. It was your idea, wasn't it? You wanted to get Lewis on your own.'

'No, Janus,' I say firmly. 'It was Lewis's idea that you stay in Ireland. And I haven't told him any lies about you.' I hesitate, wanting to stand up. Feeling vulnerable sitting down. 'I haven't told him anything.' I pause and he looks at me. 'I thought it was the best thing to do. To keep quiet. For both of us to keep quiet.' I stumble over the words. Look away. 'To try and forget. All of it. Even though what you did was a crime.'

'A crime?' he says with a little smile.

'I don't want to talk about this any more.' I get to my feet, my back against the table, facing him. 'You know what I mean. And you know that if any of it, *any* of it, gets to Lewis, we'll both lose him.'

He takes another step towards me, close enough that I can smell Lewis on him, or rather Lewis's Ralph Lauren. I look towards the door, judging if I can make a run for it. But hoping I won't have to try. Hoping he'll go before Lewis gets here.

'He's my brother,' Janus says. 'Why should I lose him? You can have someone else. Leave Lewis alone and find someone else.'

I want to shout at him, tell him that it's not a case of leaving Lewis alone, but I don't dare. He hasn't come all this way, a journey that can't have been easy, and risked Lewis's anger, to hear me tell him that his brother says he's in love with me.

'You chased him from the start, didn't you? Babysitting. Asking for a lift to your cottage.'

'No, Janus, you were the one who started it.' I can't keep quiet now. 'You were the one who wanted to stay that first night.'

He stares at me frowning slightly, as though he's trying to remember. I ease along the table, a step at a time. But the second I'm clear of him his hands shoot out and land on my shoulders. I freeze. He's not hurting me, not even gripping me. His fingers are resting very lightly on me, his thumbs on my collarbone. The memory of his face this close to mine is painfully fresh. I can't look at him without thinking of it. I see him sitting on the quay. Looking at me over his shoulder. Laying his arm across my legs. And I'm afraid. And ashamed. But still I don't move. I wait, my eyes fixed on the door. Waiting for Lewis to come, just as I gazed out to sea and hoped a boat would come sailing into the lough.

'You have to find someone else,' he murmurs. He slides one hand round my neck. Caressing it. Then both hands. Taking hold of me, tilting his head towards me as though he's going to kiss me. One thing he didn't do. And I'm thinking of what he said. We'll be together, the three of us. And asking if it appealed to me. Why did he say that? I wonder. And when? Before he banged the mud from my sandals? Before he picked up his coat? All these details blur together. They make me squint, my eyes watering as though I'm affected by the glare from the lough. When did he change? What moment?

'You tried to drown me,' I say very quietly. My voice sounds sad because I've realised, no, I've known all along, that it's possible, easy, to have sex with someone, and then kill them. 'You tried to kill me.'

He shakes his head. Goes on shaking it and I realise something else. That I want him to convince me. I want to believe I was wrong. Then his hands are on my shoulders again. Pressing me down. Under the water.

'No,' I say, twisting away from him, and he puts both hands tight round my neck and squeezes. I give a short high scream and drag at his wrists. He tightens his grip for a second before letting me go. I stand there, rubbing at my neck, too shocked to speak. Not only shocked at Janus, but shocked at myself.

'You're shaking,' he says.

'I want you to go.'

He pulls out his cigarettes, takes one from the packet and sticks it between my lips. Forcing it in until it bends and breaks. The pieces fall to the floor. I wipe the shreds of tobacco from my lips. He's right; I am shaking. I can't stop myself.

'Lewis will be home soon,' I say. 'If you go now I won't tell him you've been here.'

'I wasn't going to hurt you. You can tell Lewis what you like, but he's my brother, he'll believe me not you.' He takes out another cigarette and puts it in his own mouth.

'I don't want you smoking in my kitchen,' I hear myself say. Clinging to some last vestige of control. Bracing myself to run. Knowing I'll only have one chance. I watch as he lights the cigarette, then tosses the match towards a fruit bowl that stands in the middle of my table. It's a large bowl with only one wrinkled orange in it, so I can't be sure whether he meant to miss it or not. But the match, still burning, has fallen on to my letters. I make a dive at it, but he's too quick. He throws an arm round me, pinning my own arms to my sides.

'So you don't want me smoking in here?' he says, and flicks the cigarette into the air. It lands alongside the match, and his other arm whips round me, holding me fast. On the table an envelope turns black and begins to curl at the edges.

'Janus, don't,' I plead. 'Don't do this.' I wrench a hand free and dig my nails into his arm. But he doesn't even notice. His body is rigid. His eyes fixed on that black paper, slowly curling as the centre dissolves in flames.

Other papers catch fire. The flames spread, devouring letter after letter and blackening the table. Fragments of charred paper float in the dark smoke. The cushion of a chair starts to smoulder. I'm screaming and crying, and begging him to let me go. And finally he does. His arms fall away from me and he backs towards the door. I dash to the sink, start filling cups and jugs with water, throw them over the table, run back to fill them again. Through all this Janus sits slumped against the front door. The flames have spread to the pile of things I emptied out of my bag earlier. The tissue wrapping from Miss Campion's tablecloth, the books that I bought in Ireland. A tea towel lying next to them catches fire. I snatch it up, flap it hard against the table, stop as burning paper flies everywhere. A fire extinguisher, I think, I must have a fire extinguisher. But of course, they're upstairs. I stand motionless for a moment, sobbing with the sheer irony of it. Over by the door, Janus gets slowly to his feet.

I rush at him. 'Help me!' I scream. 'Help me!'

He puts up both hands to ward me off. 'Get away from me, you witch,' he shouts. He starts to brush frantically at his chest and arms. Beating at the flames that will soon reach him? Brushing off spiders? I don't know. But it's then that I know I've lost. I can't control this. And Janus has slipped into some dark little place from the past. I have to get out. I have to get him away from the door. But he bars my way, pressing back against it with outstretched arms. I make for the window, but he blocks that too. In desperation I pick up a burning chair. I hold it by the leg and fling it at him. He dodges but it hits him in the chest. He stumbles and lands on top, scattering the burning wood.

There's one other way out. The stairs. I grab a knife and try to lever away the wooden partition. But it won't budge. I stab at it and it splinters. A jagged split appears. It's not wide enough to crawl through, but it's wide enough to let in a fresh draught of air. I feel it against my face, cool as water. Watch helplessly as it blows across the burning room. Janus is on his knees, cradling a hand to his chest. His sleeve is turning black. He jerks forward and staggers to his feet. I back up against the splintered wood as he comes towards me. He has his arm stretched in front of him like the fiery sword of an avenging angel. His hand is stretched out too, the palm wide open. And in the centre, like a wriggling red spider, I can see dark bubbles of blood.

I know I'm screaming. I can't stop. And I can't help thinking how much easier it would have been to drown.

Chapter 20

I flew here this time and paid Mr Doyle to fetch me from the airport. It was a much longer journey in his old car, trundling along at a steady forty miles an hour. I tried not to think of last time, and the way we raced along those same roads, the four of us.

He dropped me at the cottage door where I thanked him, paid him and assured him I'd be perfectly all right on my own. I haven't told the Doyles that Lewis intends to join me. Because I don't know when he's coming, and it will look bad if I have to wait too long for him.

So here I am in the last days of August, watching the tourists, the walkers, the day trippers and the groups studying marine biology. And I'm completely alone. Each morning I get up early. Perhaps because I sleep well. A fact that amazes me. I walk to the little beach and sunbathe, religiously smearing myself with cream first. And I'm already a nice pale gold; it looks good with my sun-bleached hair. And I read. And I wait for Lewis. Sometimes I think I hear someone calling me and I sit up, shade my eyes, look for a parked car and a big man running down the path. He hopes to bring the girls. Nicole has promised he can. So I look for a man with two little girls running beside him. But so far he hasn't come.

I stayed with Evie for a few days after the fire but my head began to throb with her questions. She woke me in the middle of the night once to ask me something that was bothering her. With all my warnings, she said, why did you go on such a long walk with him? Evie, I told her, he was being fine with me, how could I guess what would happen? How could I? But she soon came up with other questions, making me go over details again which I didn't dare because I'd forgotten exactly what I'd told her.

The interior of my flat is wrecked. Not quite a blackened shell – the fire spread up through the partition before it reached my bedroom – but it won't be habitable again for weeks, months. Part of the ground-floor is also badly damaged. And every floor will need redecorating. If Lewis hadn't arrived when he did, I think the whole house would have been destroyed. And maybe Janus and me with it.

Lewis plans to make do living in the bedroom for the time being. He wanted me to stay with him but I couldn't bear the thought of waking each morning to see my beautiful house, Gerald's beautiful house, in such a pitiful state. It's not just the material damage; it's something more than that, something that is deeply upsetting to me. I feel as though I've betrayed Gerald, as though he entrusted me with so many beautiful things and I've spoiled them all. That's as far as I want to go in my analysis of what happened. I don't want to delve any deeper into that part of me which must share some of the responsibility. A part of me which I think Gerald always knew was there. Even if I didn't. Maybe he recognised it that time he caught me terrifying myself with the Henry James novel.

I thought of going to stay with my parents. And then it came to me. The one place where I could find some peace. And it will be easy enough to write my column at the cottage and fax it from Skibbereen. Lewis has to stay in London because there's a chance of saving the restaurant. He has someone interested in going into partnership with him. They plan to give the place a new look. I know that his father is putting up some of the finance. It's all in the early stages, of course, and he'll be free to come here for a holiday once the preliminary arrangements are made. He has also come to a fairly amicable arrangement with Nicole about the girls. Until they move to France, that is. But I think Lewis can handle it now. He still hasn't mentioned his suicide attempt. I think he's ashamed of it. And I don't talk about my confrontation with death either. I'm ashamed too, but for very different reasons.

There is another reason why he wants to remain in London for a while. Janus. I have been to the hospital with him once.

Janus is in isolation because of his burns; Lewis and I had to wear special sterile gowns. Janus was sedated and I stood at the end of the bed and watched the tears run down Lewis's face. And I vowed not to go again. But I did. On my own. Janus was awake but wouldn't talk to me. I went close up by his head. You wouldn't know there is anything wrong from his face, except for the feverish flush of his cheeks. But he is badly burned down one side and has to have plastic surgery. He's lucky to be alive – I suppose we both are. I tried to help him. I tried to tear away his burning sleeve. But he was hysterical and I was frightened he'd turn on me. Then Lewis was there, breaking the window, smashing his way in. I will never forget the scene that followed. Of Janus incoherent and frozen with pain. And of the way Lewis comforted him. Other neighbours were there by then, and the fire brigade. Miss Campion was trying to lead me away but I wouldn't move. I wanted to be with Lewis. I was desperate to be with him. I wanted to run up and push Janus out of the way and have all the comforting for myself. I wasn't injured; Janus needed him far more than I did, but all sense of reason had left me. Later on, when I had calmed down and gone with Miss Campion, I thought to myself, now I know how Janus feels about me.

The nurses have cut his hair. I think it may have got singed. It looks very dark and glossy against the stark white of his pillow. Lewis says they fuss over him, especially the young ones. No doubt they recognise his potential.

There was no nurse around when I leaned over him. He turned his head away from me. We have all agreed to say it was an accident. I told Lewis the truth. A sparse and doctored truth. I told him how Janus had come down to the flat to warn me off. And I told him that Janus had intended to flick the match into the fruit bowl and missed. 'I think,' I said, 'that when he saw the flames, he had some kind of brainstorm. He wouldn't let me put them out.' I left the rest to him. Waiting for him to start questioning me. But all he said was, 'You're far more charitable than Nicole.' And I was worried about the insurance. Worried about what Janus would tell him. Worried about my own state of mind and how, once again, I was having trouble in separating what was real and what I'd imagined. What could be revealed and what must remain secret. So I held back, and I didn't tell him what had happened at the lough either. And it was too late by then. How could I suddenly say, Oh, by the way, Lewis, your brother tried to drown me last week but I didn't tell you at the time because I wasn't sure if he really meant to kill me? And there's another thing, I was scared to mention it in case he told you what we did beforehand. And in case he tells you that when he came down to my flat and put his hands on me, I didn't stop him. And if I was to describe to you how I felt when he touched me, how I felt when I knew that I was in terrible danger, you wouldn't believe me. But I can't describe it anyway. And now I only want to feel safe.

And Lewis has made me feel safe. He said I must leave everything to him. And he seems to have it all under control, including Janus. Deep down he may suspect the truth, even have come to terms with the fact that should we stay together, I shall always need protection from Janus. But the bond between them is too strong to be broken by doubts and suspicion alone. And so I shall have to come to terms with something too. But for now, I feel safe.

But I still had to go to the hospital. I had to make sure that Janus wasn't going to ruin it all for me. At least remind him of the consequences if he tried to.

'Don't forget,' I said, bending as near to him as I dare, 'if you tell him, you'll lose him too.' He pressed his eyes tight shut and wouldn't say a word. I went round to the other side of the bed and crouched down so that my face was level with his. 'You know what I'm talking about. Not trying to kill me. Not trying to drown me or burn me.' I felt compelled to say these things. His eyelids trembled with the effort of keeping them so tightly closed, and I noticed his fist was also tightly clenched. I couldn't remember whether it was the one whose palm was cut, but I did remember it was the one on which I had placed that little yellow spider. And why would I have any trouble remembering? It was only a short time ago. Looking at him in that hospital bed, it felt like an age; another lifetime. His breathing sounded very laboured. I wondered if he was in pain, or just tortured with jealousy at the thought of me going home to Lewis. 'Oh, Janus,' I said with a long sigh. I touched his quivering eyelids with the tip of my finger and left.

Evie wanted to know how he looked. OK, I told her. He'll be OK. I know she'll go and see him. After a suitable time has passed, she'll go.

There are boats on the lough today. Two rowing boats, long ones crewed by teams of young men. I've been watching them, the way they skim so easily across the water, the harmony of the oars, the little splashes. Janus may never be fit enough to do anything like that. But he'll work for his father in Kinsale. He's promised Lewis. Whether Lewis threatened him, coaxed him, or begged him, I don't know. But I have to believe Janus will do as he says. That he will never be a danger to me again. Because I am quite sure now that I do not want danger in my life.

Maybe he'll save up and buy a car; visit Anne Marie and take her out. And maybe he'll steal her virginity in the woods beneath the grotto. Tenderly, the way I know he could be.

Lydia and Mimi will love it here. They'll paddle, fish with nets, putting any catches straight back in the water, of course, and we can go for walks. Not too far. Perhaps a little way in the woods, or up the first slope of the mountain path. And we'll drive out to other places, other beaches, wide sandy ones. Maybe a boat trip from Baltimore to the islands. The four of us. And maybe we'll walk as far as the donkeys.

I've collected a heap of shells for them. I know about shells now. They're a bit like dreams. The ones that you hold against your ear to listen to the sound of the sea – they are the ugly ones, the big whelks with their ridged and blistered surface. The beautiful ones – the limpets and the ormers with their rainbow patterns like spilt oil, and the fan-shaped scallops – they don't hold any secrets.

But I mustn't think about secrets because I want it to work. The four of us together. And then Lewis and I on our own. I'll be ready by the time he comes. I'll have dreamed and thought, and thought and dreamed until I've mixed up the dreams with all the things that I want to forget. Until I can't tell what is real any longer. And I'll empty it all out, rake out all the guilt and the lies so that my head's as empty as the shells.

And it'll be all right because dreams don't have memories. So I won't remember. Not even if we should take that long walk and stand there watching the tide as it shifts relentlessly back and forth between the lough and the sea. Holding our breaths as it gathers force to surge through that narrow channel once more.